THE PREY
THE SHAMAN
SEDUCTION

Kimberly Zant

Erotic Romantic Suspense

New Concepts   Georgia

Be sure to check out our website for the very best in fiction at fantastic prices!

When you visit our webpage, you can:

* Read excerpts of currently available books
* View cover art of upcoming books and current releases
* Find out more about the talented artists who capture the magic of the writer's imagination on the covers
* Order books from our backlist
* Find out the latest NCP and author news--including any upcoming book signings by your favorite NCP author
* Read author bios and reviews of our books
* Get NCP submission guidelines
* And so much more!

We offer a 20% discount on all new ebook releases!
(Sorry, but short stories are not included in this offer.)

We also have contests and sales regularly, so be sure to visit our webpage to find the best deals in ebooks and paperbacks! To find out about our new releases as soon as they are available, please be sure to sign up for our newsletter (http://www.newconceptspublishing.com/newsletter.htm) or join our reader group (http://groups.yahoo.com/group/new_concepts_pub/join) !

The newsletter is available by double opt in only and our customer information is *never* shared!

Visit our webpage at:
www.newconceptspublishing.com

The Prey/The Shaman/Seduction is an original publication of NCP. This work has never before appeared in book form. This work is a novel. Any similarity to actual persons or events is purely coincidental.

New Concepts Publishing
5202 Humphreys Rd.
Lake Park, GA 31636

ISBN 1-58608-672-3
© copyright Kimberly Zant
Cover art by Jenny Dixon, © copyright 2004

All rights reserved, which includes the right to reproduce this book or portions thereof in any form whatsoever except as provided by the U.S. Copyright Law.

If you purchased this book without a cover you should be aware this book is stolen property.

NCP books are available at special quantity discounts for bulk purchases for sales promotions, premiums, fund raising, or educational use. For details, write, email, or phone New Concepts Publishing, 5202Humphreys Rd., Lake Park, GA 31636, ncp@newconceptspublishing.com, Ph. 229-257-0367, Fax 229-219-1097.

First NCP Paperback Printing: 2005

Printed in the United States of America

Other Titles from NCP by Kimberly Zant:

The Invitation
Thief of Hearts
Thief of Hearts: The Return
Thief of Hearts: Stolen
Doctor, Lawyer … Police Chief
Four Play
The Sex Philes: Haunting Melody
The Sex Philes: The Howling
Goldilocks

The Prey

Chapter One

Emerald Green knew the moment she swam toward consciousness in a sickening wave that she'd been chloroformed. She tried to open her eyes and found that she couldn't. Something was tied around her head ... fabric she realized. It felt thick--a T-shirt, maybe? It occurred to her quite suddenly that it was probably the knit dress she'd worn to the dance. Cool air wafted around her, trickling over parts of her body where it would not have touched her if her dress had still been on her instead of tied around her head.

Her mouth was covered too. Her lips and cheeks felt compressed against her teeth. Tape, she realized from the smell of it.

She remained perfectly still, trying to master the nausea. She was in real trouble if she threw up.

To distract herself from the threat of strangulation by her own vomit, she concentrated on trying to conjure her last conscious memory. After a few moments, it came flooding back to her. She'd been chaperoning the seniors' graduation dance. Someone--Mike Todd?--had told her he thought Chrissy Stevens might have OD'd, that she'd gone into the teachers' lounge and collapsed. Alarmed, she'd rushed to check on the girl, never considering it might be nothing more than a ruse to get her away from the crowd.

She hadn't made it to the lounge, though. She'd barely stepped three feet into the darkened corridor when someone had grabbed her from behind and smothered her with a cloth coated in a sickly sweet liquid. Beyond that, she couldn't remember anything except the feel of the body that had pressed so tightly against her. It had been male ... probably Mike ... although he'd been beside her, she thought. One of his lapdogs?

The more real question, though, was why had they done it? And, more importantly, what did they have in mind for her?

She was afraid she was going to find out. The nausea, which had mostly subsided, threatened once more and she forced herself to take slow, calming breaths, turning her mind to the task of trying to figure out where she was, how dangerous her situation was, and how imminent the threat--no easy task when she could hear little and see less.

She lifted her head slowly, realizing as she did so that she was sitting upright--there was something hard and painfully unyielding behind her, something soft beneath her. The muscles in her neck protested as she lifted her head. Obviously, she'd been unconscious for a while, her head hanging down against her chest.

The stilted movement seemed to elicit a chorus of snickers and her heart jumped into her throat, thundering in her ears until she had to strain to hear above the clamor. She twisted her head, trying to figure out if she had interpreted the sounds correctly, or if the cloth wrapped around her head had distorted some other noise.

But she knew it hadn't and a shiver skated along her spine at the thread of malice in the laughter.

Unnerved by the realization that she had an audience, she tried to sit up higher, to move her arms, her legs, and found she couldn't move any part of her body except her head. Panic wafted through her, accelerating her heartbeat, and she struggled harder for several minutes until she realized that her efforts were not only useless, they seemed to be exciting whoever was watching her.

As the panic subsided fractionally, she realized the snickers belonged to four different people. One sounded female. She was almost certain the other three were male.

"Snotty bitch!" someone said, their voice vibrating with hatred.

"You fucked up our lives. Now we're fucking yours up. How does payback feel, bitch?"

She was certain she recognized the last voice. It was Mike Todd. The first one had sounded like his girl friend, Chrissy Stevens. There were still two she hadn't quite figured out, though their malicious snickering sounded very familiar.

She conjured a picture of the class troublemakers who always congregated at the very back of her classroom, talking, laughing, heckling her when they felt nervy enough--Mike, his girlfriend,

Chrissy, David Bennings, Charley Moyer, Tina Patterson and Jeffery Miller. Mike was the only one of the group that had graduated--by the skin of his teeth, which wasn't going to take him far when it came to college--and it was probable he wouldn't even have managed graduation at all except that he was better at cheating than the others, although he was bright enough he might not have had to, even though he rarely paid attention and never handed in homework assignments.

As the accusation sank in, her fear yielded to anger. *She'd* screwed up their lives? By delaying graduation a year? Because *they* were too spoiled and lazy to do their work?

It occurred to her, however, that she really didn't know what this group was capable of. They were students, she was certain of that much, but she didn't know whether to be more frightened, or less. It was hard to believe any of the teens she knew, that she'd taught, might cause her serious injury--but she wouldn't have thought they would use chloroform on her, and it certainly would never have occurred to her that they would abduct her. They might be satisfied with merely humiliating her--and they might not.

Mike had a cruel streak--all but two members of the gang--Jeffery Miller and David Bennings--were from wealthy, over-privileged families--the kind who produced offspring that had had everything handed to them all of their lives, never paid the price for any infraction because mommy and/or daddy always bailed them out of everything, and therefore had come to believe that the world and everything in it was already theirs. All they had to do was take whatever they wanted. They didn't have to work for it. It was supposed to be handed to them because it was theirs by right.

Regardless, it was hard to understand how they thought they'd get away with this. Surely they had to know that she would recognize their voices? Or, maybe they didn't. Maybe they thought she was too stupid to figure it out? They'd ambushed her from behind, knocked her out. They'd tied her up, blindfolded her.

She wished she felt safer, but the truth was, she didn't really believe her reasoning. She was quite sure they thought they were going to get away with it or they wouldn't have decided to do it. The threat to her was in just how they thought they were going to manage it.

A click, followed by a bright light made her jump. It took her several seconds to realize it was the flash of a camera.

The surface beneath her moved. She felt the heat of someone's breath moments before that someone spoke in a harsh whisper near her ear. "Nice pussy for an old woman," he said, and snickered. She felt something hard brush her femininity, running along her cleft, then parting the flesh surrounding her body opening and thrusting up inside of her, which lacked even a drop of moisture to ease the way of the sudden intrusion. Pain and fear rushed through her as he dug around inside of her with a rough finger.

Until that moment, she hadn't fully realized her situation. Blinded by the cloth, numb from having been tied so long, her body had given her little to go by. He'd gouged her with his finger, however. There'd been no tugging her panties aside, no forcing her legs apart. The only conclusion was that they'd stripped her completely naked, bound her so that her legs were spread wide in some obscene way. She tried to envision what they'd done to her, trying to focus her mind on the puzzle rather than the intrusion of his finger, but she could barely feel her arms and legs.

She couldn't ignore was he was doing to her, couldn't escape it. No matter how hard she concentrated, she could not pull her legs together to protect herself. He became more frenzied, she supposed because he wasn't satisfied with her reaction. Finally, unable to contain it, she moaned in pain. He grunted in satisfaction. "Yeah, bitch. I knew you liked it." He snickered, either because of her feeble attempts to draw her legs together, or because he was enjoying himself so hugely--she wasn't certain.

The flashing continued, however, and she knew most of his actions, and reactions, were for the benefit of the camera.

Despite the pain and fear, it made her realize that they weren't quite as stupid as she'd thought. They were taking pictures. No doubt they figured it would be insurance against her talking--it wasn't hard to imagine how the pictures might be interpreted. Pictures of her tied naked to the bed while one of her teenage students performed sexual acts 'with' her. For all she knew they were filming it as well, catching her 'moans of pleasure'.

She had no idea whether it would prove to be important or not, or if she would even have the chance to use it, but she had managed to recognize the third voice--Jeffery Miller was the one violating her body. The fourth was almost certainly his shadow,

David. He proved it the next moment by biting her on one nipple almost hard enough to draw blood and then snickering when she screamed against the gag. "Nice tits, too. How old are you, teach? Thirty?"

She was too frightened, and in too much pain, even to register his insult, much less be disturbed by it. In any case, her students were well aware that she was only a few years older than they were. She suspected that was the reason many of them resented her, maybe even hated her, her status as an authority figure over them when she was only in her mid-twenties.

Their prodding, pinching--painful abuse of her sensitive areas galvanized her into renewing her efforts to protect her body by covering herself. She struggled, trying to close her legs. She couldn't move her feet, but she finally managed to put her knees together and she realized they'd tied her somehow with her knees drawn up. There wasn't enough slack to straighten her legs in any direction her body was capable of, or to pull her feet together.

Her relief in covering herself was short lived. In the next moment, she felt someone grip her knees brusingingly and pry them apart until her groin tendons protested. Despite the pain, her heart leapt suffocatingly against her chest wall and she braced herself, certain rape would come next.

One of the two that were tormenting her moved close. She could smell him, feel his body heat. Something nudged her nose and she tried to twist her head away. He grabbed two handfuls of hair, forcing her head back so that she was facing him. She didn't have to be able to see to know what was thrust in her face. She could smell the musky odor of his cock, could feel the prickle of his pubic hair as he crushed his groin against her face.

"Maybe I should take the tape off her mouth and stuff my cock in it?"

"Stupid! You want to give her the chance to bite it off? This is good. Can't see the tape from here. Looks like she's giving you a blow job.

Abruptly, the door slammed open and Emerald heard a new voice. "What the fuck? Son-of-a-bitch! Get the hell away from her before I break you in half!"

For several heartbeats it seemed everyone was too frozen with surprise at being caught even to move. Suddenly, however, the mattress beneath her shook violently as the two teens dove off, landing on the floor at a run. She heard the stampede of footsteps, followed almost immediately by grunts, thuds, cussing, falling objects and bodies. Chrissy screamed.

Emerald's heart was hammering so hard she thought she'd pass out. Hope had surged through her when she heard, and recognized, the new voice as Reece Yeager's. Although he had his own 'bad boy' image at the school, he was not malicious, merely more interested in school as a place to party and socialize than an institute of study. He was big--well over six feet and muscular enough he might well have played football at the school he'd attended before, though he'd shown no interest in sports since he'd transferred--not sports of that nature, anyway.

Regardless, no matter how big, it was still three against one and she didn't know whether she was more afraid he'd be hurt trying to rescue her, or that he'd be defeated, leaving her once more at the mercy of a group that obviously had none.

He might have engaged in some sparring with the two boys who'd been on the bed with her, but she thought David and Jeffery had managed to elude him and run ... either that or he'd hit them so hard they weren't currently in any shape to move. The scuffling sounds had been reduced to the grunts and blows of two. Unlike Jeffery and David, who were cowards, Mike was the sort who could take punishment, and would, if it gave him the chance to mete out some.

To her knowledge, Reece had not been involved in any fights since he'd transferred. He seemed far more interested in making love, not war, and was so big that that alone seemed to intimidate most of the other students. Perhaps Mike thought Reece was a physical coward, despite his size--or too slow and clumsy to be much of a challenge. Apparently, he'd been wrong. It sounded as if Reece was hell bent on breaking everything breakable in the room--with Mike's body. She assumed so, anyway, because it was Mike who was cursing and grunting. Reece wasn't doing anything but growling.

He was not one of her students, not in any of her classes. She shouldn't have been able to recognize his voice, much less have known his name, but he was not the sort of man, even at nineteen, that any woman could ignore, and his voice--deep, husky, drawling--was not only memorable, it elicited tingles of sensual awareness in every female near enough to hear it. Since he was perfectly willing to flirt with any female that was interested in flirting with him, and nine tenths of the female student body was interested, she'd become all too disturbingly familiar with that lazy drawl even before he'd begun to take an interest in her.

She would never have admitted to anyone that she found him attractive, not even to herself if she could've avoided it. She'd done her best to convince herself that she wasn't attracted, not as a woman, that she held a purely subjective appreciation of a young man that was well above the ordinary in both looks, physical appeal and animal magnetism. It was nothing to concern herself about.

That worked right up until he decided to toy with her--She was certain of *that* much any way, that his interest in her was purely mischievous, spawned by the fact that he was well aware that she found him attractive when she shouldn't have and that she was struggling hard to ignore it.

It seemed to draw him like catnip ... her determination to resist his charms ... as if he felt challenged by it and needed to prove to himself that he could win her, be she ever so reluctant. For all that, he had never shown her anything but the sweet side of his nature, had always behaved in a gentlemanly way, and spoke respectfully, and a twinge of embarrassment skated along the fringes of her mind that he would see her in such a state, despite the pain, the fear, and her hopefulness of being rescued.

Finally, the sounds of battle resolved into the meaty thud of a body slamming against the wall and more running feet as Mike departed, screaming profanity and threats of retribution for Reece's interference.

Emerald thought for several horrifying moments that Reece had departed on his heels, giving chase, that she'd been abandoned. Finally, as her heart slowed to a more normal rhythm, she realized she could hear heavy breathing that was not her own.

Her heart began to accelerate again as she heard the person approaching. A heavy weight settled on the bed. If she hadn't been tied, she would have pitched forward. Several moments passed. "Sorry," Reece said, his voice raspy. "Guess this is what I get for smoking, huh?"

She had the uncomfortable feeling that it was more than the need to catch his breath, no matter how reasonable it sounded. Something about the tone of his voice told her he'd been studying her for several moments. Abruptly, she dismissed the suspicion. If he had been, she didn't want to think about it.

She felt a tug on the cloth around her head and a sharp sting as several hairs were plucked from her scalp. He was leaning close. She could feel the heat from his body. His cologne, or aftershave, tickled at her nostrils, sending a dizzying thrill of relief through her.

She was certain that was what it was that made her feel hot and close to fainting.

The blindfold came off. She blinked. A face swam into her vision, blurry at first, but quickly coming into focus.

Reece tossed the piece of cloth aside, never taking his gaze from her.

His hair was mussed, his right cheek swollen and red. He'd be lucky if he wasn't sporting a black eye by tomorrow. His expression was … strained … full of concern … but there was a gleam in his eyes that accelerated her heart rate once more.

His fingers were shaking slightly as he began picking at the gag. He pulled one edge loose, but then stopped. "This is going to hurt like hell, baby," he said gruffly.

She nodded, closed her eyes, bracing for it.

She gasped when he snatched it off. She opened her eyes again, blinking against the stinging tears as she felt his warm fingers along her jaw, cupping her chin. With a large index finger, he traced the chaffed skin around her lips. He released her when he saw she was looking at him and came up on his knees.

She felt a tug at her wrist. Vaguely, she realized he was untying her, but she had a hard time focusing on anything beyond the huge bulge in the jeans that he'd pressed almost to her nose as he leaned over her to reach the restrains. Closing her mind and her eyes to that hardened ridge of flesh, she turned her head, feeling it brush along her ear as she looked to see what he was doing.

He was frowning as he struggled with the cord that had been knotted around her wrist. His expression was more of anger, however, than concentration. After a moment, she glanced down and saw that the cord they'd used to secure her wrist had been tied to the post of the headboard, looped down and wound around a lower turning on the bedpost and then was threaded back through and tied to her ankle. Turning her head, she saw she was bound similarly on the other side. It explained why she hadn't been able to put her ankles together.

Embarrassment flooded her. They'd displayed her with a blatant sexuality that had not left her one ounce of modesty. No wonder Reece had had to nerve himself to release her. He was probably as disturbed at having a teacher posed before him like a female in a porn magazine as she was to find herself on display to a student … one she'd previously been far more attracted to than she should have been, but whom she hoped now that she would never see again.

Defying all logic, the combination of her awareness of her vulnerability, the blatant sexuality of her position of submission, the heat of Reece's body and the impossible-to-ignore erection, brought a flood of wetness to her femininity.

She closed her eyes again, trying to ignore it as she felt the cord slacken finally and her arm drop limply to the bed. In a moment, he had her ankle freed as well.

He stopped, adjusted his erection and reached for the other tie.

Emerald did her best to pretend she hadn't noticed that surreptitious adjustment, but the ridge that had strained against the fly of his jeans until it looked as if it threatened to pop the teeth from the zipper, now formed a straggeringly large ridge down one jeans clad leg.

Thankfully, she was distracted from both embarrassment and desire by the incredible pain of returning blood flow. She could barely lift her arm or move her leg, but the circulation assured her that she hadn't permanently lost sensation. She bit her lip, but groaned.

He glanced at her and she reddened. "Stings."

He nodded. "I'll have this loose in a minute."

She would have fallen when he finally released her, but he caught her against him, lowered her carefully to the bed and began rubbing her arms and legs. As the pain of returning circulation slowly subsided, she found herself shivering.

"Cold?"

She shook her head, but he was already half way out of his shirt. Draping it over her shoulders, he gathered her close to him, pulling her across his lap. She hadn't realized until he did so just how big he was. She felt dwarfed by him. It unnerved her and she stiffened, trying to pull away.

"Hey. It's OK. I'm not going to hurt you, baby."

Emerald looked up at him, startled, trying to decide how to handle the situation she'd found herself in. It was the second time he'd called her baby. Could it possibly be that he didn't know who she was? Was the lighting that bad in the room?

"Do you know what they did with your clothes?"

She shook her head and, to her horror, felt tears rush to her eyes as the realization struck her suddenly of just how close a call she'd had. They'd intended to frighten and humiliate her, perhaps even to blackmail her--but it could easily have escalated way out of hand if Reece hadn't shown up.

"T..thank you for helping me," she stammered finally.

He cupped her face in one huge hand that was big enough it could have covered her whole face, threading his fingers through her hair. "Did they hurt you?" he asked, his voice carrying an edge of fury.

The question brought her closer to tears. She sniffed, shook her head. He studied her trembling lips for several moments and then, before she even realized his intention, he covered her mouth with his own. Startled, she gasped and his tongue invaded her mouth like a conquering warrior, exploring every inch of the sensitive inner flesh. Faintly, she tasted cigarette and rum as his tongue raked along hers. It alarmed her--the realization that he'd had any alcohol at all. It alarmed her far more that, far from being repelled by his taste and touch, the caress of his tongue along hers sent a blinding wave of unexpected heat through her, sapping the strength from her limbs, bringing a flush of acute sensitivity to her skin. Her nipples tightened, hardening into two sharp, pouting points, throbbing for his touch. Her clit began to throb in anticipation, as well, gathering moisture into the walls of her sex for him.

She put her hands against his shoulders, intent on pushing him away, but he used the opportunity to pull her flush against his chest. She could feel the thunder of his heart against her breasts and it sent a fresh wave of heat through her. Her nipples, rubbing against his chest with each gasping breath, throbbed harder, making her breasts feel swollen and achy.

She was dizzy and breathless by the time he released her mouth, so weak she couldn't seem to lift her head. Instead of pulling away, he nuzzled her cheek, nibbled his way down her neck and then up again, thrusting his tongue in her ear, tracing the whorls of flesh that formed the shell. A shudder went through her, a rash of goose bumps lifting the fine hairs on her body in search of more stimulation.

"I'm so sorry, baby. I didn't have a clue. When I noticed you'd disappeared and went to look for you they'd already snatched you. I had to beat the shit out of Charley to find out what was up."

"You looked for me?" Emerald asked, wondering why she couldn't make any sense out of what he was saying. Her mind had gone to mush as his hands began to skate over her skin in a restless caress, tracing the column of her spine from her neck to her buttocks, the curve of her waist. He reached around, cupping one of her full breasts and massaging it gently and she bit her lip to keep from moaning.

He twisted, lowering her to the bed and she looked up at him in confusion.

"God, baby! You're so beautiful. So beautiful."

She cried out as his mouth covered the pebbled tip of one breast and the muscles in her sex clenched almost painfully in reaction. "Don't! You mustn't do this," she managed to gasp as he suckled her nipple, trying to ignore the pleasure that cascaded through her with the scalding heat of his mouth, the spasming muscles of her sex as he tugged on the sensitive tip, flicked it with his tongue and then sucked again.

His hands seemed to be everywhere at once, touching off waves of pleasure as they stroked her restlessly, learning every inch of her flesh. She felt the nudge of his hand between her thighs, and then his finger sought and found the little nub of her clit, sending a shaft of need through her that was almost painful. He grunted in satisfaction when he delved inside her and felt how wet she was. Shifting, he caught her mouth in another searing kiss as he pushed her thighs apart and settled over her, almost crushing her with his weight, insinuating his hips between her thighs, forcing them wider. Something very hard, and very big nudged her cleft and her heart almost suffocated her with its painful flutter of excitement.

She gasped, breaking the kiss. "We can't ... you can't."

He caught her lips again, lifting off of her. She was so dizzy, so disoriented, it was several moments before she realized he was fumbling for his zipper. She pushed against him, but in the next moment felt the head of his cock nudging her cleft, parting the petals of flesh.

Again, she broke the kiss. "Don't!" she gasped shakily, but it didn't sound convincing even to her own ears.

"Shhh, baby! Let me," he murmured coaxingly, grinding his hips against her so that his cock nudged and stroked her clit, sending debilitating waves of pleasure through her.

"I can't," she gasped. "You can't."

"I've wanted you so bad … so long. I get hard every time I look at you."

Her body responded, ignoring the warnings flashing in her brain. Moisture flooded her sex even as the head of his cock nudged her, finding the haven it sought at last. The hot moisture eased his way inside of her, but he was huge, stretching her to her limits, threatening to stretch her beyond her limits. She gasped, panting in an effort to force her body to relax and yield to his invasion, digging her fingernails into his shoulders as he pushed slowly, inexorably until she felt his cock plumbing her depths.

He went still then. She lay gasping, fighting the tension she knew would cause her pain, feeling her body struggling to accept his girth. Slowly, he pushed his upper body up to look down at her, gasping hoarsely as if he'd run a mile, tension in every muscle of his body. He was shaking with the effort to hold himself still, to allow her time to adjust, moisture beading his brow, his face taut as if with agony.

As she looked up at him, he groaned. "You're so tight, baby. So hot." He closed his eyes, fighting a battle. "I can't hold it, baby."

The words sent another flood of moisture through her, made her muscles clench around him. He groaned again, as if she'd mortally wounded him and began to move as if he couldn't control himself any longer, jerkily at first, pulling away slightly, then thrusting again, pushing her up the bed with the power of his thrusts, filling her so tightly that not one inch of the sensitive inner surface of her vagina lacked for stimulation.

"Oh God," she gasped, twisting her head from side to side as mindless bliss filled her, forcing little moaning gasps of pleasure from her throat as she felt her body rushing toward an explosive release. She lifted her knees, dug her heels into the bed as her body began to buck against him with a will of its own, meeting each thrust.

The movements sent him into a mindless sort of frenzy. Scooping his arms under her, he gripped her shoulders and pumped his cock in and out of her in short, hard thrusts.

He bent his head, sucked a love bite on her throat, then sought her mouth, kissing her deeply, mimicking the thrust of his cock with his tongue. She whimpered as her body convulsed around him in waves of ecstasy that rocked her to her core, her sex clenching his cock as tightly as a fist closing around him. His cock jerked inside of her as he growled his release into her mouth, spilling his seed in a hot tide inside her body.

She went limp when the tremors finally, slowly, began to fade, leaving her only semi-conscious. His body lay hot and heavy atop her, crushing her. Finally, he gathered himself and moved away.

He'd just adjusted himself and zipped his pants when the door of the room burst open, slamming back against the wall.

"Police! Freeze where you are!"

Chapter Two

The hot Florida sun beat down on Emerald as she left the air conditioned building and headed toward the staff parking lot. Within two minutes her clothes were clinging to her uncomfortably and she was struggling to breathe the hot, moisture laden air.

It had been as hot, and sometimes hotter, in north Georgia, but the humidity had not been as high. After five years, Emerald began to wonder if she'd ever get used to the north Florida climate.

She still missed home--missed Georgia, but not nearly as badly as she had when she'd first fled the sly looks and thinly veiled innuendoes that had followed her through out the trial and dogged her steps even after she'd left Atlanta to settle in Augusta.

She was lucky even to have a teaching job after that debacle.

As she rounded the corner of the building heading toward her car at the back of the lot, the growl of a motorcycle startled her. Jumping, she whirled in time to see the leather and jean clad rider whip into the driveway behind her. She was so startled, she merely gaped at him as he drove past her.

After a moment, she started walking again. School was out. Friday would see the last of the seemingly endless rounds of meetings that followed the yearly grind and then she would have nearly four weeks of vacation before the pre-school planning and meetings began.

He was no student from the school. It was impossible to tell how old the man was, but it occurred to her that he might be a college student, without a parking pass, and looking for a place to park his cycle.

She decided if the security hadn't run him off by the time she caught up with him, she'd give him a nudge.

As she cleared the first lot and crossed the raised median strip between the student parking lot and the staff lot, true outrage surged through her, however. The rider pulled the motorcycle up behind her car, parked it and shut the engine off.

She strode toward him purposefully. "You can't park that here. This is the school parking lot."

As if he hadn't heard her, he flicked the kick stand down with one boot shod foot, and pulled one leg over the seat, then settled back on the seat sideways, watching her approach, one leg splayed casually, his boot resting on the ground, the other propped on the motorcycle, his arm draped over it. "You've blocked me in!" Emerald said a little breathlessly as she came to a halt less than a yard away from him.

He lifted one hand to his chin strap and unsnapped it, then gripped the helmet with both hands, pulled it off and set it on the back edge of the long leather seat. His expression was impassive, his stance appeared relaxed, but his whole attitude was watchful and tense with waiting.

Emerald stared at him blankly for several moments, but it was the shock of recognition that held her rooted to the spot, not the lack of it. Unable to stop herself, she searched his face. If anything the years had only made him more devastatingly handsome than ever. He was heavier than he had been before, but there was nothing about him that suggested it was anything other than more muscle. The protective lightweight jacket he wore was open, revealing only a thin T-shirt beneath that faithfully followed every contour of his muscular chest. His jeans fit him like a second skin, cupping the bulge of his sex in a way that made it impossible for Emerald to ignore, even though she managed to refrain from looking directly at it. Memories tumbled through her brain, most of them painful, embarrassing, or both, but superseding all of them, to her dismay, was the memory of his body moving inside of her. Her belly clenched almost painfully in remembrance. She felt blood rush to her cheeks.

"It's been a long time, Em."

"Emerald," she corrected automatically, speaking with an effort, then shook her head when she realized, belatedly, that he'd called her by her first name. "Ms. Green."

One dark brow rose. His sensual mouth hitched up a notch at one corner.

Irritation flooded through her, ousting her embarrassment, but she wasn't about to inform him she wasn't married because she liked it that way. Men could say such things and no one ever doubted it, but just let a woman claim she preferred to be single and everyone around her smirked, certain she was secretly devastated that she hadn't been claimed by a male.

"I missed you."

The blush returned. "Reece ... there was nothing to miss. There never was anything between us except a ... mistake, which we both paid for dearly." She almost choked on the lie, because the truth was he had not just claimed her body that day, he had touched her so deeply no man had ever been able to even come close to arousing her interest since.

He flushed. "Did you?"

Guilt prompted a surge of anger, though why she should feel guilty, she was at a loss to know. None of what had happened had been of her doing. "I didn't leave Georgia because I wanted a change of scenery. Don't ... please don't ruin this for me."

He cocked an eyebrow, but his eyes narrowed.

"I came a long way."

Emerald looked at him skeptically. "Your parents live in Florida, don't they?"

Pain flickered through his eyes. "Did. They were killed in a crash a couple of months ago, less than a month after I got out. Anyway, you and I both know I've been ... residing in north Georgia."

Dismayed, Emerald could only stare at him for several moments, could think of nothing at all to say to such a terrible tragedy.

Again, the flush of guilt mounted her cheeks. "I'm so sorry ... about your parents, about everything. I tried. You know I did."

He looked away from her. "Have dinner with me. You owe me that much."

It was an outrageous demand, and completely unjustified. She was surprised to discover, however, that she was torn. She wanted to talk to him. Just being near him made her heart rate accelerate. Moreover, she felt the need to talk about what had happened to her with someone, and she had never dared to speak of it for fear that it would bring the new world she'd built for herself tumbling down around her ears.

One the other hand, she wasn't certain she dared risk being seen with him in public. The incident might have happened far away, but his parents had lived in Florida. She couldn't risk the chance that someone might know him, might know that he'd spent time in jail. A teacher's reputation was everything if she wanted to keep her job.

"You've got no right to ask it of me," she said numbly.

"Don't I?"

Sighing her defeat, Emerald glanced around. "I'm headed home. Leave the motorcycle. You can ride with me."

He shook his head. "Come with me."

"Not on your life!"

He shrugged. "I'll follow you then."

She was about to argue with him, but it occurred to her that they'd been talking for some minutes and that, any moment, one of the teachers still in the building might come out. Moreover, she could no more stop him from following her than she'd been able to fend him off the day he'd forcibly seduced her. It would be like trying to stop a train with a pickup truck.

"Fine. Follow me."

* * * *

The neighborhood she lived in was one of the older neighborhoods in Tallahassee. Tremendous live oaks festooned in long, trailing moss, lined both sides of the streets, their branches nearly meeting overhead to form enormous green canopies, casting deep, cooling shade over the street and the front yards of the homes. Grand old Victorians, carefully restored during that period of budding awareness of the historical significance of such architecture, created a parade of architectural beauty. They had faded somewhat in the years since, but they were still beautiful, providing Emerald with a sense of comfort and permanence that she craved to the depths of her soul. The house she lived in had been divided into half, forming a duplex. Her friend and fellow colleague, Maureen Steiger occupied the other half.

It had been Maureen who'd helped her to get her teaching job at the high school. She'd transferred to Florida herself about the time Emerald's world had fallen apart and when another teaching position had opened up, had called her up and offered to put in a word for her if she was willing to relocate to Florida. By that time, Emerald had been desperate to escape the reputation that she'd failed to shake, even by moving to another town. She'd seized the offer eagerly, packed up her few belongings and left north Georgia.

She'd looked back, though, with yearning. She supposed she was always going to miss home.

And she hadn't been able to escape her memories by leaving.

Reece turned into the driveway behind her, pulled his cycle up beside her car and parked it.

Emerald glanced at him nervously, gathered up her files and paperwork, and headed for the door. Acutely conscious of Reece's long-limbed stride behind her, she moved rapidly, trying to put a little distance between them.

Reece leaned against the door frame as she struggled to get her key in the lock, grinning down at her. "In a hurry?"

She blushed. "I always walk fast," she retorted stiffly. "It comes from having short legs."

He straightened away from the wall as she finally managed to get the door open and pushed inside, following her into the front parlor.

"Make yourself at home," she murmured at about the same moment he sprawled on her love seat, taking up most of it. She stumbled over a boot the size of a small cooler on her way to the desk, and he snatched his foot back.

"Sorry," they murmured at the same time.

"This is a nice place," he said, tossing his jacket aside and gazing around while she dropped her purse on the desk top of her secretary and deposited the files she was carrying next to it.

She turned, gazing around as well, trying to see it through a stranger's eyes. "I love it. Just wish it was mine ... but I rent. Someday, maybe."

"It's an awful big house for a little gal like you," he murmured in amusement.

Emerald shrugged. "I know, but they didn't build small Victorian's ... not very small ones, anyway. This one was remodeled into a duplex. I just have the half."

"No live-in boyfriend I should know about?"

Emerald blushed, mostly from irritation. "If I had, I wouldn't have invited you here."

Both of his dark brows rose and Emerald felt her blush deepen. "What I meant was...."

He chuckled. "I know what you meant."

Emerald looked away. "I should go see what I've got that I can put together to make a meal. You can watch TV if you like."

He didn't, though. He followed her into the kitchen, leaning against the counter while she scouted the refrigerator in hopes of finding something that would be relatively quick to fix. The freezer was full of freezer meals and little else.

"Eat alone a lot?"

Emerald turned and glared at him. "Actually, I do. Look, I'm sorry. I don't really have anything to fix, unless you'd be interested in an omelet?"

He studied her for a long moment and finally reached out and grasped her wrist, tugging her toward him. As if she was mesmerized, she allowed him to draw her forward until she was standing between his spread legs. "I've got a better idea," he murmured, looking down at her, his eyes glittering with an emotion she couldn't begin to fathom.

She moistened her dry lips. "What?"

"We'll order in."

It took several moments for the comment to sink in. When it did, Emerald didn't know whether she was more tempted to slap him or laugh. "Good idea!" she said on a nervous laugh, pulling away from him. "I'll grab the phone book."

They ended up ordering Chinese, and then settled in the front parlor while they waited for the delivery.

An uncomfortable silence fell between them once they'd placed the order.

"How have you been, Em?"

"What did you mean...." She stopped when they both spoke at once. "I'm OK. I've managed. What about you?"

He shrugged. "I managed."

Unnerved by his gaze, Emerald rose from her seat. "Look ... Reece ... I don't mean to sound cold and unfeeling, but I've put that whole ... everything behind me. It took a lot of work to do it. I just want to get on with my life."

"Are you?"

"What?"

"Getting on with your life?"

She moved to the window, chewing a fingernail as she watched for the delivery man. "Yes. Actually, I haven't even thought about ... about it in years now."

"Liar."

Startled, she glanced around at him. He rose and moved toward her. Unnerved, she backed up a step. "What do you mean?"

"The moment you looked at me, I saw all of it in your face, Em. You haven't forgotten a thing, and it's for damn sure you haven't forgotten me."

Chapter Three

Emerald was saved from having to respond to his uncomfortably accurate observation by the arrival of the delivery boy. As she glanced away from Reece, she saw the guy coming up the walk.

"It's the delivery boy," she said quickly and scooted around Reece, heading for her purse. The doorbell rang while she was still fumbling to get her wallet out. She heard Reece stride from the room and the sound of the front door opening. Grabbing her wallet quickly, she headed for the hallway.

"How much is it?" she asked, digging for a twenty.

"I took care of it," Reece said, closing the door.

"Did you tip him?" Emerald asked without thinking.

He gave her a look. "A quarter. Think that was enough?"

Emerald gaped at him.

"I've been in prison, not on the moon," he said dryly. "I've been out for months. I've got a pretty good idea of how the outside world works."

Emerald turned bright red. It was something those who hadn't been born blond didn't properly appreciate … the fact that very fair skin generally went with very blond hair and when she blushed, she looked like a neon sign lighting up. It was the bane of her existence that 'poker faced' wasn't a part of her anatomy. Her students had always taken great delight in making her blush at every opportunity.

"I guess I still think of you as a kid," she said uncomfortably. "Anyway, I invited you. It's my treat."

He glared at her a long moment and finally strode past her towards the kitchen instead of commenting on her remark. "I invited myself. It's my treat."

It was true, of course, but she had a feeling he didn't have much money. Even if he'd been out as long as he claimed, he had a record and he'd only graduated from high school. Getting a job couldn't be easy. Finding one that paid would be even harder.

On the other hand, she'd already stuck her foot in her mouth. She didn't really want to insult him again by suggesting he couldn't afford to pay for the take out.

He was digging the containers out of the bags when she arrived in the kitchen and setting them out on the small island. "We forgot to order anything to drink," he said as she came in.

"I've got tea and cokes."

"No beer?"

She gave him a look.

"I'm twenty seven, Em, not nineteen."

In spite of all she could do, a faint blush tinged her cheeks. "I know ... well, I hadn't thought about it. But I don't drink beer."

He shrugged. "I thought you might have some for male friends."

She whirled abruptly and went to the cabinet to get plates out, hoping he wouldn't notice her color fluctuation. The truth was, she hardly dated. She had hardly ever dated, at all, even before the abduction.

It wasn't that she didn't get plenty of appreciative looks from the opposite sex. She did. There'd been men from time to time who'd asked her out, and, occasionally, she went. She was devoted to her teaching career, however, which didn't leave her a lot of time for extra curricular activities. Most of the male teachers who'd been single when they began teaching out of college had long since settled down with a wife and one point five kids--her hunting grounds had been virtually hunted out long before it had occurred to her even to consider marriage--and meeting someone outside her chosen field was even harder. Aside from work, there were only two places for singles to meet--bars or church-- and she hadn't been interested in either extreme. "I don't have one at the moment," she said, with perfect truth.

"I always wondered about that."

She set the plates down on the counter and went to get eating utensils and glasses. "What?"

"You didn't date back then, either."

Emerald threw him an amused look. "How would you know?"

"I knew."

She put her hands on her hips. "How?"

He moved around the counter, grasped her around the waist and, before she could protest, sat her on the countertop so that they were almost eye to eye when he braced an arm on either side of her and leaned toward her. "Because I watched you."

She stared at him, feeling blood creep into her cheeks.

"You know I had a hell of crush on you from the moment I first laid eyes on you."

She considered pretending ignorance, but she could see he wasn't in the mood for coy answers. "Did you? I thought you might, but then I decided it had either passed or I was wrong to begin with and you were just flirting to gauge my reaction."

A gleam of amusement lit his eyes. "When did you arrive at that?"

The blush was back. "I … uh … well, it was impossible not to notice you had half the females in the senior class mooning over you from afar and the rest stalking you."

To her surprise, he blushed. She stared at the dark tide that crept into his cheeks, intrigued.

"I wasn't *that* much of a player," he said irritably.

"I wasn't suggesting you were, only … Well, I knew you'd just transferred and I know how hard that usually is on kids-- leaving all their friends behind and having to start over new somewhere else. I figured you were just … lonely when I noticed your interest, but you made a lot of friends fast, and you didn't lack for female companionship. When you stopped hanging around, I figured you'd gotten over it or I was mistaken."

He stared at her a long moment. "If I'd been 'over it' I wouldn't have ended up spending seven years in prison as one of your abductors … Anyway, I only did it for your benefit … obviously, if you noticed, it worked."

Emerald gaped at him at the admission, but guilt swamped her at the comment about why he'd ended up in prison. "I'm sorry. I told them you had nothing to do with. I tried to keep you out of it. I *lied* to the cops for you. I told them we'd been seeing each other for weeks before that!"

"Why?"

She was taken aback. "What?"

"Why did you risk your whole career by telling them you and I were lovers?"

She looked away. "To keep you out of jail!"

"Why was that so important to you?"

She gaped at him. "Because you were innocent! I knew you were. And I ... couldn't bear to think of your whole life being ruined, only because you'd saved me from God only knows what."

He leaned back, studying her. "That's all it was?"

"That wasn't enough?"

His gaze searched her face. She wasn't certain of what he was looking for, but she had an uneasy feeling that he would find it if it was there to see. After a moment, he lifted one hand, cupping it beneath her chin and moved closer. "I could almost believe that was all there was to it. I know you've got a good heart, Em. I know you have a strong sense of what's fair, and what isn't, but I also know you're fiercely loyal to those you care about, even if it means you have to sacrifice for their sake.... Why would you fight so hard to protect me when I raped you?"

Emerald swallowed. "It wasn't rape."

"If I recall correctly, you said no. I wasn't in the mood to listen, but I heard it just the same."

She tried to look away from him, but he wouldn't allow it. "I was ... I was as caught up in the moment as you were. After everything that had happened, or almost happened, I needed ... needed the comfort. It wasn't your fault. You were just a kid, a slave to raging hormones. I was old enough to know better. It was my place to stop it. I didn't and you paid for it," Emerald said quietly.

"I was nineteen, Em. I was a slave all right, but it had nothing to do with being a kid. I'd had a hard on for you for almost a year. I just couldn't resist seizing the opportunity that presented itself, even though I'd gone to help you with the best of intentions. The problem was, I could never be certain afterwards whether you'd wanted me as much as I wanted you, or if it was just a matter of needing a warm body after what you'd just experienced."

Emerald stared at him a long moment. "Is that why you came? Because you felt we had something ... unfinished between us?"

He stared at her a long moment and finally shook his head slowly. "I came because I *knew* we had unfinished business between us. And we do, don't we, Em?"

She couldn't think of anything to say. It occurred to her that she should tell him there never was anything between them, and never would have been, even if not for that disastrous night. The problem was, she wasn't a very good liar ... and she knew it would be a lie. She had convinced herself that she looked upon him as a cute kid, because she knew it would mean throwing her whole career away if she even considered taking him up on his none too subtle hints and allowing herself to be swept away by his considerable, youthful charm. Deep down, she knew she'd made excuses for herself for yielding to him that night, had lied to herself that she had 'really tried' to stop him, when she knew better. If she'd shown herself unwilling, he never would have forced her. Her weak protests had fallen on deaf ears because he'd known they lacked conviction, that she was merely paying lip service to morality.

"It wouldn't have worked then. It won't work now. I'm eight years older than you. People would talk about me as if I was a child molester ... and I can't afford gossip!"

He frowned. "If I was eight years older than you, neither you nor anyone else would even give it a second thought."

"If you think I like the way things are stacked in men's favor, you're wrong, but it's the way of the world. I'm not in a profession that allows me to be a free spirit, or a radical thinker ... and, despite the fact that I don't always agree with it, and I've felt stifled by the restrictions more than once, I love what I do."

"And that leaves us?"

Emerald swallowed. She knew what she needed to say, but she also knew it wasn't what she wanted to say. Crazy as it seemed, insane as it was, she'd had just as huge a crush on Reece as he claimed to have had on her. She might have been able to deny it back then, but it was as alive today as it had been then and she found it very difficult to ignore. "Nowhere. There is no us. There can't be."

His eyes narrowed. "No?" he said, leaning toward her again until his face was mere inches from hers. "I think there is. I think there always was. I think you were just as stuck on me as I was you and more than that, you still are."

The wall cabinets behind her prevented her from putting as much space between them as she needed. She put her hands on his shoulders. He caught them, curled them behind her back and handcuffed both wrists with one hand, pushing on the middle of her back until she was forced to arch it, thrusting her breasts out as if she were offering them to him. With his free hand, he captured one weighty globe, squeezing it gently. Her breath caught in her throat. "Reece...."

He'd been studying the distended nipple that had grown so hard it was evident even through her blouse and bra, poking up at him as if trying to entice him to have a taste. When she spoke, he looked up at her and for the first time she realized his eyes were a deep, emerald green, they were also hot, glazed with need. Moisture gathered in her sex at the expression on his face.

"Don't," she said without any conviction whatsoever.

He bent his head, opening his mouth over the tip of her breast and nudging her nipple with his tongue. The fabric was no barrier or protection at all. The heat of his mouth stirred currents of desire she'd thought she'd buried eight years ago. "Don't what?" he asked huskily as he lifted his head.

"Don't," she said again.

"Don't make you want me? You do, don't you, Em?"

She swallowed with some difficulty, licked her lips. "I'm a woman, Reece. It's just as natural for me to have a reaction to an attractive man as it is for your body to react to an attractive woman."

He toyed with her nipple, flicking it with his thumb while he studied her. "Teaching sex ed these days, Em?"

She was having difficulty breathing. Desire wafted through her system, heady as wine, and normal brain function seemed to have gone dormant as the sensations running through her body overloaded her circuits. "Sex ed?" she repeated blankly.

He moved closer, brushing her lips lightly with his own. "I know the difference between when a woman wants *me* and when a woman just needs to get laid."

"I ... don't understand," she said breathlessly.

He caught her upper lip, sucked it and released it, then sucked her lower lip gently. "Don't you?"

She grew tired of the teasing and caressed his lips with her tongue, hoping to encourage him. His breath came out in a rush, but he did not kiss her as she'd hoped. Instead, he blazed a trail of kisses along her cheek to her ear, traced the shell of her ear with his tongue, and then, just below her ear, he fastened his mouth over the tender flesh and sucked. The sensation sent another dizzying rush of desire through her. Her panties grew damp with want.

"Tell me," he whispered.

For the life of her, she couldn't figure out what he was asking. "I want you?" she said a little doubtfully, not because she didn't, or because she was in any doubt that she did, but because she realized, dimly, that he was looking for something else.

"Why did you give in to me all those years ago?"

The question was enough of a distraction that Emerald sat back abruptly. "Uh ... the food's getting cold. We should eat."

He didn't look disconcerted at her abrupt change of subject at all. He looked amused ... and hungry. "You're right. I'm starved. Floor or bed?"

Emerald blinked at him in confusion. "What?"

"Floor," he said, covering her mouth in a heated kiss that singed her to her toes. She couldn't think beyond his scent, his taste and the feel of his tongue as it raked along hers in a rough caress, beyond the heat that tightened the muscles in her belly and the throbbing ache of her vagina for the feel of his cock embedded deeply inside of her. She didn't even realize he'd released her hands until she felt the silkiness of his black hair between her fingers and realized her arms had come around him to clutch him close of their own volition. Wrapping her legs around his waist, he scooped her off of the counter, held her tightly a moment as he thoroughly explored her mouth and then broke the kiss and headed for the door.

"Bed," she said, breathily, her head lolling weakly on his shoulder.

He turned abruptly and headed up the stairs. "Which door?"

"Second."

He kicked the door to behind them, releasing her and allowing her to slide to the floor, reaching for the buttons on her blouse the moment her feet touched the floor. His fingers were shaking. He frowned, fighting the tiny buttons, and finally gave up. "Take it off," he said impatiently.

He grabbed her before she'd done more than release the buttons, tossing her onto the bed and following her down, kissing her deeply while he thrust aside the clothes that impeded his access of her body. Shoving her skirt up to her waist, he slipped one hand inside her panties while he scooped one breast from the cup of her bra. His mouth covered the distended nipple at the same moment his questing finger discovered her clit.

Emerald cried out as pleasure jolted through her from the suction of his mouth and the teasing stroke of his finger, colliding in her belly and making it clench in anticipation.

He rubbed his finger along her slit, grunting in satisfaction when he found she was wet for him. Cupping her mound, he pushed a large index finger slowly inside of her as he released the nipple he was tormenting and nudged aside her bra, captured the other nipple gently between his teeth and then sucking it. Emerald groaned, arching her hips and pushing against his finger.

It was all the encouragement he needed. Gripping her panties, he tugged them off and pushed her thighs apart, moving between them. She gripped his shoulders, and then shoved her hands down his chest, gripped his T-shirt and burrowed beneath it, peeling the fabric up so that she could feel his bare chest against her own.

He leaned away from her only long enough to unfasten his jeans and free his erection. Taking his cock in his hand, he nudged her wet cleft with it, moistening the head of his cock with her body's juices and finally aligning their bodies. He looked up at her as he breached her opening with the head of his cock.

Emerald gasped as she felt him spreading her flesh almost to the point of pain. She'd forgotten how big he was--had thought it had been her imagination. She hadn't expected to feel her muscles protesting the penetration she wanted so badly. Panting, she spread her thighs wider, pushing up against him anxiously. He dragged in a shuddering breath, clamped his hand on her hip to hold her still. "Be still. I don't want to hurt you."

She clutched his shoulder when she sensed he was gathering to withdraw. "Don't. Please. Don't stop."

He closed his eyes, groaning as her kegel muscles gripped him reflexively, tugging at the head of his cock. Burying his face between her breasts, he gripped her hips and pushed. Slowly, he sank a little deeper and stopped again, waiting for her body to adjust to him before he pushed again. Emerald panted, her heart thundering in her chest until she could scarcely breathe, fighting the urge to lift against him and force her body over his erection.

Realizing she was digging her nails into his shoulders, she released him, gripping the sheets in white knuckled fists. "Oh god," she gasped as he sank his flesh to the hilt inside of her at last and went still, panting with the effort to hold himself still and allow her body to adjust to him.

His head jerked up at her outcry, his face twisting. "I'm hurting you," he said through clenched teeth.

Emerald wrapped her arms and legs around him, pulling his head down and kissing him feverishly. "Don't you dare stop now!" she gasped against his mouth, biting his lower lip. A shudder went through him and then, as if he couldn't hold himself back any longer, he pulled away and thrust again.

"Oh god!" Emerald gasped, struggling to push him away from her so that she could thrust against him. "Like that! Yes!"

Gritting his teeth, he rose up on his knees, grasped her knees and thrust into her again and again, moving faster and faster as she lifted her hips to meet each pounding thrust. She writhed in ecstasy, her body on fire for him. He groaned, went still for a moment, shuddered and then his body convulsed, his hot seed spewing into her in a fiery stream. His jolting thrusts sent her over the edge. She screamed as her climax caught her and tumbled her into mindless oblivion and then went limp beneath him.

Gathering her to him, he rolled onto his back. She lay draped over him, panting as she strove to catch her breath, her ear pressed to his chest. Finally, the thunderous pounding in his chest subsided to a more normal rhythm. Her own heart slowed, and still she was reluctant to move. She could still feel him inside of her. She was a little amazed to realize just how welcome the feel of him inside of her was.

"Em?"

"Mmm?"

"You OK, baby?"

"Mmm."

He caught her face, forcing her head up so that he could look at her. With an effort, she opened her eyes. Lifting his head, he kissed her tenderly on the lips, so sweetly, a knot of tears appeared from no where, tightening her throat.

With an effort, she dismissed it, kissing him back.

When he broke the kiss, she leaned down, kissing his chest. "I hope you're not going to make me wait another eight years for a return performance."

He stiffened, then, chuckling, grabbed her and tossed her onto her back on the bed, moving up so that he rested on his elbows, hovering just above her.

He became serious, however, as he studied her face. "I missed you, Em."

Emerald reached up, caressing his cheek. He had been a devastatingly handsome boy. If possible, he was even more handsome now, and yet it made her ache to think of all the years he'd lost between boyhood and manhood that should have been his. They'd been stolen from him by Mike Todd's lies, naming him as one of the conspirators--the leader, in point of fact--and the police had refused to accept her testimony to the contrary. "I missed you, too, Reece," she said finally.

He turned his head, kissing her palm, then leaned down, nuzzling his face between her breasts, breathing deeply of her scent. "I've thought of this every day for eight years," he murmured. "I was afraid I wouldn't have the patience to make it good for you."

Warmth filled her at his words, and at the doubt in them. Her heart tightened almost painfully. She wrapped her arms around his head, cradling him to her for several moments before she pulled away, placing a hand on each of his cheeks and urging him to look at her. Honesty deserved the same. "It's been a long time for me, too."

Something gleamed in his eyes--fire, triumph. He looked down, tracing a finger around and around one nipple until it stood erect. "But not eight years."

Emerald swallowed, wondering if she dared tell him the truth, but when he looked up at her again she found she couldn't do anything else. "Yes."

He glanced away. "Waiting for me?" he said almost jokingly.

Emerald swallowed with some difficulty. "I don't think I realized it till now ... but, yes. I believe I was."

The look he gave her was doubtful and hopeful at the same time. After a moment, he rolled to his side, propping his head in one hand and running his hand lightly down her body. "You're beautiful, Em. More beautiful than I remembered. That first time ... I wanted you so bad I hardly spared the time to look at you ... and then they took me away and all I could do was try to imagine."

"Didn't you?"

He glanced up at her sharply.

"I thought ... I felt that you studied me while I was bound," she confessed.

He reddened slightly, swallowed with an effort. "I could not drag my gaze from you, could not think." He slipped his hand between her legs and slid a finger along her slit, parting the folds of flesh, seeking the nub of pleasure. Emerald gasped, her eyes sliding half closed as his questing finger sent a jolt of pleasure through her.

"I saw this pretty little thing and I couldn't think beyond filling it with my cock. I didn't trust myself to touch you at first. Finally, I thought I'd mastered it, but the moment I held you I lost it." His lips curled faintly. "I didn't really take the time to look my fill at you."

Emerald couldn't help but wonder if she was a sucker for pretty words, if he was merely telling her what he thought she wanted to hear ... and still it moved her. "We've got all the time in the world now ... But I want to see you too. Twice we've made love and both times you were still fully clothed," she added teasingly, tugging at his twisted T-shirt.

He reddened, but slid off the bed and tugged the shirt over his head, tossing it aside. His jeans and shorts were halfway down his hips. He hooked his thumbs in them and pushed them down, stepping out of them, then, propping on the edge of the mattress, peeled his socks off and tossed them aside. When he stood erect once more, Emerald saw his cock was hard and ready. It took an effort to drag her gaze from it and study his body. She came up on her knees, placing her palms on his chest and skating them over the hard bulge of his pecs and down along the washboard of his belly.

She clasped his cock, pushing the foreskin down as she stroked it slowly. He jerked slightly as she grasped him, sucking in a breath, but held perfectly still as she caressed him. Moving to the edge of the bed, she lowered her head and took the head of his cock into her mouth. He caught her hair, groaning as she sucked him. Pleased with his reaction, feeling excitement thrumming in her own veins, she took him fully into her mouth, caressing him, sucking him more greedily as her passion mounted.

She was disappointed when he stopped her.

"My turn," he said hoarsely.

Obediently, her heart thundering in her chest, she lay back on the bed.

Placing a knee on the bed, he shook his head. "Not like that." Pulling her to a sitting position, he urged her back until she was leaning against the headboard then took her hands and spread her arms wide. Understanding dawned, and she grasped the headboard on either side of her. Taking her ankles, he spread her thighs wide. He settled on his stomach then, examining her femininity with one finger, lightly parting the petals of flesh. "It is beautiful," he murmured thickly, moving forward and placing his mouth over it.

Emerald gasped at the heat of his mouth, reaching to grasp his head and cup him to her. He tugged her hands loose and placed them on the headboard again, then caught first one breast and then the other in his mouth, sending mind numbing waves of pleasure shooting through her. She was so weak by the time he began to make his way down her belly that she had to hold on to the headboard tightly to keep from falling. Sprawling between her legs again, he scooped her buttocks into his hands, lifting her hips from the bed and tilting them up to his mouth, as if serving himself a dish, and opened his mouth wide over her pussy, sucking her. Emerald gasped at the hot abrasion of his tongue as he explored her cleft from her clit to her body's opening, sending a rush of sensation throughout her body, felt as if she were falling into an abyss of pure sensual delight when he returned his attention to her clit, sucking, teasing it with his tongue. She was nearing climax when he withdrew.

Rising up on his knees, he pulled her to him so that she was straddling his lap and pushed his cock into her, impaling her. She gasped, gripping his shoulders, squeezing her eyes closed as he imbedded himself so deeply inside her she thought she might be rent in two. Slowly, her body adjust and as it did, she began to move, lifting and lowering herself, glorying in the near pain of being stretched to her limits. On her third downward stroke, something glorious exploded inside of her, shaking her to her core. She cried out, flinging her arms tightly around his neck as her climax spasmed through her. He caught her hips, lifting her and pounding into her hard and fast until his own climax burst explosively inside of her.

When the quakes finally subsided, she lifted her head with an effort and kissed the side of his neck, stroking his back. He kissed her, but chuckled shakily. "OK, lady. One more like that tonight and I'll die of a heart attack."

Emerald laughed. "Poor baby. I should have fed you first."

He lifted her away from him and collapsed on the bed. "I'm not sure I've got the energy to make it down the stairs."

Emerald leaned toward him, kissing him in the middle of the chest. "Wait here. I'll bring sustenance."

Chapter Four

Emerald was a little alarmed when she woke the following morning and tried to get out of bed. The moment she stood up her legs shook as if she had palsy and her femininity throbbed painfully, as if it had been used for a punching bag--which she supposed, in a way, it had. Her first step almost brought her to her knees as her groin tendons screamed in protest. She sat back on the bed, holding herself, torn between the urge to laugh and the need to cry.

Reece had left after they'd eaten their belated dinner the night before so she could at least be thankful he wasn't lying in her bed, watching her creep around like an old woman.

Upon reflection, she had to be glad, too, that she'd been so sated by two bouts of lovemaking she'd begged off on thirds ... but he'd been oh so sweet, and she'd been oh so tempted. It was nice to know that at some point her brain had kicked into gear again and saved her from making things any worse.

After a few moments, she rose determinedly, crept into the bathroom and ran a tub of hot water. The first dunking of her badly abused femininity almost made her faint, but she finally managed to settle and soaked until the water cooled and the throbbing eased off.

She wasn't quite as stiff when she climbed out, but she still ached enough that it was impossible to drag her mind from her soreness long enough to concentrate on anything else.

She was running late by the time she'd managed to grab a bite of breakfast.

As luck would have it, her friend and neighbor, Maureen, was also running late.

"Emerald! I thought you'd be gone by now!"

With an effort, Emerald turned and smiled. "I overslept," she lied.

Maureen's brows rose, but she merely nodded. "You OK?"

"Why do you ask?"

Maureen frowned, but finally shook her head. "I could've sworn I heard ... something last night. I was tempted to check on you, but I thought if there was any kind of problem you'd call...."

"No," Emerald said quickly. "No problems."

"I couldn't help but notice you had a visitor last night. Someone new?" she prodded teasingly.

Emerald made an effort to walk to the steps without flinching. "Uh ... no. Actually, it was a very old friend. Someone I hadn't seen in a while. We were up till all hours catching up. Guess that's why I overslept."

Maureen was studying her as she made her way around the car. "Sure you didn't fall ... or anything? You look like you're in pain."

Emerald forced a smile. "I ...uh... slipped in the shower. Must have thrown something out."

"Maybe you should call in sick today?" Maureen suggested, pausing beside her own car, which was parked behind Emerald's, with her key in her lock.

"It's tempting, but I think I'll be fine in a little while. I just need to walk it off."

Maureen nodded and opened her door. Something in the edge of the flower bed caught her eye and she left the car again and reached for it. "You didn't get the paper this morning."

Emerald had managed to get into the driver's seat. She looked up as Maureen shoved the newspaper under her nose. "I overslept," she reminded her. "Thanks. Guess I'll have to read it later."

Tossing the rolled paper onto the seat beside her, she closed her door and started the car. After a moment, Maureen took the hint and got back into her own car. Emerald watched her back from the drive from her rear view mirror.

Ordinarily, she never gave Maureen's nosiness much thought. Today, it irritated her. It was just as well Reece *had* left, not that she'd made any attempt to convince him to stay. She had, in fact, been relieved when he'd said he had to go. The fact was that as much as she enjoyed his company--and his lovemaking--she was in no position to allow any man to stay with her. Tallahassee was a city, but it had not completely lost its small town ways-- something she ordinarily found very charming about the north Florida city--but it also meant that her neighbors would notice, and talk, if she allowed a man to stay with her, increasing the chances that the school board could get wind of it, which could get her fired.

And Reece was not just any man. She shuddered to think what might happen if it was ever discovered just who her male friend was and that he had served time in prison.

She knew he was innocent of the crime he'd been convicted of, but she hadn't been able to convince anyone else of it.

She didn't want the two of them 'on trial' again, and the best way to avoid that was to make sure she used discretion in seeing

Reece ... always assuming he intended to hang around for a while.

She frowned when she realized he hadn't said anything about the possibility of staying a while. All he'd said when he left was that he had some things to take care of. She'd assumed he would get in touch with her again, but she'd had the impression when they'd first met that he was merely traveling through.

It was a daunting thought. She'd spent so much time worrying about anyone finding out she was seeing him and the potential for trouble, the possibility that he had no interest in seeing her again hadn't even crossed her mind ... until now.

Would she see him again? Or would she be left to wait and wonder until, finally, she had to face the fact that he'd breezed through her life and gone away? And the realization sank in that she was merely a one night stand?

She felt a little sick at that thought, mostly because she'd wanted that 'forbidden fruit' as long as she'd known him and it hadn't taken more than a little encouragement from him to push her over the line into an emotionally devastating infatuation, even though she'd thought she was way too practical and sensible for such a thing to happen to her--and why shouldn't she? She'd never been in any danger of it before in her life.

She'd known the first time she ever laid eyes on him, though, that Reece Yeager wasn't just a teen heart throb, he was a heart breaker. He'd done absolutely nothing after that first impression to dispel it, moving from one female to another throughout that long ago school year as if he was the only stud in the kingdom and required to service all the mares.

Not that she had any certainty that he'd slept with the females she'd seen draped over him, but she couldn't see any of the girls fighting him off ... *They* had been following him around as if he was catnip, not the other way around. On the other hand, Reece was a young man at the prime of his life. There were few, she didn't doubt, that could resist sex when offered.

When she'd parked her car at the school, she merely sat, staring out the windshield, thinking back over everything that had happened the night before.

After some minutes, she arrived at a very unpleasant conclusion.

Reece Yeager must be laughing his ass off right about now.

It wasn't bad enough that she hadn't made any attempt to fend him off. She'd told him, like a complete moron, that she'd been waiting for him.

It was the truth, of course, even though she'd never realized it before, but even a young, inexperienced girl knew better than to tell a man he'd conquered, particularly with so little effort. *She* certainly should have known better, even with her slight experience.

Blood flooded her cheeks. She dropped her head to the steering wheel, trying to fight off the awful sense of shame, embarrassment--and if she was honest with herself, the pure misery of the lovelorn--that flooded her at the realization that she'd been a complete and utter sucker for a modern day Casanova.

She didn't know whether she wanted to cry or scream curse words worse, but she realized she couldn't afford to do either. Pride aside, she was supposed to be a mature, responsible woman. She couldn't afford to behave like a thwarted, lovelorn teenager. After a moment, she lifted her head, smoothed her hair and got out of the car. It was Casanova's revenge, however, that filled her mind with every step she took on the way to her classroom and it wasn't until she was able, finally, to settle in a chair, that she managed to--mostly--put Reece from her mind and concentrate on her work.

Maureen tapped on her door at lunch. "Coming down to the cafeteria to eat?"

Emerald smiled wanly. "Actually, I forgot my lunch this morning, but I'm not really hungry."

"Probably just as well ... I've kind of lost my appetite. Did you see the paper?"

Emerald glanced at her, a little surprised. "I didn't think you read the paper."

Maureen shrugged. "You know I don't ... ordinarily. But I heard this on the radio on the way to work and stopped to grab one." She plunked the paper down in front of Emerald.

Emerald stared at the headline blankly. *Tallahassee woman found brutally murdered.* A shiver went through her. "How awful! Was it someone you knew?"

Maureen stared at her. "God no! What made you think that?"

Emerald frowned. "It's just ... well, you usually avoid this sort of thing. I was just wondering what there was about it that caught your attention."

Maureen tapped the paper. "Read it. I'll see you later."

Emerald nodded, waving absently as she folded the newspaper so that the story was facing up.

A Tallahassee woman was found murdered this morning in her home. A native of Florida, the petite blond was a former Miss Florida and was employed by Winton Marketing at the time of her death.

Police place her time of death sometime before dawn today. Although the police declined to give out any more information pending further investigation, an unidentified source indicated that there was a possibility that the death of the thirty five year old woman might have been the result of sexual games gone terribly wrong. The victim was discovered tied to her bed, brutally raped and strangled.

Emerald stared blankly at the paper as the words blurred before her eyes.

There was far too much about the piece that reminded her of her abduction eight years earlier.

She shook the thought off.

She was imagining things. Except for the fact that the woman was small, blond and had been tied up, there was nothing even remotely similar to her own experience, and, statistically, small women were more often victims than larger women for the simple reason that they were easier prey. She'd seen enough forensics shows to know that she fit the perfect profile of 'victim'--five foot nothing, a hundred ten pounds--an average sized man could grab a small woman, drag her into the bushes and rape and strangle her in under fifteen minutes.

Wadding the newspaper up, she stuffed it in the trash can and went back to work.

Despite her earlier doubts regarding Reece, she found as she left the building that afternoon that she was glancing around hopefully as she walked to her car. It wasn't until she got in her car and started it to head home, though, that she realized that that had been uppermost in her mind, the reason she'd kept glancing around, the reason she'd been in no real hurry to get to her car.

It angered and embarrassed her all over again when she realized just how disappointed she was that he hadn't been waiting for her. Why was it that she'd never noticed before how needy she was? What was wrong with her? She'd managed to get along just fine before without a man in her life. She couldn't ever remember actually thinking that she was lonely, or that she wished someone would be waiting for her when she got home. If she had, she'd have gotten a cat or goldfish ... or something.

She'd have gotten a man.

It wasn't like she couldn't. She'd turned down plenty of offers for short term and even for longer term relationships ... because she didn't want it badly enough to settle for what she could get if she couldn't get what she wanted.

She just hadn't realized before Reece had showed up that *he* was the one she'd wanted and had never expected to have ... and he was probably cruising down I75, heading for Palm Beach right about now.

Shaking off her depression, she went by the grocery store on her way home and stocked up on junk food, then went by the video store and rented a handful of movies.

The special 'treats' lifted her spirits. She was feeling pretty darned cheerful until she got home. The moment she walked through the door, however, the silence nearly deafened her. It was amazing that she'd never thought of the place as being big and empty until Reece had filled it with his presence, then vacated.

Dropping the movies on the love seat in the front parlor, she took the bag of junk food to the kitchen, tossed the ice cream into the freezer and dragged a freezer meal out, stuffing it into the microwave.

While she was waiting for the buzzer, she went into the front room and turned on the TV set, flipping through the channels until she found the local news. The piece about the murdered woman was running.

She sat down, listening, feeling her stomach tighten with nerves as the news woman gestured toward the house behind her and described, in gruesome detail, the crime scene. The woman had been found tied to the posts of the headboard. There appeared to have been something unusual about the way she'd been tied, but the police weren't releasing that information.

According to the coroner's report, the woman had died of strangulation. The news woman went on to speculate on the possibility of the victim having been accidentally strangled while engaging in autoerotic asphyxiation with the perp, who had yet to be identified.

There had been no signs of a break in which had led the police to believe that the woman had invited her killer into her home.

Emerald turned the TV off and went back into the kitchen. After staring at her dinner through the glass door of the microwave for several moments, she moved to the drawer where she kept the silverware, collected a spoon, the half gallon container of Butter Pecan ice cream she'd bought and went upstairs to her bedroom.

She'd eaten almost a quarter of it before she began to feel distinctly ill.

Making her way downstairs again, she scraped the last of her temptation into the sink, washed it down the food disposal and tossed the empty container. After locking up and turning off all the lights downstairs, she grabbed the bag of movies and went upstairs to watch TV in bed.

After two days of pure hell, Emerald finally took herself to task for behaving like an over-sexed teenager. It was Friday ... her last day of drudgery before her vacation. She made up her mind to load up her car and head for the beach first thing Saturday morning. The prospect perked her flagging spirits right up.

When she pulled into her driveway that afternoon, however, her whole world turned upside down again.

Reece, his back propped against one of the porch posts, was lounging on her front steps ... talking to Maureen.

If a bomb had gone off in her head, her brain couldn't have been more rattled.

Maureen was the very last person on earth she had wanted to see, or to know, that Reece had been to see her.

She was at once elated, and furious, to find Reece waiting for her.

She hadn't a clue of how she should handle the situation, but one thought took hold of her and wouldn't be shaken. She had to get Reece inside, out of view of all the neighbors, and most particularly, she needed to get him away from Maureen.

Climbing out of the car, she pasted a smile on her face and headed for the house. She had no idea what she said to either Reece or Maureen, but somehow she found herself inside with the door firmly shut behind her.

She was shaking, she discovered, when she turned around to face Reece. "I ... uh ... could you excuse me?"

She locked herself in her bedroom and paced the floor, trying to decide how she should handle the situation. It wouldn't have been so bad if she'd had the chance to decide how she would behave, what she'd say ... if she'd considered how she would feel if he actually did show up again.

He'd been gone for days. She'd come to believe he wouldn't be back. She'd convinced herself that he wouldn't, that she'd been 'had' and that she had to put it from her mind and get on with her life.

It wasn't as if he was her boyfriend, fiancé, husband or long time lover. She had no rights to him. She couldn't yell at him like a shrew and demand to know where he'd been, chastise him for worrying her.

But he had fucked her senseless on her bed less than a week ago--she couldn't go down and pretend they were just friends--or act as if he was a stranger she felt compelled to be polite to.

She jumped when he tapped at the door.

"Em?"

"Yes?"

"Are you all right?"

She thought, for several horrifying moments, that she was going to burst into tears. She cleared her throat, took several deep, cleansing breaths. "Yes. I'll be down in a few minutes. I ... uh ... I just wanted to change."

She wanted to change into someone else, but she didn't think she could manage it in ten minutes. Moving to her dresser, she dragged out the first thing that came to hand, tossed her work clothes onto the bed and changed. She made it a point not to check her appearance.

She wasn't trying to look good for him. She was just trying to stall for time ... Which was a waste of time, because it wasn't likely she was going to be able to pull herself together when the cause of her chaotic state of mind was standing outside her bedroom door demanding to know what was wrong with her.

Reece met her on the landing outside. "What's wrong, baby?"

Emerald had to suppose her smile looked as artificial as it felt. "Nothing. Just surprised to see you again ... uh ... so soon. Did you mention you'd be over tonight?"

She started down the stairs. "I don't think I have a thing in the house to cook."

Reece caught up to her at the bottom of the stairs, grasping her and pulling her to a halt. "Something's happened."

Emerald blinked up at him, dismayed that her state was so blatantly obvious, hoping he was referring to something else. "Give me a clue."

He frowned. "Baby, you're the worst actress I've ever seen. Why don't you tell me what the hell's wrong with you? You turned white as death when you pulled up in the drive and saw me sitting on your front porch."

Emerald chewed a nail, thinking. "I don't think I know," she said finally.

He studied her a long moment and finally pulled her against him. "You didn't expect to see me, did you?"

She closed her eyes, breathing in his scent. His was right about one thing ... well, a couple. She wasn't worth a shit at subterfuge ... and she hadn't expected to see him again, at all, ever. She'd almost convinced herself she was glad. "It did occur to me that you might not come back," she said, deciding on a half truth. No commitment there. No complaining. Just a straightforward--'I was surprised'.

"Why would you think that?"

"Because you left?"

He gripped her shoulders, holding her slightly away from him. "I told you I had some things to take care of."

She nodded. "Yes. I remember. I'm not complaining. It's none of my business."

He released her abruptly, frowning. "What do you mean it's none of your business?"

Emerald looked up at him. "I mean, I understand that you were just passing through and stopped by to see me. It's not like ... uh...."

"It was just a pretty good fuck, right?"

Emerald felt the blood rush from her face and then back again with a vengeance. "Don't say that, please."

"Why not? It's what you were thinking, isn't it?"

Emerald rubbed her temples, but she realized she was fighting a loosing battle with her tumultuous emotions. "No. But I figured it was what you were thinking."

He studied her a long moment, then slipped an arm around her waist and led her into the front parlor. Sprawling on the love seat, he pulled her down on his lap. She tried to climb off again, but he held her, tipping her chin up so that she couldn't avoid his gaze.

"I didn't look you up in hopes of a quick lay on my way home, Em. I came because I want you to be a part of my life. I just figured … all things considered, we should take it slow, take the time to get to know one another … to figure out if it was what we both wanted."

Emerald nodded, forced a smile. "Of course. You're right. You know how things are for me. It's difficult, but I figured you were thinking of a here and there sort of thing anyway … when you were in town. And we could be discreet." She was babbling. She knew she was. Most of what she'd said was like computer garbage--bits and pieces of information from a hundred different thoughts.

He pushed her off his lap abruptly and got up, glaring at her.

Emerald gaped up at him.

"Ashamed to be seen with me, Em?"

She didn't have to answer. The neon flash on her face told him what he needed to know. He studied her a long moment, whirled on his heel and headed for the door.

Emerald watched him, knowing it was for the best. She'd been certain he didn't really want her in his life anyway.

But she knew he wouldn't be back. If she let him walk out that door, thinking what he thought and he really did care anything about her, he'd never forgive her for it. He'd be too proud to be with a woman who was ashamed to be seen with him.

She clenched her fists on her lap, telling herself she'd live through it. She'd get over it. They'd both be much better off. She had no business even wanting a relationship with a man eight years her junior … and in the long term, it couldn't work out. He'd get tired of having an 'old lady' and want a fresh young model. Didn't men do that anyway? Even when they married women their own age, the minute they turned forty, or fifty, they wanted to dump them and find a twenty something lover.

She heard the doorknob turn.

Her heart felt as if someone had ripped it out of her chest.

She leapt to her feet and rushed into the hallway, skidding to a halt when she saw he'd already opened the door. He glanced at her, his face set, angry … hurt.

Tears filled her eyes. "I thought it didn't mean anything to you. I was just trying to cope."

He looked at her piercingly.

Emerald thought about how badly she wanted him and leapt off the cliff. "I love you."

He turned pale and for several moments Emerald thought she was going to be ill. She'd said the wrong thing! Men didn't want to hear that! It meant commitment, responsibility … the drudgery of having the same piece of ass night after night.

Could she fix it? Was there any possible line that could follow that one that would keep a man from running for his life?

"No strings!" she added quickly.

"No strings?"

He shut the door. Relief flooded her. He was willing to negotiate. She nodded.

"I can come and go as I please and you won't question me? Or complain? Or give me the cold shoulder because you're pissed off about it?" he said, advancing toward her.

She hadn't expected him to outline the terms so specifically, or thought he'd expect her to agree before she'd had time to really consider them. She nodded, though.

"What about other women?"

Emerald felt the blood rush from her face. Was he talking about playing around? Or was he asking if she was willing to do a threesome? "Other women?"

He nodded, coming to a halt when he was almost toe to toe with her. "You have a problem with that?"

Emerald swallowed. She had a problem with it, a big one, but beggars couldn't be choosers, could they? "What I don't know won't hurt me," she said feebly, knowing it was a lie. Now that he'd firmly planted the idea in her head she wouldn't be able to think of anything else when he was gone.

"Interesting. You're not jealous?"

She'd never thought she was jealous-natured, but the idea of Reece seeing someone else, anyone else, made her feel sick to her stomach.

He caught her jaw in an almost bruising grip. "I *am* jealous. I *have* strings. I love you, Em, but if I find out you're cheating on me don't think for one minute that I won't walk out the door and never look back. Understand?"

Relief was her undoing. Emerald burst into painful, wrenching sobs. He looked taken aback.

"You haven't, have you?"

Emerald shook her head, throwing herself against his chest. "You're almost as big a fool as I am, Reece. I love you. I've no interest in anyone else."

He hugged her tightly, then pulled away enough to kiss her. Emerald kissed him back, briefly, then excused herself to go wash her face. He was sitting in the front parlor when she returned, gazing morosely at his hands.

She studied him a moment, then pushed him back and climbed on his lap. He looked at her a little doubtfully. "I'm not sure I understand what just happened. I thought, when I left, that everything was settled ... or pretty much settled ... between us."

Emerald kissed him, then lowered her head to his shoulder. Pulling his arm around her, she held his hand, studying it. "You don't understand women nearly as well as I thought you did, darlin'."

He stiffened. "What did I do wrong?"

"You left me to wonder whether you meant to come back or not. When it didn't seem like you intended to, I thought it had just been a one nighter for you. You didn't tell me you cared for me."

"I told you I hadn't thought of anyone but you since I left," he said, a trace of indignation in his voice.

Emerald sighed. "But that could have meant anything ... could've just been a line to get in my pants. It wouldn't be the first time a guy came up with a line like that."

He grabbed her face, forcing her to look at him. "I ... love ... you. Is that plain enough?"

A smile curled Emerald's lips. "You look so angry."

"I am, damn it!" he said, but his lips twitched on the verge of an answering smile. "I was looking forward to a warm welcome all the way back from Palm Beach, and instead I meet this female with snakes in her head."

Emerald gave him a look. "Excuse me?"

"Oh no you don't," he murmured, leaning down to kiss her thoroughly. "You're not starting another argument with me until I get my warm welcome."

Emerald chuckled. "Well you aren't going to get it here."

He stood abruptly, taking her with him and Emerald squeaked in surprise, tightening her arms around his neck. "You first ... then food."

Chapter Five

Emerald bounced when she hit the bed. She braced herself for impact as Reece dove for her. The side rails of the bed groaned under the impact.

Obviously, the guy just didn't realize he was big as all outdoors.

To her relief, however, Reece didn't land on top of her. He landed beside her, depressing the bed so that she rolled toward him, slamming against his shoulder.

He raised up, grabbed the knit shirt she was wearing and shoved it up, exposing her bra. "You've got on too many clothes," he complained, burying his face between her breasts and breathing deeply.

"You didn't give me time to take them off," she pointed out a little breathlessly.

"Because I like to unwrap my pretty thing myself," he murmured, nuzzling his way past her bra and licking one nipple, which he could just reach with the tip of his tongue.

Her breath caught in her throat. She went still, focusing on the budding desire his teasing caress elicited. "Did you mean it?"

"What?"

"What you said," she prodded.

"Which thing I said?" he murmured without much interest.

Emerald sighed, but she wanted to hear it again. "The part about the way you felt about me."

He raised up on his elbows, studying her seriously, but a smile tugged at the corner of his lips. "No. If I catch you cheating on me, I'll kill the son-of-a-bitch."

Emerald gaped at him. "You don't really think I would!"

He frowned, all signs of amusement vanishing. "No. I don't think you're like that, but it's been a long time, Em. It occurred to me that you might have changed since I knew you before."

She touched his face. "And you?"

His lips flattened. "Prison has a way of changing people ... and rarely for the better. Does it bother you that much?"

"Of course it bothers me! I hate that it happened to you. I hate that I had anything to do with it."

"You didn't put me there. You did your damnedest to keep me out. I'm going to be pissed if I find out this has got anything to do with guilt you've been carrying around."

Emerald swallowed. "I can't help the guilt."

He frowned. "I did it to myself, Em. That's one of the things that pisses me off the most … that I did it to myself. But I don't blame you for it. It was my stupid mistake."

"A stupid mistake you wouldn't have made if you hadn't decided to play hero and rescue me," she said tartly. "And you wouldn't have had to if I hadn't been so naïve as to fall for Mike Todd's clumsy setup."

Reece sighed and turned over on his back, staring at the ceiling. "Is it guilt, Em?"

Pulling her T-shirt over her head, Emerald tossed it aside and moved over him, straddling his waist. Slowly, her gaze holding his, she reached behind her, unfastened her bra and shrugged her shoulders, allowing the bra straps to slip down her arms. Tossing it aside, she cupped her heavy breasts in her hands, massaging them, watching Reece's reaction. "Is that what you think? When I get wet for you the moment you touch me? When I scream in ecstasy every time you make love to me? You think it's guilt that makes me quiver all over when you stroke me with your hands? That makes me gasp and moan like someone dying when I feel your tongue caressing me, tasting me?"

He reached for her, pushing her hands aside and caressing her breasts, then allowed his hands to slide along her rib cage to her waist. "I can almost reach around you," he murmured, his eyes glowing with heat.

She should have just accepted the compliment, but honesty compelled her to say, "It'd be more flattering if your hands weren't as big as my head."

He glanced at her and then chuckled, flipped her onto her back and came up on his knees. Grasping the snap of her jeans, he unfastened them and began tugging them from her hips. When he'd tossed them aside, he pulled his shirt off and threw it to the floor as well, then ran his hand down her stomach and slipped it under the edge of her panties, cupping her.

She was wet … but she was also still sore. She winced.

He frowned. "What's this?"

She blushed to the roots of her hair. "I'm just a little tender, that's all."

He looked torn between sympathy and amusement. "You saying I fucked you bow-legged?" he murmured, settling beside her.

Emerald rolled her eyes. "Something like that."

He chuckled, stroking the abused area gently. "Poor baby. Want me to kiss it and make it better?"

Emerald gasped, spreading her legs wider as his caressing finger found her clit and began stroking it, sending jolts of pleasure through her. "Anything," she gasped.

His eyes darkened and all playfulness vanished. He moved over her as if he would consume her, lathing every inch of her body with his tongue, sucking a trail of love bites from her throat across her breasts and along her belly. Emerald writhed beneath his hungry caresses, intoxicated by rapture, oblivious to anything beyond the feel of his mouth and tongue ... stroking every part of his body she could reach. Finally, when she felt she couldn't wait any longer, when she began to fear she'd climax without him ever entering her, she began to clutch at him, urging him wordlessly to penetrate her.

Instead, he grasped her hips, lifting them off the bed and placed his mouth over her sex. She cried out, jackknifing off the bed. He raised her hips higher, overbalancing her, and she collapsed back against the bed, pleading with him to stop, fighting desperately to hold her climax at bay.

"Now! Please, Reece!"

He lowered her hips and moved over her, caressing her cheek. "Shh, baby. I just wanted to make sure you were ready for me."

"I'm ready," she gasped, reaching for his jeans, tearing at the snap and zipper. He pushed her hands away, shoved his jeans and shorts down his hips and grasped his cock in one hand, guiding it toward her body's opening. She spread her thighs wide, lifting her hips for him, gripping his shoulders and holding her breath as she felt the first tentative probing of his cock head.

She was still tender. She realized that the very moment his cock began to stretch her body. Anticipation of pain overwhelmed her expectation of pleasure and, abruptly, her body's juices abandoned her.

Reece thrust at about the time Emerald discovered her hair was trapped beneath her shoulders. She twisted her head, trying to dislodge it, but it only tightened painfully, pulling her head back. It was several moments before she realized Reece wasn't making any progress in penetration, he was pushing her up the bed. Her head cracked against the headboard.

Reece noticed immediately.

Grasping her around the hips, he dragged her back down the bed and thrust again. Emerald dug her heels into the mattress and grasped Reece's shoulders tightly, but she could feel herself slipping. Again, they waltzed their way up the bed until she sensed impact with the headboard was imminent. She twisted her head to one side. This time it was her shoulder that slammed into the headboard when he thrust.

She could've cried in frustration.

Reluctantly, Reece withdrew and flopped on the bed beside her, staring up at the ceiling.

"Why did you stop?"

He said nothing for several moments, but finally rolled onto his side, gathering her against him and stroking her back. She couldn't help but notice his cock was only semi-erect--still hopeful and unsatisfied, but doubtful of welcome.

She reached for it.

He grabbed her hand, kissed it and placed it firmly around his waist.

"Damn it!"

"No!"

"Why not?" she demanded.

"You know why not. You're too little for me. We need lubrication. I don't suppose you have any?"

Emerald glared at him. "On the off chance that you'd show up some day? I told you I hadn't been with anyone else," she said crossly.

He sighed. "I don't want to hurt you."

Emerald sat up and glared at him. "If you think for one minute that I'm going to let you walk out of here with that thing still cocked and loaded, you are mistaken, Reece Yeager!"

He stared at her for several moments and then burst out laughing. "I'll live, Em. Let's find something to eat."

Emerald sighed, but then a thought occurred to her. "We can go out ... stop by the drugstore on the way back."

Reece frowned. Sliding from the bed, he adjusted himself and fastened and zipped his jeans once more before reaching for his shirt. "We can't go out ... not yet, anyway."

"Of course we can go out!"

"I didn't come here to wreck your life all over again, Em, regardless of what you might think. I don't like the thought that you might be embarrassed to be seen with an ex-con, but I'm not stupid. I know what it would do to you if it became common knowledge that you were fraternizing with an ex-convict, and what would happen if I demanded to move in with you ... which is why I didn't suggest it. Not because I don't want to.

"We can't go out, because you can't afford to be seen with me until we've decided what we're going to do."

Emerald sighed, hugging her shirt to her, feeling close to tears once more. "It's going to fall apart again, isn't it? There never really was a chance that it would work out."

Reece knelt beside the bed, gripping her arms. "All I needed to know, Em, was that you love me. I'm going to make things work out for us. I promise. I'm not going to do anything stupid this time."

* * * *

Emerald was staring at the back fence, but her mind was focused a few hundred miles away. Reece had left before midnight, promising to be back in a few days. He said he had 'things' to take care of.

She couldn't help but wonder what sort of 'things' he needed to take care of. He'd implied that first day that he was passing through on his way home. She'd assumed he hadn't been home yet. She supposed she should also assume that, after an eight year absence, there would be a great deal that needed his attention, but she still couldn't imagine what it would be. She supposed he might be looking for work, but if that was the case she couldn't figure out why he'd go to Palm Beach to look for work if, as he claimed, he intended to be with her.

She didn't like the idea of him running up and down the interstate on his bike, but he'd refused to take her car. He didn't know how long he'd be gone. He didn't want to leave her stranded. She'd told him she wouldn't be stranded. She could beg a ride from her neighbor, or even call a cab.... Or walk, perish the thought!

He'd been immovable.

She was just beginning to see how stubborn the man was. Funny, but she'd never noticed that before. He'd always seemed so laid back, so easy going--of course he hadn't been but nineteen, which probably explained a lot.

Hovering near the back of her mind was a piece of advice her mother had given her years ago. "You might not be able to keep your man faithful if you give it to him every time he asks for it, but if you don't, I can practically guarantee he's going to be out hunting."

He'd been immovable about that, too ... damn him.

She'd bought an extra large tube of lubricant first thing this morning. The nasty man behind the counter had given her a look.

"What are you doing?"

Emerald nearly jumped out of her skin. Bending, she retrieved the book she'd been holding open on her lap and then looked around. Maureen was peering at her over the fence that halved the backyard, allowing each of them 'privacy'. "Just trying to unwind," she said with a smile, feeling guilty about the train of her thoughts.

"I thought you said you were heading out to the beach today?"

Emerald shrugged. "Changed my mind. I love the beach, but I just didn't feel up to fighting the crowd today. I spend nine months out of every year struggling through crowds of teens like a salmon trying to make it up stream to spawn every time class changes. I decided I'd rather have some quiet time. How about you? I thought you said you were leaving for that cabin of yours in the mountains as soon as vacation started."

Maureen shrugged. "I had a few things to tie up before I left ... Guess you don't want company right now?"

"I wouldn't mind a little," Emerald responded, smiling, although she didn't particularly want Maureen's company at the moment. She had a feeling Maureen wasn't just looking for company. She had a feeling her friend wanted to talk about Reece, and Emerald wasn't in any mood to listen to a lecture.

Maureen beamed at her. "I'll bring refreshments!"

She arrived on Emerald's side of the backyard a few minutes later, carrying two glasses filled with ice and two cans of coke.

Emerald accepted the refreshment gratefully. The patio where she was lounging was shaded and there was a fairly good breeze, but it was hot just the same. "Thanks!"

Maureen nodded. "I was wondering if you'd be interested in a backyard cookout tonight?"

"That'd be nice! I haven't had a steak off the grill in a while."

Maureen frowned pensively. "Should I get extra?"

"Extra what?"

"I only picked one up for each of us. I was just wondering if your friend would be back tonight?"

Despite every effort, Emerald blushed ... mostly from irritation. "Not tonight. He said he had some things to take care of."

Maureen nodded. "That was Reece Yeager, wasn't it?"

Emerald sat up, laying her book aside as she raised the back of her lounge chair. "Yes," she said flatly.

Maureen didn't take the hint. "I was pretty sure it was him … but I'm surprised you encouraged him, Emerald. Aside from the fact that he's a dangerous man … which you certainly ought to know if anyone does, it's … robbing the cradle!"

"He's twenty seven years old! He's no baby!"

"He's eight years younger than you!"

Emerald's lips tightened. "I may be a history teacher, but I can add and subtract," she snapped. "If it doesn't bother him, why should it bother me?"

Maureen shook her head. "Fine! Forget that! He's dangerous, Emerald."

Emerald sighed. "I told you he had nothing to do with that."

"Yes. I know you were determined to protect him, despite the fact that he'd brutally raped you … and that he'd involved those other boys in abducting you."

Emerald rolled her eyes, seeking patience. "Reece never did anything to me that I wasn't willing … No! … eager, for him to do!" she snapped. "He's a good man, Maureen. He didn't have anything to do with what those punks did to me. He tried to help me and ended up spending eight years of his life in jail! I owe him for that."

"Is that what this is about? You feel like you owe him?"

Emerald blushed. "No. It's about, I love him. I *always* loved him. I know I had no business feeling that way when he was a student, and only nineteen, but I can't help how I felt then anymore than I can help how I feel now. And I don't want to help it!"

Maureen blushed fierily. She rose abruptly. "Sorry. I was just trying to help, not make you mad. I'd really hate to see you wreck your life again."

Emerald thought about it for several moments and some of her anger dissipated. "I owe you, too. I know that. If it wasn't for you I'd never have gotten this teaching job. I'm grateful. Really I am. But I love Reece. I don't care what the cost is."

Maureen had paused at the gate. She shook her head. "You think that now. I think you're going to deeply regret your decision."

Emerald stared after her as she left, frowning. She was tempted to go after her friend and try to smooth things over. She knew Maureen was only trying to help, to make her 'see reason'.

It occurred to her, though, that the only thing that was likely to satisfy Maureen was to agree with her, and she couldn't do that.

Even if everything hadn't gone to hell back home, she knew it would never have worked out for her and Reece back then. She had another chance. She wanted it. Reece said he wanted it. She damned well wasn't going to pass up a chance for happiness because of what everyone else thought about it.

* * * *

Turning on the TV for company, Emerald went into the kitchen, fixed herself a fruit salad, grabbed a spoon and headed back to catch the evening news. She'd just reached the doorway to the front parlor when the news woman made the announcement.

Although the police are saying it's too early to determine whether there's a connection between the two crimes, another local woman was found murdered in her home today. According to police reports, the crime was reported by an anonymous caller.

A picture of an attractive blond appeared on the TV screen in the upper corner.

According to our sources, Ms. Grayson, who worked for Clausen Motors on Capitol Circle, was found bound to her bed in a manner eerily similar to the previous victim. Police have refused to release any information regarding this latest attack on a local woman, but there is some speculation that Tallahassee may have a serial rapist prowling our streets.

Emerald dropped her bowl. It shattered as it struck the floor, sending pieces of fruit in every direction.

The phone began ringing. It had been ringing for some moments before Emerald realized that the annoying noise wasn't in her head. She turned, staring at the phone blankly for several moments and finally moved toward it and picked it up.

"Yes?"

"It could've been you," someone said in a hissing whisper.

Chapter Six

Emerald was drowsing on the love seat when the phone rang the following evening. She wasn't certain she really felt like getting up to answer it. She'd had very little sleep the night before, had spent all day cleaning the house frantically to keep her mind off of things she didn't want to think about--and no one ever called anyway except telemarketers ... and breathers.

She was no longer drowsy, however. Rolling off the love seat, she headed into the hallway. The phone stopped ringing as she reached for it. Letting out a gusty sigh of relief, she started toward the kitchen. The phone began ringing again before she reached the kitchen door.

Angry, Emerald whirled and stalked to the table that held the phone, snatching the receiver up. "Hello?"

"Em?"

It took Emerald several minutes to change gears. "Reece?"

"I've got a problem, baby. I wondered if you could pick me up."

Emerald's heart dropped to her toes. "Were you in an accident? Are you hurt?"

He grunted. "I'm at the police station."

* * * *

Emerald sat staring at the building for a full fifteen minutes before she managed to gather up the nerve to go in. She'd had enough experience with the police eight years ago to last her a life time.

Shock had made it impossible to remember much of the details of that long ago night, but it hadn't spared her everything. She could still remember the looks on the faces of the cops that had burst into the room--disgusted, angry, avidly curious, even amused, depending upon their various personalities. Reece had been seized by a half dozen men, slammed against the floor and beaten when he'd instinctively tried to defend himself. No one would listen to anything she said until after she'd spent hours at the hospital waiting for the staff to do a rape kit--which had been nightmarish all by itself. And then, finally, she'd been returned to the police station and grilled for hours and hours while they'd picked apart every word, look and gesture as they forced her to tell her 'story' over and over until it had begun to sound rehearsed even to her.

And in the end, after everything that had been done to her by everyone, they had not 'needed' her to testify in the trial--the prosecution had declined to use her on the grounds that she was 'confused' over the role of the leader in the plot against her-- though they'd also hinted they feared putting her on the stand would allow the defense to put her morals in question when she kept insisting Reece hadn't forced her to have sex with him. She'd never been able to find out why the defense had had no interest in using her as a witness--they wouldn't even speak to her on the grounds of 'conflict of interest'. In the end, she'd been left feeling almost more violated by the police and the prosecutors than she had by her abductors.

She hadn't been able to drive by a police station since without feeling violated.

It made her feel ill just thinking about having to go in.

But she'd told Reece she would come and get him.

Taking several deep breaths to gather her courage, she pushed the car door open and, holding herself stiffly erect, marched inside.

It might have been a different police station, a different state and many miles away from the one that still gave her nightmares, but it looked and smelled the same. Emerald had to fight a panic attack as she made her way through the main lobby, looking around for Reece. He was collecting his belongings at the window of the property room when she spotted him.

The scene was so reminiscent of that other time that her knees went to water, almost depositing her on the floor.

When Reece turned, however, the look on his face was enough to drive out all the disturbing memories. He'd looked angry that other time, but there'd been no real tension in him because he'd known he was innocent and believed it would all be over soon and he'd be allowed to go home. She saw in his face that the boy he'd been was long gone and the illusions he'd nursed with them. He was well aware that innocence would not necessarily gain his freedom. "What happened?" she asked a little breathlessly when she reached him.

He frowned, shook his head ever so slightly. "Let's go."

There was fury in every line of his body as he strode from the police station. Emerald had to jog beside him just to keep up with his ground eating stride.

She glanced at him once they were seated in the car, but he looked so tense, and so tired, she decided to wait until he felt like telling her about it.

She didn't ask where he wanted to go. She drove straight back to her place. When she parked the car, he merely stared at the house for several moments, as if awakening from a dream. Finally, he opened the door and got out.

"Mind if I take a shower?" he asked as soon as they were inside. "I've been in that stinking hell hole for nearly twenty four hours."

Emerald nodded. "Hungry? I could fix you something to eat," she offered.

"Thanks. I haven't had anything since they picked me up."

Emerald watched him climb the stairs, gnawing on the one fingernail that remained on her left hand.

Twenty four hours. Her head hurt, but she managed to do the math. They'd picked him up the day after the last murder. Before he left town? Or when he'd come back?

She had a very bad feeling that the two were connected, but couldn't decide whether it was her own anxiety over the apparent similarity of the crime scenes and the fact that the murders had begun after Reece had arrived in town, or if it was pure paranoia.

Shaking off the worrisome thoughts, Emerald went into the kitchen to find him something to eat. She was cutting the sandwich she'd made for him in half when it occurred to her that he had no clean clothes to change into. Somehow, she doubted he'd want to put on the same clothes ... which meant he was going to be running around naked, or in a towel.

She took the sandwich and the glass of tea and went upstairs. He'd just come out of the bathroom. He was wearing a towel.

Under the circumstances, she couldn't help but feel like a nymphomaniac for even noticing how appealing he was, but it was the first time she'd ever actually seen him the next thing to naked. Somehow, they never seemed to make it to the point of undressing each other before they made love.

The flesh she'd caressed and kissed more by feel than sight, was as beautifully sculpted as her mind had told her it was. There was a tattoo on his left biceps, just below his shoulder. She hadn't noticed it before. She saw now that it was 'prison' blue, not colored like those acquired in tattoo parlors, which she supposed was one of the reasons she hadn't noticed before.

It was small, but it looked like a gemstone.

It could have been anything, meant anything, but Emerald had a feeling she knew what it represented, and couldn't help but wonder if that was why he was always so 'caught up' he didn't take the time to strip before he made love to her--he felt self-conscious about having an emerald tattooed so near his heart.

Unsettled by her thoughts, she set the plate and glass down on the bedside table and went into the bathroom to collect his clothes. "I'll throw these in the wash for you."

He nodded, but his expression told her he hadn't really heard what she'd said. When she returned she saw he he'd eaten the sandwich and was standing at the front window, staring down into the street. "What is it?"

He glanced toward her. "Patrol car. I shouldn't have let you bring me here."

Emerald frowned. "I wish you'd tell me what's going on."

Reece scrubbed his hands over his face and raked his fingers through his hair. "The cops picked me up. They do that, you know. Anytime anything happens, they check out everybody with any kind of record first. My name came up when I got pulled over, so they took me in for questioning."

Emerald was almost afraid to ask. "About what?"

"Haven't you guessed yet? The murders, Em." His expression was grim.

A shock wave went through her. "They don't think you had anything to do with it?" she asked shakily. "I mean, they released you, right?"

He rubbed his neck, grimacing. "My alibi checked out. They had to let me go. They didn't have anything they could hold me on … but you can be damned sure they aren't satisfied. Somebody tipped them off about me. And they really like me for prime suspect."

Emerald's heart skipped a beat. "What makes you think that?"

"They pulled me over on a trumped up *probable*." He shook his head. "They were watching for me."

With an effort, Emerald moved to the bed and sat down, feeling weak and more than a little sick to her stomach. "The murders … you mean the strangler?"

He nodded, turned and paced to the window. "The cops flung the photos down in front of me. They were tied the same way you were, Em … which I gather is pretty unique. What do you think the chances are that the strangler is somebody that was there eight years ago?"

For several moments Emerald thought she'd hyperventilate. She'd suspected the MO was similar because of the news reports, but she'd thought it was paranoia feeding an overactive imagination. She hadn't really believed it could be the same, hadn't accepted the possibility that someone who'd been involved in her abduction might have something to do with the current attacks ... and why should she? She was separated from that other crime by eight years and several hundred miles. "Who?" she managed to ask.

He turned and strode toward her abruptly and Emerald flinched. He hesitated, but then continued as if he hadn't noticed, taking a seat on the end of the bed. "You think I've got something to do with it?" he asked quietly.

Emerald glanced at him quickly, but she was already shaking her head. "It unnerves me that it started when you got here, that's all. Do you think it's somebody trying to set you up? That they followed you, maybe?"

"It certainly looks like it, doesn't it?"

Emerald gnawed her lower lip a moment, considering the possibility, but finally moved toward him, wrapping her arms around him. "It's so unbelievable, Reece. You must be wrong. It must just be a coincidence. The guys that did it are in jail. And, even if somebody else was involved that neither of us knew about, and knew enough to copy the crime scene ...It's still a strange coincidence that they'd show up in the same place we are. Anyway, they were stupid, mean ... total assholes, but they'd have to be completely insane to kill innocent strangers just to frame you. It'd make more sense if they came after me again. Besides, what reason could they have to even want to get even with you badly enough to do something like this? *Who* would?"

Reece wrapped his arms around her, giving her a squeeze, but then released her and got up to pace once more. "Mike Todd. And, as for insane ... Jesus, Em! What they did went a long way beyond a teenage 'prank'. I'm not so sure they were 'sane' then."

Emerald was taken aback by the name from her past. "Isn't he still in jail?"

Reece shook his head. "The police made him a deal to testify against the 'ring leader', which was when he named me. I think he was in two years, then probation … He spent less time in that the others. A hell of a lot less than me."

Anger surged through Emerald. "You'd think the bastard would be satisfied that he'd gotten even with you when it was his testimony that got you convicted."

"I broke up his party … named him and his buddies. Mike Todd likes to think of himself as somebody nobody fucks with. I doubt he was satisfied … especially since my lawyer got me off … finally."

Emerald frowned. "What about the other two, David and Jeffrey?"

He shook his head. "Maybe. I don't suppose they could be totally ruled out. They're out too. But they were just Mike's flunkies. They never did anything without direct orders from him."

"I don't suppose you mentioned Mike to the cops?"

"They said they'd check it out, but if it is Mike, he was pretty good at covering his tracks eight years ago--if I hadn't shown up, I doubt very much he'd have been caught--and I'm betting he's a lot better now."

"But … I recognized their voices. I would've told the police myself, even if you hadn't shown up."

He gave her a look. "Maybe … if you'd been able to."

Emerald swallowed with some difficulty. "You think … You're saying the same thing that happened to the two women here would've happened to me?"

He studied her a long moment and finally looked away. "I think he expected the photos he was taking would be his insurance that you wouldn't say anything."

A shiver skated along Emerald's spine. "No you don't. You think what was done to these two women--that's what was intended to happen to me, what had been planned from the start. Maybe the photos were intended to implicate David and Jeffery … after he'd finished having his fun." Emerald wrapped her arms around herself, trying to think back.

She'd done her best to forget everything about that time, to bury it completely. It wasn't easy trying to dredge it up again. It was easier than she liked, or would've thought, however, to dredge up the way Mike Todd had looked at her each time she'd criticized him, or sent him to the office for some infraction.

It had always made her uneasy--that look that was a combination of malice and something else she couldn't quite identify. She supposed that was because, at the time, she hadn't realized that that something else was cold blooded calculation-- the way a cat studied its prey for weaknesses before it pounced.

"Maybe it's got nothing to do with you at all," she said finally. "Maybe he thinks he has unfinished business with me."

Reece frowned. "I'd thought of it. I didn't want to scare you until I had a better idea of whether there was anything to my suspicions or not."

"Gee, thanks for sparing me!" Emerald retorted. "And what if he'd grabbed me while you were still trying to make up your mind?"

"Telling you wouldn't have lessened the possibility or made you any safer. It would just have made you more afraid. Besides, you could've arrived at the same conclusion, or speculation, as I did."

She might have been more likely to if she hadn't been trying very, very hard to convince herself that it was all her imagination.

"Anyway--somebody put the cops on to me. It wasn't purely by chance that they pulled me over, regardless of what they wanted me to think. They had my records when they got me to the police station--which means they'd sent for them."

Emerald frowned. "But ... your lawyer got the conviction overturned, didn't he?"

"Which doesn't change the fact that there was an arrest record ... which should still be in Georgia, but was lying on the detective's desk."

"Maureen."

"What?"

Emerald shook her head, fighting the anger that surged through her. "My neighbor. It had to have been her. She left to go on vacation yesterday, but she could've called them before she left ... *probably* called them."

"You told her about me?" Reece demanded incredulously.

Emerald gaped at him. "I didn't have to! She was there at the time. You don't remember her?"

Reece frowned, obviously struggling with it, but finally shook his head.

"She was a teacher at the high school at the time. She coached the girl's basketball team ... She remembered you. The day after you came back that second time, she asked me if you were

Reece Yeager, and, not surprisingly, she remembered the incident too."

"You think she would have called the cops on me?"

Emerald sighed. "I don't know, but it is a possibility. Like I said, she remembered ... tried to talk me into staying away from you. She's a friend. Maybe she thought she was 'doing it for my own good'."

Reece studied her a long moment, his face expressionless. "And, what did you say when she tried to talk you into dumping me?"

Emerald smiled faintly. "That you were innocent, regardless of what everyone seemed to think, you had not raped me. That you'd never done anything to me that I hadn't willingly participated in."

Chapter Seven

"In spite of everything that's happening, you still believe I'm innocent?"

Emerald stood up and moved toward him, laying her cheek against his chest and wrapping her arms around his waist. "I know you are."

After a moment, he closed his arms around her, holding her tightly. "I don't know if I'd blame you if you had some doubts. We never really got the chance to get to know each other, and I've been away a long time."

She pulled a little away and looked up at him, frowning slightly. "How could you love me and feel that you don't really know me?"

He smiled at her crookedly. "I spent years wondering if it was just a crush that got blown all out of proportion because I didn't get to be with you long enough to know if it was real, or would last. After a while I started believing that that was exactly what it was, heat of the moment ... the unattainable ... forbidden fruit and all that. Because I realized that all I really knew about you was that you were beautiful to me and I liked the way you laughed. I didn't know anything but your name and the fact that you taught history--didn't know where you came from, what you liked, what you didn't like ... what your middle name was... not even how old you were.

"But I discovered when I saw you again that the only thing that really mattered was that when I look at you, you take my breath away." He leaned down, brushing his lips lightly across hers. "If it ain't love, baby, I don't guess I know the difference."

"Emerald is my middle name," she murmured against his lips.

"Is it?" he asked, nipping at her lower lip with his own. "What's your first name?"

"Worse," she murmured.

He chuckled. "I kinda like the name Emerald myself."

"Right! That's why you always call me Em."

"I call you Em because Emerald is more of a mouthful than you are, baby ... and I'm lazy."

"I think I'm being insulted," Emerald said, smiling against his lips.

Reece picked her up and carried her to the bed, placing his knee on the edge and climbing onto the mattress with her. He nuzzled her neck. "Are you?"

"Mmm. What?"

"Insulted?"

"I'm too wet to think about anything but sex right now. Can we skip the chit chat and fuck?"

Reece chuckled and leaned back to study her. "Lady, you have a mouth like a sailor."

She gave him a look of innocence. "OK, but can we?" Rolling toward the side of the bed, she pulled the drawer out and held up the tube of lubricant triumphantly. "I'm ready."

He propped his head on his hand, a smile playing around his lips. "You've got a hell of a lot of clothes on for somebody that's ready."

Emerald slipped off the side of the bed, then, holding his gaze, unfastened her jeans snap with deliberation, slid the zipper down very slowly and began to slide the jeans down her hips with equal care. Kicking her sandals off when the jeans puddled at her ankles, she propped a hand on the bed and tugged them over her feet. Tossing them aside, she grasped the hem of her knit shirt and began to lift it, exposing her belly by fractions. When she tossed her top aside, she reached back and unfastened her bra. Placing her palms on the bed, she allowed the bra straps to slip down to her wrists, then 'stepped' out of it as she crawled across the bed towards him.

Reece's smile had faded the moment she began to wiggle out of her jeans. His eyes narrowed predatorily as she crawled across the bed toward him. He resisted momentarily as she placed a hand on his shoulder and pushed him to his back, but as she came up on her knees and placed her other hand on his shoulder, he grasped her around the waist and fell back, taking her with him and holding her slightly above him so that her breasts dangled in his face. Catching one pouting nipple in his mouth, he lowered her slowly until she was straddling his chest.

She propped her hands on the bed on either side of his head, throwing her head back and squeezing her eyes closed as heat surged through her from his mouth in tantalizing waves. When he released her breast at last, she offered him the other breast, groaning as he closed his mouth over the nipple and sliding backwards until she could feel his cock nudging her buttocks. Lifting slightly, she settled on top of the hard ridge of flesh, rotating her hips.

When he groaned, releasing her breast, she slid over him, slowly, back and forth, pushing the foreskin all the way to the root of his cock with her damp cleft and then up again. He caught her hips, held her still for a moment and then sat up, grabbing the tube of lubricant. She held out a hand for it and, when he'd squeezed a generous portion into her palm she moved back once more and grasped his cock in her hand, rubbing the lubricant over it from the root of his cock to his cock head in a slow, thorough caress.

Abruptly, he lifted her up, aligned his body with her own and pushed. Emerald gasped, felt her body resist for a moment, then slowly he pushed inside of her, burying himself deeply. A groan of satisfaction scraped past her throat. She wrapped her arms around his neck, gasping as heat flooded through her, feeling her body clench and unclench around him in pleasure. Grasping her hips, he guided her into a rhythm that pleased them both, lifting her up until he almost slipped free of her body before pushing her down again until her clit ground against the rough hair at the root of his cock.

Within moments, Emerald felt her body climbing toward her peak, felt the glorious tension drawing every muscle in her body taut with pending release. She began to move faster, rotating her hips so that his cock nudged her G-spot with every thrust, sending out currents of static ecstasy. Abruptly, her body clenched around his cock as shock waves of blinding pleasure washed through her in a tidal wave of exquisite sensation.

As she cried out her release, he tossed her onto her back and began thrusting into her fast and hard. She reached culmination again, harder than before, as she felt the first tremors of his climax, shuddering, burying her face against his chest to stifle the cries of delight she couldn't hold inside.

They lay panting in the aftermath, swapping feather light, breathless kisses.

As their breathing slowly returned to normal, however, Emerald felt the outside world intruding once more. The harder she tried to hold it at bay, the more determined it seemed to intrude.

"Stay with me," she whispered when she felt him stir.

He subsided, rising up on one elbow to study her. "You and I both know what could come of that."

Emerald sighed. "You haven't found a job yet, have you?"

He stiffened. "What makes you say that?"

"I'm not complaining ... but you've been down to Palm Beach several times and come back. I figured you were looking for work and you wouldn't have been back so soon if you'd found a job. I'm just saying you can stay here until you get a job and get the chance to get on your feet ... I'd like for you to."

He seemed to consider it for a few minutes. "You neighbors would be bound to notice and then, before you knew it, the board would be questioning your morality and whether or not you were the kind of influence they wanted on their kids."

"Does it really matter if my reputation goes to hell if that wacko comes in here and strangles me?" Emerald point out, playing her trump card.

His arm tightened around her. "I'm not going to let anything happen to you." He seemed to consider the situation for several moments. "It *would* be easier to keep an eye on you if I was here," he said slowly.

A welcome sense of security settled over her for about two seconds before she began to consider the way he'd phrased that last comment. There was just something about his wording that made it sound as if he'd been doing a little more than making sure she was safe. "You've been keeping an eye on me?" she asked, keeping her voice neutral with an effort.

He flushed. "I wasn't certain how much danger you might be in. I got ... someone to watch the house while I was away."

"Reece! Without even telling me?"

"I was trying not to alarm you unnecessarily," he said tightly.

"How long?" A curtain slid across his eyes. She knew then that he'd been watching, or had her watched, by some friend or ex-cell mate, far longer than there had been danger of any kind. She sat up and punched him on the shoulder. "You didn't trust me!"

He reddened. It was all the admission she needed and she was suddenly a good deal more than irritated.

"Damn it, Em! It wasn't that."

Her eyes narrowed and he flushed even darker.

"I was trying to take care of you ... All right! I wasn't sure I believed you hadn't been seeing anybody else before I showed up, but that was only part of it ... swear to God, Em!"

She whacked him with a pillow. "How dare you even question my word, you ass! If I'd been your girlfriend, you might have some right to question my faithfulness, but I wasn't ... and you don't!"

"Settle down!"

"NO!" she flung another pillow at him.

"You're blowing this way out of proportion, Em!"

"ME! You show up on my doorstep without ever once trying to contact me in eight years and just expect me to be waiting for you ... which I was, because I never was terribly bright where you were concerned ... and then question my veracity! If I'd screwed anybody else I would've been well within my rights and it wouldn't be any of your damn business! And I'd have told you I'd been seeing someone else!"

His lips tightened. "That was before! Now, you're mine!"

Emerald gasped in outrage. She'd run out of pillows. She looked speculatively at her lamp. She didn't like it anyway.

Reece dove between her and the bed side table, beating her to it. "Don't you even *think* about it!" he snapped.

Emerald sat back, glaring at him. "Go!"

"Be reasonable."

"I don't have to be reasonable either. I trusted you! Without any rhyme or reason except because I love you. But you didn't trust me. You didn't even take my word for ... for anything."

He glared at her. "I don't have any damn clothes!"

"They're in the washer. They should be finished by now."

"Wet!" he gasped, sounding almost as outraged as she felt.

"At least they're clean!"

"Fine! Fuck it!" he growled, and stalked from the room.

She got up when he'd stormed out of the room and went into the bathroom to clean up. She had lubricant up to her eyebrows and cum running down her legs. It was just like a man, damn his hide--give them an inch and they took a damned mile! And then they had the nerve to question whether their woman was faithful or not when nine out of ten were out looking for their next lay the minute you turned your back on them!

She heard him slam out of the house as she returned to the bedroom to get her clothes. Stalking down the stairs, she bolted the door, turned off all of the lights he'd left on and then went back upstairs to stew over it some more.

She was sorry about it long before morning, of course. Hours of tossing and turning between snatches of sleep and bad dreams were enough by themselves to convince her that, deep down, she regretted loosing her temper even if she wasn't ready to admit it on a conscious level.

She couldn't help but worry where he might be sleeping, however, whether he'd been able to find a room so late of if he'd ended up sleeping in the bus station or something. She was tempted to go look for him by the time it was morning, but a combination of wounded pride and the fear of being snubbed restrained her.

He hadn't even had his motorcycle ... which was probably still down at the police impound lot.

She had no idea how to contact him and that was the worst realization of all. She couldn't apologize if she wanted to. He'd never given her an address or phone number and she'd assumed that was because he didn't actually have one yet. He might not. Or he might not have wanted to give her one because he was still making up his mind whether or not he wanted to have a relationship with her ... just like he was still making up his mind whether she could be trusted or not.

It occurred to her after she'd been digging around in her flower bed the following day for several hours that she had no idea, really, of what Reece had been through in prison or how it might affect his personality. Of course, she didn't know from before how Reece had been in the trust department. Maybe he'd always been the sort not to trust until he had the chance to evaluate a person and decide whether he felt trust in them or not.

She was the opposite. For the most part she tended to like people she trusted, and dislike people she didn't, instinctively, from the moment she met them. If they proved to her that her instincts were wrong and they couldn't be trusted, she never made the mistake again--nothing they could do could ever earn it back.

She trusted Reece for the simple reason that he appeared to be, basically, open and honest. If she hadn't felt that way about him, she wouldn't have fallen in love with him to start with.

She couldn't understand how he could believe he was in love with her and still not trust her.

Unless he'd just been shooting her a line because he figured she'd be a lot more cooperative about sex if he romanced her?

It was a painfully disturbing thought.

She was so intent on stabbing the dirt with her trowel that it was several moments before she realized someone had come to stand close by to watch her. When she sensed it and glanced up she let out a gasping scream, jerked all over and pitched dirt into the air as her trowel flew from suddenly nerveless fingers.

She clutched her heart, glaring at the man. "What the hell are you doing in my yard?" she demanded furiously.

"I tried to get your attention, ma'am, but you seemed too intent on butchering the floor bed to notice," the man said coolly.

Emerald's eyes narrowed, though color filled her cheeks. "And you figured that gave you the right to trespass?"

He studied her a long moment. "I'm Detective Ansley with the Tallahassee police department, ma'am. I was just wondering if you could answer a few questions for me."

If he thought his cop status was going to intimidate her ... he was right. But it also pissed her off. She was tempted to tell him to get his ass out of her backyard. How dare he come in her yard without even asking!

She stood up, wiping her hands off, brushing the dirt--some of which was from kneeling and some from the knee jerk response of her reflexes--from her clothes. "Next time wait for an invitation from me before you invite yourself onto my property," she said coldly.

He flushed with anger, his lips tightening. "Certainly ma'am. As I said, I tried to get your attention...."

"But you didn't. Which means you should have waited until you did to find out if it was OK with me--what did you want to ask me?"

He was giving her a look of hostility now, not that she gave a damn. She felt pretty hostile herself. "Do you know a Mr. Reece Yeager, ma'am?"

"Why?"
"Do you know him?"
"Why?"
"Could you just answer the question, ma'am?"
"Why certainly! Just as soon as you tell me why you want to know."
"It's part of an ongoing investigation, ma'am. I'm not at liberty to discuss details."

She would've loved to slap the smirk off of his face with the back of her shovel, but unfortunately it was against the law to smack a cop--just because he was trespassing and being an asshole.

"Yes, I do."
"How long have you known him?"

That wasn't exactly an easy question to ask. "I met him about nine years ago." It irritated the hell out of her to answer his questions, because she knew damned well he wouldn't be standing in her yard harassing her if he hadn't known damn well she knew Reece ... which meant he knew about everything. She supposed he just wanted to see if he could catch her in a lie, though she was damned if she could figure out why.

"And this was where?"

Her lips tightened. "He was a transfer student at the high school where I was teaching at the time."

"Where was this?"

She gave him a look. "I don't feel like waltzing, Detective...." She'd forgotten what he said his name was.

"Ansley."

"Detective Ansley. You already know I know him or you wouldn't be here, so why don't you just tell me why you're here?"

"How well did you know Mr. Yeager?"

She was tempted to tell him it was none of his damned business how well she knew Reece. She bit her tongue and tamped her temper down with an effort. "Well," she responded shortly.

"Are you aware that Mr. Yeager is a convicted sex offender?"
"I'm aware that conviction was overturned."
"For lack of evidence."
"Because he wasn't guilty!" Emerald snapped.

His eyes narrowed. "From what I could see in the reports it wasn't lack of evidence but because you refused to testify against him. I'm curious to know why you let him walk ... to attack more helpless women."

Emerald crossed her arms, studying him. "If you're through asking me questions you already have all the answers for, you can leave."

He pulled a file from beneath his arm, dragged a photo out of it and shoved it in her face. "Does this look familiar to you at all?"

It was a crime scene photo of one of the murders. Emerald knew that immediately, although the photo sent such a shock of horror through her it was several moments before her brain could even assimilate what her eyes were seeing. There was blood everywhere. She couldn't understand why there'd be blood everywhere when they said the woman had been strangled. Her hand was shaking when she pushed the photo back at him. "I wasn't there, if that's what you're asking."

He stabbed the picture. "This woman was so brutally raped ... with God knows what ... that she would've bled to death if she hadn't strangled first. In all my years on the force, I've never seen a crime scene that was this bad. Now, what I want to know, ma'am, is if this is how you were tied up when you were abducted. Look at it again ... closely."

It took an effort to steel herself to look at the photo again, but Emerald did. "It's possible," she said finally, reluctantly.

"Is it or not!" he demanded.

Emerald handed the photo back to him, glaring at him. "The students that abducted me knocked me out with chloroform and tied me up while I was unconscious, and gagged me and blindfolded me. I didn't *see* it! It *looks* similar. That's the best I can tell you."

"Can or will?"

"Did you actually listen to anything I just said?" Emerald asked tightly. "I wasn't conscious when I was tied up. I don't know *how* they did it."

"You were conscious when you were untied, though, weren't you Ms. Green?"

"I was still groggy, scared half to death and I could barely see from having that blindfold on. If I could tell you positively, I would."

He studied her for several moments, obviously seething. "I'm curious to know how much Mr. Yeager offered you to keep you quiet."

Emerald looked at him blankly, trying her best not to think about her most recent roll in the sheets with Mr. Yeager, although 'about ten inches' popped into her head. "Reece?" she said cautiously, too surprised by the suggestion that she had accepted a bribe from Reece, of all people, for anger to filter through ... yet.
"Mr. Carl Yeager--of Yeager Enterprises--his father."

Chapter Eight

The name sounded really familiar, but Emerald was certain the detective couldn't be talking about the multi-millionaire, Carl Yeager, the one that owned a rather substantial number of media companies, which included more than a dozen newspapers, magazines, TV and radio stations ... the one who'd been killed in a plane crash a few months ago with his wife of thirty years. "I never met his father," she said stiffly. "If you're through now, leave."

She knew she must be white as death. She felt faint. She was desperate for Detective Ansley to leave so that she could sit down.

She didn't like the way the man was looking at her.

"You know ... I believe you didn't know. Curious. Kind of makes you wonder just how well you *do* know Reece Yeager, doesn't it?"

"Go away," Emerald said faintly, trying to keep a note of pleading from creeping into her voice.

He nodded and left. Emerald wilted back down onto the grass where she'd been sitting before the man had arrived.

It occurred to her that the Detective must have just been trying to shock her into telling him something. Cops lied all the time to get information out of people. The paper had said Carl Yeager Jr. had inherited. She read the newspapers. She kept up with what was going on in the world-- so maybe she had a tendency to skim more than anything else and she missed as much as she caught, but Reece couldn't be one of *those* Yeagers.

Rich people sent their kids to private schools. She taught in public school.

Besides, he couldn't have kept the fact that he was rich secret from the other kids at school, even if he'd wanted to ... and why would he want to?

She couldn't remember if she'd ever heard what his full name was, though.

With an effort, she dismissed it, but the detective's parting comment kept coming back to haunt her.

She went inside after she'd finished wrecking her favorite flower bed and went upstairs with the intention of soaking her blues away. The hot water soothed her aching muscles, but it wasn't particularly soothing to her thoughts.

She told herself after a while that it didn't really matter why, or if, Reece had lied to her about himself. She'd run him off. Even if she was interested in apologizing, or trying to make up, she didn't know how to reach him.

She didn't really think he'd be coming back to give her the chance to do either after she'd thrown him out of her house in the middle of the night, on foot, in sopping wet clothes.

She didn't care.

She'd assured herself of that every few minutes throughout the remainder of the day. By evening she decided she was starting to actually believe it.

She'd just started to take a long swig of ice cold tea when the phone rang. The sudden noise in her dead quiet home sent a jolt along her nerve endings, making her jerk reflexively and slosh icy tea in her face. She jumped when the chill hit her, sloshing more out over her hand.

Turning, she glared at the phone, but it occurred to her suddenly that it just might be Reece, calling to apologize for being such a suspicious ass. Mopping her face with the tail of her shirt, she rushed to answer it, grabbing the receiver as the phone stopped ringing.

"I haven't seen Casanova around. You two didn't have a lover's spat, did you?"

It was the same wheezing whisperer from before. Despite the fact that her hair was far too long to stand on end, Emerald felt it rise up along her scalp, all the way to the crown of her head.

"Who is this?" she demanded shakily.

"Your secret admirer," the voice whispered and laughed.

The goose bumps that had raced up her scalp changed directions and ran down her spine. "Jeffery?" she asked in a squeaky voice.

The line went dead.

* * * *

Emerald was fairly certain that even if there hadn't been a killer stalking women in the city, and even if that killer hadn't been using an MO that she was frighteningly familiar with, the phone calls would have unnerved her. Under the circumstances, they terrified her.

She spent the following morning trying to arrange to get a security company out to install electronic security in her apartment. Other than locks, she had nothing, none of the high tech devices on the market that were supposed to keep intruders out, alert her to attempted break-ins ... and certainly not burglar bars on the windows. Those things gave her the creeps and moreover, she refused to turn her home into a prison she locked herself into every night.

Unfortunately, everybody who hadn't already gotten security systems for their home before the murders had immediately ordered them. The best promise she could get was that someone would stop by the end of the following week to assess her situation and plan out a work order, the actual work to be performed at some distant, unspecified time.

Thwarted of that possibility of comfort, she left the house after lunch and went to the mall to buy two new phones equipped with caller ID to replace the ones she had. She didn't know how much good it would do her to be able to tell who was calling ... or even if she would be able to tell since she'd had friends tell her that the ID could be blocked, preventing her from finding out who was calling, but she thought it might be helpful.

She discovered when she came home and plugged the phones in that it wasn't just a plug and play sort of thing. She had to order the service from the phone company. She spent most of the afternoon being transferred from one department to another trying to get a work order, and finally discovered she could get that 'installed' later in the week.

Frustrated and furious, she was tempted to hang up on the sales person, but managed to contain herself and settle on the work order ... which meant she'd committed herself to an enormous amount of money for security and still didn't have any more than she'd had before she started.

The phone was ringing when she got to the door. She'd already nicked her knuckles getting the door unlocked to get inside and catch it before it dawned on her that it was doubtful that it was anyone she actually wanted to talk to. She was fairly certain Reece wouldn't be calling ... not that she wanted to talk to him anyway. She wasn't in the mood for telemarketers, and it was for darned sure she didn't want to talk to the whisperer.

Shivers skated along her spine just thinking of the last phone call. At the time, she'd been certain the voice belonged to Jeffery Miller. Since then she'd begun to doubt her first impression, not because she didn't think Jeffery was above trying to scare the hell out of her, or because she didn't think there was a possibility that he was involved in the murders, nor even because it didn't sound like his voice. It had certainly reminded her of his voice. The problem was it hadn't sounded like anything Jeffery would say.

From what she remembered of Jeffery, he'd leaned a little more toward dumb than bright. She had her doubts that Jeffery would have a clue of who Casanova was, or that he'd use the term to describe Reece even if he'd heard of the legendary lover.

Mike Todd might have said something like the caller had, but the voice wasn't deep enough to have been Mike's.

Of course, the person calling might have used one of those electronic gadgets that altered a person's voice, in which case it could, literally, have been anyone in the world, regardless of how likely she thought it was that it was one of the men who'd abducted and assaulted her before.

It could even have been Reece.

She didn't believe it, but she was beginning to seriously doubt her judgment where Reece was concerned.

It would almost have seemed as if thinking of him had conjured him, but the plain fact was she'd thought of little else since their fight, and certainly not since her discussion with the detective. But when the knock came at her door her first thought wasn't that Reece had come back. Her first thought was of her secret admirer and her knees went to water.

"Who is it?" she asked without approaching nearer the door than the phone table.

Whoever it was didn't answer. She wasn't certain whether it was because her voice hadn't been much more than a squeak of fright, or if they were waiting until she came closer so they could burst in and grab her. Finally, too unnerved to consider turning her back on the door and retreating, she peeked through the curtain. She couldn't see anything but one shoulder and part of a broad chest, but the man was wearing a suit. She thought at first he must be a detective, until she noticed the pale gray Mercedes sitting in her driveway.

She opened the door a crack and peered out at the man. It took her several moments to recognize him. She would never have thought an expensive suit would change his appearance that much.

"Not slumming tonight?"

"We need to talk."

She stared at Reece for several moments, wondering why he seemed so different to her. "I don't think so," she said finally and tried to push the door closed.

She discovered after a moment that his foot was in it and looked up at him.

"I know I shouldn't have … had surveillance on you without your knowledge and consent. I really was just trying to protect you, Em, whatever you think."

"I don't think you want to know what I think," Emerald said quietly. "Could you move your foot, please?"

He shook his head, grasping the edge of the door. "You told me you loved me. How can you just shut me out of your life like this?"

It took an effort to speak. The knot in her throat was painful, drawing tears to her eyes. "I loved Reece. The thing that's breaking my heart is, I still do. But I don't know who you are."

"Don't look at me like that, damn it," he said angrily. "You don't know what it's like when nobody can see beyond your bank account."

"Poor little rich boy, is that it? You've got more in common with Mike Todd than I ever realized before."

His lips tightened. "You know damned well I'm nothing like that bastard."

"Unfortunately, the problem, Mr. Yeager, is that I don't, because all I know now is that you're not who I thought you were." She shook her head. "I just don't understand why you did it, why you picked me. Was it for revenge? Because it was my fault you ended up in jail? Or was it just some kind of game? A bet? A dare?"

"What are you talking about, Em?" he demanded. "You think I used you for some kind of sick game?"

She studied him a long moment.

"You want me to beg forgiveness? Is that it?"

"No, I don't."

"What then?"

"I want you to go away. I don't want to see you anymore."

"Em! Don't do this," he said quietly. "I know now that I should have trusted you. I'll never doubt you again, I swear it."

In spite of all she could do the tears she'd been trying so hard to hold at bay flooded her eyes and washed down her cheeks. "You don't understand at all, do you? You broke my trust in you. I can't be with you when I can't trust you, and I'll never be able to trust you again."

He paled. "Em, you don't mean that."

She wiped the tears from her cheeks with one hand and sniffed. "It's for the best, Reece. Find someone in your own age group and income bracket. You'll be happier, because if you couldn't trust the love I lavished on you, you'll never really trust me, no matter what your investigators tell you. And I couldn't live with that any more than I could live with someone that I doubted every word they told me." She looked down at his foot pointedly. After a moment, he removed it, reluctantly removed his hand from the door.

"You're wrong about one thing, though, Reece. I do understand what it's like not knowing if someone loves you for yourself ... or if it's something else they want from you."

She leaned against the door for several moments after she'd closed and locked it but finally, when she didn't hear him leave, she moved away from the door and went upstairs.

She'd hoped to avoid the confrontation. When he'd been gone for days, she'd been certain that he wouldn't come back ... of course, up until she'd spoken to the detective she'd been hoping they could still work things out between them.

She didn't know why Reece couldn't seem to see that it wasn't his family's money that had changed everything. It was his low opinion of her. That opinion had forced her to accept that he'd never actually loved her.

She supposed, however, that as emotionally draining as it had been to have to discuss the situation with him, at least it had given her the chance to see that the whole charade wasn't some sort of huge joke he'd cooked up with friends. When she'd found out how deep his deception went, she'd been terrified she would discover it had been something like that, some rich boy's game. She didn't know if she could've recovered if that had been the case.

She didn't try to contain her tears once she'd flung herself down on her bed. She summoned them, allowed the pain the flow out of her. She couldn't hold all that pain inside. When she'd cried herself to the point of exhaustion, she slept.

She wasn't certain how long she'd slept, or even what awakened her, but something roused her. She sat up, listening intently to the house. Aside from the usual creaks and groans typical of an old house, she heard nothing.

Glancing at the clock, she saw that it was nearly three AM. It had been barely dark when she'd fallen asleep ... and now she was awake and it was too early to get up. Finally, she decided to take a hot shower, then see if she could catch a movie that would put her back to sleep for a few more hours.

The shower went a long way toward soothing her. She didn't realize until she stepped out, however, that she hadn't thought to bring her nightclothes in to the bathroom with her.

Ordinarily, she wasn't in the habit of strolling around the house in the nude, even though she lived by herself, but, with a shrug, she tossed the towel over the bar to dry and went in search of a nightgown.

The sound that drew her attention was almost like the scrabbling sound of mouse feet. She paused, her nightgown in her hand and looked around nervously, peering at the baseboard around the room. When the sound came again, however, it sounded as if it was above her. She glanced up, wondering if she did have mice in the ceiling, or if a squirrel, or maybe a stray cat, had found its way into the attic to bear its young.

It was as her gaze drifted down from the ceiling that it was caught by a faint glint. Frowning, she peering intently at the dark spot just along the edge of the picture that hung above the head of her bed. It didn't look like a stain.

A mouse hole?

It seemed like a strange place for a mouse hole.

Then, it blinked.

Every nerve, muscle and tendon in her body shut down as a wave of ice cold shock washed over her. For many, many moments, her brain ceased to function altogether. When, finally, it kicked into gear again it was like a motor struggling up a steep incline, sluggish, sputtering, misfiring.

It was an eye. A human eye.

She had no idea of how long she remained frozen in shock, unable to think what to do, how to react. Belatedly, her instinct for survival kicked in. Clutching her nightgown in her hands, she backed away a step, and then another.

She didn't manage to jog herself into a run until she reached the stairs. She was halfway down them, intent on running out the door, when it dawned on her that she was far safer in the house than outside of it. Skidding to a halt by the phone table, she grabbed the receiver up with a hand that was shaking so badly she could barely hold on to it and punched the numbers.

"911 what's your emergency?"

"Hel…"

She didn't manage to get the rest of the word out before someone caught her from behind, covering her mouth and nose with a cloth wet with something that had a sickly sweet odor.

* * * *

Emerald was aware of the nausea even before the fog departed from her brain, allowing her mind to begin to assimilate her sensory perceptions. She couldn't focus on anything beyond the illness, however, the cloying, sickening sweetness that clogged her throat. Ignoring everything else, she concentrated on breathing slowly, lightly, quelling the sickness that threatened to choke her.

Finally, she mastered the sickness enough to begin assessing her surroundings. Something had been bound around her head, blinding her to everything but a faint glow of light. Her lips were sealed with tape, which she thought was wound about her head, as well, because the slightest movement threatened to tug the hair from her scalp.

With an effort she lifted her head.

"You're awake."

She stiffened, trying to identify the voice.

Something warm trailed along one arm, across her collar bone and then scraped a path along her other arm … a finger.

Her wrists were tied, her arms suspended on either side of her from the binding. She understood then why her wrists and shoulders hurt.

The surface she was sitting on shifted, shook slightly. In a moment, a hot moist breath tickled her cheek. "I'd almost decided to forgive you and take you back," her tormentor whispered in her ear. "But you just couldn't leave it alone, you stupid, ungrateful bitch! After all I've done for you!"

Emerald's heart leapt and began thundering in her chest, making it difficult to breathe. She shook her head, but the gag prevented her from trying to explain, or question, or beg.

After a moment, she felt a tug on the cloth that was wrapped around her head. It loosened, fell away. Emerald stared at the blurry image in front of her, blinking, trying to bring it into focus. Her eyes widened when her vision finally cleared.

"You weren't expecting me, were you?"

Emerald shook her head slowly, frowning. She didn't understand. She didn't understand at all. What had she said about forgiving her?

"I always thought that doe eyed look of innocence was one of your charms, but you're really irritating the shit out of me right now, Em."

Emerald glared at her captor. "Don't call me that!" she raged against the gag.

Maureen stared back at her a moment and finally grabbed the edge of the tape, unwinding it with painful slowness. Tears sprang to Emerald's eyes as she felt her hair being pulled from her scalp by the tape. "What are you doing, Maureen?" Emerald gasped. "*Why* are you doing this?" A stray thought lit in her mind and her eyes widened. "You're trying to frame Reece, aren't you?"

Maureen slapped her so hard across the face her teeth cut her cheek and lip. Her head slammed into the headboard. For several moments, she thought she would black out.

Maureen grabbed a handful of hair. "I am so sick of you trailing after that cock like a bitch in heat! I've been patient with you, Em. You know I have. But I've had enough. You've cheated on me with that son-of-a-bitch the last time. When I get done with you, I'll be done with both of you."

Emerald tried to shake the dizziness, closing her eyes in hopes of fighting it into abeyance. She opened her eyes again abruptly as she felt something sliding around her neck. "What are you doing?"

Maureen smiled. "Something ingenious, really. I thought of it myself. I was going to just use the same tie that had been used on you that time, but then I thought, why not get creative? This little rope here's tied to that little rope there, goes around your neck just so and then over to the other rope. What happens, you see, is, if you pass out, the rope gets tighter. If you try to move, the rope gets tighter. So, sooner or later, no matter what, you strangle yourself. It was entertaining really, besides making it unnecessary for me to exert myself to do it. I really didn't have anything against them, you see. I was just trying to get a message through that thick skull of yours. I knew, even if I changed the tie a little, they'd still figure it was him. And you would know I was sending you a message. But you didn't figure it out, did you?" She grabbed a fistful of Emerald's hair again, yelling in her ear. "Behave yourself or this'll be you!"

Emerald's eyes widened. "You did ... you killed those women?"

Maureen shook her head. "God, Em. I never thought you were so god damned dense. Didn't I just tell you I did it?"

"But... but why?"

Maureen gave her a look, then popped her on each cheek. "What is it? Still groggy from the chloroform? Lis ...ten, bitch! I did it to warn you away from that dick swinging son-of-a-bitch, but did it do any good? No! Because you're too stupid to take a subtle hint."

Emerald found she had to fight another round with her nausea. "What're you doing, Maureen?"

"I'm taking care of my cheating bitch and her lover. I would've thought you'd figured that out by now."

"But ... we were never lovers!"

Maureen slapped her again. "Don't lie to me. I stood right there and watched you with him!" she said, pointing to the hole in the wall.

Emerald stared at her for several moments, trying to think of some way she might be able to reach the woman. "You and I ... we've been friends a long time, Maureen. I don't understand how you could possibly have mistaken a friendship for ... for anything else. We've never been lovers."

Maureen glared at her. "Say whatever you like. It's not going to make any difference now. I wouldn't take you back if you begged me."

She crawled off the bed. It was only then that Emerald realized that she wasn't wearing a stitch of clothing. Horrified, she looked away. When she looked back again it was in time to see Maureen picking up a dildo that looked as if it might have been modeled after Goliath. "Don't you dare come near me with that thing!" she screamed when Maureen turned around and looked at her, smiling.

Maureen shrugged, slapping her palm with it. "It has to look like he did it."

Emerald let loose a scream like a police siren. It cut off abruptly when she slid down the bed and the rope tightened around her throat. For several moments, she struggled to gasp air, too frantic at first to realize she needed to push herself up the bed to loosen the rope around her neck. By the time the answer filtered through to her panicked mind, dark spots were swimming before her eyes.

Abruptly, the door swung open, crashing back against the wall so hard it bounced. "Freeze! Don't you so much as bat an eyelash!"

"Em! Somebody cut her loose, for God's sake!"

It was the last sound Emerald heard before darkness claimed her completely.

Chapter Nine

Someone was rocking her, stroking her cheek. Emerald gasped, clawing her way loose from the smothering folds of cloth around her face. The gasp sent pain lancing through her abused throat and for several moments panic threatened to overwhelm her as she struggled to breathe and swallow through a throat that felt as if it had swollen closed.

"Shh, baby. It's all right. It's me, Reece."

She shuddered, but relaxed at the sound of his voice. "Get her?"

"Yeah. They got her. She's gone. We need to get you to a hospital ... get you checked out. The paramedics are on the way, so just hold tight, baby."

"It was her," she managed to croak past her damaged throat.

"I know. The detective figured it out ... almost too late, but he figured it out. We can talk about it later. You don't need to be trying to talk. Your throat's in bad shape."

Emerald pulled away enough to look around. She saw they were still in her bedroom. Someone--Reece she supposed--had wrapped her in a sheet. She was grateful for that. There were still cops moving around the room, collecting evidence, photographing the scene. "Why you here?" she said in a croaking whisper.

He stiffened. "Don't be pissed with me, Em."

She shook her head, but it made it swim. She dropped her forehead to his chest, closing her eyes. "Not."

His arms tightened. "I couldn't give up. I was totally pissed, but after I got to trying to see it from your point of view, I understood why you were so mad at me." He let out a deep sigh. "I promised I wouldn't do anything stupid to screw things up for us, but I really screwed up this time, didn't I?"

Emerald was in no mood to spare him. She nodded.

"If I promised never to do it again, do you think you could give me another chance?"

"Can't."

"I made a mistake. You said you loved me. Can't you at least try?"

With an effort, Emerald swallowed, gathering moisture into her dry mouth to try to speak. "You … can't … promise," she managed to say, trying to clarify.

"What if I promised to love, honor and cherish forever? In front of God and everybody?"

Startled, Emerald glanced up at him questioningly.

"Marry me?"

She frowned at him, torn between a surge of hopefulness and irritation that he'd picked the one time when she was least able to discuss the matter to ask her such an important question.

He looked alarmed. "Don't say no. Just think about it, OK?"

She gave him a look. "Yes," she managed to croak.

"Yes, you'll think about it?"

"Marry you."

He grinned. "You said yes?"

She nodded, smiled faintly. "Condition."

He looked at her warily. "What?"

"'Nuptial. Pre..Nup."

He flushed. "I won't ask you to sign one. I swear I hadn't even considered it."

"Want one."

"You want a Pre-nup?" he asked incredulously.

"For you … Don't trust me. Want you to have."

He hugged her tightly. "I don't need it. I'm sorry. I don't know how many ways I can say it, Em."

"I want you to have it," she said stubbornly.

The bustle of the arriving paramedics distracted them. Before they took her away, she squeezed his hand. "Promise?"

He looked distressed, but he nodded.

* * * *

Emerald woke to find Reece holding her hand. He was studying her fingers, tracing them. He leaned down and kissed her palm and she curled her fingers to caress his face.

He looked up at her, smiled a little crookedly. "You've been out of it. How're you feeling?"

"Better," she said, but her voice still came out as a croak and little more than a whisper.

"Do you remember what we were talking about last night?" he asked hesitantly.

She studied his face. "Yes."

He seemed to relax. "You meant it?"

"All of it."

He frowned. "I don't feel comfortable about this, Em. I'm afraid it'll ruin things for us."

She gave him a look, but gripped his hand. "I don't want you to have any doubts, Reece. That would be worse for us than making the agreement. I can't say I think it's romantic … but I'd rather have it between us than have doubts between us."

He scrubbed his face with his hands. "You're not really going to forgive me, are you?"

"Some things take time. In time, I think I will. In time, maybe, you'll learn to trust me and believe in me. I love you enough to try. If you love me as much as I love you, we'll figure out a way to make it work. But I think it would be a mistake to even attempt to make a marriage work as long as you had doubts about me. I'm hoping a pre-nup will remove the doubts and give us a chance."

He dropped the subject, but he looked miserable and uneasy.

"I've been lying here trying to figure out what happened the other night, wondering if it was some kind of nightmare brought on by the stuff they gave me to sleep. Or, rather, wondering if parts of it were. That was Maureen, though, wasn't it?"

Reece sat forward. "It was. And, as close a call as it was, it was still a damned good thing she was so focused on you that she didn't manage to get the phone hung up after you called 911. I don't know if we'd have made it in time otherwise."

Emerald shuddered. "How did you manage to arrive with the police?"

"I was with the detective at the time the call came in. I was uneasy about you so I figured, since you'd gotten so pissed off about me having someone watch you I'd just mention to the cops that I was afraid you'd be the next target.

"Turned out the detective had already deduced that. He told me that, once he'd become convinced it wasn't me--which took him a while, in spite of my alibi--he decided it had to be somebody that was there at the time. He knew it couldn't be a copycat--the MO was too close to be no more than a coincidence, but, except for the people directly involved in the previous crime, there was no way anybody could know the particulars.

"He checked out Mike, Jeffery and David--had them picked up and questioned, but the police couldn't get anything out of them and were pretty convinced they didn't know anything about the murders down here. There wasn't a lot of forensic evidence the police here had to go by, but they had picked up one partial print on the last one and it didn't match me ... or any of them.

"Since he met a dead end there, he started back tracking. At first, he was focusing on me ... on the theory that, if it wasn't me, then somebody wanted to frame me and get me out of the way. That led him to the possibility that you were the reason they wanted me out of the way, so he started digging, looking at anybody that might be obsessing over you.

"When Maureen's name popped up, he dismissed it at first. But he got to examining the crime scenes again and he realized there were a few little details that pointed to the possibility that the perp was a woman ... Things they'd missed before, or misinterpreted because they'd been certain it had to be a man.

"The problem was, he found out she'd left to go on vacation before the second murder occurred. He decided he'd have to drop her as a possibility, but, just to be on the safe side, he told them to check the partial against her prints. It looked like a possible match, so he put in a call to the police up near her cabin to pick her up. When they got to her cabin and searched it, they found out that she'd never arrived.

"By the time the detective got that information back, it was almost too late to do you any good ... but, as I said, the phone hadn't been hung up. Ordinarily, the operator might have thought it was a prank, or a false alarm, but since there'd already been two murders, she had it traced and called it in."

Emerald frowned. "It's still hard to believe. I never even had a clue Maureen was a ... liked me that way."

Reece frowned. "I'm not sure what Maureen is ... besides psychotic. I don't know if she knows. The only thing that there's no doubt of is that she was obsessed with you and convinced that you belonged to her. I think, in her mind, she considered that the two of you were living together, as a couple ... even though the apartments were separate."

"She told me she was doing it to teach me a lesson for cheating on her ... and to get even with you." Emerald shuddered in revulsion. "I thought she was just nosy. She was always watching me, asking me about my day. And any time I even considered dating, she always managed to convince me I didn't actually want to go out ... which wasn't too hard because I was usually too busy to really consider it anyway."

Reece frowned. "I thought you were waiting for me?"

Emerald rolled her eyes. "Don't be an ass, Reece. We weren't even seeing each other *before* all that happened. You wouldn't speak to me after you were arrested, wouldn't let me testify. I had no reason at all to expect that you'd ever be out ... if you'd served the full sentence .... And, even if I'd considered the possibility that you might get out, you didn't give me any reason to think you'd be interested in looking me up when you did. I didn't date because I was in love with you. If I'd met anybody that could've changed the way I felt about you, I wouldn't have waited for somebody I never expected to come."

"I was trying to protect you," he said irritably. "Stupid as it sounds, I figured you'd be better off if I could keep you out of it ... and I couldn't do that if I'd contacted you. Somebody would've gotten wind of it. I knew I was innocent. It never occurred to me ... until the trial was over, that there was any possibility of anything happening except that I'd get off. Then, after things quieted down, I figured I could look you up and we could do it right ... date, get to know each other."

Emerald studied him a long moment and finally tugged on his hand. "Come here."

He looked surprised, but leaned forward.

She smiled. "You're going to have to get closer if you want a kiss."

He got up abruptly and leaned over her, kissing her deeply, hungrily. When he broke the kiss, he propped his forehead against hers, nuzzling her nose with his own. "What do you say we fly out to Reno as soon as you get out and make it legal?"

Emerald put her arms around his neck. "You in a hurry?"

He grinned. "It took me eight years to get up the nerve, Em. Don't you think that's a long enough wait?"

The End

The Shaman

Chapter One

There was no word in the English language strong enough, in Special Agent, Charlotte Boyer's, mind to adequately describe the carnage. She thought she'd prepared herself. She supposed, if it had been even a little more typical of the murders she'd studied at Quantico, she would've been braced for it. There was nothing 'typical' or even to be expected about this and her stomach heaved. She turned away from the scene, taking several deep breaths, fighting for her dignity.

Concentrating, at first, on a pretense of professionalism, she searched the ground with her gaze, as if looking for clues. Finally, to her relief, her training kicked in and her mind, in truth, slowly focused on the search for clues.

The soil was too rocky to yield up anything as conclusive, or useful, as footprints. There were drag marks, however, much of the way. The victim, sixteen-year-old Chastity Owl, appeared to have been sneaking back into her bedroom window, or maybe out of it, when she was attacked. She'd been dragged for several hundred yards into the desert and finished off almost within sight of her own home.

No one had heard her scream, even though the field they'd found her in bordered a fairly sizable neighborhood.

"Looks like a puma," one of the men muttered. Turning, Charlie saw that it was the reservation police chief, George Brown, who'd spoken.

"Like the other two?" she asked.

He glanced at her. "It looks the same as the other two attacks." He studied her a long moment, his eyes narrowing. "I'm curious to know why they would've sent a field investigator out to look at an animal attack."

Charlie merely stared at him, trying to decide how much, or how little, to say. It was a Federal Reservation, but the reservation police had jurisdiction. She'd been invited, not very graciously, as a consultant because her boss had asked if she could drive out and have look.

She'd been sent because of the anonymous phone call the bureau had received. The caller had disguised his voice, had refused to leave a name, but he'd insisted the attacks weren't animal attacks at all, but murder.

Maybe it had just been someone from the reservation that was afraid his daughter might be next on the menu?

She frowned. "Weren't the other two attacks on the Utah side of the reservation?"

Brown gave her a look. "Don't give me that 'across state lines' crap. That only applies if there's a crime. No human did this."

Charlie thought quickly. "What's the typical range of a puma? I mean, they're territorial, aren't they? Would one hunt this far?"

"Not typically. If they drove him off, though, he'd mark new territory."

Charlie nodded and, without offering up any explanation for her presence, returned her attention to examining the scene.

The girl was unidentifiable. If not for the fact that there had been a clear drag path from the girl's home to the sight where they found the body--if not for the fact that it was a small community and anyone who went missing was immediately noticed--

Her face was gone, nothing more than a bloody mess of ragged flesh. She'd been ripped open from neck to groin, her entrails spilled out all over the ground. Swallowing the bile that rose in her throat, Charlie examined the girl's body, mentally tallying parts. As far as she could see, nothing was missing.

Wild animals attacked when hungry, or when threatened. It was a rare animal that merely attacked for sport. It was possible, of course, that something had spooked the animal off before it had had a chance to feed, or that it had eaten. The body was so damaged it was impossible to be certain if anything was missing until there'd been an autopsy--but it looked as if the animal had done nothing more than ripped her to shreds.

There was no reason that she could see that the animal might have felt threatened by the girl, unless it had been sniffing around the garbage and she'd happened up on it.

It had gone for her throat. Again, only a medical examination would tell for certain, but she suspected nobody had heard the girl scream because the animal had ripped her vocal chords first thing.

Again, that seemed fairly typical of an animal. Most predators went for the quick kill, but the drag marks seemed to indicate that the girl had struggled at least part of the way. She'd lost her shoes, one in the yard of her home, the other on the road below.

The one thing about the scene that really unnerved her though--which absolutely no one had commented on--was the fact that the girl looked almost as if she'd been posed.

When she'd arrived, the girl had been lying in the 'submissive' posture of a rape victim, her arms lying, palm up, on either side of her head, her knees bent and her thighs spread.

The sound of an arriving vehicle drew her attention and Charlie turned to look.

A small crowd had gathered at the edge of the road below them, held in check by two police officers. The vehicle just pulling up was an ambulance from the clinic/ hospital/ medical examiner's office.

To her surprise, a blond man dressed in a lab coat got out of the passenger's door. At this distance, he looked more like an intern than a doctor--it seemed doubtful he was more than thirty--His build suggested as much, for he was tall and slender. The man with him was a local, and pretty much a direct opposite--dark, short, either stout or chunky muscular.

It was he who went to the back, opened the doors and pulled the gurney out. Lifting it, he locked the folding structure upright and began dragging it up the hill. The blond man trailed behind him, making no attempt to help the driver with the unwieldy thing.

He, in fact, stopped to chat with a man that was leaning against one of the police cars.

A jolt went through Charlie as she focused on the man that had stopped him. He was wearing nothing beyond a pair of ragged, cut off jeans and he had the body of a male stripper, leanly muscular, each muscle lovingly defined, from his washboard stomach to his well shaped legs. His arms were folded across his chest, displaying, whether intentional or not, very nice pecs, and bulging arm muscles.

He was American Indian, she was certain, although his dark skin gleamed more golden than red in the bright sunlight.

Silvery highlights shown in the black hair that hung down well past his shoulders. For a moment, Charlie thought it was streaks of gray, but as he turned and almost seemed to look directly at her, she saw that he was probably no older than the doctor, for the 'streaks' disappeared as he moved his head.

With an effort, she dragged her gaze from the Native American to the white man beside him, wondering if either man could actually tell from this distance what had captured her gaze.

After several moments, she turned away, unwilling to make it too obvious that she was disconcerted that she'd been caught staring. The EMT came to an abrupt stop when he was level with her. She heard him suck in his breath. "Jesus Christ almighty," he muttered.

Charlie felt swell of sympathy. "Did you know her?"

The man glanced sharply at her. Charlie saw then that he was wearing a name tag on his uniform that said 'Bear'. "How the hell would I recognize her if I did?" he said roughly.

Charlie blushed, feeling more than a little foolish. In the world of investigation, the question was almost as pat as 'how do you do' in society, and in this case, at least, almost as inane. "Sorry. That was thoughtless. I'm special agent, Charlotte Boyer."

He nodded, but brushed past her as he saw the chief's impatient glare and lined the gurney up next to the body. Pressing the lever that collapsed it, he stared down at the body for several moments. "We need a body bag. No way am I going to let those people down there watch me scoop her up onto the gurney."

Chief Brown nodded and the EMT stalked past her once more.

As she turned to watch him, she discovered that the coroner had finally decided to grace them with his presence. He favored her with a once over that was blatantly sexist and a slow smile that might have charmed her under other circumstances. Up close, she saw that he was nice looking in the manner of meticulously groomed rather than raw nature, although he was far from ugly, or even plain. He stuck his hand out. "I'm Doctor Robert Morris. Most people around here just call me Dr. Bob."

Charlotte held out her hand and shook his firmly, then tugged her hand from his grip. "Special Agent Charlotte Boyer. Most people just call me Agent Boyer."

His brows rose. His smile widened to a grin. "Well, Ms. FBI, what brings you out to our neck of the woods?"

Charlotte supposed it was meant to be charming, but the comment annoyed her. Moreover, she had no intention of announcing her agenda. She forced a polite smile.

"You want to have a look before we take her?" Chief Brown called out.

The doctor looked annoyed, but he nodded and brushed past her.

Hearing the door of the ambulance slam, Charlie glanced back down the hill. She was far more interested in the man she'd seen the doctor talking to, however, than the EMT, whom she saw was struggling up the incline once more, this time carrying a black body bag.

As she glanced casually around for him, she discovered that he was still where she'd first noticed him, leaning against the police car.

He was staring straight at her, making no effort at all to appear casual about his interest.

Charlotte looked away, determined to ignore the wave of testosterone that smacked into her like a sledge hammer, making her stomach go weightless and jolting her pulse into high gear. She'd put her initial reaction to the man down to nerves. She didn't have that luxury this time and it annoyed her almost as much as it unnerved her. When the EMT came even with her, she fell into step beside him. "Who is that man leaning on the police car ... the one that was talking to the doctor when he arrived?"

Irritation flooded her when the EMT looked behind him. He might just as well have bellowed her interest to everyone present.

"Greywolf? He's the shaman."

Chapter Two

"What's he doing here, you think?"

The EMT gave her a narrow-eyed, assessing look. "Rubber necking like everyone else?"

Charlie's lips tightened in annoyance. She could see no reason for his hostility. It was obvious most of the people below weren't 'rubber necking'. This was someone most of them probably knew. They were, quite rightly, anxious and distressed about the killing, probably wondering if one of them, or one of their loved ones, would be next.

She had gotten the sense, however, that Greywolf was there for a purpose that went beyond community concern. His expression was impassive, but, without quite knowing why, she sensed that he had missed very little of what was transpiring at the scene on the hill, and that he was waiting--for something.

She didn't try to keep pace with the EMT. It was obvious he didn't feel particularly talkative. Either his hostility was a direct result of his own distress over the killing, or he resented her presence as much as everyone else ... or maybe he just didn't like nosy white people.

She moved closer to observe as the man unfolded the body bag and laid it out beside the victim. Dr. Morris was looking the girl's body over with clinical detachment ... in fact, he not only seemed strangely unmoved, but morbidly curious at the same time.

She had to wonder if her imagination was working overtime.

"...clearly an animal attack. See these marks here?" He looked up at Chief Brown. "Clearly claw marks ... from a good sized puma, I'd say."

"That's what I thought," the chief said grimly, sending her a glance that was part triumphant and part irritation.

"You don't think there's anything strange about the positioning of the body?"

Dr. Morris looked up at her questioningly.

"They've moved the body. When we first arrived on the scene, her legs were up, her feet flat on the ground."

He looked down at the body again. They'd straightened her legs, but they were still splayed wide as they had been. He shrugged. "Both sides of her hands are lacerated. Looks like she was trying to fight it off."

"She was dragged here by her throat. I don't think she was in any condition to fight by the time she got here."

The chief gave her a look. "How do you know she was dragged by the throat?"

"The amount of blood leading here, compared to much less at the scene itself. It looks like the initial attack severed her jugular. She'd bled out by the time they got to this point. Plus, nobody heard her scream. Didn't you say the girl's parents only discovered her missing this morning? If she was attacked right outside her home and she'd been able to scream, don't you think they would've heard her?"

The doctor shrugged her comments off and began scooping the entrails back into the girl's body cavity. After a moment, his assistant helped. When they'd finished, they lifted her body carefully and placed it in the body bag.

"I'll know more when I've had the chance to examine her in the lab," he said dismissively as he removed his surgical gloves and shoved them into the pocket of his lab coat.

Charlie gaped at him in disbelief. She wasn't an expert in forensics herself, and she couldn't claim to have had a lot of field experience, but this was so far off procedure it was just plain bizarre.

"I'll send my results over to you tomorrow, chief," Dr. Morris said, helping the EMT lift the gurney and holding one end as they started down the hill.

Charlie fell into step beside him. "When will you be performing the autopsy?"

He glanced at her. He was frowning, but she thought that might be because they were having trouble keeping the gurney upright on the uneven ground. "I've got patients waiting. Later this evening."

"May I attend?"

His brows rose. "If you think you can handle it, little lady."

Charlie gave him a look. "If I can handle seeing her strewn out all over this hillside, I think I can handle the autopsy," she said dryly.

He grinned at her, showing no animosity at her sarcasm. "All right then. It's a date. I'll see you around seven."

Charlie stopped abruptly, watching as they continued down the hillside and finally reached the road. The people waiting crowded close, asking questions, demanding answers. Dr. Morris fielded most of them good-naturedly, but elusively. Finally, he held up his hands for silence. "I'll have to have a look at her at the morgue before I can answer anything conclusively. Right now all I can say is that we're fairly certain it was another animal attack."

Charlie frowned, stepping aside as the chief and his men made their way down the hillside and pushed past her.

It was a small police force for a small community. They were well trained for all that, and would know procedure and techniques for studying a crime scene.

She supposed it was just easier to accept an animal attack than the possibility of a crazed killer. Maybe that was why they'd ignored the possibility. Maybe that was why they'd trampled all over the crime scene without giving it more than a cursory examination. Maybe that was why the doctor hadn't seen fit to look for possible evidence before he'd loaded the body.

It seemed plausible, and yet she couldn't help but wonder if there was something else going on here.

Shaking it off finally, she followed the police. She'd left her car at the station and ridden to the site with the police chief. She glanced at her watch. It was only five. She had two hours before the autopsy. She decided to ride back with the chief, get her car and return to the site to see if she could find anything they'd missed, or that hadn't been trampled.

It was almost six by the time she turned onto the road leading to the crime scene once more, and nearing dusk. She saw the thin pillar of smoke almost at once and an angry suspicion settled in her mind. Flooring it, she brought her car to a screeching halt at the bottom of the hill, leaping out almost before it had stopped rocking and drawing her weapon.

Fury filled her when she saw her suspicions had been well founded. Someone had set a fire right in the middle of the crime scene ... and that someone was still there, squatting beside the fire, throwing something into it.

She made no attempt to be quiet as she rushed up the hill. There was no point when she'd made such an arrival. To her amazement, however, the man didn't make any attempt to escape. It was almost as if he was deaf to everything going on around him.

She stopped when she was little more than three feet away from him. "Hold it right there! Let me see your hands!"

He stiffened, but he didn't move.

"Now!" she ground out.

Slowly, he lifted his hands.

She looked him over. "Spread your knees. Wider!"

When she was certain that he was in a position that would prevent him from leaping to his feet, she moved a little closer. "Hands on top of your head."

He complied, lacing his fingers in a way that told her he was at least passingly familiar with an arrest.

Cautiously, she moved toward him, holstered her weapon, dug a nylon tie from her purse and grasped one wrist. Placing her knees on the bend of his legs, she twisted the arm behind him and then caught his other wrist and did the same, looping the tie around them and pulling it tight. She relaxed fractionally when she had his hands bound.

Grasping his arm at his elbow, she urged him to stand up.

He was taller than she'd thought ... and much better looking, which was a feat since she'd thought when she first saw him that he was an exceptionally handsome specimen.

"What were you burning?" she said, her voice harsh with disappointment.

Greywolf's brows rose. "No pat down?"

His voice, deep and melodious, vibrated through her nervous system like a strong aphrodisiac. It irritated the hell out of her that he had her so addled she hadn't thought to frisk him for weapons.

He gave her an amused look over his shoulder as she moved around behind him and patted his back pockets. She was tempted to give him a pinch. She resisted the temptation, and the urge to examine his nicely taut buttocks, moving around in front of him again. "Do you have any sharp objects in your pockets? Knife? Needles?"

He shook his head slowly.

"You packing?"

Humor gleamed in his eyes, but again he merely shook his head.

Taking a deep breath, Charlie pushed a hand into his right front pocket and discovered it was empty. As she pushed her hand into his other pocket, however, she almost immediately encountered something hard and cylindrical.

It wasn't the barrel of a gun--unless he was packing a cannon.

Flustered, she jerked her hand out of his pocket.

He'd done that on purpose! Charlie thought indignantly. Discovering she was too self-conscious to look up at him, she turned to look at the dying fire. "What were you burning?"

"Ritual herbs."

"Evidence," she said testily, turning to look at him accusingly. "This is a crime scene, and off limits. There's only one reason you'd be here that I can see, and that's to tamper with evidence ... or destroy what might be left."

He looked her over thoroughly, that arrogant male look that made a woman feel as if she'd left the house without her clothes. Charlie had thought she was immune to 'that look'. Few men dared giving a woman that look openly any more, certainly not when she was on the job, but she'd gotten her share over the years. In general, she handled it by giving them one in return and then dismissing them.

Greywolf was smiling faintly when she'd treated him to her brand of clinical detachment. It irritated the hell out of her, mostly because she found him far too attractive to maintain a healthy detachment. "I could arrest you ... for obstructing justice if nothing else."

He almost seemed to shrug. "But can you make it stick, Ms. F-B-I?"

Arrogant male, chauvinistic pig! She thought furiously. He must be a throw back. She could've sworn they'd all died out. "So--talk. Convince me."

"It would be easier if my hands weren't tied," he drawled.

Charlie gaped at him speechlessly, but there was no mistaking the double entendre in the comment. She couldn't believe he'd had the gall to toss such a blatantly sexual innuendo out when she was on the verge of arresting him on serious charges. "Your tongue isn't tied," she snapped.

A deep chuckle rumbled from his chest, and Charlie felt her face light up like a neon sign. Worse, the timbre of his laugh, like his voice, sent a tide of warmth through her that was purely sensual. "Did you have a reason for being here that isn't obvious to me?" she said through gritted teeth, holding on to her patience with a supreme effort.

"I am the Shaman.... But you know that. You asked Bear about me."

The blush that had barely died, flooded back. She was tempted to deny she'd asked the EMT about him, but the man had turned around and stared directly at him. An idiot could've figured out she was asking about him ... and Greywolf was obviously not deficit in the mental department.

"And this has to do with trampling all over the crime scene--and destroying evidence--how?"

"What makes you think it's a crime scene?" he countered.

Again, he bereft her of speech. "That's not the point."

"That's exactly the point, from what I can see."

He had her there. Officially, it wasn't a crime scene, but the scene of an accident. Officially, the investigation was over. So far, she hadn't found anything at all that would give her the leverage she needed to supersede the local police jurisdiction.

It dawned upon her as she thought of that that it had grown dark as she stood arguing with him. It had been nearly six when she'd turned into the road. It must be close to seven by now. She was going to miss the damned autopsy!

"Turn around."

His brows rose, but he turned, presenting his back. Charlie

pulled a small wire cutter from her bag and clipped the nylon tie. "I'm going to let it go this time, but don't let it happen again."

Greywolf sent her an amused glance, but said nothing.

Charlie sent him a scathing look and turned, stalking back down the hill. Unable to resist one last look in his direction, she saw, as she started her car, that he was standing where she'd left him, watching her.

Chapter Three

Charlie had driven to the clinic like her tailpipe was on fire. She glanced at her watch as she parked. It was two minutes till seven. Relief flooded her, but the simmering anger remained, making her movements tense and jerky as she got out of the car and strode purposefully toward the clinic. She waited impatiently at the desk for a full minute before the nurse looked up and asked her what she needed.

She left while the nurse was still giving her directions to the morgue.

Dr. Morris was just closing up as she pushed through the door and stopped on the threshold. He glanced up at her arrival, his brows lifted questioningly, but returned his attention to his task almost immediately.

Charlie stared speechlessly at the clock on the wall. Five after seven--just like her watch. "Didn't you say seven?" Charlie asked, trying to hold her temper in check as she strode across the room.

He shrugged. "I finished up earlier than I expected. Brown called, asked what to tell the family about funeral arrangements so I told him I'd get right on it."

Charlie paused beside him, fuming as she watched him put the finishing stitches in the body. Taking a deep, shuddering breath, she made an effort to tamp her anger. "Did you determine the cause of death?"

He glanced at her, lifting his brows in surprise. "Like I said before--puma."

"You're absolutely certain of that?"

He smiled at her condescendingly. "Sorry. I guess you had visions of solving a big case and getting out of your desk job, but there's nothing here that I could see."

Charlie felt a streak of temptation surface to do violence. She clenched her hand into a fist, sought inner peace. "You took samples, I presume?" she demanded, trying without much success to keep an equal condescension from her own voice.

He shrugged. "I didn't find anything."

The comment took her breath and it took several moments to recover her equilibrium. "No fibers? No hair? No skin samples?"

"It was a puma," he said soothingly.

Charlie moved away from him, pacing the room, trying to force her anger into abeyance so that she could think more clearly. "How did you conclude that it was a puma?" she asked, pleased when the question came out sounding calm, merely curious.

"The lacerations are consistent in size, depth, curvature. If it had been a wolf, there would've more bites and fewer claw marks--their primary weapon is their jaws--and the claws are entirely different."

"But you didn't find any hairs to prove the theory conclusively?"

He frowned, finally jarred from his complacency by a touch of anger. "I didn't need to. You saw the body. Don't tell me you think there's any possibility at all that a man did this to her?"

Charlie's lips tightened. "It occurred to me that there was a possibility of it, yes."

His brows rose, but there was amusement in his eyes that made her grit her teeth.

"Whatever gave you an idea like that?"

Charlie gave him a look. "They moved the body before you got there, so I can understand that it might not have looked as blatant to you as it did to me, but doesn't it bother you that the girl looked liked she'd been posed? Doesn't it bother you that she was sprawled out as if she'd been sexually assaulted?"

He stared at her a long moment--and then chuckled. "Sorry. Puma's don't usually rape their victims though."

Charlie's anger surged to the forefront again. "No. They usually eat them," she said tightly. "But despite the mess he made of her, I didn't see any sign at all that anything was missing. I assume you checked?"

He studied her a long moment. Instead of answering, however, he said, almost gently, "It didn't occur to you that maybe you were looking for signs of rape and interpreted something, that was purely coincidental, as something it wasn't?"

The implication was clear. He was insinuating that she'd gone to the scene with preconceived notions instead of doing her job. She supposed, considering she'd accused him of the same thing, she deserved it. She also had to concede that it was possible--not likely to her mind, but possible--that the girl had been trying to fight the thing off and had ended up in what appeared to be the position of a rape victim. She would've been trying, assuming she'd been able to, to push the thing away with her legs since her legs were stronger. She would've had her hands over her face, or maybe even clutching the animal, trying to hold it off, which could account for her arms falling to her sides, and upward, in the submissive position.

She didn't believe it for one moment.

The girl was almost certainly in the last throes of death by the time they'd arrived on the hillside. She wouldn't have been capable of much more than twitching, weakly at that.

She supposed it was possible that he believed what he was saying. As he'd so nastily pointed out, she had done little field work. She'd been primarily tied to a desk since she'd left the academy. It was possible she was completely wrong, she knew, but she also knew she wasn't going to be able to prove it one way or another without evidence.

"It's possible," she conceded, smiling with an effort. "I don't suppose you've got much of a lab here, for that sort of testing anyway? I'd be happy to take samples to the lab at the agency if you'd collect some for me."

He smiled thinly as he removed his apron and moved to the sink to wash up. "I'll see what I can do ... in the morning before they collect her. At the moment, I'm tired enough to sleep a week, and starving. I don't suppose I could convince you to have dinner with me?"

Charlie forced a smile as he tossed her a look over his shoulder. "I hadn't planned to stay overnight."

He smiled suggestively. "I'd be happy to lend you my couch."

Not on a bet! Charlie thought, trying to maintain her smile. What was it with the men around this place, anyway? It was like they'd missed the feminine revolution altogether. "I'm sure I can find something--but thanks for the offer!"

He shrugged. "The offer of food is still open."

"Why not?"

* * * *

The restaurant was crowded. Charlie was a little surprised, considering the hour. She'd thought most small towns rolled up the sidewalks at dark.

She discovered when she crossed the threshold, with Dr. Bob's hand planted intrusively on her waist, that it was a combination restaurant/tavern and either the most popular one in town, or the only one in town. Bob guided her to an empty booth near the back and gestured toward the bench seat facing the wall. Charlie ignored him and took the seat facing the restaurant.

Smirking, he slipped into the seat beside her. Charlie gave him a look. "We'd be more comfortable, I think, if you sat on the other side."

He laughed, as if she'd told him a hilarious joke, but got up and moved to the other side. "Just checking."

Charlie smiled thinly. "Let's just keep this professional, shall we?"

His smile slipped a notch. "We're not working now. Relax. You might enjoy yourself."

"If I didn't have a rod up my ass, you mean?" Charlie asked sweetly.

He laughed, a little too heartily to Charlie's notion.

She glanced around the tavern. Her heart skipped several beats when she spied Greywolf, lounging against the end of the bar, one foot hooked on the rung of the bar stool, the other leg splayed with only the heel of his boot against the floor. His arms were back, his elbows on the bar behind him.

He'd changed clothes--or rather put some on. He was wearing a worn pair of jeans and a western style shirt, open almost to the waist. The wear pattern on the jeans was almost as indecent as the small tear near the crotch. As she stared, mesmerized, at the tiny patch of flesh visible, wondering if it was his thigh or--something else, he reached down and adjusted himself with slow deliberation.

Charlie felt the neon glow return to her cheeks even as her gaze flew upward, encountering a smoldering glance of interest. She shifted her gaze abruptly to the clock on the wall just to the left of his shoulder, then looked down at her watch.

She seriously doubted he'd fall for it, but it was worth a try.

Dr. Bob, noticing her lack of attention, glanced around.

"So," she said, catching his attention once more. "What time do you think you'll have those samples ready for me?"

He shrugged. "Let's not talk shop. It's been a hell of a day.

What'll you have to drink?" he added as he spotted a waitress heading their way.

Charlie frowned. His evasiveness boded ill. She supposed his explanation for performing the autopsy without her was plausible. She didn't like it any better, but she couldn't accuse him of deliberately excluding her--even though she suspected he had. Now he didn't even want to discuss the samples she'd asked for.

So maybe he was tired and just didn't want to talk shop, but Charlie had the distinct feeling that she was going to arrive at the morgue in the morning to discover he'd 'forgotten'.

She looked up at the waitress. "Any chance of getting an iced tea?"

"You're not going to have a drink?" Bob asked, feigning horror.

Charlie smiled with an effort. "Not on an empty stomach ... maybe later."

"The booths are for the diners," the waitress pointed out at almost the same moment.

"In that case, I guess we'll need menus," Charlie said, firmly suppressing the temptation toward biting sarcasm--shall we just guess what's available? Or can we look at a menu?

The waitress dragged a worn menu from the pocket of her apron and tossed it on the table, then scribbled on her note pad. "What're you having, Dr. Bob?" she asked, giving him a warm smile.

He favored her with a predatory smile. "You--on toast?"

She giggled, slapping his hand.

"What? You're not going to break my heart by telling me you're not available, are you?"

She smirked. "You know I'm married."

He made an attempt to look shattered and finally shrugged. "In that case, light beer, steak, potato and salad."

"How would you like that steak?" she asked, all business now.

"Just slap it on the ass and cut me a piece off as it runs by."

She grinned. "Rare. And you, miss?"

Despite the nauseating by play, and a very frustrating day, Charlie found that she was starving. "I'll have a steak, too, medium well, please--and a salad."

The waitress nodded and moved away.

Unable to resist, Charlie risked another glance toward Greywolf. There was a shapely young thing wedged between his sprawling thighs now. Greywolf's hands were each cupping an ass cheek, snuggling her firmly against his groin. The faint smile on his lips, however, coupled with the fact that there wasn't a shred of passion on his face, said 'bored'.

Charlie studied her hands, frowning, wondering if she'd misread his expression.

She had no idea what the girl looked like head on, but from the back she had a killer figure and absolutely 'to die for' hair. Sleek, and black as midnight, it hung in a cloud that just brushed her tiny waist.

A slight commotion drew her attention once more, and she looked up in time to see the girl thrust herself away and stalk off, her expression petulant.

There was nothing quite like throwing yourself at a man and being turned down.

When she glanced back at Greywolf, he was staring at her again, his expression brooding.

"You interested?"

Charlie glanced at the doctor. "What?"

He jerked his head in the direction of the bar. "I couldn't help but notice you seem mighty interested in John Greywolf."

"We had a minor dispute a little earlier over the crime ... the accident scene."

Bob's brows rose questioningly.

Charlie shrugged. "He was burning something when I got there."

Bob chuckled. "Hoodou, voodou?"

"I beg your pardon?"

"He's the local witch doctor--the shaman. He was releasing the spirit of the dead."

Chapter Four

"You're not serious."

He grinned but shrugged. "He is."

Charlie flicked a glance in Greywolf's direction again. Either the woman that had been hanging on him earlier had decided playing hard to get wasn't working for her, or another woman had decided to try her luck. The hair was shorter. This one was a little heavier, too.

Charlie frowned, staring down at her drink. No wonder the man was so obnoxious. He must have an ego the size of Texas the way the women around here threw themselves at him.

"He didn't tell you?"

"He didn't mention it, no."

"It's just as well you decided against arresting him. I doubt it would've gone over well with the locals. Particularly in a case like this."

"I don't let politics, local or otherwise, interfere with my job," Charlie said. "I didn't arrest him because I saw no reason to take him in for a slap on the wrist." She decided not to mention the fact that she'd also been in a hurry to get back for the autopsy. There was no point in emphasizing how totally pissed off she was about that ... any more than she already had.

Their meal arrived. Dr. Bob used it as another excuse to flirt with the waitress, who, married or not, didn't seem to mind flirting back--and Charlie wasn't convinced it was purely for play. If she'd been a betting kind of person, she would've been willing to bet Dr. Bob saw his share of action around here. Not that she cared. Dr. Bob was personable enough, but he was a long way from irresistible ... given the current situation.

She supposed, if she was honest, she would have been very interested under other circumstances. He was, she realized, what she generally thought of as 'her type'--a well educated professional, clean cut, personable--and fair. Most women seemed to go for the 'tall, dark and handsome', but she had always leaned more toward the beach boy type, medium height, lean or preferably athletic, and blond.

She was short and tall men, particularly big and tall, didn't thrill her. They made her nervous as hell.

Like the jerk at the bar that was currently fending off female number three. What did he do, anyway? Rub honey all over himself?

"You think he's serious about it?" she asked casually.

"Who?"

"Greywolf."

He shrugged. "I don't really know him that well. Could be. I get the impression that it's sort of a hereditary position, though, so maybe he does and maybe he doesn't. Maybe he's just keeping up the traditions. The natives are big on traditions."

Another mark in the deficit column for Dr. Bob. Given his

obvious contempt for the red man, she had to wonder what he was doing working at a reservation clinic. "I take it you're not a big believer when it comes to the paranormal?"

He chuckled. "I'm a doctor."

Charlie lifted her brows. "And this means…?"

"I don't have time for fairy tales."

Charlie said nothing, concentrating on her meal, which was surprisingly good.

"Don't tell me you believe in that voodou nonsense."

Charlie merely shrugged.

He chuckled. When she gave him a look, he stifled his amusement with an effort. "Seriously? This is a side of you I wouldn't have pictured. Mysticism?"

Charlie frowned. "I like to think I'm open minded."

"That's a little off the charts though, isn't it?"

"So was a round world a blink of an eye ago."

He shook his head. "I guess everybody wants to believe there's still some magic in the world."

Charlie frowned. She didn't particularly want to get into a discussion of her beliefs. The scrape of a chair distracted her and she looked up to discover Greywolf had sauntered across the bar and dragged up a chair. Setting it at the end of the table, he straddled it and propped his forearms on the back.

She felt her jaw go slack, wondering how she could've failed to notice him moving toward them.

If he'd been a felon, he would've had a bead on her now.

Dr. Bob, she saw, was giving him an assessing, not very friendly look.

"Mind if I join you?" Greywolf looked directly at her as he asked the question.

"Yes."

"Not at all," Charlie said politely at almost the same moment.

Dr. Bob forced a chuckle. "Why not? What brings you over, anyway? No luck tonight?"

"My ears were burning."

Charlie glanced at him a little guiltily and pushed her plate away.

"Ah!" Dr. Bob nodded. "I was just explaining to Charlie that you where the local medicine man."

Charlie glared at the doctor. She hadn't given him permission to call her by her first name, at all, and certainly hadn't encouraged him to get familiar enough to call her Charlie. Only her family and closest friends called her that.

"Is that why you kept glancing over there? You expect me to start chanting?"

Charlie gave him a withering look. "I was looking at the clock," she said tightly.

"Your watch stop working?"

She reached for the napkin in her lap. "I'm a clock watcher."

He gave her a faint small that called her a liar. Charlie felt her palm itch and clamped it around her napkin. "Guess that happens when you spend too much time in doors ... pale face."

Charlie was pretty sure she'd just been insulted, but she decided to ignore him.

She glanced at the clock again, just to emphasize that she hadn't been studying him since she'd come in. "It's getting late. I should see if I can find a room. What time should I meet you in the morning?"

Dr. Bob grinned, sending Greywolf a triumphant look.

"For the samples," Charlie said pointedly.

"You're killing me! Here I've wined and dined you in the finest establishment and all you can think of is work!" Dr. Bob said teasingly.

Charlie forced a smile at his effort, although she didn't find it particularly amusing. "Dinner's on me," she said tightly, pulling a bill out of her wallet and tossing it onto the table top.

The doctor glanced at the bill and then up at her again. His smile remained firmly in place, but there was a glint of anger in his eyes now. "Now, that's what I need, a lady that'll keep me in style."

"Around eight?"

Dr. Bob's smile widened to a grin. "Lady, you're as tenacious as a bull terrier ... Eight it is."

There would be no samples. Charlie saw that. She'd blown it, let her irritation goad her into losing her cool. It hadn't helped that Chief Tall Tree had decided to crowd her and completely thrown her off kilter. She sent him a look of resentment.

He got up abruptly and moved the chair so she could clamber out of the bench seat.

She could feel his gaze all the way to the door. She smoothed her hand over the seat of her britches self-consciously. By the time she reached the door, she felt like she'd forgotten how to walk and her ass had a bulls eye on it. She tripped going out the door. Fortunately, she had a firm grip on the door handle and her foot merely wobbled in her high heel. It gave her a start, however, realizing how closely she'd come to turning her ankle, unsettling her even more.

She was huffing like a steam engine by the time she reached her car, unlocked it and crawled in. Instead of starting it, she sat staring at the darkness beyond the hood, trying to thrust Greywolf from her mind, trying to decide what to do.

She might be misjudging Dr. Bob. She hadn't really been around him long enough to know him.

Part of her job was reading people, however.

He wasn't going to give her those damned samples. She would arrive, pretend forgetfulness and the body would already be gone.

Hindsight was always twenty/twenty. She realized she should've asked him to let her take samples herself while they were still in the lab.

She hadn't wanted to seem too pushy, though. It set people's backs up, made them uncooperative.

So much for trying to butter him up by letting him come on to her. She'd botched that smashingly.

Sighing in disgust, she fished her keys out and started the car. She'd seen a hotel back on the highway before she'd turned onto reservation land. It was a good twenty miles, but she couldn't recall having seen a hotel since she'd gotten into town.

She'd already driven past the clinic when the thought popped into her mind. She slowed the car, glanced speculatively at the building in her rearview mirror. Her heart tripped into overtime when she realized she was considering breaking into the building and retrieving her own samples.

She stepped on the gas again, but slowed at the next corner and turned. Turning at the next intersection, she drove past the back side of the clinic. Except for the bare minimum lights that had been left on to discourage burglars, the building looked dark and completely deserted.

She saw a van as she pulled into the parking lot, however.

It must be the cleaning crew, she decided. Pulling out again, she circled the block and finally parked about halfway down the block, watching the van in her rearview mirror.

"This is stupid," she muttered to herself. If she got caught there'd be hell to pay.

If she didn't get the samples, she had no case.

Movement at the door of the clinic caught her attention and

clinched the matter. The cleaning crew was leaving. She debated, briefly, just driving up to them, flashing her badge and telling them she had to go in for something.

If she did that, though, it seemed likely Dr. Bob would find out and call the agency raising hell about her after hours incursion.

She settled back, sliding low in the seat as the van pulled past her.

As soon as they turned the corner at the end of the block, she got out of the car and strode briskly toward the clinic, glancing around occasionally to make certain no one was around.

Apparently everyone was either at home or down at the tavern. The streets were deserted.

She examined the entrance when she reached it. The door had a dead bolt lock. It was wired, too. She compressed her lips in disgust and glanced around again. Seeing no one, she moved around the building, checking each window. She'd gotten made it down one side when she made an interesting discovery. The wire on the window was broken.

Excitement washed over her. The security system was a sham. Evidently, it had been functional at one time, but had deteriorated and not been kept up. In most cases she supposed it would be a deterrent anyway. She'd thought it was a working burglar alarm. Most likely anybody that looked at it would.

The window was high, too high for her to climb into it. She considered it for several moments, but she liked this window. Despite the drawback, it was pretty much concealed from either street. Since it was the service alley, it was blocked from the buildings beside it by a tall fence and there was a large dumpster near each end, providing more cover from people passing on either street.

Rising up on her tiptoes, she began shoving at the window. Slowly, it inched upward, baring a small crack. She was just trying to decide whether to hunt something to use for leverage when she was caught from behind.

She grunted, more in surprise than pain as both of her wrists were seized and her arms jerked out to each side, held with a vice-like grip than manacled her wrists to the wall on either side of the window she'd been trying to jimmy. A mixture of alarm and excitement went through her as he enveloped her in the moist heat and scent of his hard body, molding every hard, sculpted muscle on his legs, torso and arms into every inch of her own body as he captured her between himself and the unyielding wall. Her heart pounded in her chest like a jack hammer, pumping her blood through her veins in a roar that crashed against her eardrums deafeningly as he dipped his head and she felt his breath near her ear.

Chapter Five

Charlie tried to wrest free, but found she could scarcely move in any direction. Her thoughts were chaotic with the assault of sensations. The spurt of adrenaline that rushed through her sapped the strength from her limps, left her dizzy and disoriented, made her instincts sluggish. "What are you doing here?" she gasped shakily, unable to infuse any authority into her voice.

"That's exactly what I wanted to ask you," he murmured, his voice husky with both threat and promise.

From somewhere, Charlie managed to summon enough anger to lift the haze of disorientation fractionally and, as she felt him lift his head, she leaned her own forward, slamming the hard part of her skull back against him and lifting her foot to drive her heel into his at the same time.

Luck was with him, or he'd anticipated such a move. His feet were planted wide enough apart that she missed her target. Moreover, the difference in their heights made her head butt ineffectual. A meaty thunk reverberated in her ears as her skull made contact with hard, bulging pec instead of his face.

He tsked her, the amusement in his voice evident. "You'll only make this harder on yourself if you try to resist."

The word 'try' annoyed her, but as she felt him guiding first one arm and then the other behind her back, renewed alarm surfaced. She didn't know whether to be alarmed or relieved when he merely manacled her wrists with one of his hands. She felt his free hand skate over her ass, cupping first one cheek and then the other. She jerked reflexively when his hand followed her cleft and a fresh tide of alarm and heat enveloped her. "What are you doing?" she demanded, but her voice, shaky with conflicting emotions, lacked the authority she'd been aiming for.

Instead of answering immediately, he removed his hand and dipped his head close to hers once more. His hot, moist breath fanned along her ear and the skin of her neck as he rocked his hips against her buttocks. She gasped as his erection nudged the cleft of her ass. "Pat down."

Charlie managed to summon a weak dose of outrage, but it shrank away from her as his hand slipped around her waist and glided up her belly to cup first one breast and then the other. Her nipples hardened, thrusting hopefully against his massaging palms.

Releasing her abruptly, he stepped back. Charlie leaned weakly against the wall for a moment, struggling to catch her breath and finally managed to turn to look up at him in the feeble light filtering down the alley from the street lights at either end. Shadows shrouded his face, making it impossible to read his expression as she studied him, trying to decide what sort of threat he represented beyond clouding her judgment with desire that was as unwarranted as it was unwelcome.

"Lady ... don't look at me that," he said, his voice rough with both threat and promise.

Charlie swallowed with an effort, trying to bring her raging hormones under control.

"I did warn you," he muttered even as he closed in on her once more. Crowding her against the wall behind her, he slipped one arm around her, cupping her buttocks. His other hand settled on her throat, his fingers curling under her jaw and pushing her face up to meet his. Charlie gasped. Dismay and a heady heat rushed through her as his mouth covered hers in a renewed assault to her senses. As if her parted lips were an invitation, he plunged his tongue into her mouth. The moist heat of his mouth, the taste and texture of his tongue as it plundered her own mouth ravaged her with the disorienting sensation of falling into a deep, dark pit. She clutched his arms, struggling against the desire to yield her soul to the devil for the pleasure he offered, so inundated with the clamor of her body for repletion that there was little room in her for clear-headed logic.

Despite that, her sense of self-preservation kicked in and she began to push against him ineffectually.

Finally, reluctantly, he pulled away, relaxing his grip on her. She didn't dare look up at him, fearful that he'd see the desire that still pulsed through her. "Satisfied?" she finally managed to say shakily.

"Not by a long shot," Greywolf growled.

She glanced up at him sharply and slipped away from him,

putting more distance between them. To her relief, he didn't pursue her. A shiver moved through her at the loss of his heat. "I suppose you consider that getting even with me?"

He lifted a hand that shook slightly and scrubbed it over his face, then rubbed it against his chest. She looked away as he reached down and adjusted himself. "Let's just say this wasn't quite what I had in mind," he said tightly.

"You did it to scare me off."

He cocked his head to one side, studying her. "Did I?"

She wasn't sure whether he was questioning her insight about his motives, or if he was asking if he'd succeeded. "No," she said finally, lifting her chin.

He seemed to relax fractionally, which surprised her. Instead of pursuing the subject, however, he nodded toward the window. "Mind telling me what this is all about."

Charlie flicked a glance toward the window. "Yes."

His lips tightened. "But you will."

"Why should I?"

He moved toward the wall and leaned against it, folding his arms over his chest and crossing his legs. "Because I caught you trying to break into the clinic?" he hazarded a guess.

"It's your word against mine."

"And who's word carries more weight around here, do you think?"

Irritation surfaced, but she didn't doubt he was right. There was no point in trying to deny his accusation either. "I was looking for evidence."

His brows rose. "Against Doc Morris?"

Charlie frowned thoughtfully, but she really had no interest in Dr. Morris' competence, or lack of it. "I want something to prove conclusively whether that girl that was so brutally butchered was killed by a two legged animal or a four legged one."

"You're not buying the animal attack?"

Her lips tightened. "I'm not going to discuss this case with you."

"But you don't really have a case, do you, unless you can prove it was an animal of the two legged variety?"

She didn't say anything. She didn't have to.

"Curiously enough, I was under the impression that you were to meet Doc Morris here in the morning for those samples."

Charlie shifted uncomfortably, but kept her silence.

He pushed away from the wall. "Guess you'd feel more comfortable talking to Chief Brown about this."

Charlie grabbed his arm, tugging. "No! Wait!"

He turned back.

"He thinks I'm calling his competence into question and he doesn't like it. If I believed he'd give me the samples, I wouldn't be here. But I can't afford to chance it. Three girls are dead already."

He nodded and moved to the window, shoving the casement up. After a moment of surprise, Charlie surged forward, reached up and gripped the bottom of the sill. Leaning forward, Greywolf locked his fingers together, forming a step for her. As she placed the toe of her shoe on his hands, he lifted her upward and she thrust her head and shoulders through the opening. Before she could wiggle the rest of the way inside, he placed his hand on her bottom and gave her a push. She jumped, lost her balance and tumbled to the floor inside.

She turned to glare at him as he hoisted himself inside. He grinned, displaying a pair of dimples that made her heart flutter uncomfortably. "Thanks," she said tartly.

"My pleasure."

Her eyes narrowed and he chuckled.

"There's no sense in you risking a burglary charge," she said after a moment.

"There's a better chance of neither of us getting caught if I help."

Charlie shrugged. "As long as you understand that, if we get caught, there's probably not much I could do to help you."

His lips tightened, but he said nothing and finally she shrugged, moved to the door and opened it cautiously.

"They don't have a security guard," Greywolf said, pushing past her and striding purposefully down the hall.

"You know where the morgue is?"

He stopped at the door at the end of the hall and turned to give her a look before he turned the knob and went in. Charlie followed him, peering through the gloom. She jumped when the lights came on abruptly. Whirling, she saw Greywolf standing by the switch. "Do you think that's such a good idea?"

"Do you think you can work in the dark?" he countered.

Charlie shrugged. Being in the morgue unnerved her more than she'd thought it would. When she was considering breaking in to retrieve the samples herself, she'd focused on getting the samples, not how she might feel about the clandestine nature of it.

Moving to the cold storage, she opened a drawer. It was empty. She shut it and grasped the handle of the second drawer. A jolt went through her as she looked down at the elderly woman. After a moment, she pushed the drawer closed and opened the next one.

It was the girl, her mutilations looking even more grotesque against her death pale skin. Whoever had cleaned up behind Dr. Bob and placed the body in the drawer had discarded the body bag.

Charlie pulled the drawer all the way out. She went to the cabinets along one wall and began searching the drawers for the things she needed, gloves, sterile containers for the samples, tweezers and a magnifying glass. She found everything except the magnifying glass. When she'd placed them on a tray she looked up and saw that Greywolf was still standing by the door. "I need you to help me get her onto the table."

She'd hoped she wouldn't have to remove the body from the drawer, but without a magnifying glass, she wasn't likely to find much. There was a lighted magnifying glass on an adjustable arm over the examination table.

Without a word, Greywolf surged forward, slipped the gurney beneath the drawer and moved the girl's body to the table, his face set in grim lines. She glanced at him. "You OK?"

"Are you?"

Charlie took a deep breath and closed her mind to the body, focusing on her search. "Not especially," she admitted.

Pulling the lamp down, she held it, moving it slowly over the body. She found a hair stuck to the coagulated blood on the girl's neck and tugged it free with the tweezers, examining it under the magnifying lens. "Looks like an animal hair," she muttered, then placed it carefully in a sterile envelope, sealed it and, after a brief search for a pen in her purse, wrote a reference on it. Shoving the envelope in her purse, she continued the search, coming up with another animal hair and two pubic hairs. Very likely, they belonged to the girl, but she couldn't determine that so she collected them. When she was certain she covered the entire body, she stepped back, thinking. Finally, she returned to the storage cabinets, searching for a lamp.

She was disappointed but not really surprised when she didn't find one. There might be one in one of the examination rooms, but she didn't dare take the time to look. Instead, she returned to the body, picked up a scalpel and lifted one of the girl's hands. Holding it over a sheet of paper, she carefully scraped beneath each of the girl's nails on both hands. Several dried flakes of blood and tissue dropped onto the paper and, when she'd finished, she very carefully collected it into another envelope and sealed it.

Stepping back, she mopped the beads of sweat from her brow with the back of her hand, trying to steady her nerves for what she needed to do next. The body was just coming out of rigor and still stiff. It took an effort to lift her legs and bend them.

"What're you doing?" Greywolf asked sharply when she picked up a cotton swab.

She glanced at him. "Looking for semen."

"She was attacked climbing out of, or into her bedroom window. If there's semen, it's probably her boyfriend's," he pointed out dryly.

"I won't know, though, if I don't get it checked, will I?"

When she'd dabbed several swabs over the area and sealed them, she fished her camera out of her purse and moved to the end of the gurney, leaning in for a close up of the girl's genitals. She photographed both sides of both hands next and finally the girl's face and throat.

She felt more than a little nauseated when she'd finished, but strangely elated, as well.

Tossing the camera back into her purse, she repositioned the body and called Greywolf to help her return it to the storage drawer.

She was shaking all over from reaction when she finally reached the alley again.

Greywolf studied her a long moment and finally grasped her arm just below the elbow.

"Where are we going?" Charlie asked, trying to wrench free.

"My place."

Chapter Six

"Your place?" Charlie echoed disbelievingly.

"Unless you'd rather sleep in your car?"

"I'll find a hotel, thank you," she said firmly, peeling his fingers loose from her arm.

"You won't. Not at this time of night."

Charlie studied him assessingly, her hands on her hips.

A faint smile curled his lips. "I won't jump your bones--tonight." He gave her a smoldering once over. "No promises beyond that."

Charlie gave him a look. "I'm not sure I trust you that much."

"Me, or yourself?"

She rolled her eyes. "Please! Don't flatter yourself. I'm not one of your ... uh ... worshippers."

He studied her a long moment and finally moved toward her. Charlie inhaled a gasp and took a step back. A slow, wicked grin dawned. "If you aren't worried about it, why the retreat?"

Charlie crossed her arms. "Look, cowboy, I've no interest in becoming another notch on your belt. As long as we're clear on that, then ... thanks. I could use a few hours sleep before I head back to the agency."

He walked her back to her car and then climbed into his truck, which he'd parked directly behind her. She waited until he'd pulled out, wondering if it wouldn't have been smarter, and less hazardous, if she'd just decided to make the drive back tonight. It occurred to her, though, that she should probably go through the motions of presenting herself at the morgue in the morning. She'd done her best to leave the morgue just as she'd found it, but she'd had to take containers for the specimens. Dr. Bob might notice they were missing anyway, but he wasn't as likely to, she didn't think, if she didn't arouse his suspicions by taking off in the middle of the night.

Besides, now that the adrenaline rush had subsided, she was too tired to attempt a drive back without endangering herself and other motorists.

To her surprise, he led her out of town. They drove for several miles before he turned off onto a long, narrow unpaved drive between two posts. A sign hung from the cross piece above the drive, but she couldn't read it. Dimly, she could see the outline of a house at the top of a sharp rise.

It looked like a big house for one person, and a sense of uneasiness settled over her. Was she about to be confronted by an irate wife? His parents?

He parked his truck in front of the house and got out, waiting for her.

"Your wife doesn't wait up for you?" she asked, none too subtly, but then she wasn't currently in any condition for subtleties and moreover, she wanted to know what she was up against.

Instead of replying, he merely grunted and strode up the walk, crossed the wide porch and unlocked the door, shoving it open. She stepped across the threshold just as he flicked the light switch. Blinking against the sudden light, Charlie peered around the room cautiously.

She discovered that they were standing in a great room the size of her apartment. It was spotless, but completely bare of any frills--clearly a bachelor pad.

When she turned to look at Greywolf, he was looking her over in an assessing and none too friendly manner. "If I was married," he said coolly, "I wouldn't have been fooling around with you in the alley."

Charlie blushed guiltily. "Sorry."

He lifted one brow.

"I mean it. I'm usually a better judge of people ... but I'm tired and ... well it's a big house."

"I like open spaces ... Bed or couch?"

She looked a question.

"There're three bedrooms, but only one bed ... mine."

"The couch is fine," she said, moving toward it with a sense of relief and taking a seat.

Greywolf disappeared, returning several minutes later with a blanket, a pillow, a towel and a men's undershirt, still in the pack. "The bathroom's down the hall."

Charlie stared at the bounty, both surprised and pleased by his thoughtfulness. When she glanced around again, however, he was heading up the stairs. "Thanks!"

He nodded but kept going. Shrugging mentally, Charlie grabbed the towel and T-shirt and headed down the short hall that led to the bathroom. She was almost tired enough to just fall on the couch and sleep, but she felt almost as unclean from being in the presence of such brutal violence as she did from handling the body. She'd been wearing gloves, of course, but nothing short of a hot, thorough scrubbing was going to remove the sensation of having touched dead flesh--if even that would.

Her hair was thick and dried slowly. She would've preferred not washing it since she knew she'd have to sleep with wet hair, but, not surprisingly, there was no shower cap. When she'd finished, she washed her panties out and hung them over the shower rod to dry. The T-shirt came down almost to the middle of her thighs. In any case, Greywolf had already gone to bed and she planned to be up before him in the morning.

Returning to the great room, she grabbed her purse then crawled onto the couch, folding her legs Indian style. She'd just finished brushing the tangles from her hair when the creak of a floor board made her look up with a startled jerk. Greywolf was standing no more than six feet from where she sat, staring at her fixedly. As she stared at him in stunned surprise, she saw his adam's apple bob on a convulsive swallow. Slowly, almost like a sleepwalker, he leaned over and placed a blow dryer on the coffee table in front of her. "I thought you might need this," he said gruffly.

"Thanks," she said, smiling. It wasn't until she leaned over to pick it up that she remembered she'd left her panties hanging over the rod in the bathroom. She looked down at herself quickly and discovered the T-shirt had ridden up her hips when she sat, baring her to the breezes. By the time she looked up again, Greywolf was headed back up the stairs.

Snatching the towel up, she, belatedly, covered herself, glaring at his retreating back. He paused at the top, gripping the balustrade in white knuckled fists as he leaned over it and looked down at her. "Remember what I told you," he growled, then turned and disappeared before she could think of anything to say.

Charlie stared after him blankly, wondering what he meant by the cryptic remark.

The remark in the alley? She shrugged it off. In all likelihood she'd be gone before he even woke up in the morning and unless forensics turned up something it wasn't likely she'd be back.

* * * *

Something brushed between her thigh, nudging her knees apart and parted the folds of her sex, rubbing against her clit, making the muscles in her belly clench in a spasm of pleasure. Charlie felt a moan straining against her chest, felt sleep drifting beyond her grasp. She lay perfectly still, enjoying the pleasure that seeped through her lethargy, making her heart beat faster, the blood rush through her veins, as warmth and pleasure.

Slowly, she opened her eyes.

Greywolf was kneeling beside the couch. Still groggy to a state of near drunkenness, she pushed herself up on the couch, turning to face him. Still uncertain whether she was dreaming or awake, she watched him through half closed eyes as he caught her ankles. Spreading them wide, he bent her knees and hooked her heels on the edge of the couch.

She blinked at him, still dazed with sleep and desire, looked down as he pushed the T-shirt she wore higher. When she looked at him again, she saw that he was staring at her genitals. He lifted a hand, brushed the curls of her bush, ran a shaking finger gently over the parted petals of flesh. She inhaled on a gasp as he rubbed his finger lightly over her clit and he looked up at her, his face taut, his eyes glittering. Scooping a butt cheek into each hand, he lifted her hips, lowered his head and opened his mouth over her.

The heat went through her like a shock wave. She cried out, no longer caught between dream and reality, no longer simmering on the edge of desire, but on fire from it. She caught his head with both hands, trying to push him away, but felt desire lance every ounce of strength from her muscles as he sucked her clit. "Oh God! John!" she gasped shakily. "You gave me your word."

He lifted his head. "Only for the night."

She forced her eyes open and looked at him dizzily, uncomprehendingly.

"You want me to stop?" he asked hoarsely.

She nodded, swallowed. "Yes."

He lowered his head again, ran his tongue along her cleft and teased her clit.

"You're certain?" he murmured.

"NO! I mean, yes!" she stammered.

He leaned down and sucked her clit again for several moments, sending sharp arrows of pleasure knifing through her. Charlie felt her belly spasm, felt her body escalating toward release.

He lifted his head, sat back on his heels.

Panting, almost sobbing for breath, Charlie stared at him in confusion.

"I wanted to taste you."

At his words, a shock wave of pleasure went through her. The muscles in her sex clenched, aching for the feel of him. He was waiting, she finally realized, allowing her to decide--forcing her to. It was unfair. Her body was humming for his touch, reeling from the caresses he'd already bestowed, aching for the feel of him filling her. He'd taken unfair advantage, caught her while she was sleeping and vulnerable.

She could almost hate him for that ... but she wanted him.

She was going to have a hard time living with herself if she gave in to his underhanded ploy.

She was afraid she would deeply regret it if she didn't.

She slipped off the couch, straddling his thighs. "You're a sneaking asshole, Greywolf," she murmured, wrapping her arms around his neck and staring him dead in the eyes.

He caught the back of her head. "So I've been told," he growled, opening his mouth over hers and kissing her with an almost angry, savage intensity that boiled the blood in her veins. Her head swam dizzily as he twisted, laying her back against the carpet and following her down. She ran her hand down his bare chest, slipped her fingers beneath the waistband of his jeans and cupped his sex. He pulled away, unfastening his jeans and tugging the zipper down.

Freed from the restriction of his shorts and jeans, his cock landed heavily in her palm and she glanced down at it, a little alarmed. He pushed her back onto the floor, shoved her T-shirt up, kneading her breasts, tugging at her nipples with his lips, sucking them.

Gasping, she reached blindly for his cock, stretching, trying to capture it in her hand once more. He shifted upward, pushing her thighs apart and she caught hold of him at last, rubbing the head of his cock against her clit, searching a little frantically for her opening. Pushing her hand away, he aligned their bodies and thrust, his cock slipping in the juices of their bodies. Charlie gasped, digging her fingers into his shoulders as she felt herself slipping along the carpet.

He cursed, grasped her waist and thrust again. She locked her legs around his waist, pushing in counter to his short thrusts as he slipped slowly inside of her. They lay panting for a moment when he had sunk his cock fully inside of her. After a moment, he lifted his head. Sweat beaded his brow. His teeth were clenched. "Christ, you're tight, baby."

The desire in his expression and his words sent an echo through her. Charlie swallowed convulsively against her dry throat, feeling the muscles of her passage clench around him, feeling every muscle in her body tense as if she were gathering herself to leap. He groaned, ground his teeth and began moving, striving for a rhythm that yielded the most exquisite sensations. Charlie released her grip on his waist, dropping her feet to the floor and thrust in counter to the ram of his cock, leaning up to kiss nibbling bites along his chest, then tilting her head back to reach his throat.

He twisted, leaning down to cover her mouth with his own, plunging his tongue and retreating in like rhythm to the thrusts of his cock. After a moment, groaning in frustration at the difficulty in reaching her, he scooped an arm beneath her shoulders and held her to him as he rolled up onto his knees once more.

Charlie gasped as he slipped an arm around her buttocks, pulling her close, settling his cock more deeply inside her. Sensual delight seemed to arc inside her like an electric current, fusing her pleasure centers together, building toward release. She gripped his shoulders as he bent his head and sucked love bites along her throat and along her collar bone and shoulder. She arched her back as he moved lower, offering her breasts. The impetuous of his mouth suckling her nipple ripped her climax from her in an explosion of warmth that flooded her sex. The muscles inside of her convulsed, massaging his cock. He released her breast with a groan, his arms tightening around her almost painfully as his own release jolted through him, his cock jerking against the mouth of her sex as his hot seed erupted inside of her.

Chapter Seven

The problem with one night stands, Charlie realized even as she floated upwards from spent ecstasy, was the awkwardness that immediately followed having sex with a virtual stranger. Was there a graceful way to exit? Nothing came immediately to mind, but as she clung to him in the aftermath, staring at the morning light seeping through the drapes, providence smiled upon her.

"Oh my God! What time is it?" she cried, clambering off of his lap and looking around for a clock.

"Seven or there about."

"Shit!" she exclaimed inelegantly and dashed for the bathroom. The moment she slammed the door behind her she collapsed back against it, covering her face with her hands. Her mind seemed incapable of grasping what she'd just done and after a moment, she lurched toward the shower and turned it on full blast.

The T-shirt smelled like him. She was on the point of ripping it off and tossing it onto the floor when it occurred to her that she could use it as a shower turban to keep her hair from getting soaked again. Tying it around her head, she got into the shower and began scrubbing a little frantically, trying not to think about what she'd just done.

She found it impossible. Her nipples were still sensitive from his touch, her sex even more so. The steam from the shower seemed to activate his scent on her skin and her pussy throbbed with fond memory.

It wasn't bad enough that she'd behaved recklessly, and totally unprofessionally. For all she knew, Greywolf could turn out to be a suspect in the case ... if she had a case.

It didn't bear thinking on.

He beat on the bathroom door and she nearly jumped out of her skin.

"Yes?"

"Are you all right?"

What kind of a question was that? Hell no, she wasn't all right! "I'm fine! I just ... uh ... I was supposed to meet Dr. Bob at eight. I don't want to be late."

"You're sure?"

"Positive."

"Would you like some breakfast?"

Go away! For God's sake, her mind screamed. "No thanks," she chimed merrily.

With relief, she heard his tread as he walked away.

She'd turned off the shower and stepped out when she realized she'd left her towel in the great room.

The door knob wiggled. "I've got you a towel."

How thoughtful of the predatory bastard! "Uh. Just leave it on the knob, please."

She listened, shivering as she stood dripping on the bathroom carpet. Finally, she heard him leave again. Tiptoeing to the door, she listened for a moment and finally snatched it open, grabbed the towel and closed it again.

She'd left her purse in the great room, too.

Fuck it! She was too damned jittery to apply makeup anyway. Her hands were shaking as if she had palsy. Her skin was still damp, but she struggled into her clothes anyway. Tossing the T-shirt aside, she finger combed a little order to her hair while she did some quick relaxation breaths.

Finally, knowing she was as composed as she was going to get, she opened the door and strode purposefully toward the great room. To her relief, she discovered Greywolf was no where in sight. Slipping her feet into her heels, she grabbed her purse and hit for the door. She was so busy trying to dig her keys out of her purse while she walked that he caught her completely by surprise. When his arm snaked out of no where, grasping her around the waist, he literally swept her off her feet. With a squeak of alarm, she fell against him, clutching at him in an effort to regain her balance.

He cupped her face, forcing her to look at him. "You're not OK, are you?"

She tried to brush the silly question aside with a smile, but even she could tell it looked fake. "I have to go," she said in a brittle voice.

He frowned. "What's wrong?"

She gaped at him disbelievingly. "Hey, it was ... uh ... nice, but I really have to go now."

Anger flickered in his eyes. Slowly, he released her. "So, was it all you thought it'd be?" he asked coolly.

"What?"

"Banging an injun."

She felt like slapping him. "I'm surprised you can walk with that chip you're carrying around," she said tightly.

His gaze flickered over her face. "If it's not that, then what the hell is it?"

Charlie felt her chin wobble alarmingly. She sucked in a calming breath. "Hey, I know it was just another scalp for your teepee, but I don't do ... that! OK? I don't know why ... but it's OK, you know, because I'm a big girl. I take responsibility---But I'm just this close to hysteria," she added, holding up two fingers pinched together, "so just leave me the hell alone."

She stalked out then. To her relief, he didn't follow her to her car or try to stop her, but as she turned the car around, she saw that he was lounging against the frame of the front door, watching her.

She'd regained enough self-control by the time she reached the clinic to refrain from going ballistic when Dr. Bob met her with the 'oh I'm so sorry it slipped my mind and the body's already been taken' story she'd been expecting. She had her specimens, of course, but his smirk infuriated her all the same.

After staring at him for a full minute, she finally nodded, turned on her heel and left.

She didn't so much as glance toward Greywolf's ranch as she headed out of town although it took a supreme effort to refrain from cranking her neck to see if his truck was still parked out front.

By the time she reached the city, she'd managed to pretty well put everything from her mind beyond the case. Handing the samples over to the forensics lab, she shut herself in her office and concentrated on her case load. The lab tech had promised to have the results back on the tests by the end of the week. She'd felt like gnashing her teeth, but it wasn't a high priority case. She was lucky they weren't too busy. Otherwise it might have taken weeks to hear anything.

Two days later, as she was finishing up for the day, the phone rang. She picked the receiver up a little absently. "Agent Boyer."

"Hi."

It was Greywolf. She would've known that velvet drawl anywhere. Charlie dropped the phone from suddenly nerveless fingers. She had to scramble to catch the receiver before it slid off the desk and hit the floor. "Sorry," she said, chuckling a little nervously, when she finally managed to get it to her ear again. "I dropped the receiver. Can I help you?"

He was silent for a moment. "I wondered if you'd heard anything back about the specimens you collected."

"Greywolf?"

"Yeah," he said dryly.

"Actually, I haven't, but you know I couldn't discuss it with you even if I had."

He was silent for several moments. "I'm in town."

Charlie almost dropped the phone again. "Here?" she asked, trying to keep the alarm out of her voice.

"I thought you might like to have dinner."

To Charlie's surprise, she realized she wanted to go almost as much as she wanted to avoid him. She was still pissed off about the way he'd taken advantage of her, even though she had to admit that the end result was completely her fault. She'd known he had to be a player even before she got the chance to see him in action with the ladies at the tavern. And she'd still agreed to go home with him. That had sent mixed messages, she knew-- not no, but maybe--and then she hadn't stopped when she'd had the chance.

She didn't believe for a moment that he would have continued if she'd said no.

It didn't matter that he'd teased her until she'd lost the will to say no. She'd still had the option of leaving.

"I'd like to start over."

She hadn't realized she hadn't responded. "I don't think that's a good idea."

"Why?"

"You know why."

"I don't think I do. I'm a dumb injun. Why don't you explain it?"

"Don't think for one minute you're going to lay a guilt trip on me, Greywolf."

He sighed gustily. "Why don't I meet you at your office? You've got to eat, right?"

"Uh ... Actually, I'm not at my office. I ... uh ... I had my calls transferred to my cell. Tonight's just not a good time for me. Why don't you give me a call the next time you're in town?"

He was silent for several moments. Finally, he said, "Sure. I'll do that."

Relief flooded her as she hung up. She stared at the phone for several moments, fighting the depression that followed the relief. He was, without a doubt, the best looking man who'd ever shown interest in her, and the sexiest .. . but he was a player. As tempting as it was to allow herself to get swept up into a fantasy world, she knew she'd end up regretting it.

Shrugging it off finally, she straightened her desk and left her office. Her car was in the parking garage and she took the elevator down. She'd just shoved her key into her door lock when an arm snaked around her waist, making her knees go weak with pure terror.

Chapter Eight

"Hi, baby. Miss me?"

"Jesus Christ, Greywolf! You scared the shit out of me!" Charlie snapped angrily, turning to glare at him. "What are you doing here?"

His lips tightened. "I was about to ask you that."

Charlie gaped at him guilty, feeling her face turn bright red.

She quickly realized, however, that lying probably wasn't an option. "I ... uh ...I just didn't feel comfortable about seeing you again ... after...."

"Well now that we've gotten that out of the way...." Catching her upper arms, he pulled her against him, leaning down and capturing her mouth in a scalding kiss that made her toes curl. In an instant, all the fight drained out of her, the fright from a moment before transmuting into heated desire. She found herself leaning weakly against him, his hands moving over her restlessly.

He kissed her slowly, thoroughly, exploring every inch of her mouth with his tongue before finally setting her away from him. She stared up at him dizzily, trying to set her jumbled thoughts in order.

Taking her keys from her limp fingers, he placed one dinner plate sized hand in the middle of her back, walked her around the car, opened the door and helped her in, then moved around to the driver's side. She stared at him with a mixture of irritation and surprise when he got in and started the car. "How did you get here?"

"I was at the pay phone across the street."

She looked away uncomfortably. "I mean *here*. How did you get past security?"

He slid a glanced at her. "Shadow walking."

Her head whipped around. She studied him for several minutes, trying to decide if he was joking. He didn't look like he was. "You mean you kept to the shadows?"

A faint smile curved one corner of his mouth. "Something like that."

"It was a hell of a feat. They keep this place lit up."

"Thank you."

"That wasn't a compliment."

"I know."

"You're not going to tell me, are you?"

"I already did."

Charlie studied him skeptically. "Shadow walking?"

"Where would you like to eat?" he asked, changing the subject as they left the parking garage.

Charlie turned to study the traffic while they waited for the light to change. She'd never been really comfortable about dates. The whole, 'who'll pay, where will we go, how much can I spend' thing felt awkward, particularly when you'd just met someone and knew next to nothing about them--their tastes, preferences, finances. There were clever ways a woman was supposed to figure it all out and avoid uncomfortable situations, but she hadn't dated enough to develop a knack for it. She'd set her sights on a career with the agency and that didn't leave a woman a lot of time for a social life.

Greywolf seemed pretty laid back, but he could also be prickly. If she picked a quiet, out of the way sort of place, he was liable to decide she didn't want to be seen with him.

Or worse, that she'd picked an intimate spot so that they could be alone. "You pick."

He shrugged. "I'm not really very familiar with the city. Why don't we just drive around till we see a place we like the looks of?"

She nodded, instead of pointing out that it might be better if she drove considering she *was* familiar with the city. She didn't particularly care where they went, so long as she didn't end up defending her choice.

To her surprise, he picked a small, but popular, Cajun restaurant. The moment they entered the restaurant and stopped to wait to be seated, it seemed every eye in the place fixed on Greywolf. She was used to being ignored. As short as she was, unless she wore something provocative, no body ever seemed to notice her. Somehow, however, she didn't think it was Greywolf's height that commanded attention. He *was* tall, probably around six two, but it wasn't all that unusual to see men that tall--not unusual enough to attract so much attention.

She supposed it might've been his hair. Almost nobody wore their hair long anymore, especially not men. But she didn't think it was that, either, or the beaded, obviously Indian, choker he wore around his neck for that matter.

As they were escorted to a table near the back, every female in the place either gaped at him openly, or cast quick, nervous glances at him--and that included grinning, toothless infants and grandmas. For that matter, every gay man in the place looked him over like he was strolling through the place buck naked.

He gave her the seat facing the restaurant, and sat down with his back to his audience. His expression when she looked at him was stern, almost angry, his color faintly heightened.

He'd noticed and he wasn't happy about it.

"What'll you folks have?"

Greywolf didn't even look up at the man that was beaming at

him. He looked at her. "Do you know what you want?"

"What ever you're having's fine."

He ordered two steak and seafood platters. She caught the waiter and ordered a smaller version for herself.

"So--how are things on the ... uh ... down your way?"

"Settling down some. Every man with a gun's been out hunting puma."

Charlie's eyes widened. "But--they're protected."

"Not on the Res."

Charlie held her tongue while the waiter set their salads and drinks on the table. "I suppose I can't blame them."

"But?"

"I don't think it's a puma. Even if it is, there's no sense in slaughtering all of them."

He studied her a long moment. "You one of those bleeding heart animal rights nuts that figure people ought to come second?"

Her lips tightened at the challenge in his voice. "Not hardly. I just don't think it ought to be up to people to decide what lives and what dies. I suppose, when it comes right down to it, I just hate waste and I don't think we can really afford to be so wasteful anymore.

"If it was my child, I'd shoot the thing myself before I'd let something like that happen ... I don't care if it *is* the cat's territory. But killing the wrong animal isn't going to make these attacks stop."

He shrugged. "As it happens, I agree with you. But they're not listening to me. Not on this one. They're scared and they've got every right to be. It's not going to stop. Whatever it is, it's doing it for sport."

He was silent for several moments. "The animal rights people've got wind of it. They're demanding the government put a stop to the slaughter. The tribal council want the cats all rounded up and killed. The government wants them rounded up and moved to placate the animal rights people. Looks like we've got a real storm brewing."

Charlie frowned. "I hadn't realized it was that bad."

"It's that bad. The news hounds got wind of your trip down to the Rez and started nosing around, and naturally got everything stirred up."

"I didn't have anything to do with that, if that's what you're thinking."

He shook his head. "It's not. Generally, what happens on the Rez, stays on the Res. Some tourist probably heard about the girl and started talking. Maybe somebody just saw the GOV on your plate and started nosing around. Who knows?"

She was relieved he kept the conversation revolving around neutral subjects, or the situation on the reservation, instead of directing it to more personal conversation and found she actually enjoyed herself.

Afterwards, he kept her so involved in the case that they'd arrived at her place before it occurred to her that she should've been directing him back to his truck, not her apartment. She looked at him a little accusingly.

"Can I come up?"

She wasn't falling for that one. "I've had a really rough day...."

"I need to call a cab to take me back to my truck," he said casually, before she'd managed to fully formulate her excuse.

"Oh. I should take you back."

He got out of the car and walked around, opening her door. Charlie was so surprised, she got out before she thought about it. "I don't want to put you out. Anyway, it's late. It's not safe for you to be out by yourself so late."

He was right, of course. She fit the perfect victim profile, and training only lessened her danger a little. Besides, she couldn't help but be charmed by his concern for her safety.

"Sure. I'll make coffee if you like."

He dropped his arm around her waist. It remained on her, as if attached, throughout the walk up to her second floor apartment, riding her waist, her hip, cupping one elbow to help her up the stairs. Charlie was a nervous wreck by the time she managed to fit her key into the lock and rush into the apartment ahead of him. "The phone's over there," she said, pointing and then turning to drop her purse on the table near the door.

"Nice place."

She glanced around as if seeing it for the first time and smiled. "Thanks. It's just one bedroom and bath--back there--a small kitchen over there--It's small, but I don't need much room."

He nodded, smiled faintly. "Because you're a runt."

She gave him a look. "Because I'm not here much anyway," she corrected, irritated.

He held up his hands in feigned surrender. "I didn't realize you were touchy about it."

"I'm not, but that was hardly flattering."

He caught her around the waist and dragged her up against him. Charlie placed her hands on his chest, pushing, without much effect. "I like my women tiny."

Charlie's lips flattened. "I'm not one of your women."

"No, you're not."

She was slightly mollified.

"But you are my woman," he said, walking her backwards until she bumped against the door.

Charlie opened her mouth to annihilate him. She was certain that was what she'd had in mind. Before she could get a word out, however, he'd planted his mouth firmly over hers and shoved his tongue into her mouth. A red haze descended on her instantly, and anger had nothing to do with it.

In the two days that had passed since she'd left his ranch, she'd almost managed to convince herself that it hadn't felt nearly as good as she remembered. It was nothing but abstinence that had made her so susceptible, and the fact that he was obviously a very experienced, and very proficient, lover. Despite the kiss in the parking garage, she'd clung to the illusion that she had developed an immunity to him.

She was wrong. With his first touch, he enveloped her in a sensual haze. She dissolved into mindlessness the moment the scorching heat of his mouth covered her own. Without quite knowing how it happened, she discovered she was stretching up on her tiptoes, her arms locked around his neck, pressing herself as tightly against him as she could. Shoving her skirt up around her waist, he caught her ass in both hands, lifting her clear of the floor and parting her thighs. She wrapped her legs around his waist at the silent command, shuttering with delicious sensation as the hard bulge of his erection nestled in her cleft, rubbing against her clit in a way that made excitement pound through her.

Chapter Nine

Charlie was gasping for air when he released her lips and dragged his mouth downward, placing sucking bites on her throat, nudging her blouse aside to nuzzle the tops of her breasts and the cleft between them.

The sound of ripping fabric barely penetrated the fog. Briefly, irritation surfaced as she felt his hand on her bare thigh and realized he'd ripped the crotch of her pantyhose, but she forgot it in the next instant as he brushed the wedge of fabric between her legs aside and ran his finger along her hot, moist cleft, then delved inside of her.

He groaned against her throat. "You're so hot for me, baby. So wet."

"Yes," she gasped mindlessly.

Her heart thundered against her chest as she heard him slide his zipper down. She tensed, wading for the probing touch of his cock. A shudder went through her when she felt him, felt the mouth of her sex stretching. He caught her shoulder, pushing, using her weight and gravity to help him work his way deeply inside of her. She almost climaxed when he struck bottom. Panting, trying desperately to hold it at bay for just a few moments more, she leaned down and bit his shoulder. Steadying her, he pulled away and thrust again. She tightened her arms and legs around him, trying to move with him, to counter his thrusts. He slipped his arms around her, shielding her from the wall as he began pounding into her hard and fast.

She buried her face against his neck, uttering little, gasping cries as her climax rocked her. He jerked, shuddered as he found his own release.

For several moments, they remained where they were, Charlie draped weakly over him, her thighs quivering with the effort to hold on, Greywolf leaning weakly against the wall, struggling for air.

Finally, he stood away from the wall, hefted her and headed for her bedroom. She gave up the effort to hold on as he lowered her to the bed, collapsing gratefully. He moved to the other side and sat down, nudging his boots off, tugging his socks off and tossing them down, struggling out of his shirt. Finally, he stood up and stripped his jeans and shorts off.

She was half asleep when he pulled the covers back and climbed in beside her, but still awake enough to complain when he began removing her clothes. Weakly, she pushed his hands away. He ignored her, stripping her naked and then dragging the covers from beneath her.

The heat of his mouth on her breast roused her. "No," she muttered plaintively. "Can't."

He chuckled, but ignored her weak protest, sucking her nipple lazily until she felt fire pouring through her veins once more. When he'd kissed and tasted her with his tongue from neck to thigh, setting her on fire for him, he shifted, pushing her legs apart and settling between them. His cock seemed to find its own way home, nudging against her and then gliding deeply inside, aided by the slick juices from before and her arousal from his kisses. To her surprise, she found herself climbing toward release even as he began moving slowly in and out of her. Gasping, she tightened her arms around him. She dug her heels into the bed, rising up to meet each thrust, striving to meet the promised ecstasy, crying out sharply as it caught her up in a wave that jolted through her entire body.

The complete absence of tension, the inability even to think, was pure bliss. Charlie couldn't even find it in her to protest when he collapsed half on top of her, pinning her to the bed with a tree trunk of a leg and arm. She was just drifting to sleep when he slapped her ass soundly, jerking her wide awake.

"Let's grab a shower."

She closed her eyes again, grunted irritably, but he dragged her out of the bed anyway and into the bathroom. Grabbing her shower cap, he pulled it down over her head, stuffed her hair into it and shoved her under the steaming hot shower. The water revived her somewhat. He came up behind her, lathering her breasts, massaging them, then slipping his hand down between her thighs.

She groaned, half in protest, and partly because she just couldn't help herself. Pushing her against the glass door, he nudged her from behind.

Charlie stiffened. "There is no way you're shoving that ... pole ... up my ass, buster!"

He chuckled, slipping his rock hard, fully erect cock between her thighs, bending down to bite the side of her neck.

Christ! He was insatiable, she thought with a touch of panic. He must be nearly thirty. Wasn't that too old to have this kind of stamina?

She quickly found, however, that she could no more resist his teasing caresses than she could stop breathing. Within minutes, he brought her to another shattering climax.

Her thighs were quivering so badly, she barely made it back to the bed and crawled in. He slid in beside her, threw one arm and one leg over her and promptly fell asleep. Charlie's last thought just before she lost consciousness was that he could easily become addictive.

She was almost as tired when she woke the following morning as she had been when she'd fallen into the bed. She wasn't used to sharing her bed, particularly not with anyone as big, and sprawling, as John Greywolf. He'd spent most of the night draped over her. He was still draped over her.

She was afraid to move. At the moment, his cock lay dormant, but she knew from experience that it didn't take much to arouse the beast. Irritation filled her as she realized that she hadn't even invited him. Holding him back was like bracing oneself against the tide, he just washed over you like you weren't even there.

She did hate confrontations, but it was easy to see that he'd decided she was his current lay and he wasn't going to be discouraged easily.

So, maybe she'd given him plenty of reason to believe she found him irresistible ... because, in point of fact, she did. There was no room in her life for a relationship, however. Relationships, even short term ones, took work and time and she couldn't spare it.

And then there was the inescapable fact that he was a player. It was all very well for women to talk about using even as they were used, but that didn't work for her. She didn't want to use anybody just to scratch her itch, and she didn't want to be used that way either. She would become attached--it didn't take any imagination at all to see that she would--and then he'd break her heart, because men like Greywolf had all the women they could handle and found no reason at all to limit their diet.

It had distressed her to see all the women drooling over him the night before at the restaurant. She wasn't about to let herself get caught up in the fantasy/hope that he would settle on her and never stray. She'd be an emotional wreck in no time at all, worrying, eaten up with jealousy, broken hearted the moment she discovered her worst fears had been realized and he'd found another woman that was irresistible.

The moment she felt him stir, she rolled out of the bed and hit the floor, snatching a suit from the rack in the closet and heading for the bathroom. "There're breakfast bars in the cabinet in the kitchen, if you're interested," she called back to him as she slammed and locked the door.

She had no underwear, she realized in consternation.

She was also occupying the only bathroom, and he would probably need to use it.

She wasn't about to leave the bathroom naked.

Heaving a long suffering sigh, she dressed without her underclothes. She could put them on while he was in the bathroom, she decided.

He was propped up in the bed, grinning at her lazily when she left the bathroom.

"Forget something?"

He looked good enough to lick.

She decided to ignore him. "Bathroom's available," she said brightly.

He studied her a long moment and finally took the hint. The moment the door closed, she snatched a pair of panties from her drawer and pulled them on. Dragging a bra out, she decided just to stuff it in her purse. She could put it on when she got to work.

She was putting the finishing touches on her makeup when he came out ... naked.

It took an effort to refrain from staring at him. She concentrated on raking the knots out of her hair and binding it with a hair thingy in a pony tail at the back of her head. It wasn't a particularly attractive way to wear her hair, but she was supposed to look professional. Fancy hair styles didn't really go with the job. She couldn't be fussing with her hair all day. "I'm running a little late."

He sat down and put his socks on. "Running period," he muttered.

She stiffened, but decided to ignore that, too.

She was standing by the front door, glancing nervously at her watch when he sauntered out of the bedroom with that lazy, long-legged gait of his that made her stomach muscles clench. How could a man just walk and be sexy? She wondered a little distractedly.

Neither of them said anything as she made the drive to the office. Instead of getting out when she pulled alongside his truck, however, he turned and looked at her.

"We're double parked."

"So. Go ahead and park."

She'd hoped, since he hadn't said anything, that he was going to make things easy for her. She saw now that he had no intention of it. Feeling a combination of irritation and pure fear, she drove to the parking garage and parked.

"What's the deal here?"

She let out a deep sigh of anxiety. "There's no point in lying. I find you very attractive. And I enjoyed the time we spent together...."

"But you want to leave it at that?"

She felt the sudden urge to cry, but resolutely squelched it. "I think it would be for the best, yes."

"For me? Or for you?"

She glanced at him. "You've got women falling all over themselves for your attention--I just don't want to get caught in the stampede, OK?"

His lips tightened into a thin line. "Sure," he finally said. "No problem."

He got out of the car abruptly and strode away. Charlie watched him, feeling suddenly as if she'd made a terrible mistake.

Finally, she dragged in a deep, shuttering breath. She had. She was already far more deeply attached to him than she'd realized. It hurt. She'd thought she was going to escape getting hurt.

After a moment, she got out of the car and locked it. She'd made the right decision. If it already hurt, how bad would it have been if she'd allowed it to go on, weeks maybe, before he began looking for greener pastures.

She'd probably never see him again anyway.

Chapter Ten

"All right," the pathologist said, "now this is where it starts getting really weird."

Charlie moved closer, studying the picture he was pointing at.

"This looks like a human bite--or at least more like a human bite that any animal I could compare it with. If I'd actually seen the body, I probably could have told you exactly what it is, but...."

"On her throat? You're sure?"

"I'm as sure as I can be with what I have to work with."

Charlie felt like hugging the man. She contented herself with giving him a smile of appreciation. "Anything else interesting?"

"The hair samples--we identified the animal hair as puma. The two pubic hairs came from two different males, both are microscopically similar to American Indian--which would be consistent with a serial rapist--they usually work within their own ethnic group."

"Thanks! You've been a tremendous help."

Gathering the pictures and his report, she hurried to her supervisor's office and asked his secretary if she could speak with him.

She'd almost resorted to chewing her nails by the time she was admitted.

"You've got the report?"

She nodded and handed it over to him, waiting impatiently while he read it.

"She was raped then?"

Charlie nodded. "The pathologist said he found two types of semen --which wouldn't necessarily mean anything, but the tearing in the genital area are a dead giveaway that she was sexually assaulted. Either she'd been out with her boyfriend and was assaulted by the other man later, or there were two assailants. He also said the bite here on the neck looks like a human bite."

Her boss frowned. "Any theories?"

"She might already have been dead when the puma came along--which might also explain why it didn't appear as if the puma had ... eaten her."

"I think I need to get somebody down there."

Charlie stared at him in dismay. "I thought--that is, I expected this to be my case."

"This looks like a bad one--and she's possibly the third such victim--which means a serial rapist/killer. This is going to take someone with a little more field experience."

"Is there any reason why I can't be included in the investigation--I'm not going to get field experience at my desk."

He gave her a look. After a moment, however, he looked down at the pictures again. "This was a little unorthodox."

Charlie blushed. "I know, sir, but it was clear I wasn't going to get anything to go on going through regular channels. They're convinced it's animal attacks--not that I can blame them for preferring to think so--but they're not looking for anything else and they don't like being told they might've made a mistake."

"Or they might be our perp or perps."

Charlie didn't comment, though she found it hard to imagine Dr. Bob, or Chief Brown being capable of such savagery.

"I'll think about it."

Charlie's shoulders slumped, but she merely got up and reached to collect the photos she'd taken. "You can leave these here."

Again, she nodded and then left the room. She was fuming by the time she returned to her office, but she knew there wasn't a damn thing she could do but wait.

* * * *

When Agent Richard 'Rusty' Stephens, nicknamed for the color of his hair, tapped at her door and then poked his head in before she answered, Charlie looked up with a mixture of irritation and, when she recognized him, distrust.

He had the build of a weight lifter, the grating voice of a crow, the libido of a stud bull, and the personality of pudding--He'd made it clear he'd settled upon her as his chosen and he was certain it was only a matter of time before she gave in and fell for him.

He grinned. "You're in."

Charlie stared at him with a mixture of revulsion and incomprehension. "In?"

He jerked his head in the direction of the director's office. "They put me on the Reservation rape case. I asked for you as an assistant."

Such mixed emotions flooded through her that she was speechless. Fortunately, Stephens was certain she was speechless with gratitude and excitement. "*You* did?"

He nodded. "I'll pick you up in the morning."

It *was* possible he'd asked for her ... unfortunately. It was also possible that he was only claiming credit to make points with her and that her boss had decided to honor her request. She might never know either way, but it really irritated the hell out of her to be assigned to assist on a case that she'd discovered.

She would be stuck with Rusty for God only knew how long.

And she was bound to run into Greywolf.

She was tempted to beg off the assignment, but she finally decided she could handle Rusty. She'd been holding him at arm's length for almost two years after all.

As for Greywolf ... no doubt he'd found someone to console him, but she doubted she'd see much of him and there was no reason to think she couldn't handle seeing him with his newest conquest anyway.

* * * *

He was lounging against his truck, talking to a young woman

when Charlie stepped out of the police station. Her heart beat a little war cry as she glanced over, drawn by the color of the truck, and saw him. It was no more than a second, but long enough to notice that the woman probably wasn't a day over twenty, was exceptionally pretty, and had his full attention.

Rusty's hand on the small of her back was an almost welcome distraction. She turned to glare at him even as he leaned down to speak to her in a low voice. "I don't think they'll be very forthcoming in the investigation."

Her lips curled in a determined smile as she looked away. "It could've been handled a little better."

He shrugged, sliding his hand higher in the old 'is she wearing a bra?' move. Charlie stepped out of reach just before he found his target and reached for the door handle. "I assume we'll be starting with Chastity Owl's parents?"

He nodded, moved around to the driver's side of the car and got in. "I'd like to have a look at the scene, too."

Chastity's parents greeted them at the door with almost identical expressions--basically none, except for the glitter of distrust in their eyes. The didn't seem to know anything about their daughter--the names of her closest friends, where she spent her free time, who she was seeing. Charlie and Rusty left the residence virtually as empty handed as when they'd arrived.

They girl's father stood in the yard as they walked the crime scene, as if he suspected they might steal something if he wasn't keeping an eye on them.

They weren't even out of hearing before Rusty voiced his opinion. "They're lying. What do you make of it?"

"We're Feds. I doubt we're going to have much better luck with anyone else around here, especially not after the bureau had the girl's body exhumed and shipped off. If I'd known...." She broke off. If she'd known, she would've been expecting resistance, but she would've taken the case anyway.

It had been over a week since the body was discovered. Charlie didn't expect to find anything, but she knew Rusty needed to get a picture of the scene fixed in his head. He noticed the remains of the ceremonial fire immediately and squatted down to examine it, using his pen to pick through it. "I wonder if forensics could get anything out of this?"

"I doubt it would be all that helpful even if they did," Charlie said.

He glanced up at her. "What makes you think that?"

She was almost sorry she'd brought it up, but it was possible they would eventually trace it back to Greywolf anyway. "It's a ceremonial fire--intended to free the girl's spirit--from what I understood. The shaman was here."

Rusty stood up, frowning. "I think we should have a little talk with the shaman. Any idea who he is?"

"His name is John Greywolf," Charlie said, feeling her past rush back to haunt her.

Rusty nodded. "I'll see if I can get an address from Chief Brown."

Charlie studied the toe of her shoe. "We might as well interview as many of the neighbors as we can while we're out here."

Rusty nodded, pulled his cellphone from his jacket pocket and called Brown for directions to Greywolf's home. Uneasiness assailed her. It was a small community. She'd left early the morning after, but that didn't mean no one had seen her car parked in front of Greywolf's house. She was a slightly relieved when Rusty didn't make any comments suggesting Brown had mentioned it, but that didn't mean it wasn't a problem.

For all she knew one of his local lady friends might have cruised by his place. It could be common knowledge that she'd spent the night at Greywolf's.

There was no sense in kicking herself over it now, however.

They stopped at every house along the street facing the hill, then backtracked along the alley, then knocked on every door up and down the street where the girl had lived. They spoke to someone at ninety percent of the homes they canvassed, but the story was the same. They'd already spoken to Brown or one of his officers, and nobody had seen or heard anything.

Chapter Eleven

It was already dark when they pulled up in front of Greywolf's house. The porch light was on. His truck was parked near the barn.

Charlie had been hoping he wouldn't be home. She'd hoped this confrontation might be put off indefinitely.

Bracing herself, she got out of the car as Rusty started up the steps to the porch.

The door was opened before she'd crossed the porch. Greywolf stood in the opening, his shirt unbuttoned to the waist. It was still partially tucked into the waistband of his jeans, but it looked like he'd been in the act of pulling it off.

A wave of nausea washed over her as the thought slammed into her that they'd interrupted him in the middle of something she'd rather not know about.

His gaze zeroed in on her instantly. It took an effort to look him squarely in the eyes without flinching--an effort she discovered was beyond her. His face was expressionless, but the glitter in his eyes told its own tale. She glanced at Rusty, the toes of her shoes, the room beyond Greywolf and finally, finding she just couldn't help it, looked at Greywolf again, her gaze dawn to the sprinkling of dark hairs she could see just above his low riding jeans.

A wave of heat washed over her as he hooked one thumb into his waistband. She glanced up at his face, saw that he was staring straight at her, and turned to focus her gaze on Stephens.

"Good evening. I'm Special Agent Stephens and this is my associate, Agent Boyer. We'd like to speak to Mr. Greywolf."

John's gaze flickered to Stephens, summed him up. He leaned against the door jam. "I'm John Greywolf."

She'd forgotten what his voice felt like as it slid over her. She swallowed convulsively against a throat that suddenly felt as dry as desert dust.

Stephens frowned. "Is there a John Greywolf Senior?"

Greywolf crossed his arms, a faintly contemptuous smile curling his lips. "Why don't you tell me what this is about?"

Stephens' lips tightened. "We're looking for the ... uh ... shaman?"

"You found him," he said, making no pretense to address the answer to Stephens. Instead, he stared pointedly at Charlie.

Obviously disconcerted, Stephens looked Greywolf over skeptically. "I wonder if we could come in and ask you a few questions?"

Greywolf studied him a long moment and finally stepped back, turned and strode toward the worn easy chair that was obviously his favorite. Stephens crossed the threshold and looked the place over. Reluctantly, Charlie followed up the rear, afraid to look and afraid not to.

More than half expecting to find a naked, or partially clothed female sprawled on the couch, she stopped only a little way inside the room, watching Stephens head for the couch and take a seat. Memories she'd have preferred not to think about at the moment, flooded through her as she stared at the couch and the rug beside it.

Self-consciously, she glanced at Greywolf. His impassive mask had slipped a notch. She thought he might be remembering that time, as well--until she glanced away and something caught her eye on the balcony above them.

It was the young woman, she thought, that she'd seen hanging on his earlier.

Her gaze flew from the woman to Greywolf. The sick feeling that had assailed her before was as nothing compared to the avalanche of emotion that hit her like a ton of bricks. She thought for several unnerving moments that she was going to faint.

Any hope she might have nursed that no one would notice her distress was immediately dashed. Greywolf reached her while she was still trying to decide whether to look for a place to fall or try to make it out the front door again. "Are you all right?"

Almost as if time was moving in slow motion, she glanced down at the hand he'd wrapped around her upper arm, then up at his face, feeling strangely bewildered. Rusty thrust him aside, grabbed her around the waist and led her to the couch, pushing her down. "Charlie! Are you all right?"

Charlie blinked at him, still more than a little dazed but feeling the numbness slowly ebbing. "Sure," she managed through stiff, awkward lips. "I'm fine. .. Really," she added when he looked at her doubtfully.

"Maybe I should get you some water?" he said, straightening and glancing at Greywolf.

"The kitchen's through there," Greywolf responded, although he didn't take his eyes off of Charlie.

"I'm sure it's just the heat," Charlie muttered, embarrassment edging out her shock. Two bare legs appeared beside Greywolf's Jean clad legs and Charlie glanced up to discover the female had come downstairs and was studying her assessingly, one arm looped possessively through Greywolf's.

Charlie studied the body language for a moment, then glanced up at Greywolf. To her horror, his image blurred. She looked down at her hands, his feet, breathing slowly to regain her equilibrium.

Rusty returned with a glass so full of water that it was sloshing over the sides. As grateful as Charlie was for the distraction, and his thoughtfulness in getting her the water, she wished he'd refrained from filling it so full. The water that dripped from the glass as she lifted it to take a sip dampened the entire front of her suit jacket.

She set the glass aside, brushing at her jacket.

"Have we come at a bad time, Mr. Greywolf?"

Drawn by the comment, Charlie glanced at Rusty. He'd made the effort to sound polite and courteous, but he was smirking faintly as he divided a glance between Greywolf to the woman.

Greywolf frowned. "She was just leaving."

The woman gasped indignantly. "But ... I just got here!"

Greywolf slid a glance over her and then began speaking rapidly to her in his own tongue.

The woman gaped at him disbelievingly for a moment, then her face slowly contorted into a mask of rage. She spoke heatedly to him in the same language, then whirled and stalked out the front door, slamming it behind her.

Charlie watched the woman's departure almost with a sense of envy, wishing she could run out the door and all the way back to the city without stopping. "I wonder if I could use your bathroom?"

Fortunately, Greywolf wasn't suffering mental meltdown. He nodded, pointing toward the hallway. Charlie felt a fresh wave of faintness wash over her as she realized how closely she'd come to giving away her familiarity with his house.

She was so relieved when she made into the bathroom without disgracing herself that it was all she could do to keep from bursting into tears. Turning the lavatory faucet on, she sat on the edge of the tub and put her face in her hands, breathing slowly and deeply, trying to empty her mind of thought.

"That went well," she muttered under her breath and then had to clap a hand over her mouth to contain the hysterical giggle that threatened. She'd made a complete fool out of herself. No way could she delude herself into the hope that Greywolf hadn't realized exactly what was wrong with her. She wanted to sink into the floor.

She wondered if it would've been any less of a shock if she hadn't arrived at his door to find him with a woman.

Fat chance of that happening!

In the back of her mind, she knew she'd been more than half

expecting it, which made her wonder how it could've effected her so badly.

Her conclusion wasn't a pleasant one. It had already been way too late for her when she'd given him the brush off.

She would almost prefer to believe that he'd put some sort of spell on her than to accept that she'd fallen for him the moment she set eyes on him. How could something like that happen? It completely defied logic. It was more than that. It was insane. Lust was one thing. She could see where two people could fall instantly into lust. It was a simple matter of chemical and physical attraction. Greywolf had it in such abundance it was almost as if the man bathed in pheromones.

But emotional devastation shouldn't follow a bad case of lust. Possessiveness, maybe, jealousy almost certainly--but she hadn't felt anything at all but a horrible sense of lost that could only be equated to death.

Realizing that she couldn't hide in the bathroom forever, she got up abruptly and began to splash cool water over her face. When she decided she was probably as calm as she was going to get, she dried her face, straightened her clothing and left the bathroom.

Greywolf looked up as she returned to the great room, but she ignored him, returning to the seat she'd occupied before. Rusty glanced at her a little absently, his look questioning.

She nodded slightly and then ignored both men, sipping her water and staring blankly at the carpet, allowing their voices to diminish into no more than an indistinguishable drone. When Rusty finally put his notebook away and rose, she rose. Greywolf and Rusty shook hands. She held out her own robotically, felt the warmth of his hand as it seemed to swallow hers, and then tugged her hand loose, shoving it into her pocket.

Leading the way out, she crossed the porch, descended the steps and headed for the car while the two men were still talking.

"If there's any more I can do to help...."

"You've been very helpful. If we have any more questions, we'll contact you."

"It's possible people might feel more comfortable about answering your questions if I went with you."

The suggestion brought Charlie up short, penetrating her shield as nothing else he'd said. She paused with her hand on the door, glancing at him sharply. He was staring straight at her, but he looked away once he'd caught her gaze.

Rusty was frowning, apparently considering the offer--not seriously, Charlie was certain. Rusty didn't like anyone sharing the limelight with him.

"We'd appreciate that," Rusty said. "Maybe you could meet us for breakfast in the morning and we could work out a strategy?"

Charlie climbed in the car and slammed the door, cutting off Greywolf's reply.

Chapter Twelve

"You still look a little pale. You coming down with something?"

Charlie forced a smile. "I'm fine. Actually, I think it must have been lunch coming back to haunt me. I feel OK now."

"You did look a little green."

Lovely! Could she possibly have looked any less attractive? Not that there was a chance in hell of competing with a woman like that anyway, always assuming she had any desire to--which she didn't, but she was certain she'd never hated the pale freckles that had accompanied the blond hair she'd been born with quite as much as she did at that moment. The woman wasn't just beautiful, she had a flawless olive complexion.

Long submerged insecurities surfaced as her mind did a side by side comparison despite her efforts to squelch it.

It wasn't much of a contest. She knew she had a good figure--she worked on it constantly, dieted habitually--If one discounted the freckles, she thought her face fell a little over the line between plain and pretty.

Greywolf's latest conquest could've been a pin up, however.

"You think it's a good idea to bring him in?"

Rusty shrugged. "If there's any chance having him along will help the investigation, I'm willing to try. So far, we've got nothing. I'd like to have something when I have to call in our progress report.

"If it doesn't seem to make any difference, we'll thank him for his time and dismiss him."

She wasn't going to make it, she realized, trying to fight a panic attack. One more episode like the debacle tonight and even Rusty, who was completely convinced she was his for the plucking, was bound to notice. The whole town was going to be talking about it if she couldn't remain within his vicinity without falling to pieces.

She should excuse herself and head back to the city. She was going to be useless in the case.

Given time and distance, she knew she'd be all right. She was twenty five, way too old to be suffering from school girl crush, but then she hadn't met her waterloo before--had made it all the way through high school and college without loosing a moment's sleep over a single male. She supposed everybody eventually went through that first case of 'kill me and put me out of my misery'. It was just her bad luck that it had to be the one man west of the Mississippi that every female, single or attached, wanted for their own wigwam.

"He seemed particularly interested in you," Rusty said abruptly. "Did you meet him when you were here before?"

Charlie made a point of staring out of the window. "He was probably just worried I'd puke on his carpet," she muttered, trying to infuse some humor into her voice.

She heard a rustle of clothing as Rusty shifted in his seat and realized he was looking at her speculatively. "He barely took his eyes off you from the moment he opened the door--I had to ask him half the questions twice just to get his attention. Now that you mention it, though, he looked almost as sick as you did for a little bit there."

"Maybe he had lunch the same place I did?"

Rusty chuckled. "If that's the case, I think we need to find us a different restaurant while we're here."

* * * *

Charlie didn't sleep particularly well that night, but by morning she'd managed to rediscover her backbone. She arrived at the restaurant on Greywolf's heels. He'd only just sprawled in the seat across from Rusty when he looked up and their gazes locked. He got up, gestured toward his seat. Ignoring him, she slipped onto the bench beside Rusty.

He settled once more, anger flashing briefly in his eyes before he turned his attention to the cup of coffee steaming in a mug in front of him.

Charlie risked a glance at him when she noticed his attention was focused on his coffee. He didn't look like he'd gotten much more sleep than she had, if as much. She refused to speculate on *why* he looked as if he'd been up half the night. She was fairly certain she could live with not knowing a hell of a lot better than she could handle knowing.

To her annoyance, she discovered Rusty was a morning person. Never having had the good fortune to work quite this closely with him before, she'd been previously spared that knowledge. Resisting the urge to plug her fingers in her ears, she focused on her coffee while he ordered a man-sized breakfast. Either Greywolf wasn't feeling particularly hungry, or, like her, he couldn't handle solids so early in the morning. Like her, he contented himself with coffee.

By the time Rusty finished his meal, she'd had enough coffee to kick her brain into gear. As they left the restaurant, she suggested that, instead of accompanying him and Greywolf, she could stop by the police station and see if they'd gotten the files on the other two victims yet.

Rusty vetoed the idea, deciding to walk over to collect the files himself before they left.

Irritated, Charlie stalked over to the car and got in. Before she could close the door, Greywolf caught it. Pushing it open, he squatted beside her, leaning back against the open car door.

She gave him a wary glance, saw that he was looking particularly displeased, and focused her gaze on the wind shield, urging Rusty to get his ass in high gear before she found herself in another uncomfortable situation.

"Yosemite Sam over there seems to have a lot of trouble keeping his hands to himself. Something going on between you two?"

The idea revolted her more than the surprisingly astute characterization amused her. "No!" she said sharply. "Not that it's any of your business either way."

His lips tightened. "You were pretty clear on that the last time I saw you."

Charlie felt a headache coming on. "Then why are we having this conversation?"

He was silent for several moments. "Nothing happened, Charlie."

She glanced at him, but she didn't even try to pretend she had no idea what he was talking about. "Right," she said dryly. "I'm sure there's a perfectly reasonable explanation for why she was in your bedroom and you arrived at the front door half dressed."

"Not that you care, either way."

She blushed, irritated to realize how easily he'd baited her into admitting she was suffering from an unhealthy dose of jealousy. She sent him a reproachful glance.

He sighed impatiently. "You're enough to drive a man crazy, Charlie. Does it matter to you, or not?"

She'd die before she would admit it did.

He caught her jaw, forcing her to look at him, studying her for several moments.

"We dated a couple of times. I hadn't seen her in over a year. She's been living back East. We just ran into each other--that's all there was to it."

She glared at him. "You're a piss poor liar, Greywolf. All? She was in your damned bed! What did she do, trip up the stairs?"

He ground his teeth. "You're no so hot at it yourself. *You* gave me the brush, remember? That means I don't owe you an explanation. I can damn well fuck whoever I please."

"And vice versa," she said sweetly.

For several moments, he looked alarmingly violent. "Baby, this is a dangerous game you're playing," he growled threateningly.

Her heart beat uncomfortably fast as she stared at him. "I don't want to play any games at all--that was the whole point," she managed finally. As she glanced away, she saw, with relief, that Rusty was striding rapidly toward the car.

Following the direction of her gaze, Greywolf rose to his feet. She'd already released a sigh of relief, when he leaned toward her. "We're not through, baby. Not by a long shot."

Chapter Thirteen

It was immediately apparent that Greywolf's presence was going to be a boon to the investigation. The residents of the community continued to look upon the two Feds with suspicion, but several of the Owl's neighbors admitted to having heard a commotion in the alley the night of the girl's murder. No one saw anything. They'd thought the noise was dogs, trying to get into the garbage cans, or possibly wild animals. By the time they'd gotten outside to investigate, however, there had been nothing in sight. Nobody had noticed the trail of blood.

An old man who lived near the hillside where the girl's body was discovered said that he'd heard what he had believed at the time was the scream of a puma. That was Greywolf's translation at any rate.

The downside to having Greywolf along was that nobody bothered to speak English, instead carrying on the entire conversation in their tongue. Something told Charlie, however, that the old man had said much more than that. She might not understand the language, but she did understand body language, and she knew the old man had told Greywolf something that had made him uneasy.

The Owl's supplied them with a list of the girl's friends and the name of the boy they believed she had been seeing. They didn't look the least bit guilty about lying before, when they'd said they couldn't think of anyone. In fact, they gave a good imitation of never having set eyes on Charlie or Rusty before.

Rusty was so pleased with their progress, he suggested that Charlie sit in the back and familiarize herself with the files. Under other circumstances, Charlie would've been ready to bite nails over being relegated to the back seat while the men 'handled' things. As it was, she was glad for the excuse, having felt Greywolf's burning gaze on the back of her head for long enough that her nerves were frazzled.

Her relief was short lived. No sooner had Greywolf settled in the front seat than he turned, placed his back against the door and looked her dead in the face.

Disconcerted, Charlie picked up the files and concentrated on studying them. She discovered fairly quickly however that reading in the back seat of a moving vehicle was a good recipe for motion sickness. Within a very short length of time, her head was swimming sickeningly. Laying the reports aside, she closed her eyes, leaned her head back and concentrated on keeping her lunch. The queasiness subsided after a little while, but it left a blinding headache in its wake.

As soon as they returned to the hotel that afternoon, Charlie bailed out of the car and headed for her room. After popping a dose of painkiller, she took a long, hot shower and then fell into bed without bothering to crawl under the covers.

It was dark when she woke. Disoriented, Charlie pushed her hair out of her face and looked around the dim room, wondering whether it was dusk or dawn.

Greywolf was sitting in the easy chair next to the door, studying her.

A jolt went through her. Her gaze jumped from him to the

door, but she could see it was still locked and bolted.

"God damn it, Greywolf! How the hell did you get into my room?"

Instead of answering her, his gaze wandered over her almost like a caress. When he finally met her gaze once more, his eyes were glittering with anger and something else that set her heart to fluttering wildly in her chest. "Feeling better?"

Charlie raked her fingers through her disheveled hair, trying to think what he might be talking about. Memory crashed in on her abruptly, and she looked down at her towel--which was lying on the bed. Belatedly, she snatched at it, but discovered she was sitting on top of it. She only managed to drag a corner across her breasts. Jumping to her feet, she fought the towel and finally managed to get it around her. "I don't know how you got in, but you can go out the same way," she snapped. "I don't feel like talking and I damn sure don't want everybody in town talking about me."

"Is that why you pretended you'd never set eyes on me before?" he asked tightly.

Charlie stared at him for a long moment and finally looked away guiltily. "What did you expect me to do?" she asked sullenly.

He got up and advanced on her. "I didn't expect you to show up at my door with another man--the same one I saw fondling you in the street earlier--acting like you didn't know who I was--and then giving me accusing looks as if you'd caught me cheating on you."

"He was *not* fondling me!"

Greywolf leaned over, his face only inches from hers. "It was a damned fine imitation then."

"You should talk! That ... female was twined around you like she was planning on growing there! And I didn't let him, anyway. I have to work with him--If I complain of sexual harassment, they'll slap him on the wrist and give him a promotion and write me up as a paranoid feminist and give me a closet to work in. I've worked damn hard to build a career. I'm not about to throw it away because some man can't keep his dick in his pants, or his hands in his pockets!"

His eyes narrowed. "What the hell do you mean by that?"

Charlie gaped at him for several moments before it occurred to her what he was asking. "That is too insulting even to deserve an answer!"

"Answer it anyway," he growled.
"I'm not sleeping with him!" she snapped.
He looked slightly mollified.
"Not that its any of your business."
His eyes narrowed, but after a moment he seemed to relax, looking almost amused. "We're not making a lot of progress here, are we Charlie?"

She looked at him a little distrustfully and finally sighed, smiling faintly. "No, I guess not."

His gaze flickered over her face, his own amusement vanishing. For a moment, Charlie thought that he would close the small distance between them and take her in his arms. Instead, he shoved his hands into his jeans pockets. "You don't trust me, do you, Charlie? That's what all this is really about, isn't it?"

Instead of answering, she shrugged. "It's a bad time for me--I spend most of my time working." It was true, not all the truth, but certainly a big part of it. "I need to get dressed," she added, turning and heading for the bathroom.

"Charlie."

She stopped and turned to look at him.

"You have to take what life offers when it offers it to you--if you want it. Life isn't order. It's chaos."

She frowned. "I'm not sure what you mean."

"Yes, you are."

When she left the bathroom a few minutes later, he was gone. Disconcerted, she looked at the door and saw it was still locked and bolted. The only windows were at the front of the room, next to the door, and they were locked too.

Chapter Fourteen

All three victims had been between fifteen and sixteen years of age, five foot to five foot two inches, one hundred to one hundred ten pounds. The third victim had been attacked right outside her own home. The first one had been on her way home from a party with friends and had taken a short cut through a park. The second had left home on a date. Her boyfriend had been found in the car where they'd gone to park and fool around.

She was found a half a mile away--which meant that there had been four victims already, not the three they'd believed.

There were only a few, badly focused pictures of the earlier victims, and it wasn't likely any amount of tweaking on the photos was going to help much.

The parents of the first two girls were still fighting the order to exhume the bodies. The Owls, still in shock, had been too bewildered by their daughter's death to defend themselves. They'd signed the exhumation papers and then complained that they hadn't understood what they were signing.

In all likelihood, they'd been too upset to understand. Charlie felt badly about it. She realized that that was probably the main reason nobody would talk to them, but she knew it was necessary. The body had already been embalmed. They might not get any evidence from it at all, but there was always a chance that they might ... and they needed all the help they could get.

They had no leads. After days of questioning everyone even remotely connected and every potential witness, they hadn't managed to come up with a single thing that tied the victims together. The girls were from three different communities. They didn't go to the same school. They didn't have the same friends. The youngest had been a girl scout. The last victim a cheerleader, but the remaining victim hadn't been involved in any extracurricular activities.

They knew they had a serial rapist/murderer on their hands. They knew he would strike again. He had been preying on girls on the reservation, but it was a very big reservation--he could strike anywhere, at any time--unless they could figure out a where and when, there were going to be more victims.

There had been almost six months between the first and the second attacks, only two between the second and third. He was escalating and, they knew, could attack again any time. They desperately wanted to prevent a fourth victim from falling prey, but they couldn't do that unless they could get ahead him.

The report from the pathologist was almost as confusing as it was enlightening. He was no longer certain that the marks he'd thought were bite marks actually was a bite. If it was, it didn't match a human or a puma--too large for one, two small for the other--wrong teeth. He was positive the girl had been raped. The semen samples had been compared with the boyfriend and they now knew that he had definitely had sex with the girl--but they couldn't determine whether it had been consensual or not--

He was as certain as he could be, given what he had to go on, that the puma attack, and the rape, had taken place at the same time. He couldn't absolutely rule out the scenario that the girl had been mauled by the puma after being left there, but he didn't believe it could've happened that way. Combined with the other two attacks, the possibility was even more remote--one incident of a puma happening up, or even drawn to, a fresh victim was farfetched. Three separate but virtually identical such attacks became astronomical odds.

Specialists in animal behavior that had been contacted had insisted that the behavior was not typical of a wild puma--they weren't scavengers by nature and the distance separating the scenes was more than a single puma usually hunted.

There was only one conclusion to draw from it. The puma wasn't a coincidence. It was the weapon.

For a week and a half they worked their way through the reservation and through the communities and farms nearest it, asking everyone they met if they knew of anyone who owned a pet puma, if anyone had been seen with one, or if there were anyone they knew of who bred, and or trained, pumas.

Coming up empty handed, they decided to see if they could scare anything useful out of the Owl girl's boyfriend and brought him in for questioning. It was then that they discovered the one thing the three girls had in common, something that had been staring them in the face all along--Earlier on the same night that she was killed, Chastity Owl had been at the same lover's lane where the boy and girl, who'd become victims two and three, were killed. When they questioned the boy the first girl had been seeing, they found that she, too, had been at the lane on the night that she was killed.

Finally, they'd caught a break. Charlie was elated. "All we have to do now is to get the location and keep an eye on the place."

Greywolf and the officers in the meeting room with them exchanged glances. Chief Brown cleared his throat. "As far as I know, there's only one--we patrol it pretty regularly, rousting the kids out, but---they always come back. During the week, we do one drive through. On the weekends, when the kids are out of school, we do two."

Charlie glanced around at the officers. A couple of them were smirking, no doubt remembering their own exploits. She looked at Rusty questioningly. "Fine," he said. "Keep to the routine. We want to catch him, not scare him off. We'll go out and inspect the area, find the best place for a stake-out and see if we can catch the son-of-a-bitch."

The officers exchanged a look.

"What?"

"You're talking about you and Agent Boyer?"

"Yes."

"In the government vehicle?"

"He's saying we'll stick out like a sore thumb," Charlie muttered. "Two white people in a government vehicle."

"He attacks at night," Rusty pointed out.

"Most of the kids around here drive old, beat up trucks," Greywolf said. "We need a truck and two people that will fit in a little better."

Charlie didn't like the sound of that, and neither, apparently did Rusty. "It's our show."

The safety of the young girls was their first concern. Patrolling wasn't keeping the kids out of harm's way. Two of the girls had been killed on their way home from the lane, not in it, but they believed the lane was where the killer was choosing his victims, which meant any girl who went could end up being the next victim.

They were also fairly certain the killer was American Indian, however, which meant a reservation wide announcement might warn him off.

It seemed unlikely the killer would strike during the week--few kids ventured out to the lane during the week, and all of the victims thus far had been there over the weekend. They decided the best they could do would be to go directly to the schools and speak to the teens. Officers frequently visited the schools, and were more trusted, in any case, than federal agents, so Brown selected men to go out and speak to the teens. Charlie also made up several posters and took them to the school to post on the school bulletin board. At Chastity's school, she pinned the poster up directly beside a public service poster encouraging safe sex and planned parenthood. The irony of it wasn't lost on her, but she hoped Chastity's death would be enough to make them take it seriously.

They took it seriously--but not quite in the way Charlie had envisioned.

****

Stake-outs were often the most dangerous part of law

enforcement. They required long hours of watching, and waiting, sometimes for days, weeks, or months. No matter how much training, or even experience, one accumulated, it was almost impossible to maintain the necessary level of alertness for such extended periods of time. Rotating, when possible, helped a great deal, but even so there were long stretches of time doing nothing but waiting and watching that allowed boredom and inattention to infiltrate one's defenses.

The first weekend they spent on stake-out, Rusty, just by virtue of being his wonderful self, managed to keep her on high alert. About half way through their first shift, when he decided they weren't likely to see their perp, he decided they might as well use the time to become a little better acquainted. They were at lover's lane, after all. They'd been observing teens at play for hours with their night vision field glasses.

She'd managed to hold him off and keep her temper the first night. The second night she'd had to resort to being nasty.

She was not looking forward to another weekend cooped up in a car for hours with randy Rusty!

The moment he parked the car at the spot they'd chosen, Charlie opened the door, climbed out, and then got in the back seat. Rusty swiveled around in his seat and looked at her as if she'd lost her mind. She favored him with an artificial smile. "Just so we have this straight between us, Agent Stephens, I don't expect a repeat of last weekend. Let's just keep this professional, shall we?"

Even in the dimness of the car, she could see his complexion fluctuate. "What are you talking about?"

"I'm talking about touchy feelly, damn it! I'm here to do a job, not save you from boredom!"

He sulked for the next hour. Charlie was irritated, but as long as he didn't get it into his head that her climbing into the back seat was an invitation to join her there, she was satisfied. She had no desire to play musical chairs with him.

At two o'clock, when they'd just been discussing calling it a night, a scream rent the night air that made the hair stand up all over her body. Her arms, back and neck goose fleshed at the same instant. Even the flesh on her scalp contracted. She broke three nails getting the car door open. "Did you get the direction?" she called in a harsh whisper to Rusty, who'd bailed out the driver's door and, like her, was standing by the car in shooter stance, scanning the woods.

A shot gun blast answered her. In an instant, she and Rusty were racing toward the sound, guided by a girl's hysterical wails. Rusty, taller, and muscle bound from his neck to his toes, took the lead. He was agent in charge, but Charlie didn't let that hold her back. The plain fact was that her damned short legs made it a hell of a lot harder to get over the brush. She tripped, sprawled out and Rusty pulled ahead.

The trip saved her life and cost Rusty his. The shotgun blast was closer this time and lifted Rusty clean off his feet, slamming him back against a tree. Charlie watched his flying backward in slow motion. "FBI," she screamed, scrambling toward Rusty. "Hold your fire!"

The blast had caught him in the middle of his chest, peppering his throat, as well. Blood was oozing from dozens of holes in his neck and chest. He'd been wearing a jacket, but he was a broad man.

He coughed, spitting up blood, looking at her with a pleading, bewildered expression. "You're going to be all right," she said automatically. "Hold on. I'll get help."

The words were barely out of her mouth when the girl screamed again. Charlie whirled, leading with her gun. The teenage boy, his shotgun now aimed at the dirt at his feet, was still gaping at her and Rusty in horror. His girlfriend, half in and half out of the truck, was staring at something racing toward them from the brush in front of the truck. As Charlie watched, something huge leapt from the woods. The boy turned, almost in slow motion, bringing his shotgun up to fire. Charlie raised her own weapon. Before she could fire, the thing slashed the boy across the face and throat. Blood spurted in every direction as the boy's jugular was severed. The thing leapt over him and into the woods on the other side of the clearing even as Charlie laid a bead on it and began firing, over and over. Jumping to her feet, she raced after it, firing until she'd emptied her clip.

Gasping for breath, she stopped abruptly when she realized she was out of ammunition. In front of her, she heard it thrashing through the woods beyond her view.

She grabbed her radio. "The perp's headed just north east of the trail. We've got two down here--a teenager and Agent Stephens."

The boy was dead long before help arrived. Rusty managed to hang on until they'd made it to the clinic and through hours of surgery, but he died on the table. Charlie merely nodded when the surgeon they'd brought in gave her the news. She thanked Chief Brown. He'd radioed ahead to get a surgical team in. Dr. Bob was a general practitioner, he knew, and wouldn't be able to handle it, and it seemed doubtful they could get Stephens to a big hospital fast enough.

Greywolf drove her back to her hotel, where she called the director with the news. He would handle all of the arrangements that needed to be made, contact Stephens' family, and get back with her Monday, he said, on what the next step would be.

"Did he have family?"

Charlie turned and stared at Greywolf blankly for several moments. She hadn't even realized he'd followed her into the room. She sat down on the bed. "I don't know. I've worked with him for almost two years, and I don't know."

Greywolf studied her for several moments and finally got up and crossed the room. Settling beside her on the bed, he pulled her against his chest. She resisted at first, but it felt good just to be held. She hadn't realized how cold she was until the heat of his body enveloped her.

"I saw it."

"It?"

She clutched his shirt, looking up at him. "It wasn't a man."

Chapter Fifteen

"You're upset," Greywolf said soothingly.

Anger surged through her abruptly. "You're damned right I'm upset. But I know what I saw. That ... *thing* ... was no man! At first, I thought it was. It looked like a man wearing an animal skin. But it didn't move like a man, John. It moved like an animal."

Greywolf stiffened. "Could you see it well enough to describe it?"

Charlie got up and began to pace. "We were using field glasses with night vision, but when we heard the screams we left them-- we should've had the goggles. It was dark as hell in the woods, but the truck was parked in a clearing. I was still bending over Rusty when the girl screamed. I saw--something, really more like shadows, at first--coming through the brush--something huge. My first thought was that it was a bear. It was standing up right, running, but I realized it couldn't be a bear. They can walk upright, but they're clumsy. The run on all fours. This thing was running--fast. It *leapt* into the clearing--fifteen, maybe twenty feet--caught the boy before he could raise his gun, almost taking his head clean off. Then it leapt over him and into the woods. I was chasing after it, firing…." She broke off, picturing the scene in her mind.

"I hit it. I think I hit it. I heard it fall and then get back up."

"Maybe. And maybe it just stumbled."

"I'll know in the morning."

"Yes. In the morning--we'll go back, check it out. Right now, you need to sleep."

She *was* weary. She felt like she was ready to drop, but her mind was running on overtime, racing. Images kept flitting through her mind, like a movie reel in fast forward, zipping to the end and then starting over again.

She didn't protest as Greywolf removed her jacket, then her gun and holster and pushed her to the bed. She sat, watching him as he squatted in front of her, feeling strangely detached as he removed her shoes and massaged her feet one by one. Finally, he crawled onto the bed beside her and tugged her down, gathering her close against his chest. She lay stiffly at first, but slowly, as he stroked her back in a soothing, almost hypnotic caress, she felt herself relaxing.

Strangely enough, it was the first time he'd touched her that she wasn't instantly on fire with arousal. Instead, she felt something equally alluring and as rare as the fiery passion he generally inspired in her, warm, safe, comforted.

It was the first time he'd touched her at all since the night he'd entered her room and confronted her. She'd been both relieved and disconcerted that he'd kept their relationship impersonal after that, always polite but coolly distant, as if they were in fact strangers, not merely pretending to be. She'd caught him studying her a few times, but his expression had always been unreadable and he had taken great pains to avoid even the most casual touch.

She'd told herself she was relieved that he seemed to have moved on, but she wasn't. She regretted loosing what they'd had together.

She didn't want to think about regrets, though. She wanted to think about how to catch the bastard that had killed four teenagers ... and her partner.

"I saw it," she murmured as she descended to the edge of sleep. "It was ... so strange...like a man and a puma fused together...."

"Skin walker."

* * * *

They found the girl the following day when they returned to the scene to recover whatever evidence they could find. Charlie was studying the clearing around the truck, searching the ground for prints when one of Brown's officers let out a yelp of alarm. She was on her feet in an instant, whirling toward the sound.

"Victim!"

Everybody went stock still, exchanged a glance of stunned surprise and then surged toward the officer.

The girl was sprawled on her back, her arms on either side of her head. Her clothing had been shredded from her body. Her legs, bent at the knee, were splayed wide. The men gaped at her for several moments, and then looked away uncomfortably.

Charlie moved forward to examine her more closely.

Her throat was crushed, like the other girl, but she hadn't been gutted. Charlie stood, backed away a little and began searching the ground around the girl. A discarded condom lay on the ground between her legs. Pulling an evidence bag from her belt, Charlie looked around for a stick and fished the condom from the ground, holding it up to study it a moment before she bagged it. She looked up at Brown. "No semen. Looks like they were caught in the act. You better send somebody to look for the boyfriend."

Brown nodded and motioned to two of the men. Charlie stood up, staring toward the clearing, trying to piece together what had happened. After a moment, she moved back toward the truck, taking care not to disturb the broken brush the perp had left when he'd rushed the boy. When she was standing beside the truck again, she turned and looked toward the car where she and Rusty had been. She could just make out a patch of dark color.

They'd been listening to vehicles pull in, park, then start up and leave all night, seen headlights. She didn't remember seeing the truck's headlights, though. Either she'd been looking in another direction when they pulled in, or he'd switched the lights off before he turned in.

She remembered hearing the engine shut off, though. Less than a minute later, the scream, the first two gun blasts. The boy had been reloading when they jumped from the car. She replayed the scene in her mind.

"They caught him in the act--that's why she wasn't butchered like the others. The girl in the truck saw him, screamed. The boy grabbed his gun and jumped out of the truck, pulling off two shots. The perp ran, but not far.

"He came back to kill the witnesses. Why? It was dark. They couldn't have gotten a very good look at him."

She realized the officers had all stopped to look at her.

"They knew him?"

Charlie stared at the man for a long moment, feeling excitement flood through her. "He knew them ... well enough that he recognized them, or the truck. He didn't want to take the chance that they'd recognized him."

Brown frowned at her, his hands on his hips. "We figured it had to be somebody on the Rez or living near it."

"Yes, but we assumed he was hanging out here--that it was more a crime of opportunity than that he was actually stalking his victims. We missed something. We must have."

As they were packing up to leave, she stopped Brown. "He'll strike again ... soon."

Brown shrugged it off. "He got one last night. And he knows we're on to him now. He could be halfway across the country by now."

"He didn't finish," Charlie said tightly. "The kids interrupted his orgy. He didn't get his 'fix' and he's not going to be able to restrain himself. He'll hit again, soon--maybe even tonight."

Brown studied her a long moment and finally clapped her on the shoulder. "I know it's been rough--with your partner dead-- You need to take a rest, step back from this a little."

Anger surged through her, but she saw it was a waste of time trying to talk to him. He'd made up his mind, thought he knew more than she did--He'd dismissed her as a hysterical female, like men always did if a woman showed any sign of emotion whatsoever.

Striding to her car, she climbed in and slammed the door, staring at the hood of the car blindly while she allowed her mind to play back all the data she'd collected. She glanced at Greywolf as he climbed in beside her, momentarily distracted.

It occurred to her that he'd been ghosting her, always distant, but always there.

"That word you said last night--skin walker--What did you mean by that?"

Greywolf said nothing for several moments. Finally, he sighed, turning to stare out the window. "The old man mentioned it--the day we were questioning witnesses. It's superstition."

Charlie frowned. "The one that lives near the hillside? The one that said he'd seen a puma?"

Greywolf looked at her. "He didn't say he'd seen a puma. He said he saw a skin walker. *I* said it was a puma."

"So--you're saying you lied to us?"

He frowned. "You wouldn't have believed me if I'd told you."

"Maybe not, but I'd at least like the consideration of an honest answer," she said tightly.

"In the old days, we believed it was possible to absorb the powers of one's enemy. The skin walkers were shaman who could steal the powers of the animal skins they wore."

"Like that thing I saw, you mean? It wasn't just a man wearing an animal skin. It moved with him, like it was part of him--a puma skin."

He nodded.

"So--either we've got a maniac running around that thinks he's a puma--or we have someone capable of actually becoming part man, part puma."

"I found a blood trail. Looks like you were right. You hit him."

Charlie stared at him a long moment. "Would a skin walker have stronger powers of healing than an ordinary puma?"

"You're not taking this seriously, are you?"

Charlie gave him a look. "When I asked you how you managed to get past security in the parking garage, you told me you'd shadow walked. I didn't take it seriously then. You spoke as if you were joking. I thought you just meant that you'd kept to the shadows and avoided detection. But you were in my room. You left it with every door and window locked. Either you walked through the wall--like a shadow--or you're a hell of a magician."

Greywolf said nothing for several minutes, finally he looked at her again. "Am I a suspect?"

She studied him, slowly, thoroughly, her heart thudding painfully in her chest. "It never once crossed my mind."

She started the car and headed back, stopping at Greywolf's ranch to drop him off.

He was reluctant to get out of the car. "What have you got in mind?"

"At the moment? Nothing. I need to think. I need to be alone to think."

He didn't look like he believed her, but after a moment, he climbed out. He was still standing in the yard, watching her, as she reached the road and headed for the clinic.

She wasn't really surprised to discover that no one had checked into the clinic with a gunshot wound, but she was disappointed. Either she'd hadn't wounded him badly enough to drive him to a clinic for help, or he was trying to doctor his own wound. Greywolf hadn't found much blood, so she was leaning toward the former.

She thought of the evidence bags in her trunk as she left. Brown had volunteered one of his men to deliver it to the agency, but she saw little point in it. She fully expected to be called back on Monday morning--and that was the earliest anyone was likely to begin examining them anyway. She could drive up and deliver them, but they'd just end up in the evidence room until Monday morning anyway.

Returning to the hotel, she grabbed the box from the trunk and carried it to her room. Pouring the contents in the middle of her bed, she sat with her back to the headboard, picking up each, examining, dropping it back in the box and checking the next.

Not surprisingly, they'd found a number of condoms in the area. The lab was going to have their work cut out for them sorting through them all. Evidently, the kids paid more attention to the 'safe sex/planned parenthood' posters than they'd paid to the posters she'd put up--Actually, Rusty's death was proof that they hadn't completely ignored the warnings.

She deeply regretted that they hadn't adequately considered the possibility that the teens, instead of staying away, would go armed.

In the end, she supposed it wouldn't have made much difference if they had considered it. They'd heard the gun shots. Instead of rushing up on the kids, they should've approached more carefully, but then both of them, she supposed, had been focused on the catching the killer before he got away--not on the kid with the gun.

It had been a stupid, stupid thing to do--and Rusty, who'd had more experience than her and should've known better--had paid for it with his life.

Shaking the thoughts off, she poured the evidence bags onto the bed once more. Instead of picking them up, she spread them out, staring at them. Four condom wrappers had been recovered.

She stared at them, trying to figure out why they seemed significant.

Abruptly, like a falling stack of dominos, everything fell into place.

There wasn't a single brand name condom in the lot.

They were generic--because the kids had gotten them all from the same place. The clinic. Every single victim had been to the clinic.

Their killer worked at the clinic.

Her heart was thundering in her ears so loudly as she leaned over and picked up the phone that she barely heard the voice on the other end of the line. "This is Agent Boyer. I'd like to speak to Chief Brown, please."

"Yeah?"

"Can you do a couple of background checks for me?"

Chapter Sixteen

Charlie checked her watch as she killed the engine. It was still early, not much after eleven. All of the other killings had taken place between one and three.

Her gut instinct was that the killer would be back. Everyone else was convinced that he'd been 'scared off', but she didn't think their killer scared easily. To her mind, he was just brazen enough to come back the very next night to try again--she knew he had to be furious that he'd been interrupted. They'd found no semen, and the girl had not been savaged as the others had. If he'd been hungry enough to 'feed' again so soon, he had to be in a rage now.

Maybe it was conceited to think she knew more than the others--they had a lot more experience than she did--More than likely they were right and she was wrong. She'd probably end up spending half the night in the woods and come up empty handed, but she'd rather take a chance on being laughed at than sit in her room, doing nothing, and then discover he'd killed again.

She'd borrowed clothes from the witness. There was no telling whether the killer would recognize the clothes or not--and even if he did, a reasonable person would know it for a trap. The killer wasn't reasonable, however. Moreover, it had occurred to her that if, as John suggested, the killer absorbed the powers from the animal skin he wore, it could also follow that his mind became more beast than man. If that was the case, he might merely jump at the chance without considering that it wasn't likely the girl would come back the next night when he'd killed her boyfriend.

Or he might not realize he *had* killed her boyfriend.

In any case, she'd needed clothing that fit in with the local teens. The black wig and dark make-up she'd bought had completed her disguise. In the daylight, she doubted she'd fool anyone into thinking she was American Indian, but it wasn't daylight.

Reaching under the dash, she pulled the fuse from the dome light. Dropping it to the floor, she opened the car door and got out, looked around to get her bearings, and then began her first 'stroll'.

The girl's clothes fit like a second skin--a T-shirt style spandex top that ended just below her boobs and a spandex skirt that was so short it fanned her ass to the breezes if she bent over more than 35 degrees. It was actually surprisingly comfortable if a gal didn't suffer too much from modesty, but trying to figure out where to hide her gun had been a challenge. She'd finally decided not to. There was no place she could think of that wouldn't make a noticeable bulge, except between her thighs and she wasn't about to stash a 45 between her legs. She'd bought a pair of cowboy style boots to go with the get up--hardly sexy, but the boots were loose enough at the top she could slip a small caliber pistol in them and still have some hope of getting it out in case of need.

She palmed the 45. It was the best she could do, because there was no way in hell she was trolling for a killer without having a cannon close to bring him down.

Fortunately, it wasn't a part of the country that supported lush woodlands. The 'woods' consisted of a lot of rocks, cacti, scrubby brush and undernourished trees. It was enough to make things difficult after dark--a lot to trip over and limited visibility-- but it could've been worse.

It was too large an area for her to have any hope of 'patrolling' it alone. She didn't even try. She walked around for about twenty minutes, pretended to take a pee, and then headed back.

She'd just reached for the door handle when someone slammed into her from behind, grabbing her arms. Her heart jerked painfully in her chest. "What are you trying to do, get yourself killed?" he growled in her ear.

She was tempted to grind the heel of her boot down on his toes anyway--knowing who it was the instant he spoke--but she refrained. "If I had a weak heart, I'd be dead already," she said through gritted teeth. "I swear to God, Greywolf, one of these times you're going to sneak up on me and I'm going to end up making us both sorry."

She elbowed him in the stomach when he relaxed his hold on her. He grunted and moved back a step. "You didn't answer my question," he growled.

"Was that a question? It sounded more like an accusation to me--but the answer is, I'm doing my job. This is what I get paid for--and I don't intend to stand here arguing with you about it until we alert the killer. Go home. Stay out of my way."

Snatching the car door open, she climbed inside and locked the doors, dropping her gun onto the dashboard within easy reach.

Greywolf glared at her through the window for several moments, his hands on his hips. Finally, he leaned over, placing his hands on either side of the window. "Unlock the door."

"Go home."

"I mean it, damn it!"

"Keep your voice down! --I'm just as serious as you are, so unless you think you can shadow walk into my car, you might as well go."

He stepped back from the car, glared at her for a long moment and--vanished. Charlie, who'd been staring angrily at the front wind shield, glanced quickly toward the side window, thinking he'd moved away. There was no sign of him. When she turned to look to see if he'd gone around the back of the car, a hand came down on her shoulder.

If she'd been able to, she would've screamed her head off. Fear turned into pure fury when she whirled toward the threat and discovered in was Greywolf. She launched herself at him, her fingers curled into claws. He caught her wrists, dragged her across his lap. "Stop it!"

She stopped when she'd exhausted herself trying to reach him. She was shaking all over, partly from anger, and partly from the adrenaline rush of fear that deserted her almost as abruptly as it had surged into her system. Slowly, he released his grip on her wrists and slid his arms around her, holding her tightly. "I didn't mean to scare you. I'm sorry. But I'm not leaving you out here alone."

Charlie lay weakly against him, fighting the surge of warmth that inevitably consumed her whenever he held her close, trying to wrap her mind around what he'd just done. She supposed she hadn't truly accepted that he could do it. Somewhere in the back of her mind she'd been certain it must be some sort of slight of hand, a trick, maybe some sort of mental manipulation.

Maybe it was, but it was no easier to believe he'd hypnotized her into opening the doors and then allowed her to wake with no memory of having done it than it was to think he'd merely walked through.

Finally, she pulled a little away from him and looked up at him. Before she could think of anything to say, he slipped his hand around the back of her neck and descended upon her as if he meant to consume her, sucking her lips, plunging his tongue into her mouth, dragging it possessively along hers then along the sensitive inner flesh of her cheeks. It was an assault upon her senses that drove past her defenses before she could even erect them. Desire blazed a debilitating swath through her, became a conflagration that consumed will, thought and the strength from her muscles. It drenched her vaginal passage, made the walls contract with need.

The primal urge to feel and taste him replaced reason. She tore at his shirt, shoving her hand inside when the snaps parted, leaving his shirt open to his waist, running her hands over his bare chest, his belly. He slid lower. With his free hand, he grasped one cheek of her ass, dragging her higher. Arching his hips, he ground his erection against her thigh. She spread her legs as wide as she could in the confined area, trying to angle her body so that he was rubbing against her throbbing clit. He grazed her clit with each undulation of his hips, teasing her until she was shaking with need.

She broke the kiss, replaced her hands with her mouth, licking his skin, nipping at him, fighting his belt and the fastening of his jeans with shaking, clumsy fingers. She slid off him, into the floorboard when she finally managed to free his cock. He flinched all over when she put her mouth over the head of his cock and sucked. Gripping her shoulder, the back of her head, he let out a ragged groan that was part protest, part ecstasy.

She ignored him, sucking him greedily. He twisted after a moment, caught her under the arms and dragged her onto his lap again, kissing her. For several moments, he struggled to situate her on his lap, brushing the head of his cock up and down her cleft. Finally, it filtered through both their minds that there wasn't enough room for his legs and her feet between the seat and the dash. He twisted again, laying her down on the seat. She bumped her shoulder on the steering wheel on the way down, and then bumped her head on the armrest of the door. The pain, slight as it was, broke through her haze, but she ignored it, reaching for him as he tried to move over her. His head made painful contact with the rearview mirror, knocking it sideways, as he tried to maneuver over her.

"Shit! God damn it!" he swore, subsiding, resting one hip on the edge of the seat.

Charlie giggled a little hysterically, panting with both desire and effort. Struggling, she managed to drag herself up the car door so that Greywolf could sit down again. He rubbed his head, glared at her and finally grinned a little sheepishly. He slid down in the seat after a moment, thrust his throbbing cock back into his shorts and scrubbed his hands over his face, making no attempt to fasten his jeans again. "That was an exercise in futility," he muttered.

Charlie sat up straighter and tried to adjust her own clothes. Her entire body was throbbing with unrequited desire, but her mind had cleared enough for reality to intrude. "An excise in stupidity, more like," she muttered.

He glared at her. She shook her head. "I just can't figure it out."

He frowned, his lips tightening with anger. "What?"

"Why it is that all you have to do is touch me and I completely loose my mind. This is a dangerous situation."

Greywolf sighed, the anger leaving him. "You really think he'll show?"

"Yes. That wasn't what I was talking about though."

Before she could say anything else, something landed on the trunk of the car with a crash that made it bounce on its springs. Charlie grabbed the gun from the dash, releasing the door lock at the same time. Wrenching the door open, she dove out, landing on her back, her gun trained on the top of the car.

He bounded away even as she fired her first shot. Scrambling to her feet, she raced after him, ignoring Greywolf's warning shout as he, too, bailed from the car. Dimly, she realized he was hampered by the fact that his pants were still unfastened. She had no intention of waiting for him, however, and loosing sight of her quarry. In any case, he was unarmed.

The skin walker had bounded into the brush some fifteen feet from the car. She skidded to a halt, watching for movement. He erupted from the brush abruptly, leaping straight at her. She fired, then dove for the ground. He caught her a glancing blow on one arm and pain exploded through her. Her gun flew from her hand as she hit the ground jarringly.

As she scrambled for it, he caught her by one ankle. Whirling, she kicked him in the face with every ounce of strength she could put behind it. Blinding pain shot through her ankle and up her leg to her knee. Her back up pistol fell from her boot. Jackknifing up right, she grabbed for the pistol. She'd barely stunned him however. He reached for it first. Even as he did so, something huge materialized out of the darkness, bowling him over. Charlie's heart jumped into her throat. It was Greywolf, she saw, struggling to hold the man/beast at arm's length, his teeth gritted as he dodged the skin-walker's snarling bites toward his throat.

Whirling, Charlie looked around frantically for her pistols and finally spied the 45. She launched herself toward it, screaming in pain when she tried to use her throbbing ankle. Her scream distracted both of them, but the skin walker was far less concerned about her than Greywolf. The distraction cost him. He lost his grip and leapt backward as the skin walker swiped at him with his claws, slicing his upper arm. In pursuit now, the killer launched himself toward Greywolf.

"Get out of the way!" Charlie yelled, grabbing up her gun at last and rolling so that she had the gun aimed directly at the skin walker. Greywolf vanished abruptly and the skin walker landed hard on the ground. Stunned, he glanced quickly around, but he didn't waste more than two seconds looking for Greywolf. He growled when he spied her, gathering himself to leap at her.

"I'll kill you if you so much as move in my direction, you son-of-a-bitch."

Something flickered in his eyes, perhaps a moment of doubt, but it vanished almost as quickly as it had appeared. Snarling, he launched himself at her. Greywolf's shot caught him in the shoulder. Charlie fired one into his lung and one into his thigh.

He landed on top of her, stunning her.

Greywolf rolled him off of her with a sharp kick in his side. He struggled to get up but finally subsided, breathing harshly.

Charlie pushed herself upright as Greywolf knelt beside her, keeping her gun leveled on the doctor as he slowly transformed once more from man/beast, to no more than a man garbed in the skin of a puma.

"You all right?" Greywolf asked sharply.

"I think I sprained my ankle when I kicked the son-of-a-bitch in the head--can you get my cuffs while I watch him?"

Greywolf straightened, studied Doctor Bob for several moments and finally nodded.

"I need help," Doctor Bob gasped when he'd left.

"Don't worry. You'll get it."

He subsided, laboring for breath. "Why didn't you just kill me when you had the chance?" he gasped.

"You think I'd let you off that easy after what you did to those kids? You're going to sit in jail, waiting for execution. I want you to have plenty of time to think about it before the fry your ass."

Chapter Seventeen

Greywolf shouldered his way into his bedroom and strode across to the bed, settling Charlie carefully. "How's the ankle?"

Charlie sighed. "The painkiller's kicked in. It's still throbbing but it doesn't hurt nearly as bad as it did. How's your arm?"

"Probably about the same as yours," he said dismissively, turning and striding into the bathroom that opened up off the master bedroom. She settled back on the pillows, closing her eyes as she heard the sound of running water.

He was back in a few minutes with a damp washcloth. Urging her to sit up, he carefully removed the wig and tossed it aside. Then, catching her face in one hand, he began carefully removing the makeup. He smiled faintly as he washed the makeup off. "There's one freckle."

Charlie glared at him. "No wisecracks about my freckles."

"I love your freckles."

Charlie looked up at him quickly, suspecting he was teasing her. His expression was serious, however.

He frowned, returning his attention to removing the makeup. "You're going to be laid up with that ankle a while. You could stay here--with me."

"I couldn't impose--besides, the women around here would be

ready to cut my throat," she added, only half joking.

Anger glittered in his eyes. "I'm not going to apologize for anything I did before I met you, Charlie."

"I'm not asking you to."

"If you just don't feel anything for me, I guess I can learn to live with it--guess I'll have to, but if this is all about women I've got no interest in--it just pisses me off, Charlie."

Charlie sighed. "I just don't think I'd be any good at this, John. I don't want to get hurt."

"You know I'd never hurt you on purpose."

"But that's exactly the point! I love you. I fell for you like a--ton of bricks and the more I'm around you, the worst it gets."

Greywolf glanced at her sharply, his expression arrested. "Say that again."

Charlie frowned. Her mind had begun to wander just a tad from the medication. "What did I say?"

"You said you loved me."

"I did?" she hedged.

He growled, shoving her back against the pillows and kissing her. When he lifted his head at last, Charlie had to struggle to open her eyes.

"Say it," he commanded grimly.

"You didn't say it to me," she pointed out.

"You crazy white woman! Do you think I'd be chasing you all over the state if I didn't?"

Charlie felt her heart speed up. "Is that it? You're not even going to say those three little words?"

He studied her for several moments. "Will you marry me?"

Charlie stared at him. "That's four."

He stood up abruptly and began to strip his clothes off as he moved around to the other side of the bed. More than a little startled, Charlie merely gaped at him for several moments, but heat suffused her as she watched him. When he'd finished, he placed a knee on the mattress and crawled toward her, a predatory gleam in his eyes.

Charlie reached for him, rolling to her side to meet him half way. Desire burgeoned inside of her as it always did the moment he touched her, but the residual effects at their aborted attempt earlier fueled the fire in her even more. She was tugging at him before their mouths even connected in a searing kiss, demanding his weight on top of her. He moved closer, his hands shaking with his attempt to restrain himself and move carefully. Despite that, he bumped her ankle. She gasped, but gripped him tighter when he stiffened, tried to move away again.

She reached for him, sliding her hand down his taut belly to wrap her fingers tightly around his engorged member, massaging him, guiding him toward the aching wetness between her legs. He caught her thigh, draping her injured leg over his hip, nudging her opening. The throb in her ankle warred with the throb in her sex. Firmly, she closed her mind to it, shifting, moaning with pleasure when she felt him rubbing her cleft and finally pushing inside of her.

It was torture, trying to get close enough to feel him deeply inside her as she needed to. As he reached between their bodies and began to tease her clit, however, she forgot about everything else, arching against him, gasping each time he slid inside of her and out again.

He bit down on her shoulder, sucked it. "Tell me you love me."

Charlie groaned.

"You love me."

"Yes!"

He kissed her, thrusting his tongue roughly into her mouth, sucking her tongue into his own. The sensation sent wild jolts through her, brought her near the brink. She tensed all over, cried out as she felt it explode through her. He sucked her tongue harder, thrust harder inside of her and abruptly shuddered with his own release.

Gasping, he dropped his head to her shoulder. "I love you, Charlie. Marry me."

"Yes," she gasped.

He lifted his head. "You'll marry me?"

She managed a smile, nodded.

"Because you love me?"

"Because I'm tired of fighting."

He frowned.

She lifted her head and nipped him on the chin. "I already told you I was mad about you. I--love--you, John Greywolf."

He grinned, finally settling back against the pillows. "Tomorrow."

Her head came off the pillow. "Tomorrow!" she echoed.

"I'm not giving you time to think it over."

She'd was drifting off when he spoke again.

"You knew it was Dr. Morris?"

Shaking herself awake, she nodded, then yawned. "It was the

condoms. I kept staring at them, trying to figure out what didn't seem to fit about them--finally, I remembered the posters at the schools, and the one at the clinic--and I realized the condoms didn't look right because they didn't have any brand names on the packaging. I knew then that they must have come from the clinic, and that tied all the victims to a common link. At first, it still didn't seem to fit. I figured the skin walker had to be American Indian, and Dr. Morris couldn't be the killer. I called Chief Brown and got him to do a background check--which is when we found out he's half--his mother was Seminole. He grew up on a reservation in Florida."

"So ... you got your man, Ms. FBI," he said, smiling faintly.

She lifted an arm and draped it around his neck. "Yes, I did."

The End

SEDUCTION

Chapter One

Amanda Fitzgerald frowned, trying to focus on the court brief she had in her hands as her fellow assistant DA, Cole Macguire, sauntered through her office again. She'd been an assistant DA for years. She was used to working in an overcrowded office humming with activity and ordinarily she was able to filter out most of the activity around her and concentrate without a lot of trouble.

Today, it was different, but she wasn't sure why.

Removing the hated glasses she'd started having to wear just to get her eyes to focus so she could read, she dropped them onto her desk and pinched the bridge of her nose.

"Headache?" His voice was deep, husky and it tingled along her nerve endings like a mild jolt of electricity.

Her head snapped up and she blinked to focus on the man who'd spoken. "What?" she asked distractedly.

His dark brows rose slightly, his gaze assessing her in a way that made her uncomfortably aware of how small her office suddenly seemed.

"I've got a bottle of painkiller in my desk if you've got a headache."

She stared at him for a full minute before the comments finally sank in that he'd noticed her concentration was off. Or maybe he'd noticed she was massaging her eyes?

The surprising thing was that he'd noticed at all.

They worked in an office full of overworked people who had little or no life beyond their work. They were fortunate when they made it home in one piece at the end of the day without being hit by a semi-tractor trailer.

The most surprising thing, though, was that Cole had actually been paying enough attention to her to notice anything that might suggest she had a headache.

Actually, the most surprising thing was that he'd noticed *and* initiated a conversation.

She was about to tell him thanks, but no thanks, when it dawned on her that the throbbing she'd been trying to ignore actually was a headache. "Thanks, I'd appreciate that."

When he'd left, she simply stared at the open door.

Cole Macguire had been working in the office nearly a year and she was pretty sure that that was the longest 'personal' conversation she'd had with him. It said a lot for him that she even knew how long he'd been working in the office. With the exception of Cole Macguire, she seriously doubted if anybody in the office knew how long anyone else had been there.

There were a grand total of five women in the office, three secretaries and one other assistant DA like herself. She'd be willing to bet every single one of them knew to the day when Cole had first been introduced around as the newest assistant DA.

He was the office 'baby', not quite fresh out of college, because he'd come to them with an already impressive resume, but he was still shy of thirty.

He was an absolute heart stopper, however, and she doubted any female of any age was immune to the charm that went along with his dark, smoldering good looks. The vacuous looks the women in the office, who ranged in age from twenty two to fifty, had cast his way for the first six months he'd worked with them was a testament to that.

She wasn't immune, and she'd never looked at a younger man with any interest at all in her entire life. As far back as she could remember, she'd had a taste for 'older' men. In her teens, that had been the older guys on campus, but she hadn't actually dated anyone closer than five years older than her in years. She rather thought that was because she had no patience, had never had any forbearance, with immaturity, irresponsibility, or pure stupidity.

If she'd wanted a baby, she would've had one.

She qualified that thought. She did want a baby. She'd finally woken up to the fact that she was damned near too old to have one anymore, and the realization in itself was enough to make just about any woman panic, especially one like herself who'd been wanting a baby for years and kept putting it on hold for her career.

What she didn't want was a baby that would never grow up, i.e. immature male that had to be babied forever.

She'd dated seniors when she was a freshman in high school, college men before she got to be a junior, and gone upwards from there. She'd been married, and divorced, three times before she'd finally given up on the whole concept. She'd never considered herself particularly pretty--although she did have a good figure and worked hard to keep it that way--but attracting men had never been a problem for her. She was a strong woman. She attracted two kinds of men; the ones who wanted the challenge of dominating a strong woman, and the ones that were looking for a mother. After three tries, she'd decided she just didn't have the patience for a relationship.

She'd been single again for a whole two years.

Maybe, she thought as Cole strode into the room once more and her heart did a strange little flip flop, that was the problem... because that also meant she'd been celibate for two whole years.

Where had the time gone!

Talk about a suppressed libido! She was shocked and horrified when she realized she hadn't had a piece of meat in that long.

And what a hell of a time to think about it with the office 'too young for me' hunk standing by her desk with his groin virtually eye level!

He caught her hand, to steady it, she supposed, as he tapped a dose from the bottle into her palm. She stared at the capsules as they dropped, trying not to think about the warm, tingly feeling running down her arm. "More?"

Ah the workings of the human mind when they had fire in their pants! She dismissed the images that flickered through her mind. "No! The regular dose will probably do me. I don't take drugs."

To her surprise, he chuckled. It had roughly the same effect on her as his deep voice in general did, except double. It made her stomach clench.

"Most people don't consider nonprescription medicine as drugs."

She was still holding the pills, wondering what to wash them down with. "There are prescription drugs and nonprescription drugs. They're all drugs and they all have side effects and they're all addictive, if for no other reason that a person gets used to taking something to handle something they'd probably be able to handle on their own if they weren't too wimpy to try."

When she looked up, she saw that he was studying her intently. She hadn't seen him up close before, hadn't noticed he had eyes the color of emeralds--black hair, green eyes, dimples--definitely

Irish--but as mundane as the thoughts were, the rest of her didn't feel at all ho-hum about the discovery that he'd invaded her 'space'.

"So law isn't your only--passion?"

She was getting seriously hyper-sensitive. She thought. She was an ADA through and through, though. She couldn't help but wonder why he'd paused before he used that particular word.

"It's just a personal preference," she said, rising abruptly and putting a little distance between them. "Not religious and not fanaticism. I just don't like the concept of drugs. If I really need something, I take it. Otherwise, I don't--Thanks! I'll just go get something to wash this down with."

He was at his desk when she headed back to her office from the water cooler. He glanced up, but she 'discovered' a stain on her sleeve at that precise moment and managed to concentrate on it until she'd passed him.

Her boss was grooming her to take over after he retired. He'd given her the task of grooming 'wonder boy' for her position. Neither decision had been officially announced, but, unofficially, there wasn't much that happened in the office that everyone else didn't notice and there were several who weren't happy about the boss' decision.

She could relate. There were two ADA's that had been working here longer than her, who'd had their sights on the position it seemed probable that she would land.

Cole was at the bottom of the totem pole and shouldn't have even been considered to fill her position.

But Cole *was* a 'wonder boy' and she knew he'd won the boss' respect or DA Murray Johnson wouldn't have considered it.

She was a female. She'd worked damn hard at her job and she was good at it, but in the back of her mind, she knew that the only thing that really mattered was that she'd been born with a pussy, and it would make the boss look good, politically speaking, to nominate her.

Unfortunately, everyone else felt the same way. Even the other female ADA looked at her as if she suspected Amanda had been sleeping with the boss.

Johnson was married, however. She avoided involvement with married men when she knew they were married. Even if she hadn't, she made it a policy *not* to get involved with her fellow workers. It was unprofessional. More than that, it was just asking for trouble…. And to have everyone snickering and talking about you behind your back which could be uncomfortable and disruptive.

On a personal level, she didn't particularly give a damn what anybody else thought, but it irritated the hell out of her when a room suddenly fell silent at her approach and talk started up again in her wake, and she knew gossip would reduce her chances of getting to be top dog. Not that the position itself made her feel warm and fuzzy--she wasn't a status kind of gal--but it meant more money, and if she was going to work her ass off, she wanted the money.

She was just finishing up a review of the cases she had coming up when Cole came into the office again. It took an effort but she resisted the urge to release an exasperated sigh.

He was supposed to be sitting second chair. She was supposed to be keeping him up to date on her strategy. It wasn't his fault that it irritated her to find herself tripping over someone else when she'd grown accustomed to handling cases solo.

It wasn't his fault that he'd somehow triggered her catatonic libido.

She glanced at her watch. Then she did sigh.

She'd skipped lunch and now it looked as if she wasn't going to get within sniffing distance of food before eight o'clock.

"Too tired to go over the cases?"

She looked up at him and managed a tight smile. "I'm going to have to run down to the vending machine before we start. Otherwise, my concentration's going to be non-existent."

He stretched. "I'm pretty washed out, too. Why don't we decamp to your place to go over this stuff? I'll stop and pick up a food type substance on the way over."

She almost said no before she even had time to consider it. She knew her instincts were right on target and she should say no, but the offer was so tantalizing she hesitated. She could take a nice, relaxing shower--put on something less professional, which guaranteed it would be more comfortable, and she wouldn't even have to drag herself into the kitchen to stare at the bare refrigerator. "We should probably just go over this and be done with it. It's sweet of you to offer, but I don't want to take advantage of your good nature."

He smiled faintly. "You wouldn't be. I'm starving, too. Besides, I'd like to get out of the office, even if I can't get out of the work."

"You're absolutely positive?"

"Positively positive."

"I'm going to go for it. My tail's dragging. I'll buy if you'll fly."

They argued over it briefly but finally settled that she would buy since he was doing the fetching. Gathering up the case files, she gave him directions to her house while they walked to the garage.

It wasn't until she'd headed home that it occurred to her that she'd just let a coworker talk her into fraternizing after work... in her home.

Chapter Two

By the time Amanda pulled into her garage she was suffering from an acute case of paranoia. Had she said, or done, something to give him the idea that she would welcome a good fuck?

She dismissed it as absurd. He was just a kid. He probably didn't even consider her a woman--she knew she was well past the 'nailing' stage for men below forty. Not that many forty-something men gave her a glance anymore for that matter. She was thirty-seven and they were still looking at the twenty somethings. The thought had probably never crossed his mind.

Just because it had crossed her mind to think of him as a good looking man was no excuse for such a ridiculous case of paranoia.

All the same, she went out of her way to make sure she didn't give him the impression that she was one of those hopeful, nearing forty and desperate to get laid, females. When she'd finished showering, she washed the last of her make-up off, raked a comb through her wet hair and dragged on the biggest, sloppiest T-shirt she could find over her jeans.

She debated on the bra. She really ought to put one on, but the T-shirt hardly touched her. He probably wouldn't even notice.

Her hair hadn't dried enough to tie it back when the doorbell rang. She left it loose to dry and went to answer the summons.

A shock wave hit her when she opened the door.

Apparently, Cole had dashed home to lose the suit for something more comfortable and take a quick shower, as well. His cologne hit her before the smell of the food. She'd always had a weakness for that particular cologne. It worked on her like a particularly potent bottle of wine, submerging her instantly in a quagmire of burgeoning desire.

It wasn't only the scent that mired her senses, however. The T-shirt he had on faithfully conformed to every bulging muscle in his arms and upper torso, yielding the vague thought that he must spend a great deal of time in the gym. His faded jeans were the coup de gras. Riding low on his hips, they cupped his sex in a way that the dress pants he usually wore didn't, making it instantly, abundantly clear that he had hither to unsuspected assets--at least unsuspected by her.

"Can I come in?"

Amanda blinked, dragging her gaze from his crotch to his face with an effort. "Sorry. I think I'm still half asleep. Would you rather eat in the dining room like civilized people? Or would you prefer to just go on in the living room and get to work? We can lay it out on the coffee table and munch."

Something flickered in his eyes when she finished. She frowned, mentally reviewing what she'd said. Paranoia reared its head again as she thought it over. Was it just in her head? Or had that sounded like an allusion to sex?

"The living room sounds good to me if you're not worried about it."

His voice sounded a little deeper than usual, but he gave no indication that he'd misconstrued the comments. Relieved when he didn't come back with a suggestive remark, she turned self-consciously and led the way to the living room.

Pizza wasn't the most nutritional thing they could've chosen, and certainly not a food for anyone careful about their weight, but they'd decided to go for something quick that didn't require as much attention as a meal that had to be eaten with utensils.

Amanda was almost as anxious for a distraction as she was for food. When he'd settled the box on the coffee table, she grabbed a slice and bit into it. The cheese formed a string from her mouth to the piece of pizza and sauce oozed onto her fingers. Catching the wayward strings, she stuffed those into her mouth and sucked the sauce from her fingers. When she looked up, Cole, who'd just popped the tab on a can of beer, was watching the slide of her fingers in and out of her mouth, his expression taut.

"Sorry. Didn't mean to gross you out, but I'm starving."

She stared at the can when he held it out to her. She didn't particularly care for beer, but it was good with pizza and she thought she might need something to relax her just a little bit.

On the other hand, she hadn't eaten anything all day.

"I probably shouldn't," she said hesitantly.

"I didn't think to pick up cokes."

Shrugging she took the can he'd offered. He'd brought a six pack. She didn't think he ought to drink the whole thing by himself and then drive home.

She was doing a good deed.

Right.

The pizza was fabulous, but messier than she'd thought it would be. She was going to have sauce all over her files, she reflected wryly. Opening the first case file on the floor beside her, she leaned back against the sofa and stuffed her face. Instead of moving the file closer to him, he scooted close enough to her to read the top document.

As he did, his scent wafted over her like a cloud of airborne desire. Her senses sharpened, expanded.

When he reached to adjust the page he was reading, his arm brushed lightly along her bent leg. Her attention snagged, her gaze followed the movement of his arm to the page and then back again as he draped his wrist on his knee.

His hand, dangling limply, was well groomed, his palm broad, his fingers long and thick. Her stomach shimmied as she stared at them and she dragged her gaze back up his arm, past his muscular forearms to the bulging biceps that strained the seams of his T-shirt.

Her appetite vanished abruptly but she'd managed to finish her slice by the time he'd read the page. Sucking the sauce off her fingers, she grasped the page carefully at one corner and moved it while Cole worked on his own slice. When she'd settled the sheet, she reached for another piece of pizza and sat back.

Cole's gaze was on her when she sat back. "You dropped some on your shirt," he commented, his eyes fixed on a spot on her shirt.

"Where?" She glanced down automatically and discovered she'd dropped cheese on the end of her boob.

He scooped it up with his finger before she could find a clean spot on her napkin to dab at it. Her nipple--poor stupid supplicant--instantly stood erect, trying to drill a hole through her T-shirt. She glanced at him quickly to see if he'd noticed. He was sucking the glob of cheese he'd captured off the end of his finger, staring at the little nub poking through her shirt like a canary's dick and a hard knot lodged in her throat.

For several moments she lost all ability to think. As he blinked, however, her brain kicked into over time with the realization that his gaze was about to shift to her face.

She knew if she hunched her shoulders he'd instantly notice that she'd noticed that he'd been staring at her nipple. She leaned forward instead, set the slice of pizza on the box and glanced over the paper in the folder. "That's a little background on one of our witnesses."

He dragged his gaze back to the page she was poking with her finger.

Or he simply followed her movements. She wasn't certain whether he was staring at her, or the page.

When he had turned his attention on the page once more, she pulled her T-shirt away from her skin and tried to wipe the sauce off. Unfortunately, she only managed to rub most of it in.

She now had a big red bull's eye over her left nipple.

Cole couldn't seem to keep his eyes off of it. Every time he glanced in her direction, his gaze seemed to zoom in on that red spot as if it was a magnet. It was almost ten o'clock before they managed to get through the first case file.

Between Cole's cologne, the beer, the bull's eye on her nipple, her suddenly overactive libido and... well, Cole himself, Amanda discovered she couldn't concentrate on the case to save her life. Finally, she leaned back and rubbed the tension in her neck muscles. "I can't concentrate anymore. I shouldn't have had that beer. It has relaxed me into zombie-ism. We're just going to have to go over the other cases tomorrow."

"There's something that's been bothering me," he said thoughtfully.

Feeling her neck muscles unclench fractionally, Amanda leaned a little further back, stretching the kinks from her back. "What?"

Even as she began to sit up to look at him, she felt something hot and wet fasten over her left nipple, or, more precisely, the bull's eye of sauce on her T-shirt. Her heart slammed into her ribcage so hard she felt for several moments as if she'd been shot.

Chapter Three

Even through her T-shirt, Amanda could feel the heat and suction of his mouth, the grating of his tongue back and forth across the sensitive tip. It crushed the air out of her lungs as forcefully as if he'd slammed his fist into her solar plexus. The adrenaline that shot into her blood stream joined the alcohol and turned her brain into a swirling, dizzying mass of useless gray matter.

She didn't realize he'd settled one hand on her belly until she felt the pressure of his fingers cupping her mound through her jeans. That assault to her already overwhelmed senses further debilitated her. When he lifted his head, releasing her at last, all she could do was stare at him open mouthed, the air grating through her throat as she struggled to bring her galloping heart into control.

He must have studied her for a full minute, breathing almost as harshly as she was, but she was still trying to prod her brain into functioning again when he caught her shoulders and pushed her to the floor, pressing his body tightly against hers and covering her mouth almost in the same movement. She managed something vaguely like a moan of protest as his tongue skated along the seam where her lips met and then charged beyond the fragile barrier, filling her mouth with his taste, but even that weak effort to regain her sanity vanished when he thrust his hips against hers, grinding his cock against her cleft. Heat and moisture and anticipation stampeded through her vaginal passage with the force of a small a-bomb, mushrooming through her and kicking off seismic waves that brought her to the verge of coming right then and there.

Sanity surfaced briefly when she felt his hand on her hip but her mind sank once more into primal, animal need as he skimmed his palm upwards beneath her T-shirt, raising prickles of acute sensation along the skin of waist and ribs with the faint roughness of his palm. Pausing briefly when he reached her breasts, he rubbed his thumb back and forth across her nipple until a fresh gush of moisture raced to join the moisture already dampening her panties.

The groan that clawed its way up her throat that time was one of pure need.

Apparently he spoke the 'fuck me' language fluently. He left off teasing her nipple and skimmed his palms higher, breaking the kiss long enough to dispose of her T-shirt, his body trembling now with his own barely controlled need.

It flickered through her mind, briefly, that she should protest, but he blasted brain cells into oblivion once more with another shot of endorphins by opening his mouth over her nipple and raking his teeth back and forth across the distended tip. She caught a fistful of his hair mindlessly, clenching and unclenching her fingers.

The tug of his hand at the waistband of her jeans should, by rights, have spurred her to action. It did, but not the action she should have taken.

As he succeeded in opening them and slipped his hand inside her jeans, she groped him until her hand closed over the hard ridge of flesh pushing against his jeans. He shuddered when her hand closed over his sex.

Sitting back on his heels abruptly, he caught the waistband of her jeans and tugged them off, taking her panties with them.

He was still fully clothed.

As she stared at him, however, he unfastened his jeans, pushing them down his hips until she saw the dark nest of hair surrounding his cock. She sat up, intent on helping him out of them, reaching through the front opening of his jeans and past his shorts to clasp his heated flesh in her hand. As she did, he bore her back against the floor once more, opening his mouth over hers and thrusting his tongue into her mouth without preliminary.

Beyond any thought by now, Amanda sucked his tongue hungrily, bumping her pubic bone against his groin in a silent demand to feel his cock surging into her. He groaned, pushed her hand from his cock and nudged her cleft with the head. She opened her thighs wider and lifted against him. The head of his cock slid along her cleft, connecting with the mouth of her passage. She rocked her hips forward to meet him at almost the same moment as he countered with his own hips. Slipping through her juices, he seated himself firmly. She gasped as her body adjusted to his possession, curling her fingers into his sides.

Grunting, he withdrew slightly and pressed forward again. She spread her thighs wide, heaving upward to meet him, gasping as she felt him fill her completely with his third assault. Slowly, he withdrew and thrust again, slowly, as if to allow her body to adjust to the girth of his cock. Each stroke sent a sharp pang of dizzying sensation through her, spiraling the tension of her body upwards toward release.

Sinking deeply inside her again, he hesitated, gasping hoarsely.

Impatient, feeling herself hovering on the brink of climax, Amanda dug her heels into the carpet and arched against him. He ground his teeth, groaned. Abruptly, he shoved his hands beneath her hips and slammed into her, setting a harsh, pounding rhythm. She lifted her legs, squeezing her eyes closed as he pounded into her over and over, hovering near her crisis for so long she feared she would miss it.

The convulsions of rapture caught her off guard, tore a sharp cry from her throat. Dropping her feet onto the carpet once more, she bucked beneath him frantically as it seared through her, meeting his thrusts with desperate lunges of her own as her climax reverberated through her. A shudder ran through his length as he was caught up in his own crisis.

She was still gasping hoarsely when he collapsed on top of her.

With an effort, she lifted her heavy arms and wrapped them around him, stroking his damp hair from his forehead, stroking his back in appreciation.

That was when it dawned on her that he hadn't taken anything off.

A prickle of uneasiness went through her even before he rolled off of her.

She shivered when his heat left her. Feeling exposed, strangely violated, she sat up, wrapping her arms around her knees. He was studying her, but his expression was unreadable when she looked up at him. After a moment, he pushed himself to his feet, adjusted his genitals in his jeans and fastened them once more.

The sound of the zipper closing seemed obscenely loud in the silence that engulfed them in an uncomfortable web. She didn't look up at him. Instead, she remained as she was, wishing she could just vanish altogether, resisting the urge to drop her face in her hands and groan her regret aloud.

Good God! She'd just fucked the office baby!

"I should go," he said on a harsh breath.

Amanda nodded without looking up. God only knew what he thought about what had just transpired, but he could keep it to himself. She was sure she didn't want to.

"Are you all right?"

"Sure!" Amanda said quickly. Maybe too quickly?

"I'll see you tomorrow then."

She glanced up at him before she realized he was talking about in the office. A flush crept up her neck and into her cheeks. "Right. Good night... and, uh..." On second thought, thanks might be polite, but she just didn't feel comfortable about it. "Drive carefully!"

He looked at her hesitantly, as if he wanted to say something else and finally turned and left.

The moment he cleared the doorway, Amanda made a dive for her T-shirt and dragged it on. She felt better once she wasn't quite so exposed, but not a lot better. Spearing her fingers through her hair, she dropped her head to her knees once more as embarrassment and despair swept through her. Why had she done it? What had she been thinking?

The soft footfall on the carpet startled her. She glanced up quickly and saw that Cole had returned. He looked at her uncomfortably. "I dropped my keys."

Reddening, Amanda looked around on the floor and finally dragged the set of keys out from between her feet and her bare ass, realizing the key's had fallen out when they were grinding pelvises on the floor. When she'd handed the keys to him, she got up, following him to the door to lock up.

He paused in the door, studying her face.

Determinedly, she stared back at him with as much unconcern as she could muster. When she felt the warmth on her inner thighs, she glanced down, saw what it was, then quickly jerked her head up again.

She couldn't imagine what expression was there, but after a moment, he caught the back of her neck, kissed her soundly and then departed before she could even catch her breath.

She didn't slam the door. She resisted the urge and closed it quietly before she bolted it.

The urge was strong to give way to a fit of hysterics. Instead, she sailed into her bedroom and through it to the bath. He was all over her. She couldn't take a breath without smelling his skin, his cologne, the scent of their lovemaking.

"Fool! Fool! Fool!" she chanted to herself as she bathed, trying to ignore the sparks and flashes of heat that went through her every time she touched herself, trying *not* to think about how absolutely wonderful it had felt fucking him.

The problem was, she wasn't certain if he'd fucked her, or if he'd *really* fucked her. Had there been some motive other than just getting laid?

She was being too paranoid!

No, she wasn't! She was thirty seven for cripe's sake! He was...what? Twenty six? Maybe. And drop dead gorgeous. And a chick magnet. He couldn't have just wanted to. If he was horny, he could've gone out and picked up a *young*, attractive woman.

By the time she'd gotten out of the shower, she'd discarded the question of motive for the scarier question of repercussions.

She'd never heard any talk around the office regarding his sex life. If he had a habit of bragging about his conquests, surely she would have?

But did that mean she could trust him to keep his mouth shut? Just because she hadn't heard anything before didn't mean this wouldn't be the first time.

Yeah, I fucked tight ass. She wasn't half bad...considering. Heh, heh, heh. All I did was give her a couple of smoldering looks and she couldn't get her pants off fast enough.

Finally, she climbed into bed and turned off the light. She found, however, that she couldn't close her eyes. She kept staring at the ceiling while visions played in her head. It varied each time but the basic theme was the same.

She would arrive at the office the next day. Cole would already be there, and every time she walked through the office, she'd notice little knots of people tittering.

Banishing those images, she tried to figure out how it was that she'd managed to get herself into this mess to start with.

Her first mistake, of course, was in allowing Cole to talk her into inviting him over for a cozy dinner at her place, but then she hadn't had designs on his body, be it ever so appetizing. Why would it occur to her that he'd have something in mind?

Or had he? Maybe he'd been as innocent about it as she had been? Maybe, because she'd been turned on by him early, he'd noticed, and then he'd noticed after he arrived that she was putting out 'lay me' signals and he'd tuned into them.

"*God*! It was the damn bra! I *knew* I should have put on a fucking bra!"

Chapter Four

After rehearsing exactly how she would behave for half the

night and all the way to work, Amanda arrived at the office to discover Cole would be out most of the day. Feeling deflated and oddly ill used, Amanda spent the first hour at work trying to focus. After a while, she was able to dismiss the 'day after' confrontation that she'd been dreading so much she'd hardly slept. Upon later reflection, however, she realized putting it completely from her mind so that she could concentrate had been a serious strategic mistake.

When she looked up from her work halfway through the day and discovered that Cole was standing in front of her desk, the jolt that went through her decimated her. It wouldn't have been so bad if he hadn't been looking directly at her. She might have had an opportunity to recover, at least a little. Instead, she received a full frontal impact and found herself staring up at him like a fish on the end of a fishing line--eyes gaping, mouth open and working to drag in air.

The smoldering look he'd bent upon her slowly dissolved into a puzzled frown and then one of irritation. "That doesn't look like a 'happy to see you' expression," he said coolly.

Amanda turned fiery red. She saw as she glanced sharply toward the drapes that they were closed, but the glass wall they covered had never seemed particularly private and seemed less so now. Abruptly, she closed her mouth. It took her a full minute after that to sort through her scrambled brain for 'the plan' she'd formulated, and several minutes after that to figure out how to launch it and compose herself enough to do so.

She smiled coolly. "Ready to go over these files?"

In the scenario she'd mentally rehearsed, Cole was thrown into complete submission by her cool, older woman facade and became putty in her hands, too cowed by her attitude to even consider overstepping the boundary she'd established.

In actuality, Cole planted his palms on the front of the desk and leaned toward her with an expression that was mid-way between anger and that smoldering look that made her insides quiver like jelly. "You're wasting your time trying to freeze me out… now. Last night you damn sure weren't cold."

Amanda gaped at him again, sent another nervous glance toward the glass partition and felt the color in her face fluctuate several times. "This isn't the time or place for… for personal discussions," she finally managed to say.

He straightened. "Your place? Or mine?"

Amanda blinked at him rapidly for a moment, trying to get her mind around the fact that he appeared to be demanding a return performance. "I... uh... I'm busy tonight."

"Tomorrow night, then."

Frowning, she looked down at the file on her desk. She simply couldn't concentrate looking at that face. Why was it, she wondered, that she hadn't noticed before that, behind that beautiful facade that looked like it should have belonged to some model or movie star, there was cold steel? Because she was an idiot? Because she hadn't stopped to consider that he was very good at what he did *because* there was a great deal of intelligence and ruthless determination wrapped up in that pretty package?

"I can't," she said, and was gratified that the delivery was both cool and decisive.

He sprawled in the chair in front of her desk. "I was under the impression that you didn't like to discuss personal subjects at the office, but it you'd prefer...."

Amanda glanced at him sharply. "I'd just as soon not discuss it at all. Let's just... uh... put it down to an interesting experience and leave it at that, shall we?"

His eyes narrowed. "Let's not."

She stared at him, but all she could think about was that someone was liable to pass close enough to overhear them at any time. They wouldn't even have to pass very closely if this continued and one or the other of them lost their temper and raised their voice. She smiled with an effort. "All right, then. Why don't I meet you at your place?"

He studied her suspiciously. "What time?"

She blinked a couple of times. "Around seven?"

He nodded, rose, gave her directions to his apartment and left. She breathed a deep sigh of relief, but she had the uncomfortable suspicion that he didn't believe her.

Finally, she dismissed it. She had no intention of going, of course, but she'd placated him. When she didn't show tonight, he'd get the message and mark it down to experience. He was more determined to pursue the matter than she'd expected--truthfully, after their uncomfortable *dismount* she'd expected him to pretend it had never happened--but it wasn't likely it would be a huge blow to his ego. He'd be off in search of greener pastures and they could both put their little indiscretion behind them.

Amanda had begun to feel more like her old self by the time

she arrived at work the following morning. Despite her decision, she'd been a little uneasy about it. Cole had shown a surprising resistance to being given the brush off given the fact that they'd done nothing more than shared a night of wild sex. She supposed she understood the anger. Men always preferred to be the dumper rather than the dumpee. It wasn't any fun either way, but it was a matter of pride and, of course, it always put men on their medal. If things had been different she might have been willing to allow the situation to run its course and let Cole save face by dumping her when he'd decided he was ready to move on--she was older and wiser and could probably handle it better after all.

It would've been nice, actually. She couldn't deny that he really rang her bell but she simply couldn't afford to take the chance.

She'd been a little surprised when he hadn't shown up at her door, hadn't even called. After the uncomfortable little scene in her office she'd more than half expected something like that.

Truth to tell, she'd actually been more than a little thrilled when he'd insisted he wanted to see her again, more than a little disappointed that he'd given up so easily, but she'd managed to put her chagrin behind her by morning and consider it a good thing.

She hadn't slept much better, however, and she was still more than half asleep when she collapsed in her chair and looked over the work on her desk, trying to decide where to start.

She thought that was probably why she was so completely vulnerable and defenseless when Cole strode into her office, closed the door behind him, and advanced on her purposefully. She couldn't seem to do anything beyond gaping at him through red-rimmed, bloodshot eyes as he rounded the desk and planted his palms on the arms of her chair, staring down at her.

She licked her lips uneasily. "This is all very masterful," she managed to get out when he dragged her knees apart and knelt between them, "but so unnecess--"

He cut off the remainder of her cold, deliberately emasculating speech by the simple expedient of covering her mouth with his and plunging his tongue inside. His kiss was both angry and possessive, but also carried the hunger of full blown arousal. Her body responded almost instantaneously to his urgency, sweeping her from zero to sixty in six seconds flat. Her heart revved. Her lungs felt like she couldn't drag enough air into them fast enough. Her brain shut down and her pussy did a Chernobyl.

Fortunately, his brain was functioning a little better than hers. The first she realized that danger was imminent was when Cole broke the kiss abruptly and ducked beneath her desk. Stunned, she stared down at him. "Amanda?"

Her head jerked up so quickly at the sound of Murray Johnson's voice, she felt a bone in her neck pop. Cold collided with the molten fire inside her body. Like the collision of the Atlantic and the Pacific, it created a monster storm instantaneously as each strove for dominance. The overall effect was to make her both hyper sensitive and hyper aware of her surroundings at the same time. Surreptitiously, she nudged Cole with her toe and rolled her chair closer to the desk. "Yes?" she said a little breathlessly, wondering if he'd actually seen anything or if he was merely staring at her strangely for another reason.

On that thought, she became aware that her lips were tingling and knew she must look as if she'd just been thoroughly kissed. Propping an arm on her desk, she covered her mouth casually with her hand.

"Have you prepped the witnesses in the Mulroni case yet?" Johnson said, frowning as he paced before her desk.

It took an effort to gather her wits, particularly since Cole chose that moment to pry her knees apart. Briefly, they struggled, but he was stronger and more determined. He forced her knees wide and jerked her hips forward at almost the same moment, almost unseating her. "Yes," she finally managed, "but I want to go over it with them again this afternoon and tomorrow before court."

Johnson nodded. Instead of leaving, however, he glanced around and finally sat down in the chair facing her desk. Amanda swallowed with an effort. Fortunately, the knee hole of her desk wasn't open. The side facing Johnson was solid. "What's on your mind?"

She felt the heat of Cole's breath along her thigh a second before she felt his mouth. A shock wave went through her. She dropped her hands to the arms of her chair, gripping them tightly as she leaned back. She could neither pull herself upright, however, or close her thighs as Cole worked his way upward in a leisurely fashion and planted his mouth over her cleft. A gasp escaped her. She followed it with a feigned cough.

Chapter Five

The heat that went through Amanda brought the skin all over her body into a massive, prickling of awareness as goose bumps chased goose bumps up and down her legs, her arms, and her body from neck to groin. Moisture flooded her sex, dampening her panty hose, the only barrier between Cole and his goal, and that a flimsy one that scarcely qualified as an impediment at all.

He proved that in the next moment by parting the panty hose at the crotch seam.

"I was wondering if you'd given any thought yet to how you'll manage your campaign?"

Amanda's eyes widened as Cole thrust his tongue through the opening and licked her cleft from the mouth of her sex to her clit. A shudder went through her. "Some," she managed to say with an effort, "but, frankly, campaign funds could be a problem for me."

Johnson shrugged. "They usually are, but I know a few people. I'll have a talk with them and see what we can do."

It took a supreme effort to smile in appreciation and an even greater one to refrain from panting as Cole dragged her closer and sucked her clit into his mouth, flicking his tongue back and forth across it. Her knuckles whitened on the arms of the chair as she felt her body struggling toward an explosive climax.

Johnson rose and moved to the door. "You haven't seen Cole this morning, have you?" he asked, turning back.

Amanda gulped. "No."

His brows rose. "Sampson said she thought she saw him come in here a little while ago."

"I guess that was before I got here."

Johnson nodded and went out, closing the door behind him.

Amanda gasped shakily, but she was well beyond the will or the ability to call a halt by now. The moment the door closed behind Johnson the arousal she'd been fighting to hold at bay consumed her like a flash fire. She bit her lip, struggling to refrain from groaning out loud. The effort to contain herself only seemed to build the tension higher and faster, however, as Cole sucked and teased her clit feverishly.

She whimpered as her climax swept her up and over the edge. Instead of allowing her to come down from the heights, however, Cole continued to suck and tease her clit and her culmination went on and on until it was all she could do to keep from screaming or passing out.

Finally, she managed to gasp out a shaky, "Stop! Please."

She went limp in the chair when he stopped, feeling as if she would ooze out of it and onto the floor. She found she couldn't even lift her head as he pushed the chair out and stood up. Bracing his palms on the chair arms, he leaned over her, covering her gasping mouth with a deep, thorough kiss.

She tasted herself on his mouth, the scent of her satiation, and her body convulsed again in a faint echo of her release.

Finally, he broke the kiss and stepped away from her, studying her while he adjusted his erection in the front of his trousers. He said nothing and Amanda wasn't able to. It took all she could do just to drag her legs together and sit up weakly.

He paused at the door, turning to study her enigmatically. "I'm glad we talked. I'll see you tonight around eight. Don't cook. I'll be bringing diner."

It didn't even occur to Amanda to protest until the door had closed behind him. By the time it did, it also occurred to her that the one thing she definitely did not want was any sort of confrontation with Cole in the middle of the office.

The remainder of the day passed in a blur. She hid in her office until the witnesses arrived to go over their testimony again. She caught a glimpse of Cole as she moved from her office to the conference room but she managed to ignore his intense gaze.

Calm did not settle over her as the day wore on. Instead, she found that the nearer she came to the end of the work day the more tightly the knot of nerves in her stomach wound itself. By the time the doorbell rang, she had been pacing the floor for almost twenty minutes.

Anger instantly came to her aid and she strode purposefully to the door and snatched it open. Cole pushed past her and strode toward the living room. She stood gaping at his rapidly retreating form for several moments and finally closed the door and followed him. When she reached the living room, he'd already settled the packages on her coffee table. He straightened and turned to look at her as she strode purposefully toward him.

"Now look, Cole," she said tightly. "I don't know what you thought you were doing this morning, but...."

He caught her upper arms and dragged her against his chest, cutting her off with his mouth. Heat immediately washed through her but she wasn't about to allow him to get the upper hand again.

She dragged her mouth from his.

He skated it downward and sucked a love bite on her neck.

Her nipples stood erect as sensation sloughed over her like flowing fire.

"I can still taste you on my tongue. It's been driving me wild all day," he murmured huskily against her throat.

"That's... we need to talk about that," Amanda said shakily.

Tracing her ear with his tongue, he slipped his hands downward until he reached the edge of her T-shirt, then burrowed under it and skated his palms up her ribcage.

She was prepared for him tonight. Briefly, a sense of satisfaction flickered through her as he encountered her bra. He hesitated, then slid his hands behind her back and pinched the opening together. The sense of satisfaction vanished as the bra loosened, her breasts falling heavily from the cups. He slipped his hands to the front again, cupped her breasts and began brushing his thumbs back and forth across her nipples.

Her breath caught in her throat. Heated arousal burgeoned inside of her, blossoming within moments into a full blown tumult of her senses.

"We can't," she gasped, without conviction as he guided her backwards until her knees connected with the edge of the couch and pushed her down on it. Following her, he sprawled on top of her, wedging a knee between her thighs even as he thrust her shirt upwards and substituted the tease of his thumbs on her nipple with his tongue.

She was writhing beneath him within moments, too caught up in the fire he generated inside of her with his mouth and tongue to think to protest further beyond protesting when he moved his mouth from one nipple to the other, and then down her stomach. When he sat upright and unfastened her jeans, tugging them down her legs, she lifted her hips.

Pulling his shirt off, he covered her once more. The brush of his bare flesh against her belly and breasts sent her senses spiraling into a deeper, drugged haze of passion. She reached between them as his lips sought hers once more, cupping his sex through his jeans, massaging him. He made a sound in his throat that was equal parts satisfaction and discomfort. Brushing her hand away, he unfastened his jeans, worked them down his hips and guided her hand inside his briefs. His cock filled her hand gratifyingly. She stroked him from the root to the head of his cock.

A tremor traveled all the way through him. Grasping her leg behind the knee, he pushed it upwards, settling between her parted thighs. She guided him to her body eagerly, lifting up to meet him when he thrust, embedding his rigid cock, then worked his way deeply into her in a series of thrusts and retreats. They were both gasping for breath and coated with a light sheen of sweat by the time he'd claimed her fully and set a pace that drove them both quickly to an explosive culmination.

He settled heavily against her as the tremors of his release slowly died down.

Feeling wonderfully sated, Amanda lifted her hand to stroke his back before she thought better of it. He tensed slightly at the first brush of her hand, however, and she fell still, remembering abruptly that he'd seemed as coldly distant the previous time.

The uneasiness of before crowded into her mind, chasing the last glow of satisfaction from her. After a moment, he lifted slightly, placed a brief kiss on her lips and climbed off of her. She drew her knees up and then sat up as he settled at the end of the couch. A shiver skated over her, cooling her flesh and she glanced around for her shirt.

At least, she thought wryly as he found his own shirt and pulled it over his head, this time he'd taken some of his clothing off.

The mixed signals she got from him were almost as disturbing as they were confusing. Twice now, he'd fucked her as if he couldn't get inside her fast enough, but she wasn't to touch him? It wasn't that she minded the idea of a strictly sexual relationship. It would actually be preferable at the moment and under these circumstances. If that was what he'd had in mind for the two of them, she might be willing to reconsider keeping company with him.

Except for the little 'desk' incident, he seemed willing and able to keep it out of the office, to limit their contact to after hours back scratching.

And he was damned good at it.

But the 'fuck me but don't touch me' thing still made her uncomfortable. Either he'd misunderstood the lover's caress and was afraid it meant she was getting too attached, or he couldn't stand to be touched like that... or he couldn't stand for *her* to touch him, and that was the part that worried her.

She glanced at him as he stood up to adjust his jeans, wondering if he was about to pull a disappearing act like he had the last time. The shirt he'd pulled on while he was sitting on the couch was caught in a fold that left his back bare almost to his ribs and the bare patch of skin drew her gaze.

When he twisted slightly, trying to straighten it, she saw the scar.

"Have you got a microwave?"

"Huh?" she jerked her gaze toward his face when he spoke, but uncomprehendingly because the image she'd just seen had completely stunned her.

He smiled faintly. "I imagine the food's cold by now," he said, picking the bags up from the coffee table and heading from the room in search of the kitchen.

She watched him, but her mind wasn't on what he'd said or even the fact that he'd apparently decided not to fuck and run.

She'd only gotten a quick glimpse of the scar on his back. Like a shutter flash, the image had been impressed on her mind, but not deciphered right away. When her mind finally did interpret the image it had picked up, something far more uncomfortable than uneasiness moved through her.

It wasn't merely a scar, unidentifiable, some sort of childhood war wound from a careless accident. The pattern was not something easily misinterpreted nor something that could be dismissed as an accident.

It was from a very bad burn and formed the perfect three cornered impression of a steam iron.

Chapter Six

When Amanda arrived in the kitchen, Cole was propped against the island, watching the food revolve on the turn table in the microwave. He glanced at her. "I got Chinese. I hope that's something you like."

With an effort, Amanda shook herself and forced a pleased smile. "Actually, I love it. Did you get egg rolls?"

He pointed to one of the bags and she moved to the island, pulling the boxes out and checking them. She put the egg rolls in the broiler to heat up. The rest of the food would heat well enough in the microwave, but she liked her egg rolls crusty.

When she'd set the temperature, she moved to the cabinet and pulled out some plates and glasses. "What would you like to drink?"

He removed the box from the microwave and put another one inside. "What've you got?"

Amanda glanced in the refrigerator to inventory. "Fruit juice-mixed, water, milk, and iced tea."

He glanced at her with interest as he settled on a stool at the breakfast bar. "Home made tea?"

She nodded.

"I'll take the tea."

She brought the pitcher to the counter and set the plates down.

He initiated a discussion regarding an upcoming case while they ate. Amanda was perfectly willing to follow his lead. As much as she would've liked to question him about what she'd seen, obviously it was not a subject he would welcome or he wouldn't go to such pains to hide his scars.

There would almost certainly be more. It wasn't self-inflicted, not on his back. It was possible that it could be from an accident, but she doubted it--not when he was so uncomfortable about being touched--which made her wonder if it had been sexual as well as physical abuse or if it was simply a matter of not knowing how to handle affection because he'd never received it and didn't know how to return it.

She wondered if it was sheer human perversity that she, who'd always gone out of her way to avoid needy men, felt a nearly overwhelming urge to mother him and try to erase the childhood pain he didn't want anyone to see.

The wonder was that he'd survived childhood at all. There weren't many children that suffered abuse that severe that did.

Had he been 'rescued' then? Dragged from his prison and thrown into the overworked social care system where he would've spent the remainder of his childhood free from torture but unloved and ignored.

If she'd given it any thought before--which she hadn't--she would have supposed he'd grown up as somebody's darling boy. He was smart and most any parent would be so proud of that alone that they'd be overindulgent. As good looking as he was, though, he had to have been a beautiful child and beauty in this world generally equaled spoiled brat.

He hadn't been adored, however. He'd been abused, and although that wasn't limited to poverty stricken households exclusively, the chances were probably better than even that he'd also grown up dirt poor, which meant he'd had to fight physical abuse and poverty to get where he was.

It occurred to her on that thought that he was probably one of the most remarkable men she'd ever met. It was amazing that he seemed so self-confident, so well adjusted. She was certainly not complaining, but she had to wonder if his sexual aggressiveness stemmed from the abuse. She supposed it must, and maybe part of it was to maintain his distance from any sort of tenderness?

So much for flattering herself that she turned him on to the point that he lost control, she thought wryly.

Empathy aside--and she couldn't deny that the discovery had undermined her entire perception of him--the real question was, how safe was she in being with him? He hadn't shown any tendency toward physical violence at all, even when he was angry with her though.

She'd prosecuted enough violent criminals to know the most subtle signs of imminent explosion. She simply couldn't believe she was in any danger from him, but could she really trust her judgment when she was so deeply involved with him already?

Had it been his mother? Was that why he'd focused on her?

It was an unpleasant thought.

"You seem pensive."

She glanced at him guiltily. Finally, she shrugged and got up to clean up the remains of their meal. "I've got things on my mind. Sorry. I didn't mean to be rude."

He got up and helped her. In a few minutes they had the kitchen clean and their dishes stacked in the dishwasher. He was leaning back against the counter studying her when she straightened from filling the dishwasher.

"I'd like to stay the night."

Amanda blinked at him in surprise, feeling her heart skip a beat. "I'd don't think that's a good idea."

"Why?"

She frowned, trying to read his expression, but she realized fairly quickly that she wasn't going to discover anything in his expression he didn't want her to know. Finally, she turned and headed toward the living room. "You know why."

He caught up to her in the living room, sprawling on the end of the couch opposite her. "Why don't you explain it?"

"I thought we'd established that this was going to be casual sex?"

He studied her speculatively for several minutes, then caught her leg, dragging her across the couch toward him as he levered himself up and sprawled on top of her. "Did we?"

A shiver skated through her as he sucked a love bite on the side of her neck.

"I can't think when you do that," she protested.

"And this is a bad thing?" he asked, propping his arm on the couch beside her head and dropping his head onto his hand so that he could study her.

Actually, just having him so close made it nearly impossible to think. She should've been used to that remarkable face, immune to it by now. But then, he hadn't looked at her like that before. As long as she was looking at him from a distance, it wasn't any different that looking at anything else that was pleasing to the eye, it pleased one in a distant, impersonal sort of way. Up close, when his beautiful green eyes gleamed with predatory hunger, it was an entirely different matter. "I'm too old for mind games, Cole."

His brows rose. He traced a pattern along the center of her T-shirt, and then over her breast, circling one nipple. "Afraid I'll get hurt? I'm a big boy. I think I can handle it."

He certainly was--all over.

His flippant dismissal of her concerns irritated her, however, effectively offsetting the drugging effects of his nearness. Her lips tightened. "There's no need for sarcasm. I only meant that it'll be easier to keep things simple if we limit ourselves to brief encounters."

He frowned, but it wasn't thoughtful so much as it was irritated. "Is that what we're going to do? Keep it simple?"

"I thought that was the idea."

"Why?"

Amanda felt like she'd been caught up in a chess match and she didn't particularly like the sense of having to study each move carefully before she took a step. "Why don't you tell me what you had in mind?"

"When it started?"

"Yes."

One dark brow arched upward and a faint smiled curled his lips. "Fucking you until you screamed and begged me to fuck you some more."

Heat curled in her belly. It took an effort to gather enough moisture into her mouth to swallow because all of it was in her pants. "You will keep things strictly professional at the office?

No more of that…. What happened earlier."

His eyes gleamed. "You seemed to enjoy it."

She reddened. "That's beside the point."

He shrugged. "I didn't seem to be getting through to you. You've got this barrier thing."

She considered herself a strong woman, but she wasn't super woman and she wasn't stupid enough to think she was completely impervious. If she had been, she wouldn't have been married three times. The 'barrier thing' was added armor and she didn't like the idea of taking it off. Especially around a man like Cole. He didn't seem to be a player, but she knew that was probably just because she didn't know him that well, not on a personal level. He had the way, and definitely the looks, of a player.

Even if that wasn't the case, allowing herself to become deeply involved with a man so much younger was just asking for trouble. She considered herself a realist. She took care of herself, she looked young for her age, but she wasn't twenty something and she didn't look it. Women showed their age faster than men anyway, or maybe it just looked worse on them.

The bottom line was, it was herself she was worried about, not Cole, and she had a pretty fair notion he knew that. He should anyway. If he'd just been a pretty face, she wouldn't have worried about it at all, but Cole was much more than eye candy. He was an intelligent, complex man and all of that together boiled down to extreme danger.

"Well," she said at last, "to be perfectly honest, I make it a policy not to get involved with people I work with. It can make working with that person uncomfortable when the relationship goes south, and it usually does. If you mean to keep it simple, though, I can handle it."

He studied her a long moment. "So--you don't have a problem with me spending the night?"

Amanda gaped at him in disbelief. It was like he hadn't heard any part of her argument beyond her agreement to continue. "You're damned pushy. You know that?"

"I'm an attorney."

"I think that's putting the chicken before the egg."

"The cart before the horse, you mean?"

She gave him a look. "I think you went into law *because* you're pushy, not the other way around."

He smiled faintly. "You think so?"

She studied his face, realizing with unpleasant clarity that he'd already pierced her armor. The chances weren't good that she was going to keep the cool head she prided herself on through this. He was like the tide, though, inevitable once he set his sites on a goal. Bracing yourself just didn't do a lot of good when something washed over you anyway and kept going.

The path of least resistance, in this case, could be disastrous for her, however.

"I'm a bed hog," she said weakly.

He smiled. "You'll get used to me."

She sighed. That was what she was afraid of. There was nothing worse than getting used to something when you knew you were only going to have it temporarily.

* * * *

Despite the fact that he'd fucked her to the point of exhaustion before he fell asleep, Amanda found that she was having a lot of difficulty doing the same. Cole appeared more long and lanky than muscle bound, despite those great muscle groups he hardly allowed her a peek at. Obviously, however, he was *all* muscle, which was considerably heavier than fat, because his arm and leg felt like two one ton logs draped over her.

He'd undressed in the dark. She couldn't decide whether he was that embarrassed by the scars he carried or if he just wanted to avoid having questions thrown at him.

She'd begun to suffer some doubts about her assessment, though. Except for the clothing thing, he just seemed too self-confident to have emotional scars. He certainly wasn't shy about dragging that big cock of his out and shoving it into her.

She'd just begun to doze when he jerked in his sleep. She thought at first that it was one of those falling dreams, but he began to moan almost at once, and mutter completely unintelligible words and she realized he must be having a nightmare.

When he broke into a sweat and began thrashing around on the bed, she was no longer in any doubt. She was wary, however, about waking him. Some people reacted violently to being wakened suddenly and she didn't want to have to go into work tomorrow and explain why she had a black eye.

She lay staring up at the ceiling, listening to him and counting off the seconds. Finally, she couldn't stand it anymore. She rolled toward him and scooted close enough to lay her head on his shoulder, stroking his chest lightly. To her relief, he grew calmer almost at once. After a moment, he wrapped the arm next to her around her and dropped his other hand on her head, stroking her hair. "Mandy?"

Amanda resisted the urge to grind her teeth. She hated the diminutive of her name worse, if possible, than the name itself. Amanda sounded like a stuck up bitch. Mandy sounded like an empty headed teenager, or worse, a street walker.

Unfortunately, there was no middle ground when you were stuck with a name like hers.

"Mmm?" she murmured finally.

"Sorry I woke you. I had a nightmare."

She was silent for several moments. "Want to talk about it?"

He disentangled himself and sat up, throwing his legs off the edge of the bed. A shudder went through him as he scrubbed his hands over his face. "I don't remember it, actually--what time is it?"

Amanda glanced at the clock. "Three."

He got up and started pulling his clothes on. "I should get back to my place so I can get ready for work."

"Now?"

He glanced at her. "You'll sleep better."

"Not if I'm going to be lying here thinking about you driving to your place at three in the morning, still half asleep," she said dryly.

He looked at her sharply. "I'm awake. I'll be fine."

She was torn. On the one hand, she really wanted her bed to herself. On the other, she *would* worry about him.

She seriously doubted he'd give in to her coaxing, however.

Yawning sleepily, she rolled over, putting her back to him. "Don't be a complete ass, Cole. Come back to bed."

He didn't move so much as a muscle for several moments. Finally, now wearing his shorts and shirt, he slid into bed beside her, dragged her across the bed and tucked her against his belly as if she was a sleep pillow, threw an arm and leg over her and went back to sleep.

Amanda stared at the clock, wondering how it was that men could just drop into unconsciousness with such ease. She'd always thought it was just her husband that had the ability and that age contributed.

So much for thinking you had everything all figured out.

Chapter Seven

Exhaustion, Amanda reflected the following day while she struggled through court, was something women never truly understood until they had a baby--or took on a new lover.

Cole looked well rested, relaxed, and fresh as a daisy.

That irritated her, particularly when she got a look at the dark circles under her eyes. Concealer stick or not, she was surprised nobody had asked her about her two black eyes.

"You look done in," her boss commented when she returned to the office. "Is it going that badly?"

Acutely conscious of Cole standing behind her, Amanda dismissed his concern. "It's going as well as I expected. I'm confident I'll get a conviction."

He nodded, but studied her piercingly. "It's the Garner hearing, isn't it? I'm just surprised you didn't beg off to go down there."

Amanda felt a shock wave run through her. She was instantly completely wide awake. "Garner? You're not talking about Lyle Garner?"

Johnson frowned. "You didn't know? He's up for parole."

"Son-of-a-bitch! When's the hearing?"

Johnson looked at his watch. "You don't have time to get down there now, Fitzgerald. It's four o'clock. With the traffic, it'll take two hours at least."

"Watch me!" Amanda said grimly. Whirling on her heel, she strode toward the exit.

Cole fell into step beside her. "Let me drive you."

Amanda glanced at him distractedly. "I'll drive myself."

He caught her arm when they reached the parking garage. "You're dead on your feet. You're totally pissed off and your judgment is shot to hell. I'll drive."

Amanda tried to jerk her arm free. "Stay out of my way, Macguire. This has got nothing to do with you."

He held on grimly. "You're not going to stop anything if you don't get down there in one piece. I'll drive. You rest. You'll be in a better frame of mind when you get to the hearing."

The truth was, her eyeballs felt like they'd been boiled. As scared as she was--and contrary to what Cole thought, she *was* scared, not pissed off--she knew he was right.

"How could I have missed the memo?" she ground out, more

to herself than to Cole as he settled her in the passenger seat of his car.

He shrugged. "You've got a lot of work in your lap right now."

She knew it was unreasonable, but it infuriated her that he was so damned calm about it. "They'll let that bastard out as sure as shit!" she muttered.

Instead of commenting, Cole closed her door and moved around to the other side, concentrating on negotiating his way through the parking garage.

Johnson had been right, Amanda saw with dismay. The traffic was horrendous.

"I know some back roads that'll probably allow us to make better time," he said grimly when he saw the cars that were inching along a foot at a time.

"No! We'll be better off going with the flow than to risk getting lost."

"I know what I'm doing. Trust me."

Amanda glanced at him sharply. After a moment, however, she settled back in her seat. She was far from relaxed, but there seemed little point in arguing with Cole and none in biting his head off. It wasn't going to change anything. She still couldn't figure out how it was that Johnson had known and she hadn't. He knew how she felt about Lyle Garner. Surely, even if he'd been too busy to stop by himself, he would've sent over a memo?

Or, maybe he'd been too distracted? Maybe he thought he had?

Did it really matter now?

Lyle Garner was up for parole, and he was a wily psychopath. He'd have the parole board convinced he'd changed his ways.

Violent rapists never changed. Never.

"Looks like this one's personal."

Amanda glanced at him sharply. "Maybe." She leaned her head back against the headrest, rubbing her eyes. "Let's just say the world is a better place so long as he's behind bars."

Cole said nothing for several moments. "Have you considered he might be rehabilitated?"

"You didn't tell me you were a dreamer," she retorted dryly.

"You don't believe in the system?"

There was an edge to his voice.

"The system works as well as can be expected, all things considered--those things being that it was designed by people, it's run by people and it's at the mercy of the judgment of the people. I'm not saying we should quit trying. I'm not saying everyone isn't doing the best they can. All I'm saying is sometimes it works and sometimes it doesn't. If it had been left up to me, I'd have executed the son-of-a-bitch."

"For rape? You know as well as I do that one of the reasons the rape laws are the way they are is because of women."

Amanda sat up and looked at him. "What is that supposed to mean?"

"It means, they get pissed off, they scream rape. Then, at least half the time, they recant."

"That's because half the time they're scared to death of the bastard and they allow him to intimidate them into recanting."

"And half the time they're in love with the guy and just pissed off and looking to get even with him about something."

Amanda scrubbed her hands over her face. She knew she was making a wreck of what was left of her makeup but she was too tired to care anymore and too worried. "I don't think we're going to be able to agree on this particular subject so why don't we drop it?"

He fell silent, but she could see he was as angry about it as she was. What had she expected? He was a man. He was bound to see it from a different perspective altogether. On one level, she knew he was right. There were just enough really stupid women out there to fuck everything up for everybody else. It was the vindictive bitches who lied through their teeth and got caught at it that made it so hard to get a rape conviction. Nobody, not even a jury, wanted to risk ruining a man's life by convicting him of a sex crime if their was a shadow of doubt, and there so often was. Except in those cases where the woman was clearly a randomly chosen victim, it mostly boiled down to his word against hers.

She fell to chewing her nails off. It wasn't a habit, not something she regularly did, but she was too nervous to sit still.

True to his word, Cole negotiated the back roads and found his way to the freeway again. Unfortunately, they still weren't far enough out from the city for the traffic to have thinned a great deal.

The lot was vacant by the time they reached the prison. Amanda bailed out as soon as the wheels stopped rolling anyway and raced to the doors. Without surprise, she saw that the board had already convened.

She felt sick as she made her way back to the car and climbed in.

"What happened?"

"We were too late."

Cole scrubbed his hand along his jaw. "What do you want to do now?"

"Go back for my car, I guess."

"Why don't you just let me take you home? You can get your car tomorrow."

Amanda shrugged. "Fine."

He kept glancing at her as they made the drive back. Finally, when they pulled up in her drive, he turned to look at her. "Still mad?"

Amanda glanced at him blankly. "Mad?"

"Yeah. You still pissed off?"

"No. I wasn't mad."

He gave her a look. "Sounded like it to me."

She turned to study him for a long moment. "That's what terror sounds like, Cole."

"Even if he did get paroled, and you don't know he did, the guy's probably a lot more interested in getting his life back together than bothering you."

Amanda swallowed. "He'll come after me," she said with conviction.

Cole caught her arm and dragged her across the seat toward him, wrapping his arms around her. "Why would you think that? My God! Of all the people you've convicted in your career, why this one?"

She looked up at him. "Because this one promised he would, and I believe him."

Chapter Eight

"I don't feel like having company tonight, Cole, if you don't mind," she said when they reached the front door, turning to put her palm in the middle of his chest.

He caught her hand and lifted it to his lips, kissing her palm "What you need is some TLC."

She couldn't help but chuckle. "I'm *old*! I've had all the TLC I can stand... at least for a couple of days," she amended.

He grinned. "Still after my body? I was thinking more along

the lines of cooking you something to eat, maybe a thorough massage, a hot bath."

It sounded so heavenly, Amanda felt as if she would dissolve into a puddle of bliss on her steps. Taking that as a yes, Cole took her keys, walked her into the living room and pushed her down on the couch, then disappeared into the kitchen. She fell asleep to the rattle of pots and pans in the kitchen.

She woke to a persistent tickle on the tip of her nose. She swatted at it and rubbed her nose. It came back the moment she put her hand down again. With an effort, she lifted one eyelid. Cole was bent over her tickling the tip of her nose with the corner of a kitchen cloth, his green eyes alight with suppressed laughter. "Very funny," she said sleepily.

Dragging her up despite her protests, he guided her to the kitchen and helped her onto one of the stools. He'd cooked a simple meal but it was surprisingly good. After they'd eaten, he made good on his other promises. She was asleep before he'd worked his way past her calves.

When she woke, she was sprawled across Cole's chest, one arm around his waist, one leg entwined with his. He was stroking her back. Stifling a yawn, she glanced up at him. When he felt her movement, he glanced down. They studied one another for several moments.

Her first thought was that he looked sexy as hell first thing in the morning with his tousled hair and the dark shadow of his beard shading his cheeks. It was a sight she could get used to way too quickly.

Her second was that she probably looked like the wrath of God.

She pulled away and sat up, dropping her head in her hands. "You should've woke me."

He looked like he'd been awake a while and she wondered what had woken him and what he'd been thinking about. It was just the sort of thoughts she shouldn't be thinking if she was going to try to keep some emotional distance between them.

"It's early yet."

Nodding, she glanced at the clock and scooted to the side of the bed.

"I figured I'd drop you off at work and then run by my place to change."

She glanced back at him in surprise before she remembered she'd left her car in the parking garage the day before. His comments pushed the last dregs of sleep from her mind and her anxieties about Garner swamped her. She'd been so exhausted from three days of very little sleep and numb from the crash of the adrenaline rush that had followed her discovery of the parole hearing for Garner, she'd barely registered anything afterward. "Sorry. I should have thought about that last night when you offered to bring me home." A thought occurred to her just then, however, and she pointed to her ex-husband's closet. "There might be something in there you could wear and save yourself a trip."

When she came out of the bath, Cole was dressed in the clothes he'd worn the day before, standing at the closet, studying the clothing her husband had left. She frowned, shaking her head at herself. The clothing her ex had worn probably wouldn't come close to fitting Cole. Gary had been short and stocky.

"Looks like he expected to be coming back."

His voice sounded strange. She glanced at him but he had his back to her. Shrugging at his comment, she selected a suit for herself and tossed it onto the bed while she dug around in the dresser for a bra and panty hose. "I've got no idea what he might have been thinking, but that shouldn't have crossed his mind. When I'm done, I'm done. I told him that."

"When did you two split?"

"The divorce was finalized almost two years ago, but we split the year before that. I was busy. It took me a while to get around to the divorce."

"But, you kept his clothes."

"I didn't keep them. I just haven't gotten around to getting rid of them yet."

Closing the closet, he turned to study her while she dressed, leaning back against the door, his arms crossed over his chest. "How long were you married?"

She glanced at him. "The last time?"

Briefly, he looked surprised, but it was replaced very quickly with a taut expression of displeasure. "How many times have you been married?"

"Three. The first one hardly counted though. I don't think we even made it through the first year. Seven the second time. Two the last."

"You don't have much luck with men."

There was something about the way he said it that irritated her. Or maybe it was just the fact that he was questioning her at all. It wasn't as if *they* had a relationship or even planned on having one. Even if they did, what she'd done before wasn't any of his business.

It wasn't mere curiosity. He was hiding it fairly well but he was pissed off. She could tell. "I didn't have any luck with *him*," she corrected. "I was married to Gary three times."

He said nothing for several moments. "So he had reason to believe he could come back."

Amanda let out an irritated huff and stood up to straighten her panty hose and slip her feet into her heels. "Like I said, I don't know what he had in mind, but I told him when I let him talk me into trying just 'one more time' that it wasn't going to work. If we could've made it work we wouldn't have gone through the second divorce.

"We got married right out of high school. Then he decided he was too young to settle down and wanted to go to college, so we split and went off to college. After we graduated from college, he decided he was ready to settle down, so we tried again. Three years into it, I knew it wasn't working, but we kept on trying for another four before we threw in the towel. I realized almost as soon as we got married the third time around that he was never going to grow up. I haven't seen him in two years. But, no, he wasn't the only man in my life. I dated between marriages.

"I'm thirty-seven, and I know damn well you knew that to begin with, or at least had a pretty good idea. So don't tell me you didn't have any idea that there'd been men in my life. I've never pretended to be a nun or a saint."

"Gary Fitzhugh?"

She glanced at him, coloring faintly. "Why?" she asked cautiously.

"You took his name and you kept it."

She looked around for her purse. "I didn't feel like going through the headache of another identity change," she said tightly. "The first time, I reverted to my maiden name and it was a real pain in the ass changing back, and then five years later I ended up going through it all over again. If it'd been legal to keep my maiden name back then, when I first married, and I'd know what a headache it was, I never would've changed it to start with."

His expression was taut when she looked at him. "So... it just all boils down to whatever happens to be convenient for you?"

She stared at him for a long moment. "Why don't you tell me

why, or what, we're really arguing about here? Because this is an argument, isn't it?"

He said nothing for several moments, merely studying her in tight-lipped silence. Finally, he scrubbed his hand along the stubble on his jaw. "We should go," he said shortly, pushing away from the wall.

They drove in silence. Amanda broke it when she saw the fast food sign two blocks from the office. "Just drop me up here."

He slid a speculative look in her direction. "Afraid to be seen getting out of my car this early in the morning?"

Amanda drew in a calming breath, trying to subdue the guilty blush she felt rising in her cheeks. "I thought I'd grab a bite to eat since it's still early," she lied.

He pulled into the drive through and ordered coffee and breakfast croissants for both of them--just to be an ass--then dropped her in front of the office. She stood on the sidewalk, her little paper bag and cup of coffee in her hands, watching him drive off.

When she turned toward the building, she looked up. Johnson was standing at the window of his office, staring down at the traffic, or, more specifically, watching Cole's car as it wove through morning traffic.

"Pure paranoia," Amanda muttered, balancing her breakfast as she entered the building and strode to the elevators.

Johnson was watching for her when she arrived in the office. He crooked his finger at her. "Could we have a word?"

"Let me just set this down in my office," she said, feeling a sinking of dread.

He was sitting behind his desk when she arrived. He motioned for her to take the seat before it. "Was that Macguire I saw dropping you off?"

She adopted a look of unconcern. She had a glib lie handy. "We car pooled today. He drove me down to the prison."

He nodded. "He's not coming in today?"

"Of course he is. He just… uh… he said something about an errand he had to take care of first."

He knew she was lying. She could tell by the way he was looking at her. "Any luck with the hearing?"

"You were right. I was too late."

He picked up a pen from his desk and began to study it. "There's always a chance that he didn't make parole."

"There's also a chance he did. We'll know in a few days."

He nodded, glanced at her speculatively and then looked down at his pen again. "I try to keep my nose out of other people's business, but I'm thinking if you happen to be seeing anybody right now, it might be a good time for it. I'd feel better knowing you weren't alone. I could get a patrol car to step up the drive bys in your area, but that won't deter Garner if he decides to make good on his threat."

A cold sweat washed over her. "It's been ten years. That's plenty of time to forget it."

"Unfortunately, prison inmates have a lot of time on their hands to mull over their sins--and their promises."

Amanda nodded jerkily and stood. "We'll just have to hope for the best."

"Just watch your back," he said, waving a hand in dismissal.

What little appetite she'd had had vanished during the course of their conversation, but Amanda dug the breakfast sandwich out and nibbled on it anyway while she played her voice mail from the day before.

The last message almost made her throw up.

"Hi, Mandy. A buddy of mine asked me to give you a call and let you know he's looking forward to seeing you real soon."

Chapter Nine

It said a lot for the level of fear Amanda was experiencing that two days passed before she tumbled to the fact that Cole was assiduously avoiding her. She was so busy watching the clock and waiting to learn whether or not Garner had been paroled, and then, when she learned he had, counting the time for processing and release, that she didn't think much about two no-shows in a row beyond a considerable amount of disappointment.

Wild sex would've been a welcome diversion and would've helped relieve her stress, if not her fear, but a warm body in her bed would've been even more welcome.

She'd thought, the night after their argument, that it was typical of men that they were never around when you really needed them, but he *had* been angry. She still wasn't entirely certain why. It hadn't been lost on her that he wasn't pleased about her long history with Gary. She just didn't see why it would matter to him. That was the past. It was over, regardless of what it might look like to him. And, in any case, *they* didn't have a relationship and he'd seemed content enough to leave it at casual sex.

The plain fact was, she missed him. In spite of all her rationalizations, she knew it meant more to her than just sex, casual or otherwise. They hadn't spent enough time together to get 'used' to it, and she shouldn't have been, and she'd thought she'd been guarding herself from getting too deeply involved. After two miserable days she was forced to admit she hadn't been, and she *wanted* to get used to having him around.

It was just as well. It had been a bad idea to start with.

Obviously, the sex had been better for her than it had been for him or he wouldn't have lost interest so quickly.

She decided just to let it slide. The main reason she'd been trying to avoid involvement to start with was because she didn't want her personal life to overlap her career. She didn't want to be involved in any embarrassing scenes at her work place, in front of her coworkers. She certainly wasn't going to say anything that might set one off.

The only thing that could really be said for abject terror was that it was impossible to maintain for any great length of time. It was just too intense an emotion. When a week passed and nothing happened, Amanda decided she'd allowed her imagination to run away with her. The message she'd gotten either hadn't had to do with Garner at all or he'd just done it to throw a scare into her without any real intention of following it up.

Misery was another matter. It seemed to grow with time. It might not have if she hadn't had to see him every single day, but she couldn't look at the cool, distant stranger without remembering the way he'd looked at her before.

It had been her call. She had no right to be upset, particularly when it seemed that it had been her fault he'd withdrawn. He'd known she didn't want to be seen getting out of his car so early in the morning that it was obvious they'd spent the night together and he hadn't liked it. It also seemed that he'd gotten the impression that she still had a 'thing' for her ex--maybe because she'd gotten irritated that he'd even asked?

Maybe he'd wanted more and he'd decided he didn't have a chance if he was going to be doing battle with her ghosts?

Right!

Most likely he'd just lost interest. Or, maybe, since they'd had several disagreements right in a row, he'd decided things were getting a little too emotional and it was time to bail?

Almost a week to the day after their mutually silent agreement to break things off, she arrived at the elevator to go home and discovered Cole was already waiting for it. She would've pretended she'd forgotten something and turned around and gone back to her office if anyone else had been waiting at the elevator, making it unlikely he'd notice her reluctance to share such cramped quarters with him. By the time it had occurred to her, however, that it was going to be even worse when it was just the two of them in that cramped little box, the elevator had arrived.

I can do this, she thought, taking a deep breath as if she was diving into a pool and stepping onto the elevator. After wracking her brain to try to think of something inane that she could say to support her 'I'm totally cool with this' act, and drawing a blank, she glanced at him. He glanced at her at the same moment. She pasted a fake smile on her lips. "God, it's been hot lately, hasn't it?"

As absolutely stupid as the remark was, he didn't so much as crack a smile.

She looked away uncomfortably, staring at the digits that displayed the floor number that they were passing and wondering just how long the damn elevator was going to take to get to the parking garage.

"Hell!" he ground out.

Amanda looked down at his briefcase when it hit the floor of the elevator and then glanced up at his face just in time to see him surge toward her. He absorbed her gasp of surprise with his mouth as he pinned her against the wall of the elevator. If she'd been hit with a hundred ten volts of electricity at that moment, it couldn't have stunned her more, or fried any more brain cells. His tongue, skating possessively across hers, set her on fire.

He caught her waist, lifting her up and perching her buttocks on the handrail and then pinning her there by driving his hips against hers. The hard ridge of his cock dug into her cleft as he thrust against her. Blood flooded her labia, bringing it to throbbing sensitivity and the moisture of desire followed.

"I thought I could do this," he muttered as he lifted his lips from hers and gnawed a path across her cheek and down her neck.

She moaned in pleasure as he sucked a love bite along the

curve where her neck joined her shoulder. "I've missed… you," she whispered dizzily.

He stiffened at that and lifted his head, his face taut as he studied her. After a moment, very deliberately, he ground his cock against her again, watching her face. She tightened her arms around his neck, leaning toward him to trace the swirls of his ear with her tongue. "This too," she murmured.

A shudder traveled through him. "What happened to 'let's keep this simple'?"

She leaned back to study his face. "I hadn't counted on you being more than a pretty face," she said, smiling faintly.

He grinned, nudging her nose with the tip of his. "No?"

She ran her tongue along his lips. He opened his mouth, sucking it in and sending currents of fire through her blood stream.

The ding of the elevator startled both of them. He released her abruptly. Her feet had barely settled on the elevator floor when the doors began to open. Adjusting himself, Cole leaned down and swept his briefcase from the floor, holding it in front of him.

Amanda found it amusing until it occurred to her that her face was stinging from whisker burn and her suit was rumpled. Looking down, she moved hastily out of the elevator as two people got on.

Cole caught up to her at her car. Pushing her against the door, he kissed her thoroughly before he released her and allowed her to get in. "I'll meet you at your place."

To her surprise, he followed her. She'd expected him to swing by his place first to change.

He slipped an arm around her, pulling her tightly against him and lowering his mouth to hers before they were halfway through the door. They stumbled through, falling back against the wall.

Cole kicked the door closed with his foot. Catching her hand, he guided it to his genitals, cupping it around his erection. She stroked his cock as he caressed her tongue with his own in a deep, thorough kiss. Finally, he tore his mouth from hers and kissed her neck. "What would you like first? A little piece of meat about this size?" he asked hoarsely as he pressed her palm against his cock. "Or dinner?"

She snorted. "*This* isn't little--I'll take the meat, thank you."

He chuckled. "Smart girl! But I'm saving it for desert. I've got to keep my strength up." He slipped his hand down over her hips and squeezed a buttock, then slapped it lightly. "Get dressed. I'm taking you out."

Amanda looked up at him, torn between amusement and irritation. "We could always have an appetizer, then go out, and then desert."

He kissed her. "I don't want interruptions."

That sounded promising. "Since you put it that way… dressy? Or casual?"

He studied her a long moment. "Dressy. I haven't seen you in anything slinky yet."

Chuckling, she left him and went into her room to pick out something 'slinky'. When she'd chosen the dress, she laid it on the bed and went into the bathroom to take a quick shower.

She'd already undressed before she noticed a pair of her panties lying on the vanity top of the lavatory. She frowned, but dismissed it, deciding she'd tossed them toward the clothes hamper and missed.

As she stepped out of the shower ten minutes later, however, and glanced at the foggy mirror above the lavatory, her heart just seemed to stop in her chest. Someone had been in her home. Someone had taken their finger and written a single word on the mirror. 'Cunt!' Below it was what looked like the imprint of a tongue.

Chapter Ten

How long she remained frozen in place, simply staring at the mirror, she had no idea. Eventually, however, she glanced down at the panties lying on the lavatory. Feeling as if she would pass out, or throw up, she took a step closer.

Someone had masturbated on her panties.

Panic freed her body from its frozen state and she turned blindly and fled the bathroom. Cole was pacing her bedroom. When she opened the door he turned to look at her.

Her mouth worked but she couldn't seem to get a sound out.

He stared at her for a long moment and abruptly strode toward her, grabbing her and pulling her close. "What is it?"

It took her several tries to get anything past the knot of terror in her throat. "The mirror."

Cole walked her to the bed and pushed her down on the edge. "Stay here. Don't move."

She nodded jerkily. Her teeth were chattering. She looked down numbly at the water still dripping off of her and wrapped her arms around herself.

Cole went into the bathroom, paused for several moments, apparently studying the mirror. Then she heard him checking the window. He came out of the bathroom several moments later, his face grim, his hands shoved into his pants pockets. "The window's locked."

Noticing she was shivering, he turned abruptly and went back in the bathroom. Returning a few minutes later with a towel he draped in over her shoulders. "Stay here while I check the rest of the house."

"B...be c...careful."

She watched while he checked the windows in her room, then the closets. When he'd left the room, she gathered the towel tightly around herself and got down on her knees to make certain he wasn't under the bed.

She knew it was Garner.

He wouldn't be in the house. He was playing a cat and mouse game with her. He wanted to torment her for a while before he got around to torturing her to death.

"He came in through the back," Cole said, coming back into the room.

She nodded. "It was him. It was Lyle Garner."

He moved toward her, gathering her against him as he sat on the edge of the bed. "You don't know that."

"I do! You think that's just a coincidence in there? He had a cell buddy call me right after the hearing to tell me he was coming to see me."

"You didn't tell me that. Why didn't you say something?"

She gave him a look. "You weren't talking to me. I figured it was my problem. It *is* my problem."

He caught her face between his palms. "It's our problem. I'm not going to let anything happen to you. Whatever it takes, I swear to you I won't let him hurt you."

Amanda slid her arms around his neck, burying her face against his shoulder. He stroked her back soothingly and finally nudged her chin up and kissed her. She shuddered as heat went through her, thawing the ice in her soul. Acute desperation seized her as his heat and scent flooded her senses. Shifting, she straddled his lap as she sucked hungrily on his tongue, rocking her hips against him as she felt his cock become engorged in response, pressing up into her cleft.

He caught the fever, kissing her with equal fervor, delving his tongue into her mouth to stroke her intimately, and then moving over her face and her throat with hot, opened mouthed kisses that sent quakes of delight through her.

She reached between them, tugging at the fastening of his trousers with shaking hands. The zipper resisted her efforts, and finally she shoved her hand beneath his waistband, grasping his cock tightly and massaging him.

He gasped, released her long enough to push her hand away and unzip his trousers and then caught her buttocks in his hands, pressing her tightly down against him and then loosening his hold in a kneading motion that drove them both beyond the edge of control.

Grasping his turgid flesh once more, Amanda lifted up and aligned their bodies, impaling herself on his throbbing shaft. He caught her hips, guiding her as their flesh merged, expelling a hissing noise of pain and frustration as her flesh clenched him so tightly it impeded his possession. Lifting her away slightly, he bore down on her hips again, thrusting upward, groaning. "Baby, you're so tight," he growled hoarsely, squeezing his eyes tightly shut. "I feel like I'm going to come now."

Amanda shuddered, feeling her body clench and spasm at his words. Panting, she lifted away and pressed downward again until she could feel him filling her to her depths.

They paused, panting, exchanging heated kisses.

Wrapping his arms tightly around her, he bore down on her hips, sinking deeper still. It tore a groan of pleasure from her. A tremor went through her. She felt her body quaking on the verge of release. Lifting her slightly, he thrust upward again and then groaned as if he was dying and began arching against her in short, hard thrusts that sent her spiraling into ecstatic oblivion. She went limp against him as he plunged deeply inside her and then went still, holding her tightly and gasping hoarsely as he struggled to catch his breath.

After a moment, he fell back against the bed, carrying her with him. She snuggled her face against his neck, breathing his scent, feeling his heat wash the last vestiges of terror and revulsion from her, replacing them with warmth, satiation and a comforting sense of safety.

He stroked her back comfortingly. "I'm sorry, baby."

She shivered. "It's better now."

"I'll make it up to you. I just couldn't hold it."

She lifted her head and looked at him blankly. "Hold what?"

"I didn't mean to leave you hanging."

It dawned on her then what he was talking about. Chuckling, she snuggled against him again. "You didn't leave me."

He rolled over so that she was lying on her back and levered away from her to study her face. "You're just saying that so I won't feel like such an ass."

She lifted a hand to stroke his cheek. "I'm saying it because it's true. And I wouldn't think you were an ass even if you hadn't satisfied me. I'd just make you do it again until you got it right."

He smiled faintly. "Would you?"

She sighed, lying back against the bed and covering her eyes with her arm. "I just needed you inside of me."

He climbed further into the bed, pulled her close and then dragged the cover over her. "I'm not going to let anything happen to you, baby. I promise."

It made her feel good to hear him say it. His tall, muscular physique comforted her with his strength, but he had no idea of what they were dealing with and she was as afraid that he would be hurt as she was fearful for herself. She molded herself tightly against him. "Garner isn't a man, Cole. He's monster."

"Even monsters have their weaknesses," he said after a moment.

She dragged in a shaky breath. "I got him convicted on rape, but I know that was just the tip of the iceberg. We just couldn't pin anything else on him."

Lifting away from her slightly, Cole reached for a pillow and thrust it beneath his head. "Did it ever occur to you that, maybe, if you couldn't find evidence, that the only thing he was guilty of was the rape he was convicted on?"

"If you'd seen the woman after he got through with her there'd be no doubt in your mind that she wasn't his first, either," Amanda said, sitting up. A shiver skated down her spine and she pulled the coverlet over her shoulders, hugging it to her. "She wasn't his girlfriend. This wasn't an isolated case of a man loosing it and beating his girlfriend nearly to death.

"She'd come here from out west somewhere, searching for her sister. Her sister and her baby had gone missing and she was convinced Lyle Garner was responsible. She'd been trying to track him down for years to find out what happened to her sister. We'd found her sister almost fifteen years earlier, but the body was mutilated beyond identification with the means available at the time and she'd been tagged as a Jane Doe and buried. The baby was never found. Nobody even knew there was supposed to be a baby until the sister showed up, so no one ever looked."

Cole sat up, adjusted himself and fastened his trousers. "What makes you think he had anything to do with the Jane Doe?"

"The Jane Doe was his ex-wife. From what her sister said, he'd nearly beat her to death several times before she managed to escape him. She moved away, started a new life and then one day she just disappeared. It doesn't strike you as just being too much of a coincidence that she was found murdered right here?"

Cole looked ill. She didn't blame him. It made her skin crawl just thinking about the man. "But you couldn't find any evidence linking him to the murder?"

She shook her head. "The body had been in the water for almost a week. Anything that might have been on it had long since washed away. Forensics was barely a hope back then anyway. Her hands and feet had been cut off, so there was no way to get prints, not that they would've done us any good anyway since she didn't have any kind of record. Her head had been cut off, too--no way to identify her with dental records. If not for the sister's determination, we would probably never have identified her."

Cole frowned. "If the body was in such bad shape, how did the sister identify her?"

"They'd taken photos. She had a unique tattoo. Just above her pubic bone were the words 'eight ball's cunt'.

Chapter Eleven

Cole scrubbed his hands over his face and finally dropped his arm across his eyes. He said nothing and finally Amanda lay down beside him once more, slipping her arm across his chest. He jumped when she first touched him, stiffening, and she hesitated. After a moment, however, his hand closed over hers, squeezed it and then he pulled her closer.

"What happened to the woman he raped?"

"She still lives here."

"Shouldn't she be notified that he's been released?"

Amanda shrugged. "I'm sure notice was sent. I don't know how much good it did. She's not... right anymore."

He fell silent again and she wondered what was going through his mind.

"What are you going to do about the break in?"

"Report it," she said promptly. "Not that it's likely to do much good."

"It'll get him off the streets."

"I doubt he left any evi--" Amanda broke off, sitting bolt upright and then scrambling off the bed and heading toward the bathroom. She was back in a moment. "The panties are gone."

"What panties?" Cole asked, sitting up.

"The ones on the vanity. He left semen on them."

"I bagged them."

Amanda stared at him uncomprehendingly for several moments. When it did sink in that he'd moved the evidence, for whatever reason, she was still stunned. "You shouldn't have moved them at all."

His lips tightened at the note of accusation in her voice. "I wasn't thinking straight. I just didn't want anything to happen to the evidence--this isn't going to get him off the street long, you know. It certainly won't keep him off."

"If I can prove he broke into my home they'll revoke his parole."

He sighed and got off the bed. "You get dressed. I'll call the cops."

It was nearly midnight by the time the police finished investigating the scene and questioning them. An APB was put out to pick Garner up but Amanda was far from satisfied. Now that she'd had time to calm down and consider things more rationally, it had begun to sink in that Garner had been too easy to catch.

When the police had finally left, she glanced at Cole, wondering if she looked as haggard as he did. "It was too easy," he said, echoing her previous thoughts.

"What do you mean?"

"Don't you think he's too cunning to leave evidence behind that would get him thrown right back in jail?"

Amanda stared at him, feeling her heart sink. "You think it wasn't his semen?"

"Honestly? I don't think it was semen at all."

Until he'd said it, she hadn't considered that she hadn't actually looked that closely at the panties. She'd been so terrified when she realized Garner had been in her house and so frightened by the connotations of his message, she'd assumed that what she'd seen was semen. She hadn't stopped to consider that Garner hadn't even left semen at the rape scene. He'd worn a condom and he'd sanitized with bleach when he'd finished.

The following morning, as she was getting ready for work, Amanda got a call from the police station. They'd picked Garner up and brought him in for questioning. She called her boss and explained the situation, then rode down to the station with Cole.

She was standing in the hallway when they took Garner from his holding cell to an interrogation room. He leered at her and Cole as he passed them, his eyes gleaming with malicious amusement as he looked them over.

Naturally, he disclaimed any knowledge of the incident. She watched for a while through the one way mirror, but it became obvious he wasn't going to make a mistake and let them trip him. Finally, frustrated and depressed, she decided to go on in to work.

She got a call just before she left the office that Garner had been released. The results had come back from the lab and the substance on the panties had not been semen. There were no fingerprints and Garner had an alibi.

She'd been expecting it all day and she still felt the urge to cry out of sheer frustration.

Instead of starting the car once they'd settled inside, Cole turned to study her. "Why don't we drive over and talk to this woman you were telling me about?"

She shook her head. "Gayle Carlson? I doubt if it would do any good."

He shrugged. "It couldn't hurt."

When they arrived at the nursing home and asked to visit Gayle, the nurse looked them over suspiciously. "She doesn't get many visitors."

"We're from the DA's office. We just want to talk to her for a few minutes."

The woman studied their ID's, but she didn't look terribly impressed. "You're not likely to get anything out of her, particularly if he goes in. She doesn't react well to men."

Cole's lips tightened. "I'd like to see her just the same. If it upsets her, I'll leave."

Finally, the woman walked them to Gayle's room. She made them wait in the hall while she went in to speak to her and explain that she had visitors. When she came out again, she nodded. "She's already had her medication for the evening. She won't be awake long."

"We won't take long," Amanda assured the woman again.

When the nurse finally left them, Amanda pushed the door open slowly and went in.

Gayle Carlson was sitting up on the edge of the bed, her feet dangling over the side. She looked up at them as they came in. Amanda heard Cole's sharp intake of breath and her hand tightened on his. "Ms. Carlson? I'm Amanda Fitzgerald and this is Cole Macguire. We're from the DA's office. I hate to bother you but we wanted to ask you just a few questions if you're willing."

She was blind in one eye. One side of her face had been crushed, the bones too shattered to heal in any semblance of normalcy. The blow to that side of her face had damaged her eye so badly she'd lost the use of it. The other half of face was paralyzed from the brain damage, which had given it a mask like quality since she had difficulty forming expressions. She turned her head sideways to peer at them through her good eye.

To Amanda's surprise and dismay, tears gathered in the woman's good eye. "Danny?" she asked in a slurred voice.

Cole halted abruptly, staring at the woman stone faced.

Amanda followed the woman's gaze to Cole and then back again. "It's all right," she whispered to Cole. "You remind her of someone, that's all." Releasing his hand, she moved a little closer to the woman. "Ms. Carlson, I'm Amanda Fitzgerald. Do you remember talking to me a long time ago? After you were... after you were hurt?"

"I'm going to wait outside," Cole said abruptly, his voice strained and harsh.

He strode from the room before Amanda could do more than glance toward him in consternation.

She found him an hour later, propped against the hood of the car, staring into the distance with an indecipherable look on his face. She didn't need to be able to read it, however, to have a fair idea of what was going through his mind. Her work was making her far too callous. She should have realized that the woman's appearance was liable to throw Cole for a loop. It had stunned her the first time she'd seen the woman and she had no childhood horrors to be resurrected by such a sight. "You okay?"

He glanced toward her when she spoke but he still had a faraway look in his eyes as he caught her hand and dragged her into his arms. Considering the difficult interview she'd just conducted, she was grateful for the comfort of a hug, but she knew Cole needed it more than she did and it warmed her immeasurably that he was willing to seek comfort from her. "It bothered you that she thought she recognized you, didn't it?"

He shuddered, gasped several deep, shuddering breaths as if he'd been holding it in. After a moment, however, he seemed to shake off the images that were troubling him. "It's hard to believe anybody could have survived what she must have gone through."

Amanda felt a shudder run through her as his words evoked the memory. "It was purest luck that she survived. Someone heard her screaming and finally got around to calling the police, otherwise I don't think he would've left until he was sure she was completely dead--or maybe he thought she was and he was in too big a hurry to leave to check.

"I know it sounds cruel but I think she's better off that she hasn't got much mind left. She hardly knows what's going on and she doesn't remember the attack itself. If it had been me, though, I'd rather be dead."

"How did you even convict him of rape and assault if she was your only witness?"

Cole asked harshly.

"It was mostly circumstantial. I told you, he doesn't leave evidence behind, despite the brutality of his attacks. Ms. Carlson had been at the police station and talked to the detectives several times about him, so they knew she'd been looking for him. She'd identified her sister's remains. He didn't have an alibi. He'd been spotted in the area and... she screamed hysterically when she saw him and kept on screaming until they took her out of the room.

"The judge was not happy with me and threatened a mistrial, but I managed to convince him I'd had no idea she would react so violently to seeing him and that, as the victim, she should be allowed to testify in the only way she was capable of. She convinced the jury that we had the right man. It didn't take them an hour to deliberate."

He nodded, still looking pale and sick to his stomach. Finally, he redirected his thoughts to their reason for coming. "Did you get anything useful?"

Amanda sighed and shook her head. "I couldn't get her to talk about anything but her sister, poor thing. She must have had her on her mind when we came in."

Cole swallowed audibly. "What was her sister's name?"

"Danny. Actually, Danielle, but she called her Danny."

Chapter Twelve

When Cole's belongings began to appear in her house, Amanda didn't know whether to be touched, amused or irritated. She thought she would've been happy to have him in her bed even if not for the terror that waited for her in the night. Under the circumstances, he was more than welcome to camp on her doorstep, but even so, the subtle invasion wasn't something she'd anticipated and it gave her a sense of mounting dread that she was being built up to take a huge fall.

Some of it was to be expected, of course, when he spent more time at her house than in his apartment. He was determined to guard her, and it was certainly not convenient for him to sleep in her bed, then get up and go his apartment each morning to get ready for work. She completely understood that and had suggested it would be more convenient for him to bring enough of his belongings over that he didn't have to go to his apartment every day.

By the time he'd made his third trip to his apartment and back to hers, however, she discovered that everything was coming in and nothing was going out again--which wasn't that difficult to see since it arrived in boxes and stayed that way. After staring at the boxes for nearly two weeks, she asked him if he wouldn't prefer to clean out her ex-husband's closet and use that for storage.

She didn't think he particularly cared whether he lived out of boxes or not, but the closet obviously still rankled. He was more than happy to clean everything out of it and pile it on the curb for garbage pickup. Instead of making a big deal out of him throwing away such expensive clothing, she removed it from the curb and took it down to Goodwill and they were both satisfied.

She was glad enough to know that if Garner should decide to pay her another visit, she wouldn't be alone in the house, but it complicated the relationship between her and Cole even further. They'd never actually established boundaries and she still wasn't sure whether this was fuck buddy plus guard, or fuck buddy turned boyfriend, temporary, or semi-permanent.

Should she throw her whole heart into it? Or should she remain guardedly optimistic?

It was difficult to decide, but she finally realized that emotions weren't something a person could decide on. You felt them, or you didn't. Logic didn't enter in to it.

Two weeks after the break in, her uneasiness about the direction her personal life had taken was overshadowed by Garner once more when Johnson called her into his office.

Amanda knew the moment she opened the door that the news was grim. Johnson was standing at his office window, looking down at the street and he didn't bother to invite her to sit. He turned at her entrance, his expression grave. "I got a call from the police. They've discovered a body. Sounds to me like it's got all the earmarks of Garner's MO. I want you to get down there and keep an eye on things while they're processing the scene. They're not going to like it, but they've got to process it from the perspective of a fresh case and you might notice something they miss that would help us pin it to Garner... Take Macguire with you."

When she and Cole arrived at the scene, the body was being brought up the river bank. Amanda's heart sank. The river would most likely have cleaned away anything the killer had left behind, even assuming he had. Dumping the body in the river fit what they suspected as Garner's profile, but then he wasn't by any means the only killer who made a habit of dumping his victims in bodies of water when he was done with them.

She stopped the MT's when they reached the ambulance and had them open the body bag for a look. She felt faint when the MT whipped the plastic back. There just was no bracing oneself for that kind of sight and, as gruesome as some of the murders had been that she'd prosecuted, she didn't usually see the actual body. Pictures, however horribly detailed, weren't the same as seeing the work of a murderer face to face.

Swallowing with an effort, she focused on what she was looking for and checked the body over, nodding at the MT when she was finished. "At least it shouldn't be too difficult to identify her."

"No problem with that," the MT said matter-of-factly. "She had an ID on her."

Amanda exchanged a glance with Cole and turned to survey the investigation team on the riverbank below them.

"Is it his MO?"

She glanced at Cole. "The problem is, we don't have a complete profile on him. She's still got her head, and her hands and feet from what I could see, but then Danielle Johnson had been married to him. He was obliged to know we'd look at her husband and ex-husband first."

"She'd remarried?" Cole asked sharply, his voice sounding strange.

Amanda had just taken a cautious step on the sloping embankment. Despite the odd note in his voice, she was more focused on trying to keep from slipping than what he'd asked. "A couple of years before she went missing," she said absently, wondering if it might be best after all to wait until the detectives came back up. There wasn't much of a scene for them to investigate from what she could see, nor much to be overlooked.

She finally decided to wait and talk to the lead detective first and see what she could find out. When the investigation team had cleared out, she could go down and look around then.

That way, if she busted her ass, she wouldn't have nearly as big an audience.

Fifteen minutes later, the team started up the embankment. Amanda headed the detective off. "You the ADA Captain Bernard told me about?"

She nodded, studying him expectantly. He wasn't familiar to her and she wondered if he'd just transferred from somewhere else, just made detective, or if she simply hadn't run into him before. Her first assessment was that he was good at his job because he was meticulous and focused. He didn't like anybody getting in his way, especially not somebody from the DA's office.

And he despised having to work with women, particularly if they happened to hold a job he considered superior to his own.

Nothing he did or said after that quick assessment caused her to revise her opinion.

"Well, what's your take on it? Does it look like your man?"

"It's hard to say absolutely. The condition of the body looks enough like the one we put him away for--except she survived the torture and beating. The victim we believe he murdered was found in the river, and in pretty much the same condition as your victim, except he'd decapitated her and removed the hands and feet. The MT said you had an ID on this one?"

He nodded and motioned for her to follow him to the van. Dumping the evidence bags on the carpet, he shuffled through them and handed her a small plastic bag containing a driver's license. Amanda felt the first finger of coldness creep up her spine when she looked at the woman's picture. By the time she'd finished reading the woman's stats, she was shivering. "I think it's a good probability that this is Garner's work."

The detective took the ID and studied it doubtfully. "You got that from the ID? You *are* good."

Amanda's lips tightened at the edge of sarcasm in his voice. "Brenda Donaldson; five foot four inches, one hundred thirty pounds; thirty four years old; blond hair; blue eyes--," she quoted. "I'm thirty seven. I have blond hair, blue eyes. I'm five three and I weigh a hundred twenty pounds. It's a message--for me."

The detective looked her up and down with more interest this time. "The stats look close."

"She is… *was* a lawyer. That's a little too close for my comfort, all things considered."

The detective sighed irritably. "I'm going to be honest with you. We went over the body and everything that washed up with it. I'm guessing the lab isn't going to come up with much for us. She was reported missing about a week ago, so we know she hasn't been in the water more than that, but I don't know how close they'll be able to pin down the time of death… which could help us calculate where she went in and might give us more leads. Right now we don't have any.

"We'll pick him up for questioning, but unless he decides to do us a favor and confess, I don't know if we'll be able to find anything to hold him on."

"I know it was him," she said when she and Cole were in the car once more. "I feel it in my gut."

"Unfortunately, that isn't going to get a conviction."

Amanda sent him a look, but then sighed. He was right, of course. She'd been convinced Garner was a serial killer when she convicted him of rape and assault ten years earlier. "When we were investigating him before, we tracked down five other murders and a half a dozen rapes over a twenty year period that were similar--besides Danielle and her sister. Three of them had been attributed to other perps, but there wasn't enough evidence on any of them to do us any good. I think I'm going to contact them again and see it there was any biological evidence collected that might still be in good enough shape to run DNA on it."

Cole remained thoughtfully silent until they reached the office once more. When she went directly to Johnson's office to speak to him about what they'd found, he followed her, listening while she went over her findings and her plans. It wasn't until she'd finished, however, that he finally spoke.

"I've been giving a lot of thought to this situation with Garner. I have an idea. I'm not particularly happy with it, but I believe it'll work."

Amanda exchanged a glance with Johnson and gave Cole her full attention.

Cole rubbed his lower lip with his thumb thoughtfully for several moments and finally sat forward, dropping his elbows on his knees. "Amanda may or may not be right about Garner, but if she is, that presents us with two problems. One, sooner or later, he's going to come after her, and we don't know when or where that might happen, which decreases our chances of preventing it. And two, if we continue to make things hot here, he's going to decide to move on to new hunting grounds.

"We need to come up with a game plan to flush him out at a time and place of our choosing."

Chapter Thirteen

The police department did their part and Garner ceased to be amused after he was dragged in for questioning on five different occasions within a three week period. After three weeks of constant surveillance they made no attempt to hide, two searches of his apartment and the three twelve hour detainments for questioning, they withdrew and waited to see if they'd harassed him enough to goad him into making a mistake.

When two weeks passed and nothing happened, even Amanda began to have doubts that he would go for the bait. She wasn't surprised when, little by little, everyone else relaxed their guard and began turning their attention elsewhere.

As her own fear and focus on danger began to wane, she realized she had other problems close to home. With much the same subtle inevitability that Cole had found his way into her bed, and then into her home, he'd caught her with her defenses down and burrowed under her skin.

It might have taken her much longer to realize it if not for the fact that diminished fear meant greater awareness elsewhere. When it finally dawned on her that Cole was deeply troubled, fear of a different kind surfaced, bringing it forcefully home that she hadn't just grown accustomed to having Cole around. She supposed she'd put his behavior down to worry to begin with since it would be natural to be concerned about his own hide as well as hers with a threat like Garner hanging over them. As staunchly determined as he seemed to be to protect her, he knew what they suspected Garner of, and he wasn't young enough to think he was invincible.

She still thought that was probably a good bit of it. It was the unknown part that worried her. She'd spent more of her adult life with her ex-husband than any other man, but she'd certainly been around enough men to know the signs of 'moving on'--emotional withdrawal was often the first.

She wasn't convinced that that was it, but she didn't know whether it was really a lack of conviction or hopefulness. Cole had never actually been very open with her to begin with. She hadn't encouraged him to be. She'd been too focused on trying to keep an emotional distance herself.

Now, she couldn't even look back and determine whether it was a slow change, a rapid one, or if there'd been no change at all and he'd been emotionally distant from the beginning.

She very much feared, however, that their relationship was slowly winding down to a close and now that it appeared that way, she realized she wanted a lot more than just a casual fling.

The problem was, she didn't know how to go about getting what she wanted. There was only one real way to a man's heart--comfort, which seemed simple enough except that everyone had their own definition of comfort.

Making love should have topped the list, she figured, especially with a man Cole's age. She could see no notable lessening in his desire for her--in fact it was almost the opposite. The more distant he became emotionally, the more desperate and wild their lovemaking and she began to worry whether the desperation she sensed was an effort to hold onto the fire they'd had to begin with. If it was, however, she certainly knew of no way to change it. She'd tried everything her fertile mind could suggest, and yet he was no more inclined to cuddle her afterwards, or allow her to cuddle him than he had been to begin with. It was almost as if he'd felt himself slipping and dropping his guard and had set out to try to cut the tentative bond they'd formed.

She wished she could just put it down to a disinclination to cuddle. A lot of men really didn't want to be bothered with that after sex. They were relaxed. They just wanted to cool down and go to sleep.

Although he had consoled her after the break in and after the distress of speaking with Garner's victim, Cole seemed disinclined to touch her at any time unless he was fucking her senseless--or asleep. When he was asleep, he sprawled all over her.

Finally, she reached the point where she felt like she simply had to know one way or the other. She didn't want to go on for weeks more, getting deeper and deeper and waiting for the ax to fall. Either it was something they could work out, or something they couldn't, but she couldn't stand the suspense anymore.

Instead of allowing him to distract her, or drag her off to bed the moment they came in from dinner one evening, she stiffened her spine and held him at arm's length. "We need to talk."

He gave her a wary look. "About anything in particular?"

Amanda shook her head in irritation. She was going to have to pry it out of him if she got anything at all. "Something's wrong. I wish you'd just tell me what it is."

Frowning, he moved away from her, heading toward the kitchen. "I think I'll have a beer. Want one?"

The comment surprised her. He hardly ever drank. He generally kept a six pack in the refrigerator, but that would usually last him a week or more and he'd already had two at the restaurant. After a moment, she followed him into the kitchen, frowning as she watched him pop the tab and take a long draught from the can. "You're scaring me," she said finally. "This isn't… like you."

He glanced at her guiltily, but in the next moment the 'curtain' came down, that wall he had a way of putting up anytime he felt threatened. "How would you know?"

Amanda blinked at him in confusion. "How would I know, what?"

He studied her a long moment and finally left the kitchen

heading for the living room. She hesitated, wondering if she should just let it go until he was more sober. Three beers wasn't a lot, except when a person wasn't used to drinking three. Finally she decided to make at least one more attempt.

He was sprawled on the sofa, the remote in his hand. When she arrived, he'd just turned the TV on full blast.

"Don't."

He slid a speculative glance at her and finally clicked the power off button and set the remote down.

"You're suggesting I don't know you?"

He propped his feet on the coffee table, crossing his legs. She ignored it, knowing he was trying to be deliberately provoking to distract her. "I didn't 'suggest' it."

Sighing, Amanda sat down on the edge of the coffee table, facing him. "I don't know a lot of facts, that's true--you've never seemed to want to talk about your past--but I've known you long enough and lived with you long enough to know you."

"And what do you think about this facade? Do you like it? Or do you think you might like another one better?"

The comments made Amanda's heart skip several uncomfortable beats. She knew, suddenly, that at least part of his problem *was* his past. Scars like the ones he had to be carrying around didn't heal--ever. They might heal over, but they went right down to the soul and there were any number of things that could rip the tender, healing flesh away and leave a deep, gaping wound exposed to pain once more.

The question was, what had opened them? Her? Was it something she'd done? Something she'd said? She'd thought it best to leave it alone. If and when he felt like talking about it, he would. If he didn't, then he wasn't ready to and forcing him to confront it wasn't going to help him.

Was it just the threat of any kind of relationship at all?

Now was certainly not the time to tell him that she knew enough about his past that she believed she knew the real him.

She swallowed with an effort. "I love everything about you-- from your crooked, hairy toes to the funny little cow lick on the crown of your head."

His face twisted with so much pain that she thought for a moment that he would cry. In the next moment, however, he had himself firmly under control once more. "You love what you see," he said dismissively, almost accusingly.

Amanda felt like crying herself. "Do you really think I'm that shallow?"

Instead of answering, he merely looked at her steadily for several moments and then finished his beer. When he stood up and went into the kitchen for another one, she got up and went to bed.

She was still wide awake, however, when she heard the voices.

She sat up, but she couldn't make out anything that was being said, only that both were male and one was Cole's voice. She'd already climbed out of bed to go investigate when she heard the distinctive smacking sound of flesh against flesh.

Chapter Fourteen

By the time Amanda made it to the living room, there was a full scale fight in progress. Her heart slammed into her ribcage when she saw that Cole and Garner were locked in a death match on the floor beside the overturned coffee table. For several moments, she was so petrified she couldn't seem to will herself even to move.

Cole was younger and well muscled, but Garner was heavier and by far meaner--and Cole had been drinking. That realization galvanized her. She wasn't about to wait around to see which one of them would be victorious.

Glancing around for a weapon, Amanda finally surged toward the two men rolling around on the floor and grabbed the metal table lamp, yanking it out of the wall. The moment she did, she realized she'd royally fucked up. The room went black and she could no longer see anything that was happening, let alone find her target.

Turning, she groped her way blindly toward the wall, but she realized even as she finally found it that the lamp she was holding was the one controlled by the light switch. The room had no overhead light. Struggling to tamp her fear down and tune out the horrendous crashes and grunts and growls, she closed her eyes, trying to remember exactly where the other lamp was in relation to her position. Finally, it occurred to her that the kitchen light would probably provide enough illumination to see well enough to at least find the other lamp.

As familiar as she was with her home, however, she wasn't

used to negotiating it in the dark. It took her longer than it should have to find the kitchen door and the switch beside it. Even as she flicked it on and blinding florescent lights flooded the room and the hallway, spilling into the open door of the living room, she heard a sickening thud followed by the sound of a falling body.

She arrived at the living room door once more in time to see Garner standing over Cole's prostrate form, a bloodied log from the basket beside the fireplace in his hand. She screamed, in both fear and rage. "You bastard!"

He turned at the sound of her voice, but she was faster. She'd already covered the distance that separated them, the lamp swung back to deliver the hardest blow she was capable of. She caught him along the side of his head. His head jerked sideways. His knees wobbled and he pitched to one side. "I'll kill you, you son of a bitch!" she screamed, leaping after him and raising the lamp again, intent on beating his head to a bloody mass of pulpy gray matter. He grunted when she landed on top of him, but he managed to get his arm up before she could hit him again. The lamp connected with the meaty part of his forearm. He let out a satisfying yelp of pain, but unfortunately, it wasn't as debilitating as she'd hoped.

She wasn't nearly as strong as he was. She opted for speed instead and began hammering at him with the lamp in swift, short strokes. He managed to deflect the blows by covering his head with his arms. She couldn't hit him hard enough to break bones and she couldn't reach any target, except his head, that the lamp might actually be effective on.

It occurred to her belatedly, that all he had to do was to wait until she'd worn herself out battering at him. At almost the same moment the thought blossomed in her mind, he made his move, striking at her with one arm while he continued to shield his face and skull with the other. He caught her along her side hard enough to unseat her.

She rolled as she struck the floor but she lost her grip on her weapon as she slammed against the sofa. He dove on top of her, forcing the air from her lungs with the impact. Before she could recover sufficiently to find the lamp again, he caught her around the throat and began squeezing. Instinctively, she grabbed his hands, trying to pry his fingers loose so that she could breathe.

Blackness was already clouding her mind when the pressure stopped abruptly. She coughed, gagged for breath as she tried to drag air through her bruised larynx. Finally, still disoriented, still trying to bring her vision into focus, she turned to see what had drawn Garner off of her. Dimly, she saw that Cole had gripped Garner from behind in a headlock. Blood ran down his head and into his eyes. She could see, however, that he was struggling as hard to remain conscious as he was to hold on to Garner. Garner's face was red, but it seemed unlikely Cole had the strength at the moment to hold onto him long enough to render him unconscious.

Groping around on the floor blindly, her fingers finally connected with the lamp and she grasped it and staggered to her feet. Gripping it tightly by the narrow end, she moved unsteadily toward the two men. She realized, however, that she couldn't swing at Garner's head without the risk of hitting Cole again. Instead, she swung it at his ribs. It connected with a satisfying thunk against one of his ribs, but before she could draw back to swing at him again, he caught the lamp, snatching it from her hand.

She screamed as he swung it toward Cole's head, leaping to catch Garner's arm. Her fingernails dug into the arm she gripped frantically, carving four gashes, but she didn't manage to deflect the blow that she could see. He slammed the metal against Cole three times before Cole's grip loosened and he began to slide toward the floor.

"Cole!" Amanda screamed, ignoring Garner and surging toward Cole to try to catch him as he fell. Garner seized a fistful of her hair as she tried to move past him, yanking her to a halt, then dragged her backwards. When she fell, he gripped her around the waist, snatched her off her feet and tossed her through the air. She hit the back of the sofa and rebounded onto the cushions. Before she could recover enough to try to roll off, he landed on top of her. Straddling her hips, he sat up, ignoring the punches she threw at him as he took the lamp, examined it almost calmly and tore the cord from it.

Seeing his intent, she fought harder, but he managed to loop the cord around one wrist anyway, squeezing the cord so tightly her wrist went numb almost instantly. Lifting away from her, he rolled her onto the floor, twisting her arm behind her back. She struggled briefly, but he managed to catch her other wrist, twist that arm behind her and knot the two together. Her ankles came next, but she had little fight left in her and her position face down on the floor wouldn't allow for much of a struggle anyway.

Panic washed over her when he finished and stepped back to admire his handiwork. She glanced at Cole. It was still dim in the room, but she thought she could see his chest moving. She stared at him hard as Garner moved away from her, willing him to move, if only a little to reassure her that he wasn't dead. His finger twitched. A moment later, she saw his eye move behind his eyelid.

She glanced around for Garner to distract him. He'd found another lamp. She watched him, her heart in her throat, but apparently he decided he couldn't see her well enough. Instead of ripping it out of the wall and taking the cord, he turned it on.

"You've killed him, you worthless piece of shit!" she snarled at Garner.

He glanced at Cole. "He'll be fine. He's a tough little son of a bitch. I beat him worse that that when he was a kid and he healed just fine."

A jolt went through Amanda. She glanced quickly at Cole. He hadn't moved, but his eyes were open now and every word, every look, every nuance of his actions flooded her mind in sudden comprehension. Garner had used him to get close to her. The look in his eyes broke her heart--shame and absolute certainty that she must despise him now as much as he hated himself. With an effort, she dragged her gaze from Cole and looked at Garner again. He was grinning. "You never even suspected, did you?"

"Suspected what?" she said tightly.

"That he was my boy."

"That's because he isn't," Amanda ground out.

Garner laughed. "You'd like to think you hadn't been fucking my boy, wouldn't you?"

Amanda's eyes narrowed. "I don't know whose boy he is, but I know damn well he isn't yours. And what's more, you know it, too. I've seen your military record. You got your balls shot off in Vietnam. You have never sired a child in your life… not unless it was before that, and Cole isn't old enough. My guess is that he belongs to your ex-wife and her husband. He's the baby we never found after you butchered his mother."

Garner's face reddened. "That whore took off and took up with another man but I taught her a lesson. I went and got her and brought her home where she belonged."

"That's a damn lie! She was no whore. She divorced you. She married another man. That's what you couldn't handle, wasn't it? You figured she'd run off because you weren't a real man anymore."

For a moment, she thought she'd pushed him too far, that he was going to lose sight of the fact that he enjoyed his work so much and kill her without taking the time to torture her first. After a moment, however, he collected himself and grinned. Moving toward her, he bent down and picked up the lamp he'd discarded, examining the broken bulb at the end. Amanda's insides cringed.

His preference seemed to be to use a foreign object to rape women, either because he couldn't actually get an erection anymore, or because he was just plain psycho.

"I know what you're up to. You think you're going to goad me into killing you quickly, but I've been waiting ten years for this. I'm not going to make it easy for you."

Amanda swallowed with an effort. She had to keep him talking. "Why not? You took it easy on your wife, even though she'd been unfaithful to you, cheating on you with another man."

He snorted. "It took her almost a week to die and she spent the whole time begging me to give up my boy to that prick she'd been sleeping with. Is that your idea of easy?"

Amanda bit her lip. She hated having to talk about this in front of Cole. He was still barely conscious, but she knew he could hear it. "You're exaggerating," she said finally. "I don't believe that was you that did it at all. Or maybe you're trying to tell me you learned some tricks from the Vietcong?"

He grinned, this time with genuine humor. "Yes, you do. You know it was me. Her sister convinced you. If I'd just managed to shut her up a little sooner, everything would've gone along fine, but, like you, she just couldn't keep her nose out of my business. I should've cut her throat and been done with it, but she kept screaming at me to tell her what I'd done with her sister till I just couldn't resist showing her."

Cole groaned. Amanda's heart skipped a beat as Garner's attention was immediately caught. He studied Cole through narrowed eyes as Cole struggled to sit up. "You going to behave yourself, now, Junior? Or am I going to have to beat some sense into you, boy?"

Cole had managed to drag himself to a sitting position. Weak and dizzy both from the blows to his head and the blood loss, he dropped his forehead onto his knees. "I'll be good boy, daddy," he said in a meek voice that raised goosebumps along Amanda's spine.

She swallowed with an effort, trying to fight down the terror that Garner had regained control of him... or worse, that he'd damaged Cole's mind. Where were the damned cops? She'd more than half expected them to bust in before they got a confession--she'd hoped they would, but they *had* insisted that they would play it themselves until they had a confession.

They had a confession, a thorough one, so why the hell weren't there cops crawling all over her living room?

Almost as if he read her mind, Garner spoke again. "I told you to get rid of the damned cops. I had to take care of it myself. Me and you are going to have to have a little talk about that later."

Cole looked up at him then and Amanda saw that the fear on his face wasn't feigned. He really was terrified of the man, however hard he tried to hide it... and small wonder considering the bastard had tortured him his whole life--until she'd sent him to prison? Cole would've been at least sixteen or seventeen then, though. Had the reprieve come too late for him? Was she completely wrong about Cole?

Chapter Fifteen

The certainty that if she didn't get loose, she was going to die moved over Amanda. She'd long since lost feeling in her hands, however. Concentrating for all she was worth, she finally managed to twitch her fingers.

It did nothing to return sensation to her hands but it did draw Garner's attention.

He grinned at her. "Let the fun begin," he said, moving toward her with the lamp.

Cole staggered to his feet as Garner caught hold of the cord and lifted her. Agony shot through her arms and legs as the cords tightened further from the weight of her body. It was a relief when he tossed her onto the couch.

"Don't just stand there like an idiot, boy. Get her situated."

Cole staggered to the side of the couch and looked down at her. "What do you want me to do?"

"Roll her over and get rid of the panties."

Amanda groaned in spite of all she could do when he did as he was told, pinning her arms beneath her. Fire shot through her thighs and knees.

Cole refused to meet her gaze as he tore her panties from her and then stepped back.

Garner's eyes glazed. Slowly, he got down on his knees.

Cole stared down at him a moment. "Why don't you let me do it?"

Garner looked up at him. "I don't know that I want to share," he said belligerently. "But you can watch."

"I did everything you told me to do. The least you can do is let me go first," Cole said plaintively.

Garner glared at him. After a moment, however, he turned to look at Amanda speculatively. The horror on her face apparently decided the matter for him. "You'll have to go easy at first. Otherwise she'll just bleed to death before we're through having our fun," he said, handing the lamp to Cole. "Take the bulb out. The glass'll cut her up too much. We can always use it later."

Cole took the lamp and studied it thoughtfully for several moments before he glanced at Amanda. For a moment, their gazes locked. "I'm so sorry, baby."

Abruptly, he slammed the lamp, glass end first, into the side of Garner's head, gouging flesh from his cheek and neck. Blood gushed in every direction. Garner began to topple sideways. Cole followed him as he fell, hitting him twice more before he landed on the floor.

"Stop! Cole!" Amanda screamed when she saw he had no intention of leaving it at that.

He hesitated, his head jerking up at the sound of her voice, his arm still suspended in the air.

"You'll kill him. You have to stop."

Cole's eyes glazed. He turned to look at the man he had by the throat. "I mean to kill him," he ground out.

"Please, Cole. Don't do it! Please!" she added when he hesitated once more and turned to look at her. "We've got him. We can send him to the electric chair. Don't do this! You haven't done anything wrong. I can't bear it if you let him drive you into doing something that'll ruin your life."

Cole dragged in a long shuddering breath and finally tossed the lamp aside. Rising a little unsteadily, he dragged Garner across the room, tore the tie backs from the draperies and used them to bind Garner's hands and feet. When he'd finished, he stood over the man for several moments and finally moved to the couch.

After fumbling with the cord for several moments, he rose and disappeared into the kitchen. When he returned, he had a serrated knife, which he used to saw through the cord.

Amanda groaned as her hands and feet fell uselessly to the couch.

When he'd tossed the cord aside, Cole went back into the kitchen and phoned the police.

* * * *

At the hospital, Cole was taken into custody once his head had been sown up and his skull x-rayed for fractures. He had a concussion but he was alert enough for questioning. Amanda, who'd managed to get through the entire ordeal with nothing more than bruises, stood outside the door while the police talked to him, listening. Johnson, who'd been waiting at the hospital when they arrived, dropped a comforting hand on her shoulder. "Why don't you go home and rest?"

She glanced up at him tiredly. "Cole didn't do anything wrong."

Johnson sighed. "I don't want to think that any more than you do, believe me, but we've got to be sure."

Dragging in a deep breath, Amanda nodded. "How's Garner?"

Johnson smiled grimly. "He'll live long enough to keep a date with the electric chair. We've got him on two counts of murder now… three if the other officer doesn't make it."

Amanda shuddered. "Garner confessed to that on the tape, too. We got everything, right?"

Johnson patted her shoulder. "We got everything. Even if his lawyer gets the tapes thrown out, we've got you and Cole. He won't slip out of it this time. Go home. I'll let you know what I find out."

What she wanted to do was to go in and sit with Cole, but that wouldn't be allowed until they'd decided whether they had anything to charge him with or not. For now, his hospital room was his jail cell.

With great reluctance, she called a cab and left the hospital to face her empty house alone.

She spent a miserable two weeks at home since Johnson had insisted she take leave and use some of the vacation time she hadn't taken in years. It was a relief when she discovered that Cole had been cleared off all charges.

Johnson had been kind enough to drop by himself and explain what they'd discovered. Cole thought he'd managed to escape his 'father' while Garner was in prison, but he had been contacted by Garner, who demanded that he 'keep an eye' on Amanda and make certain she didn't nix his first chance of parole. Cole had refused to begin with, but Garner had been wily enough to threaten his own mother, who'd raised Cole from a small child.

Knowing Garner was just mean enough to hurt his grandmother to spite him, he'd gone along, and he'd seen to it that Amanda was distracted when the news came through about the parole. He'd been prepared to delay her as long as it took to keep her from making it to the hearing, but the traffic had done the work for him.

That boiled down to immoral behavior in the face of duress, however, not criminal.

He hadn't known anything about Garner's plans to break into her house. He hadn't believed, even as mean as Garner was, that he was a cold blooded killer, or that he'd be crazy enough to actually come after Amanda. Garner had convinced him that he had no interest in doing more than throwing a scare into her when Cole had confronted him about it after the break in.

Cole had admitted that the break in had totally unnerved him and his impulse had been to dispose of the evidence Garner had left behind, but he'd realized almost as soon as he took them that he had to produce the evidence because Amanda had already seen it… and he'd done so. Garner had thought it a great joke that the panties he'd doctored up with household products had been studied so intensively.

They weren't going to charge Cole for tampering with evidence when he'd only thought about doing it… or, to be more precise, panicked at the thought that Garner would hold him responsible for failing to clean up after him and do something to his grandmother after all.

No wonder Cole had looked so distraught, and grown gradually more and more withdrawn when he realized that he was in too deeply to figure a way out, particularly since he now had to worry about protecting Amanda as well as his grandmother.

She was pretty distressed herself. As relieved as she was that Cole would be all right and that he wouldn't have to face criminal charges or jail time, the discovery that he'd turned in notice at the DA's office in spite of all Johnson's refusal to accept it didn't help her feelings at all.

If Cole had decided to leave, she knew that must mean that he'd only seduced her to help Garner, or more specifically, to protect his grandmother. Even though she completely understood that he'd found himself in a situation there was no way out of, it was worse than a lowering thought. It was devastating.

She wondered if anybody ever reached an age where they weren't stupid when they fell in love.

By the time everything had been thoroughly examined and sorted through, at the end of yet another week with nothing but her thoughts for company, Amanda's spirits were so low when the doorbell rang she was tempted to just ignore it. She hadn't hidden her car in her garage, however, and the doorbell rang again. Finally, she dragged herself to the door and answered it.

Cole, looking pale but still more handsome than she remembered, was standing on her doorstep.

She was so stunned, she merely stood like a post staring at him.

He cleared his throat uncomfortably. "I came to get my things."

The hope that had just begun to filter through to her short-circuited brain died.

Nodding, she stepped back to allow him to enter.

She watched him until he disappeared in her bedroom, fighting the urge to follow him.

Finally, feeling the numbness slowly wearing off, she went into the living room and sat down, staring at the blank TV screen across from her. She tried *not* to think. The sounds filtering from the bedroom penetrated her brain, however, stimulating thought despite all her efforts to subdue it. She heard the jangle of the coat hangers and knew he was taking his suits out and folding them.

After a little bit, the jangle of coat hangers ceased and she could hear his feet on the bathroom tile. He was collecting his toiletries.

She loved the cologne he wore. It didn't smell the same in the bottle, though, as it did on him. She'd missed him desperately enough that she'd sprinkled it on his pillow, but found it only made her miss him more, not less.

He came out a few minutes later, carrying a box.

She'd thought he had gotten rid of them when he put his clothes in the closet. Obviously, he'd merely left them in the bottom of the closet.

Obviously, he'd known he would be moving out before long.

She didn't glance in his direction. She just sat, staring at nothing as if she'd been turned to stone.

She wished she had been.

Stones were cold. They didn't feel anything.

She was starting to feel just enough to know she was going to be dying any minute. It was kind of like the first prickles of a sunburn after too long in a tanning booth, harbingers of the pain that was soon to come.

After a moment, she curled her knees up under her and grabbed a pillow, hugging it against the pain that was starting to get really bad in her chest, so bad she could hardly breathe for it.

She tried not to hear him as he came back in and loaded another box and left again. Finally, the trips up and down the hallway stopped. She didn't move. She knew if she did she'd loose control of the pain and she had it at bay now. If she could just hold on a little longer, keep breathing slowly in and out, it was going to go away.

It was several moments before she realized Cole was standing in the doorway, studying her. She didn't want to look at him, but she couldn't help herself.

"I think I've got everything," he said, his voice sounding a little rusty.

Amanda swallowed with an effort and nodded. She thought she really ought to say something, but she couldn't think of anything to say.

He pushed away from the door frame after a moment and looked around the room uncertainly. Scrubbing his hand over his jaw, he glanced almost longingly at the front door, hesitated and finally started toward her.

He stopped in front of her.

Amanda stared at his knees.

Finally, he sat on the coffee table, facing her. "I'd didn't mean to hurt you, Mandy, but I couldn't let him hurt Granny. I didn't know you then. I didn't know it would be so hard."

Chapter Sixteen

Amanda didn't think she could say anything to save her life without just bawling like a baby. She dragged in a deep, calming breath and tried. Her voice only came out as a squeak. She cleared her throat. "I know," she managed to say, bobbing her head like one of the 'bobbers' some people put in their cars, except that she couldn't manage the vacuous smile. She wanted to tell him that she did understand. It didn't mean she wasn't hurt, but she couldn't hate him for it when she knew he'd never had any intention of hurting her.

It wasn't his fault she'd been stupid enough to fall in love with him when the objective was only to fuck her brains out and keep her distracted.

Well, he'd certainly done a damn good job of it!

He scrubbed his hands over his face. "I know you hate me now. I don't blame you but I wanted to try to explain that I did the best I could to protect both of you."

Amanda swallowed with an effort. "I don't."

He glanced at her distractedly. "You don't…?"

"I don't hate you."

He flushed. "That's something at least. I wish I could say the same. I hated that bastard my whole life. I hated my mother for abandoning me to him and finally I started hating myself because I thought I was his son. Except for granny, you're the only person who ever made me feel like, maybe, I was worth something, and then I almost got you killed because I couldn't stop the son-of-a-bitch. I thought I'd… outgrown being scared of him, but I was so paralyzed I couldn't even think at first when he came in that night. The only thing that got me through it was that I was more afraid for you than I was for myself."

The urge to cry receded with the realization that he was embarrassed that he hadn't 'performed' better and ashamed of his fear. She reached over and took his hand where it lay on his knee. "Not being afraid of a monster like that is just plain stupid! I know what he did to you. I know what it must have taken for you to overcome all of that and face him. I've never known a man--anyone--I admired or respected more than I do you."

His hand tightened on her fingers, a fiery blush suffusing his face. Swallowing a couple of times, he looked up and met her gaze. "I wish… I wish there was a way I could make things all right. I spent weeks trying to figure it out, but I was in so deep by that time I was afraid even to tell you. I should have, I know, but I just couldn't face your disgust. I know you probably won't believe me, but I love you. So much it hurts."

Amanda stared at him blankly for several moments while that sank in. When it finally did, she burst out crying. Throwing the pillow down, she launched herself at him, throwing her arms around his neck. He caught her, patting her back awkwardly. "Shhh. Don't cry. I'm sorry. I should've just left."

Amanda tightened her grip and cried harder. "Don't go!"

He stroked her back, rubbing soothing circles on it and finally gathered her up and moved to the couch. "What can I do? What do you want me to do?"

"Stay!" Amanda wailed.

He patted her back. "All right. I won't go anywhere. I promise. Feel better?"

She nodded.

"You want some tissue?"

"You won't try to sneak out?"

He reddened, but chuckled. "I won't try to sneak out. I swear."

Reluctantly, she released him. He scooted her from his lap and went into her room. When he came back he had a box of tissues. Amanda uttered something midway between a laugh and another sob, but took the box and mopped the tears off her face and blew her nose self consciously.

"Feeling better now?"

Grabbing a fresh tissue, she climbed in his lap again and settled her head against his shoulder. "Did you mean it?"

He wrapped his arms around her and sighed. "I meant everything I said. I know, after everything I did you don't trust me... but I meant it."

Amanda sniffed again. "Will you marry me?"

He stiffened. Finally, he pushed her away so that he could look at her.

She blushed self-consciously. "You didn't mean it like that?"

"You're serious?"

She gave him a look. "No! I was joking," she snapped, and pushed away from him.

His arms tightened. "You want to marry me?"

She gave him a sullen look. "Not if you're going to be like that about it."

"You already asked. You can't take it back now," he said coolly.

"Yes, I can."

"But you don't want to."

She looked at him suspiciously. "Maybe I do and maybe I don't. It depends."

He studied her a long moment and pushed her down on the

couch. Pushing her thighs apart, he settled between them. "On what?" he murmured, studying her nipples as they tented her T-shirt and finally opening his mouth over one.

Amanda gasped at the heat that surged through her. "On what your answer is."

He lifted his head. "Yes," he murmured tugging her T-shirt up and shoving his head under it.

Amanda chuckled and then gasped again as he dragged his tongue slowly up her belly to her breasts and then flicked it across a distended nipple. Pulling her T-shirt off his head, she caught his shoulders and pushed him up. He looked at her questioningly.

She climbed out from under him and stood beside the couch, undressing slowly and casting her clothes aside. When she was naked she caught his hand, tugged on his arm until he stood up, and then began undressing him.

He stiffened. Amanda looked up at him. "I love you... everything about you. I want to feel your skin on mine."

After a moment, he pulled his shirt off. She unfastened his jeans and unzipped them, pushing them down his hips. When he sat down on the couch to push his shoes off, she pushed him back and straddled his lap. "Never mind. That's enough for now. I don't want to wait anymore."

She undulated her body against him as she kissed him, luxuriating in the feel of his warm flesh against hers. He caught her hips, pushing his cock along her cleft. She allowed it to slip back and forth for a moment and finally reached down to guide his turgid flesh inside of her. The muscles along her passage undulated with excitement, moistened, swallowed him up deeply as she pressed downward.

Urgency filled her as heated pleasure vibrated along her nerve endings and passion drugged her mind to all else. She began moving steadily up and down, watching his face as his cock slid inside her and then out again. As she saw his face grow taut with need, she moved faster, grinding her clit against his belly with each descent until she felt herself riding the crest of ecstasy. When he grabbed her hips and began thrusting upward to meet her it sent her over the edge. He gritted his teeth, drove deeply inside of her and then echoed her cries of completion with a deep, satisfying groan.

They lay limply against one another for some moments in sated bliss before either of them stirred. After a few moments,

Cole pushed his pants and shoes off and shifted until he was lying with his head on the arm of the couch with Amanda draped over him.

"I wish I remembered my mother," he said after a bit. "Sometimes, I almost think I remember something, but I'm never sure."

She stroked his chest. She wanted to kiss every scar on his body and tell him she loved every inch of him, but she knew she couldn't push him any faster than he was willing to go. It was something, at least, that they'd progressed to a state of trust where he would undress completely for her and allow her to give him the affection she'd been wanting to lavish on him. "Her family might have pictures."

He stiffened. "You think she still has family living? I mean, besides her sister?"

"I'm sure we could find out."

He fell silent for a while. "Do you think my father--my real father, might still live out west where he lived with my mother?"

Amanda frowned. "It's possible. You thinking about going to find him?"

He stroked her back. "Not really... I don't guess. I doubt he'd be that thrilled to have me show up after all these years and, truthfully, I wouldn't know what to say to him."

Amanda kissed his chest, then lifted her head to look at him. "Tell him he's going to be a grandfather."

Cole stared at her uncomprehendingly. "How could..." He stopped, sitting bolt upright and grasping her shoulders. "You're...?"

She studied him a little nervously. "Yes."

A slow grin dawned. "Seriously?"

She gave him a look. "No! I'm joking!" she snapped irritably.

He chuckled and kissed her soundly on the lips, then pushed her away and placed his hand on her belly. "When?"

"Hopefully, *after* we get married."

"How about tomorrow? We can catch a flight to Reno."

She studied him seriously for several moments. "You're not upset about it?"

He swallowed. "I assumed... you want to keep it?"

Amanda shook her head at him. "Cole, I told you weeks ago that I loved everything about you. There was never any doubt about that... whatever happened between me and you. It's *your* baby. No way would I give up the chance of having a little Cole running around my feet."

He grinned, settling back musingly. "You think it's a boy?"

Amanda rolled her eyes. "I think its a boy--or a girl."

He studied her a long moment and finally pulled her tightly against him, swallowing thickly. "You think... I'll make a good parent?"

"I don't even know if I'll make a good parent--but you're not Garner's son. You already chose your destiny. There's no doubt in my mind that you can excel at anything you set your mind to."

The End

Printed in the United States
34205LVS00018B/51